END OF DAYS

ORDER OF THADDEUS
BOOK 13

J. A. BOUMA

EmmausWay
PRESS

This one's for Eddie P

PROLOGUE

MCLENNAN COUNTY, TEXAS. 1993.

What was that?

Judah flung his eyes open with a startled snap, the depths of murky slumber disorienting, and heaved an uncertain breath. Then another, his heart rapping a mean beat against his piglet ribcage, the skin stretched tight from malnourishment.

The dueling scents of grass and raspberries filled his head even as it swam with fight-or-flight impulse. The momentary confusion at jolting awake sent his hands clenching that grass into fists. The soft, scratchiness of the long switchgrass native to the prairie wilderness was an anchor for his consciousness as it processed the turn. Same for the tart tang of those raspberries he'd whiffed, the dried juices from the humble berry on his lips further grounding him in reality. His reality.

Which was...

He didn't dare answer that just yet. Brain couldn't just yet. And he didn't dare sit to find out.

The gentle lapping of water from behind and the distant call of some mangy buzzard high above oriented him to some countryside. As did a warm breeze brushing against his cheek, a stronger whipping wind native to flat wilderness drawing one side of his mouth upward.

He remembered.

Home.

Except—

There it was again.

A growly *bang*!

Somewhere beyond his feet.

Then again: *bang-bang-bang*.

Before an unmuffled growl snatched that growing grin and sent him to his knobby knees.

Was that gunfire? The final assault by Babylon promised by Daddy, perhaps? Or maybe the Babylonian whores readying for the fight. Mounting their steeds and rolling into position.

Judah suddenly felt like his midnight adventure had been a mistake. He ached for Daddy's protective arms, along with his guns. He wanted to fight alongside him. With him.

For him...

Another echo of the same grumbly bangs sounding more like mortar shells sent him recoiling back for protection against a birch tree he had leaned against earlier for a bit of shut-eye. But he knew he needed to investigate. Needed to know if Babylon was readying their assault—or if they had already launched it.

Thank the good Lord Almighty he was nestled in a thicket of tall grass and wild raspberry bushes—clearly the fruit of the vine plastered across his lips. The cocoon was tall, pressing, sheltering. He slunk forward on those knobby knees of his and pealed back the switchgrass and caught a glimpse of the retreating offender.

Just a motorcycle. Harley Davidson, if he placed it right.

He smiled at the name.

David. Son.

Seemed almost prophetic to the seven-year-old boy.

There were a mess of 'em too. Chrome handlebars glinted a brilliant gold in the rising sun, those beefy black motorcycle bodies tooting black smoke from their backsides making Judah snicker. What they were doing that far out in the boondocks, he didn't have a clue. Wondered if they'd come to join the fuss that had flared a few weeks ago. The fuss that had kept him locked up tight inside home. Which had sent him scurrying out in the dead of night for a midnight snack on raspberries.

Judah had left the other children behind at the late hour for his secret passageway he had discovered one winter afternoon during Sabbath. Daddy had been droning on and on for what felt like an eternity! And he couldn't take it any longer. So he'd slipped out the back and started exploring, when suddenly the midday light caught a crack in one forgotten wall just right.

He figured it was a sign from the good Lord Almighty himself! So he wiggled his fingers in between, catching a nasty sliver in his middle finger—a sign he had been using it too much!—and pried open a gap big enough for him to fit through. Smelled nasty. Like rotting fruit and his brother Cyrus's dirty underoos! Was real dark too, which almost sent him running for Mama.

Yet Judah pressed on, the cramped space clawing at his clothes even as hot, dry air clawed at his throat—and that dang smell of Cyrus's underoos almost sent him puking a pants load! But soon enough he had popped out the other side.

And just after midnight he had taken the same secret passageway that even Cyrus and his grubby underoos didn't know anything about. Thought the guards would catch him, and then the Texas Rangers, but Father said they weren't any bother to the family while he was still in control. After chowing on those raspberries until he thought they'd explode out his you-know-what, he'd taken a snooze in that patch of switchgrass.

Until the grunting growl of the Harley Davidson sent him jolting awake.

David. Son.

The thought spread a smile across his face again. Until the thought of Cyrus and his grubby underoos snatched it away.

Cyrus. Daddy's firstborn. The Chosen One.

Judah hawked a good loogie and sent it sailing against that birch he had rested against before toppling to the grassy ground while in dreamland. It splatted a good-size coin against the rough, brown bark.

Score!

He raised his head with pride, even as his stomach sank with guilt. Knew he shouldn't be sour toward his brother. But what was he to do? Judah played second to the Golden Boy. And when the family came out on top from the siege, as Daddy promised, Cyrus would be raised up as his right-hand prince. At least, that's what the punk went on about. Couldn't stand it when he climbed up on that high horse of his and trotted around as Daddy's Chosen One. It's what had sent him scurrying through that passageway to begin with.

That, and wanting those raspberries!

Speaking of which...

Daddy would be getting worried if he didn't return soon. So he swiped another handful of his fave treat and started back toward home.

A noisy smattering of *pop-pop-pops* and *rat-a-tat-tats* skidded clear across the still morning wilderness. Must be Uncle Steve and Daddy target practicing again. Or—

Or maybe something else...

Daddy had been prophesying Babylon's impending assault as long as he could recall. Didn't exactly understand what he meant by it all. Just that it fit together in the events that would usher in the End Times. Didn't really get that ball of ugly neither. Something about the family winning, and all the evil bastards—that's Father's foul mouth for ya!—getting what they deserved.

Judah picked up his pace at the sound, the switchgrass prickling against his open palm gently swishing through the tall grass. A mid-spring breeze kissed his cheeks and tickled his stomach. He had crawled through the passageway in nothing but his night shorts. Now his skin puckered with a bazillion tiny bumps from the cold, and he wished he'd worn more.

The sounds grew louder, more livid. As he padded through the woods toward the compound, there was a curious fog floating like a phantom across the ground. Seeping, really, among the briar patches and scrub brush of the place Judah had often retreated to.

He slowed, crinkling his nose and turning it up from the spreading, acrid fog that didn't feel right. He stooped low to the ground to investigate when another sound interrupted him.

A *thwapping*. One he had memorized the past few weeks. Those damned Feds, as Daddy had called them. Which made him snicker at the cuss word, and also recoil in fright beneath the bent boughs of a pine tree.

Two helicopters raced above him. No, wait—three! Big black buzzards with a far more menacing growl than the Harley. Looked like they were moving fast.

A rustling from behind, all around, snapped his attention to the forest floor.

He looked down at his feet—and it was like the ground was moving!

"What the..."

Judah skittered back, slinking farther beneath those prickly boughs, the scent of pine heavy and welcomed.

That's when he saw it. Saw what had been moving.

And it wasn't the ground cover!

Rabbits, foxes, squirrels. All skittering away from...something.

But what?

Then it hit him.

Home...

A rushing wind sent that pine tree waving with irritation, carrying a hot breath of morning air thickened by more of that fog that had turned a putrid black. Inky tendrils reached for those woodland animals now, almost giving chase as they scampered away from the demonic threat.

Now those phantasmic tendrils reached for him, black, bony fingers curling toward his bony legs before another rushing wind ballooned those fingers into billowing balls of demonic darkness.

The sight caused him to gasp with terror.

And recognition.

Because the sight was quickly joined by a scent.

Smoke.

Strong and acrid. Of burning wood and fuel.

Judah scampered out from his hiding place and bolted to his feet, heaving desperate breaths—for stability, for fresh air. He coughed and gagged on the invasive threat, squinting toward its source and finding a wall of smokey doom.

A muffled explosion sounded in the distance now. Not the Harley Davidson.

It was David.

And his son needed to do something!

Judah dashed down the pathway that led back home. His bare feet crunched across dead leaves and splashed through puddles. His limber legs sent him sailing over fallen branches and carried him toward the fight.

Toward the End Times.

His heart kept pace with his feet, and his mouth breathed curses down upon his head for abandoning Daddy. How stupid could he be! He would fix this. He would fight next to him and repel the infidels!

The edge of the tree line came into view, along with a flash of fiery red and orange, obscured by the deepest darkness of hell.

Bursting into a clearing across a pond, he skidded to a stop as another whipping wind smacked him in the face with a raging heat and wall of smokey wickedness that sent his stomach lurching and head spinning.

The entire compound was engulfed in furious, livid flames. Acrid smoke billowed high into the clear morning sky and sailed across the only world he had ever known.

"Daddy..." Judah muttered, hands smacking the top of his head and eyes spilling over.

The grunting growl that had awakened him flashed through his mind. The Harley Davidson. Exactly.

David's son. That's who he was!

He had to do something. Had to act.

He started off, yelling for Daddy again—

When a hand reached from behind and clenched against his mouth.

Then yanked him back from the tree line and held him tight against a solid chest of muscle.

Judah flailed, his wiry limbs groping for purchase and a mean fight. He might only be seven, but he was a scrappy seven-year-old boy who knew how to handle himself in a fight.

A deep voice commanded, "Stop fighting. Stay calm. And shut your mouth."

Not growly, not angry or menacing. More brotherly, even paternal. The tone and timbre of his words made it that the more soothing by a trace of mint on his breath.

Judah felt the tension leach from his taut, spindly arms and legs, and trust rise unexpectedly.

The mystery man seemed to sense this trust, his own arms slowly loosening his grip before easing his arms open and releasing the boy.

He took a flying leap, shoving off the man's foot with one lanky leg and stretching the other toward freedom. Nearly kept going, but something stopped him.

Not the man. A feeling. A warm blanket of comfort drawing him into an embrace toward destiny.

Judah took one more leaping step for good measure, making good and sure he was out from arm's reach, then spun around.

A surprised gasp escaped him. The mystery man was nothing like he expected.

Dark hair, dark skin, dark eyes.

Nothing like the kind of folks who were part of his people, that's for sure. And not at all like most of McLennan County, Texas. Sure, there were those folks from south of the border. Greasers, Daddy called 'em. Some historic slang for Mexicans greasing wagon axles and animal hides from back in the day.

This guy was different.

There was a foreign look about him. Especially on account he wore these curious white pants that billowed in the spring-time breeze.

Silence stood between the pair, for the longest time.

The mystery man broke it: "Your name is Mister Judah, isn't that right?" Mister came out in a funny accent. *Mis-tah*. Which he sort of liked.

A tremble skittered through him at the mention of his name. His chest rose and fell, rose and fell more quickly, and he wanted to bolt.

But he didn't. Instead he licked his sun-chapped lips still sticky with raspberry juices and swallowed before nodding sharply. "Yes, sir."

"Judah David Howell?"

Another lick, another swallow, another sharp nod.

"You will come with me. Right now, before it's too late."

The boy narrowed his eyes, head swimming with indecision.

Come with him? He didn't even know him! Although he looked like a prophet, with those pure white robes. One of the 144,000 perhaps that Daddy spoke of. The messiah's Remnant.

"Who are you, mister?" Judah whispered on a cautious, yet believing breath.

"I am—" The man stopped short, like Daddy's cat had got his tongue. Then he smiled, as if he'd gotten the right word, and he said it: "Your salvation."

"Salvation?"

"And you will be the world's."

The worlds? That made not a lick of sense!

Judah cast his gaze back upon home, billowing black smoke and a raging inferno obscuring any sense of what had been. Daddy was inside, the messiah! Along with Cyrus, the real Chosen One.

He returned to the mystery man, eyes filling with emotion again even as his head swam with confusion.

Judah shifted, discomfort burrowing into his bare feet and begging him to run. But he didn't. Instead, he crossed his arms and tipped his head back, and threw him a questioning stink eye.

"Did Daddy send you?"

The man took in a measured breath. "In a manner of speaking, yes."

Then he approached, placing two wide, heavy palms on his shoulders.

Judah stiffened but didn't run. Instead, he looked straight into that dark face, his brown eyes making a connection that would determine his fate.

"Your father is no more," the man explained. "As is your brother. Just as it had been foretold. The same forthtelling that is your own."

He let slip a gasp and silently cursed himself for the reveal.

How did he know? Daddy's prophecy. He looked off toward the inferno again, those words striking him in an ecstatic rush: *'The only one worthy to open the seals is the Lion of Judah, the heir to David's throne. Behold! He will be a Lamb that looked as if it had been slaughtered.'*

That wasn't all.

'Behold, the Lion of the tribe of Judah, the Root of David, hath prevailed to open the book, and to loose the seven seals thereof.'

Judah's heart raced at the memory. And the implications. For John the Seer's words filled him with a revelation-insight he had never before grasped.

Until that moment.

With trembling lips, he locked eyes with the mystery man again.

"The seven seals. The End of Days. Is that my purpose?"

He said nothing. Only nodded, eyes bright and alive with purpose.

Apparently *his* purpose.

A crash drew his attention to what had been his home.

The south tower collapsed in a phantasmic show of fire and fury. Sparks fluttered high, fingering flames licked the morning air, smoke continued to billow.

Judah turned his back on the scene, looked into the mystery man's dark eyes, and nodded.

He wrapped a strong arm around his shoulders and the two started off.

'The Lion of the tribe of Judah, the Root of David, hath prevailed to open the book, and to loose the seven seals thereof...'

Judah had prevailed! Had been preserved, for such a time as this.

For the End of Days, even.

Whenever that day might come...

CHAPTER 1

WASHINGTON, DC. PRESENT DAY.

Silas Grey was running late. Again. And to a very important date.

Unfortunately, it wasn't a rendezvous with his wife, Celeste Bourne-Grey. Who not only was a Bourne before that whacked-out Ludlum character was a Bourne. She was a far better Bourne than Bourne was a Bourne!

Not only because she kicked butt and took names as the director of the Church's special-ops arm, SEPIO, providing solid leadership with street-smarts and a steady hand. But also because she was his rock. A source of comfort and stability the past year finding himself after he had nearly died. And at the hand of his own brother. The past year of marriage had proven the case in spades.

She was also his fill-in, Silas having taken leave of his post as Master of the Order of Thaddeus, the Christian religious order that stretched back to one of Jesus' very own disciples. It was supposed to have been temporary. A few months, max. A way for him to recuperate, regroup, and reenter the fray of things contending for the Christian faith.

Along the way, month in and month out, Celeste hadn't complained a bit. Even though she was technically his boss, having been tapped by the Order board of directors while he took a leave of absence, she hadn't nagged him to finish finding himself already. She had been more than supportive of his therapy sessions with Doctor Konfara. Even helped pay for his globetrotting jaunt to various sites of Christian veneration—from the traditional points of connection with the ministry of Jesus in Israel to the not-so-traditional relics of Christian saints scattered across Europe. For a while, Celeste was even the one bringing home the bacon while he fried it. Which suited him fine, for a while, because there was an unsaid expectation he would return to his post.

But as time spread between their last operation finding the Garden of Eden and relic bones of Adam and Eve, and then that moment when he had found himself at the mercy of his villainous brother, Sebastian, Silas had fallen into a comfortable rhythm outside the hustle and bustle saving the Church's backside. Although his background with the Army Rangers more than prepared him for the gunfights and car chases and general special-ops mayhem that had been the hallmark of his tenure with the Order, he quite liked letting others take the lead in saving the Church's backside for once!

And Celeste was with him through it all. Beside him and behind him. Not only giving him space, but also encouraging his newest pursuit and supporting his move back to the former life he had known before he'd been tapped to join the Church's Navy SEALs for Jesus, as Sebastian himself had quipped.

A former life that he was running late for!

Par for the Silas Grey course.

Felt like the White Rabbit most of the time, perpetually running from one thing to the next—running *late* from one thing to the next. And with the Queen of Hearts waiting to lop off his head! At least that's the way life *had* been, going on half his life. Whether in basic training and then with the Army Rangers cleaning up Uncle Sam's Middle East misadventures, or in grad school burning the midnight oil and then Princeton burning the candle at both ends keeping his head above water —and then keeping his head above the Order water leading the charge to protect and defend the Christian faith.

So, yeah, add running ragged on top of running late!

Which, today of all days, wasn't a good look.

Because the date Silas was running late to was the first day of a new gig thanks to a favor from an old college buddy. Blamed Fiat Chrysler for this bout of tardiness, the multinational conglomerate's Jeep Wrangler failing him when he needed it most. The Metro wasn't much better, some commuter subway train breaking down in the tunnel between Northern Virginia and the District.

So, yeah, not the best way to start the morning—or a new job!

Nothing a little breakfast couldn't cure at his favorite cafe. Saxbys. A local haunt in Georgetown that had just the thing to set things right. Could smell the frying bacon and roasted coffee a block away before he even spotted the red sign that signaled a respite before the crazy began.

Silas threw open the grayish-blue door and was overcome with the force of brewing joe, baking blueberry muffins, and the rumble of conversations. The red-brick space anchoring the corner of 35th and O Street since the eighteenth century was packed with students grabbing a caffeine and sugar fix before class at Georgetown University up the road, same as him.

Offering a dose of cheer to the gloom was a heroic display of purple and pink flowers sitting atop a glass case filled with cookies and breads and bagels and scones, greeting and tempting patrons waiting in line. Gray plastic tables and chairs lined the walls and filled small alcoves in the back and across from the register, all brimming with folks putting last-minute touches on papers or cramming for tests, or both.

On his Metro ride over, he'd put in an order for a breakfast sandwich and coffee, adding the day's *Washington Post* to the mix. Was amazed the local East Coast coffeehouse chain had joined the land of the digital living with their order-ahead app. Supposed the corona crazy from the past few years forced their hand in the dog-eat-cat world of restaurant retail. Just wished the joint would've been around when he was a student just up the road, along with its app-ordering convenience!

"Ham, egg, and cheese for Silas!" a woman called out above the morning din a minute after he arrived.

That was quick. For which the cranky grumblings of Silas's famished stomach thanked the perky blond coed wearing a Modest Mouse T-shirt.

Not his style of music, preferring hard bop and avant-garde fusion jazz to the lo-fi indie rock band, but he appreciated her display of individual music taste. Almost felt like he should break out his "Birth of the Cool" Miles Davis T-shirt and join the show, but figured it would clash with his tweed jacket.

Grabbing his grub, his stomach threw up a cranky appreciation for the woman's service. Silas offered an actual "Thank you!" joined by a fiver at the bar. Clenching his breakfast sandwich in his one hand, if you could call it that, and a large black coffee he'd also ordered in his actual one, he brought his meal to a small gray plastic table in the back, *Washington Post* jammed under his arm. Not a Luddite in the least. But he did like his news analogue.

Settling in, he popped the top to his coffee, closed his eyes, and just took a moment to breathe. Deep, earthy notes met his nose, smelling of smoked nuts. Heaven. The first sip was equally serine, a brightness joined by a lingering herbal spiciness setting his day right.

Same for the egg sandwich, sharp cheddar oozing out as he chomped into the sandwich, the salty, fried bacon ending any complaint from his rumbly, grumbly stomach.

Now for the paper.

Holding the cup of joe in his one good hand, he snatched for the *Post* with his other—when it slipped from his grip and fluttered to the floor in a spread of loose pages. Totally misjudged his hold. Without actual sensory action in his fingers, it was any wonder he was able to grip anything to begin with!

Silas cursed under his breath and glanced around at the embarrassing show before snatching the pages from the floor. No one seemed to notice, the morning mix of flip-flop wearing students and sun-dress wearing soccer moms busy with their *Angry Birds* app or cranky child.

Was still getting used to that dang thing, his new hand. Although, he probably shouldn't curse it too badly. Had it not been for Celeste, he would look more like Captain Hook in tweed than the college professor he was. She had leveraged some of her contacts back from her days with MI6 to call in a few favors across the pond at her old place of employ. Apparently the Brits were a step ahead of the Yanks burrowed in the basement at DARPA.

The result was a highly functioning hand to replace the one that had been blown to smithereens in his last operation, thanks to the fallout from a shot aimed at Silas's gut during a fierce wrestling match with Sebastian. His right hand. His dominant hand for writing and firing, for living.

The surgeons had worked through the night to repair the damage to his side that the bullet had torn through, and the limb. Apparently, his baby brother's bullet had shattered his hand and tore through his side. Lost a lot of blood before being extracted, and the doctors had worried about brain damage, so he'd been placed in a medically induced coma, coming to three days later. It wasn't until months later that his wife had gifted him a replacement for what his brother had taken from him.

As embarrassing as it had been getting the device surgically attached onto his stump, he had grown to appreciate the futuristic tech—and was mighty grateful for his British brothers leapfrogging his American ones. The prosthetic fingers and wrist combined both tendon-driven and mind–controlled modalities for movement. He had wanted it armed with rockets and a repelling hook, but he knew those only showed up in bargain-bin Kindle yarns.

Laying the newspaper on the table, he scanned the headlines, and frowned. Nothing new under the sun, as Solomon lamented.

Or in the *Post*, apparently!

Russia downed a NATO reconnaissance plane in western Ukraine, sending the US Military Industrial Complex into a tizzy, not to mention the European Union. The Dow Jones reached another one-day low, shedding almost 5000 points as the latest recession dragged into a third consecutive quarter. Drought has ravaged California for most of the year. That wasn't even touching on the threat amassing in the East China Sea, reports of China's Liaoning Carrier Strike Group growing off the coast of Taiwan. Then snaking gas lines and renewed toilet paper shortages and brownouts out West—all of it was enough to drive a person to the brink!

Nestled between the rustling of his newspaper were the distinct chimes of bells sounding in the distance. Scanning the Business Section, the back of his lizard brain counted off nine tolls. The kind a clock tower would make tending to its duty marking the nine o'clock hour—

"Are you kidding me?" Silas muttered, tossing the paper to the table and yanking back the cuff to his Zegna blazer, a gift from wifey for his first day on the job. Way too fashion forward for his T-shirt-and-jeans uniform of late, but it was appreciated. And cherished. Another signal of Celeste's belief in him and his next gig.

A Seiko pockmarked by three tours of duty with Uncle Sam

and several more operations post-Princeton with SEPIO told him the truth of the matter.

Looked like it was about time he invested in a new watch. Because that one was twenty-three minutes off, and those bells signaled what was what.

Silas Grey was running late for his 9 o'clock morning class. Again!

And for the first day of a class that was crucial to maintaining his status at Georgetown University.

As a professor, not a student.

And by Professor Grey, that was *Adjunct* Professor Grey. Part of the pool of bottom feeders in the caste system of academia who were barely above grad assistants. Education pays, they say. Unless you end up an adjunct like Silas Grey.

It would pay jack squat if he didn't hop to it.

Muttering a curse, Silas shoved the paper in his leather satchel and slung it around his shoulder. Then he snatched his half-eaten sandwich and coffee and dashed back outside.

Ready to face the day, come what may.

At least the day was all bright and sunny and happy and warm. Though a nighttime storm that had barreled through the DC Beltway left behind a miasma of sweltering humidity that was already drawing a line of sweat crawling down his spine. Didn't put much stock in those old sailors' tales about red morning and nighttime skies. But given the sorry state of things across the world, he'd take whatever good vibes the good Lord wanted to flare up across the heavens.

His attention was snatched by some bellowing fool down the way: *"We are the music makers, And we are the dreamers of dreams!"*

Couldn't help but smile at that. A line from *Willy Wonka & the Chocolate Factory*. Father had loved that line growing up, the Grey boys wearing out their VHS copy after way too many pizza-and-movie nights to count. Loved that scene, too, when the kiddos were licking the edible wallpaper—sending him and his twin brother, Sebastian, trying out the same dream by licking the walls of their Army-issued bungalow.

His sweet memory was interrupted by some other bellowing fool: "*I said, shut the hell up, Mother!*" a passing girl in pigtails cursed into her phone. "My body, my choice you *bleepin'* moron!"

And *bleepin'* was the G version for this crazy story.

Silas was stunned by the crazy disrespect. Couldn't even react to it, though, because—

Across the street, a man was screaming at the top of his lungs!

At a trio of women standing outside a clinic. Him white, them Latino. Catholic sisters, by the look of it, their white habits swaying in a gentle breeze. The clinic was marked by familiar blue lettering and a double-leaf logo indicating it offered women's health services. The women weren't doing anything but standing with eyes closed. Probably praying. But the man wasn't having anything of it. Just screamed at them to leave, joined by another raging the same, the pair looming large over the slight, silent women.

He wanted to give those two fellas a piece of his own mind. Tell them to mind their own damn business. Get into it with them, if it came to it, to protect the women and their First Amendment freedom.

A quick check of his watch reminded him he was growing very late for his very important academic date!

Instead, Silas just shook his head and kept going.

Ironically, the next block over, someone had spray-painted a large white X over a beautiful mural on the sidewalk exhorting people to value black lives. The colorful blocky letters were obscured along with symbols of Africa, horned animals and birds and patterns. An old black man was scrubbing away the graffiti, joined by a young mother and young boy.

Silas just shook his head, flat amazed at what the country had come to the past few years, where rage and discord and a hatred of goodness reigned. Between the depressing headlines in the morning paper and the chaos playing out in the street, he could only agree with John the Seer's prayer at the end of the Book of Revelation.

Come, Lord Jesus!

Pulling up to 36th Street, a block from his newest employer, a stiff orange hand forced him to wait for late-morning traffic to clear.

"Come on, come on," Silas complained, swiping a line of sweat away beading at his hairline as he waited for the light to change.

Waiting, the bellowing man returned somewhere in the closer distance: *"The end is nigh! You are your only hope!"*

Silas smirked. Add apocalyptic hysteria to the morning's festivity nonsense.

He punched the crosswalk again, impatience growing. When nothing changed, he did the only thing that running late demanded.

He charged onto the cracked pavement, nearly tripping on a pothole that was par for the DC course.

And met the squealing tires of a Ms. Something finger-wagging behind a screaming candy apple red Mercedes.

Supposed he deserved at least one of those fingers for his urban indiscretion. But he was running late to class. Again.

Not a good look for his first day on the new job.

Scurrying across the road, the retreating Mercedes gave him another piece of her *honkity-honk-honk* mind. The vanity license plate on its backside told him all he needed to know about who he'd picked a traffic fight with.

BSYLDY.

Busy Lady.

Only in DC.

Turning back toward Georgetown, squawking brakes and squealing tires flared before a hideous crunch. A beat later, the opening of a car door and it slamming shut, then another yanked Silas's attention back to the road behind.

Where a woman dressed like a cat was exiting a silver Honda Civic and getting ready to square off with Busy Lady!

That's right. Pointy ears and a tail curled up from behind her back, wearing black and whiskers and all. Maybe she was a preschool teacher, readying to give kiddos a day of fantasy. Maybe she was one of those furries he had read about on the internet, people who identified as anthropomorphic embodiments of animals. Maybe she was readying to give someone else a day of fantasy...

A sudden string of accusations sprang from Busy Lady, the woman clearly of the sisterhood of the traveling pants variety who was pissed as pissed could be. The brawny woman stuffed inside a bright red suit that matched her gaudy car stormed toward Cat Lady now.

And reached back with a raised fist, clocking her one in the face!

Cat Lady went down like a sack of potatoes. And actually, more toppled like the stunned cow he'd sent to the ground on a late-night cow-tipping run his freshman year pledging for Sigma Chi.

Silas gasped. "Are you kidding me?"

Now Busy Lady was on top of the poor lady sprawled on the pavement.

He had to do something.

He had to save the cat!

CHAPTER 2

Silas had always been one to jump into the fray of things when injustice reared its ugly head.

Got him not a few black eyes back in his childhood day when he stepped between bratty Army brats stationed with his dad and brother in the South Pacific. Then a few more nicks when he was stationed in Afghanistan and Iraq stepping between Uncle Sam and his FUBAR nation-building operations. That wasn't even counting the bumps and bruises—the missing hand!—he'd gotten stepping between Christ's Bride and the destruction of its faith!

So, yeah, Silas had been around this merry-go-round a time or twelve.

Only thing that gave him pause throwing off his leather satchel and Zegna blazer was something worse than the black eyes and nicks, bumps and bruises, even the hand blown to smithereens.

Cancellation.

In an age of voyeuristic spectatorship, where everyone and their mother had a live-streaming weapon linked to a global audience thanks to WeNet, and its constellation of social media platforms, one had to have a death wish getting into any public altercation—as virtuous and noble as the moment was. Careers could be torched, reputations raked through the coals, livelihoods incinerated until the proper struggle session resulted in groveling repentance.

Except that same voyeuristic spectatorship had mentally sidelined the rest of the commuting public! Because instead of jumping in to save some helpless victim dressed like Catwoman getting pummeled by a road-raging Ms. Somebody, drivers climbing out of their parked cars and pedestrians were just standing around and aiming their phones like they were tasers.

Not only at the two women going at it. But also at Silas Grey clenching both hands on Busy Lady's shoulders trying to save the cat!

"Not on my watch, ma'am. Why don't we step aside, take a breath, and talk things—"

A punching jab nearly landed square in Silas's nose. A quick uppercut from Busy Lady. Didn't think she had it in her.

Lucky for Silas, he was a minor Army boxing champ back in his Camp Liberty days in Iraq.

An equally quick blocking punch batted it away. Still—

It pissed him right off!

He lunged for Busy Lady, placing firmer hands on her shoulders and yanking her back, readying to give her a piece of his Army-bred mind.

When a jutting elbow to the jaw sent Silas's head snapping back.

And Busy Lady scrambling from his grip.

She spun around on candy apple red stilettos that could do some serious damage to his manhood with him splayed on the pavement. For a second, it looked like she might!

Instead, she scurried back to her Mercedes and sped away as distant sirens wailed their direction.

Silas rubbed his jaw and winced, but he'd live. He stood and strode to Cat Lady, helping her back to her feet.

"You alright?"

She offered a weak smile and nodded. Left eye had swelled shut and a quarter-size scrape marred her right cheek. Her cat getup was all askew too: whiskers jutting this way and that, eyeliner smeared, cat tail bent at an odd angle that actually made him wince.

Thanking him, she hobbled to her car and sat inside. He went to check on her wounds when a sudden rushing shout of yelling hoots and hollers filled the air, and a mob of people flooded the streets.

"What the..."

Men and women, young adults and middle-agers and elders. Twenty or thirty, maybe more, from all directions—up and down 36th Street and O Street. All wearing black pants and bright green T-shirts with an hourglass symbol, carrying signs that offered rosy enviro-apocalyptic slogans: *Keep calm and let's save the earth*; *Treat your planet like you want to be treated*; *Let your negativity be burned, not our Mother Earth.*

They swarmed the cars now, four to a vehicle, stopped in the middle of the road thanks to the fender bender. And started slashing the tires!

Yellow box cutters, blades glinting in the morning light, sunk in then popped out in rapid succession across the street, mooring the slumping hunks of metal and deflated rubber for good.

Reminded Silas of the extreme climate activism across the pond, where hysterical activists desecrated priceless works of art with mashed potatoes and tomato soup. As if throwing a can of Campbells at the problem would save a tree, let alone Earth.

What the heck was going on with people—with the city, the world? It's like someone had added one too many crazy beans on the scale and tipped it into a full-on manic episode!

Silas couldn't help but think of Paul's words in his first letter to Timothy, his partner in ministry, describing the chaos that would swarm across the world during the last days: *'People will be lovers of themselves, lovers of money, boastful, proud, abusive, disobedient to their parents, ungrateful, unholy, without love, unforgiving, slanderous, without self-control, brutal, not lovers of the good, treacherous, rash, conceited, lovers of pleasure rather than lovers of God—having a form of godliness but denying its power. Have nothing to do with such people.'*

Have nothing to do with such people? Silas smirked. "Don't have to tell me twice."

Especially with the mob throwing punches all around now.

Which was his cue to get out of Dodge.

Adjusting his leather satchel across his shoulder, Silas let the authorities deal with cleaning up the ungodly mess and hustled off. Still a block away, and he was running late for class. Again. Last thing he needed for his first day on the job.

He shuddered, making for the university and shaking his head. What was DC coming to—the world coming to?

First some teenybopper dissing her mom. Then the raging discord between not only political opponents, but automobile ones.

Perhaps his first gut reactions were right: Only in DC!

Silas hustled through the university's gated entrance festooned with bright flowers in full bloom. Striding past the bronze statue of Bishop John Carroll, founder of the university, he thought back to his undergrad days dressing the good bishop up in women's lingerie. Not that it was his idea or anything. The boys of Sigma Chi were adept at filling the days with all manner of mischief.

And boy, were those the days!

Striding through the circular drive in front of Healy Hall, its façade weathered charcoal grey from age, Silas hoisted his leather satchel on his shoulder. Then he threw back the sleeve to his white dress shirt soaked through with sweat and raised his wrist for a look at the damage.

He was screwed. By almost twenty minutes now!

So he hiked it and hustled up a set of stairs and across a mosaic of tiny blue tiles marking Georgetown University's founding in 1789. Throwing open the heavy oak doors to Healy Hall with an echoey clatter, he made for a set of doors on the other side of a hallway paved in more of those scuffed blue-and-white tiles. He burst through those doors and hustled out into a courtyard on toward destiny.

The scent of late-summer blossoms and the warm misty morning air brought a flood of memories to the surface as he hustled through a canopy of some flowering tree smelling like honey and past a bubbling fountain before the sight of Dahlgren Chapel of the Sacred Heart faltered his steps. It was at that very chapel that it all had started. His claim to fame, his entrance into the Order of Thaddeus and its special-ops arm, SEPIO.

The chapel had been a jewel in the university's spiritual mitre, with cream-colored walls, vaulted by cherry wood beams and ceiling slats, and commanded by a massive, intricate stained-glass window of Jesus and the saints nestled between a bronze pipe organ behind the high altar. That is, until it was all blown to smithereens thanks to a terrorist plot to take out some of the Church's highest-ranking researchers.

Including Doctor Silas Grey.

He had been the keynote speaker for an annual theological conference gathering the brightest minds who researched the Church's most important relic: the Shroud of Turin. *New Revelations of the Shroud: Leveraging Space-Age Technology to Uncover Ancient Truths* had been the title of the presentation. He was about to get to the goods when it happened.

An operative with the Church's ancient enemy had exploded a suicide vest, the explosion of fire and fury shredding the chapel and killing several of his sindonologist colleagues, including a close friend, Father Arnold.

What was built in its place was a monstrosity of glass and chrome and titanium beams. Looked more like a mental wellness center than a house of prayer. Which was pretty much spot on the money with the state of the Church these days. Whether Protestant megachurches pumping fog and bass in their industrial garage-style sanctuaries to rev up their congregants, or post-Vatican II Catholic institutions that showed little sacred character through wreckovations as some congregants have quipped.

It was from the wreckage of that former Christian chapel that Celeste and her team of ecclesial operatives had drugged him before dragging him to safety. It was the inciting incident that had launched his new life as an operative of the Church, contending for and defending the faith. Since then, going on five years now, so much had happened.

Sure, he'd stopped way too many conspiracies and plots to take down the Church that would give ol' Dan Brown a run for his religious conspiracy thriller money. From a splinter Christian religious sect manipulating an American election and plots to forge false Christian texts to change the meaning of the Bible, to scams designed to undermine crucial beliefs.

He'd also scored major historical victories that would give Steven Spielberg a run for his archaeological adventure money —from proving Jesus' resurrection historical and revealing the true location of the Ark of the Covenant, to uncovering a government plot to leverage UFO technology that was really demonic and even the location of the Garden of Eden and relic bones of our ancient ancestors.

All of it had been stunning. Enough to catapult his name in lights for good.

But then there was all the loss. Rowan Radcliffe, who had been the former Order Master until he died defending Celeste.

A former friend from his tours with Uncle Sam, Eli Denton, caught up in one of those conspiracies. Greer, the faithful operative who had given his life protecting his and others.

His hand. His brother...

Silas shook away the memory—the memories—hustling toward another set of stone stairs leading to another set of heavy oak doors into another building of weather-worn, rain-streaked stone. The mustiness of old wood and aged academia greeted him, along with the muffled instructions from professors already deep in their sessions. His clattering stiff leather shoes echoed loudly, tattling on his tardiness.

He reached for the burnished bronze knob and stopped short.

Taking a breath, then another, he crossed himself and sent up a prayer to the good Lord above. A prayer of gratefulness for the job and purpose. Of grace and mercy for the new teaching road ahead.

Wherever that might lead.

Silas threw open the door, the heavy wood thudding before closing behind as he entered through the sort of portal into the next chapter of his life. Which was really a step back into a wormhole through time into a former life.

What's the saying? History doesn't repeat; it echoes. He was living proof.

Even then, stepping through the threshold into another classroom was more a step back professionally than a step forward in a better direction. Because: adjunct!

My, my, had the mighty fallen, or what?

Shaking away the thought, Silas strode with purpose into the vast hall of three hundred seats, dark cherry wood paneling rising from floor to ceiling, the carpet and taupe paint fresh and welcoming. Here it was, his new class—

Which was dead silent.

It was also dark, the lecture hall's lights having been turned low with only a smattering of dim yellow lights at the front offering any purchase for his eyes. While they adjusted, he at least smelled the signs of life. Strong coffee, unwashed college jocks, oddly popcorn. A smattering of small LED screens flared from across the seating, and groups of students were huddled together in whispering bunches in the dim light, faces illuminated by their phones inches from their faces.

Clearing his throat, he picked up his pace toward the front and announced, "Sorry I'm late, class. And thanks for waiting."

No reply. Just the same group of zombies glued to their devices. Sure, he had to wrangle with the same distractions when he had been teaching at Princeton. But not like this bunch, their technology almost an extension of their existence. Man and machine had merged into a frightful singularity. Supposed every generation had their techno distractions. His had been *Call of Duty.* But that was relegated to his dorm room, not brought into the classroom—*his* classroom!

Reaching the front now, he sloughed off his leather satchel and slung it up onto a front table with a loud *smack,* hoping to rattle the attention of the students and wrest it from those devices.

Still nothing. And now that Silas thought about it, their distracted attention seemed more like concerned, even frightened focus.

"Somebody want to tell me what's so interesting?" he asked, stuffing his hands in his pockets and wandering to the empty front row.

"It's Kiev," was the reply from a woman in a pink hoodie. Pronounced *key-ev*, which irritated Silas.

Ever since Comrade Crazy Pants launched that blasted war against Ukraine, he had insisted on correcting people's pronunciation of the capital to its Ukrainian dialect instead of its Russian counterpart. Seemed only proper, given the injustice of the invasion.

So he offered a correction: "Kyiv. Pronounced, *keave*. Like *leave*."

Nothing but the quiet whispers of a disinterested audience. Or perhaps distracted audience, their attention dialed into something from Eastern Europe that had clearly set some of them off.

"And what about it?" asked Silas.

"It's fallen," said the same woman.

Took him a beat to get her meaning.

Then he did.

Silas hustled over to the young coed and craned over her shoulder. There it was.

SUNFLOWER'S KYIV FALLS.

The headline reminded Silas of another famous—or infamous, depending on your politics—national felling: HUSSEIN'S BAGHDAD FALLS. In fact, he had been there for that moment when President Saddam Hussein's government collapsed, ending decades of ruthless Baath Party rule after they were swept aside by US troops who drove through the streets of Baghdad—including his Ranger company.

This *Washington Post* alert traded the dead dictator for the national symbol of Ukraine. Which apparently had finally succumbed to the ravings of Comrade Crazy Pants. And the West was completely impotent to stop it all. A damn shame for the Slavic nation.

"As sad a day as it is for Ukraine, and the world," Silas said, returning back to the front, "we have a comparative religion class to get to. And I have a strict no-devices rule. So follow my lead."

He pulled out his slab of glass and metal and held it out toward the class, then pressed the power button with his thumb. On cue, the class sighed with a collective groan but complied.

Kids these days...

Although, looking out into his lecture hall, Silas saw an interesting array of ages and stages of life. Most were your typical late teenager and early twentysomething, kids sent off by Mommy and Daddy to fulfill their middle-class obligations. There were a few others who looked another decade into their career, two men and three women, even an older gentleman who had aged out of collegiate life decades ago—the handful representing the continuing education cohort whom Silas had mad respect for. Was humbled, even, that they had chosen to use not only their hard-earned greenbacks but their most valuable commodity at that stage of the game.

Their time.

Which meant he had to bring it. And bring it he would.

Beginning with a standard opener he had deployed in previous classes on the same topic he had taught at Princeton.

CHAPTER 3

The hall settled into an expectant lull, coughs and shifts waiting for Professor Silas Grey to begin.

For his part, Silas took his time, taking out his laptop and folder with lecture notes. Always had printed copies, the margins annotated with additions and asides in red ink. Found out the hard way that analogue was the way to go, no matter what all the cool kids said. Definitely wouldn't want a repeat of that one time his notes disappeared from his tablet that one day!

Satisfied with his arrangement after shuffling through his papers—mostly for effect—he got to it, snapping his head up and looking out into the audience of slouching, half-sleeping post-teenyboppers.

Silas sighed, taking a swig of his coffee and bemoaning the state of the next generation, then actually got to it.

"I want to begin this class," he started, "with a popular modern-day parable about four blind men and an elephant. The story is told from the vantage point of a king who watches as these men grapple with the reality of the massive creature. It goes like this—"

He took another swig of coffee, the caramelly notes sour

now from growing stale and lukewarm, then set it aside and got back to it.

"One day, four blind men were trapped in a room with an elephant. They started feeling our massive mammal and describing what they experienced. Don't know why they were trapped with him and why they were feeling this elephant. That's just how the story goes."

Silas stepped out from behind the table and clattered across the polished hardwood floor, propping a foot up on the empty front row.

"One guy felt the tusks; he said the great beast was smooth and hard. Guy number two felt the tail; he described the elephant as thin, long, wiry."

A giggle erupted from a few rows up joined by a smattering of snickers and hushed whispers exchanged between the students in the dimmed darkness. The out-of-body-experience side of his brain told him something was up, but he didn't understand it. He withdrew his foot from the front row and took a step back, then kept at it.

"Another touched its ear and believed the animal was a soft, flexible creature."

More giggles, more snickers, more whispers.

"The final person rubbed his hands over its hide and came to the conclusion the elephant was hard and rough like clay."

Now a ripple of laughter spun out from every row, the lecture hall clearly in on the joke he was woefully ignorant of. He went silent, letting the classroom's amusement play itself out while deciding whether to inquire about it.

Finally, Silas planted his foot back on that empty front row and said, "Apparently I'm not in on the joke. What's the deal?"

A tall man wearing the smiling face of Jack the Bulldog imprinted on a navy T-shirt, the university's mascot, stifled a snicker before sitting straight. "Sorry to break it to you, teach," he explained, "but your parable sounds more like the set-up for some erotic chic lit than a metaphor for religion!"

The man's friends nodded and roared back in agreement across the lecture hall.

Heat raced up Silas's neck and bloomed with hot embarrassment in his cheeks. He'd never thought of it that way before, the four blind gropers groping for—well, something that sounded a whole lot like something other than an elephant! Long and wiry, soft and flexible, hard and rough. He shuddered at the sophomoric giggles. And to think: He'd used the parable with sweet old ladies at his church's Sunday school class!

Another shudder before he snapped his foot from the front row and shuffled back behind the comforts of the front table.

"While I see your point—and will take great pains to revise my parable for future classes—" the roaring rush of laughter died back down to a ripple now "—the point of this parable is that here are four different descriptions of the one *elephant*, coming from four different experiences. Each of these guys had a limited understanding of the elephant. Each believed they understood the elephant completely based on their own personal experience, even though that belief was based on limited exposure. Because of their ignorance of the *entire* truth of the elephant, each of these blind men assumed the entire elephant matched their own limited description."

The room seemed to finally grasp his meaning, settling back for the lecture.

"Of course, we enlightened ones know that an elephant isn't only tusks. It isn't only a long, wiry tale. It isn't just big floppy ears. And it isn't only this massive hard, rough body. No, it's made up of all of these things described by the blind men."

"So what's the point of this story?" the man from earlier asked.

"The moral of the parable is this: Each religion is like these blind men and our elephant is like some divine reality. Many insist nowadays, including progressive Christians, that each religion has only a partial knowledge of the divine reality, only a limited experience and exposure to God—just like the four blind men."

"Well, duh! All religions are merely parts of the one divine whole. That's just basic. They all describe the same elephant, just in different ways, as I gather your point being."

Silas suppressed a frown, sensing this young man's capitulation to this popular, enlightened way of thinking about religion. And at one of America's premier Jesuit academic institutions!

He replied, "This is a very popular way of talking about God and religion, of describing God."

"Well, sounds nice, doesn't it?" another man asked, the older gentleman he had spotted in the back.

"You tell me. I suppose it does sound nice. I mean, we're modern, sophisticated, *enlightened* people. How dare we claim *one* truth is the *only* truth. How dare we claim that *one* God is the *only* one true God. And yet, from the very beginning, Christians have declared: *'I believe in God, the Father Almighty, Creator of Heaven and Earth.'* That's the first line of the Apostles' Creed. Not little 'g' god. Not gods with a pluralized S. God. *Singular.*"

"Yeah, but those are Christians!" a blond woman with a ponytail replied. "What about the rest of the world?"

"Ahh, good question. The people of the Most High God, the children of Israel, recited daily a line-in-the-sand proclamation known as the *Shema*. It went like this—"

Silas threw up Deuteronomy 6:4–5 on the overhead screen, then read: *"Hear, O Israel: The Lord our God, the Lord is one. Love the Lord your God with all your heart and with all your soul and with all your strength."*

He regarded the class again, explaining, "Yahweh is our God, ancient Jews declared. And Yahweh is the one God. Not the Egyptian gods Isis or Thoth. Not Baal of the Canaanites.

Not Artemis of the Greeks. Yahweh. This belief in only one true God continued with Jesus, who equated himself with God the Father. In fact, he equated himself with Yahweh, the god of Israel. And of course Jesus' followers recognized he was God and worshiped him as such."

Silas threw up another slide with a verse from Saint Paul's first letter to the Church of Corinth, chapter 8:

We know that 'An idol is nothing at all in the world' and that 'There is no God but one.' For us there is but one God, the Father, from whom all things came and for whom we live; and there is but one Lord, Jesus Christ, through whom all things came and through whom we live.

"This is the apostle Paul," Silas explained, "citing the Shema and equating Jesus Christ with the Most High God of the universe. Elsewhere, when Paul visited the multi-god city of Athens, he acknowledged their spiritual interests, but then declared those gods false and called its worshipers ignorant."

"Bigot..." someone muttered from some row farther back, joined by a rush of whispering agreement.

Silas actually took a step back at that comment. Understood the sentiment, coming from a changed demographic of young people who were more open to non-conventional spiritualities and resistant to the prevailing institutionalized religions.

Apparently it had changed more than he realized since he last taught.

He brought a hand to his mouth and cleared his throat, gathering his thoughts, when—

"Now, son, you're just speaking about the Christian God,

right? Maybe you could tell us more about what they believe about this god."

Silas squinted, searching the dim space for the voice of assistance.

The older gentleman from earlier, a full shock of silver hair atop shimmering beneath one of the lights. He had round, silver glasses with a silver comb mustache framing a grinning mouth, as if he were encouraging him onward.

Sort of irritated Silas, the helping hand. Then again, he sort of needed it.

What a day...

"That's right," he continued, coming out from around that table and making his way to the front row again. No way would he let a comment from some pampered Gen Zer get the best of him. "That is the way Christians understand their God. They also understand him as both the Author of our human story and an Actor within it."

Ponytail Lady threw up a smirk. "A starred performance that God is giving."

She held up her phone and gave it a jiggle, the point clear.

He allowed a smile. "I suppose the latest headlines aren't the best advertisement for him, are they? But Christians do believe that as Author Jesus alone is King. He alone is high and lifted up. He alone is holy. Which means he is distinct and separate from all other things. That God is not part of creation, but is distinct from it, separate from it. He is not some sort of force that's part of the universe—thank you very much, *Star Wars!*"

"I always thought he was more an energy or spark," Funny Guy from earlier added, sitting up and actually looking like he was engaging, instead of ruining his illustration. "Like the glue that holds things together."

Ponytail Lady added, "God is love. Isn't that right?"

A smattering of agreement spread across the room. This was getting good.

Silas replied, "That is one way some Christians have talked about God. As an idea or symbol for that which is ultimately meaningful in life. But a traditional understanding is that God is an actual Being, the Creator of the universe, who is high and lifted up and separate and distinct from Creation, from *us*. He is the Author of our story. But he is also an Actor within it. And this does bring in a distinction from most religious concepts of the gods that are distant and removed from the world. For Christians, he isn't removed from what happens in life on Earth. He is a *personal* God who is involved with the world."

"Doing a pretty crappy job of it these days," Funny Guy complained, holding up his phone now with the same point.

Silas chuckled. "I suppose one could be forgiven for such a sentiment. But get this: The God of Christianity doesn't reveal himself through history and Scripture as a God come to destroy us or give us a crappy life. No, he shows up, time and time again, as the God come to rescue us."

"Bulldookie!" Laughter and a few muttered agreements echoed his sentiment.

Silas put a foot back up on the empty row of chairs. "Think about it. At the start of Israel's story, in the Book of Exodus, God showed up in a burning bush while Moses was tending his flocks on a mountain side. Why? Because he heard the cries of oppression from his people. And he came to do something about it. To *rescue* them. And then, several hundred years after this story, God showed up again in a small insignificant city while shepherds were tending their flocks outside of Bethlehem. Why? Because he heard the cries of oppression from his people. And he came to do something about it. As the Gospel of John says, God became flesh and blood and moved into the neighborhood. He became one of us!"

He leaned an elbow on a knee, staring out into the hall.

Voice a little above a whisper, he added, "God walked around on this earth. God experienced everything that life has to offer. He experienced our pain. Our fears. Our hardship and struggle. He understands this life because he *lived* this life. What kind of God does that? Chooses to become an actor in our human drama? Yet this is who God is. He came to rescue us!"

He was met with silence. Several beats ticked by before there was a cough, then another reply farther back across the room. Some shifted in their seats, looking uncertain. A few others nodded, dialed into his sermonette.

Silas glanced down at his Seiko. Supposed it was time for a break after that heavy load.

He told the class to take fifteen minutes, and he promptly did the same.

Snatching his coffee, he threw back a swig and winced. The brightness from earlier had gone cold and sour, and those toasted nuts tasted more like cardboard now. But it was caffeine, and he was spent after not even an hour. He'd need the fuel for the next hour ahead.

Slumping down in the empty first row, he closed his eyes and took a breath.

"Silas Grey," a voice interrupted.

He looked up and saw the older gentleman he had spotted earlier, the one who had helped him along with his lecture.

Silas stood and nodded, extending his hand. "Appreciated your helping the discussion along earlier."

The elder took it. A strong grip that betrayed his tucked Ralph Lauren Polo and pleated pants. Clearly a man who kept in shape and wore his average height well.

"Glad to have you in class," he continued, letting go. "What's your name?"

"Ed Pierzynski. But I was Eddie P to your father."

Took a beat to register.

Then it did.

He almost choked on another sour swig of his coffee. He coughed and cleared his throat, managing to croak, "My father?"

The man's face—Eddie P, apparently—fell and hardened, jaw setting and lips thinning and eyes narrowing. He took a step forward, a strong whiff of aftershave thrown up as he leaned in close. A pleasant mixture of citrus and sage, attached to a sweet memory. Stetson, if he placed it right.

The one his father had worn.

"I need to talk to you, Silas."

Silas took a not-so-subtle step back. "About what?"

Before the mystery man could answer, a sudden alarm overtook the room. Muffled, not blaring. But still insistent and demanding.

Recovering from the initial jolt of the wailing sound, he realized something about where it was coming from.

Not inside, like a fire alarm.

Outside.

Which was super odd.

But also super familiar.

Intimately so, from another lifetime ago.

The one before the Order of Thaddeus, then Princeton before that.

For this was no mere alarm.

It was a blaring siren of nightmares from military bases past.

CHAPTER 4

No way is this happening...

Silas hustled down the aisle up the stairs from the front lecture-hall well.

Then stopped short, not wanting to create a panic.

Glancing around, it was clear the students knew something was up, whispered mutters of confusion and shaking heads and shifting postures all signaling their growing alarm.

Taking a breath, he stood at the center of the vast hall—waiting, discerning, intuiting what sort of blasting blare that alarming sound actually was.

And what it meant.

A beat, then a few more, the coppery tang of adrenaline heavy in his mouth now as his heart pulsed with activation, the siren making another crescendoing pass as it spun around somewhere close by.

Telling him all he needed to know.

Yup. Sure enough. That was no fire alarm. No doubt about it.

A civil defense siren. More commonly known as an air-raid siren or tornado siren, though those things weren't why the District was littered with those suckers.

Last time Silas had heard the same sort of blaring siren that was sounding with a muffled moan through the thick stone walls of academia he had been the farthest thing from an academic—as *adjunct* as he was.

Sergeant Grey had been his title. With the 75th Ranger Regiment stationed in Camp Liberty, a former US military installation in Baghdad, Iraq. This was after a stint in Afghanistan chasing down the Taliban searching for good ol' Lion Sheik. Also known by his birth name as Osama bin Muhammad bin Awad bin Laden. Or better known as simply Osama bin Laden, the Big Kahuna mastermind behind the terrorist attacks that had shattered all the post-Cold War myths of American hegemony and slaughtered 2,996 people in the largest attack on US soil.

Including his own father that fateful day while he was stationed in the Pentagon.

Ironically, the same siren that should have been blaring during his junior year at Georgetown that day hadn't sounded. Not like they were now, or that fateful day in Iraq.

Back in the day, he'd been yanked from Afghanistan and handed Donald Rumsfeld's deck of cards. Officially named the "personality identification playing cards," it was a literal deck of Hoyles with the mugs of fifty-two most wanted Iraqis, and Silas was tasked with tracking them down.

Except that one day, instead of driving with Colton and his crew—while they were still alive—they'd been stuck in their bunker during a wicked sandstorm. That's when it sounded. The same blaring, muffled moan screaming for them to take cover while an incoming barrage of rockets battered the base. More than seventy of them suckers killed twenty-three of his fellow Rangers, including one of his own.

Was never reported in the media since Uncle Sam wanted to put on a victorious sheen to their nation-building misadventure that had promised they would be received by the Iraqis with open arms. But he sure as heck remembered what had happened—that sound, the panic.

The pair of which were now dancing together with a chaotic confusion in his lecture hall thanks to the civil defense sirens arrayed around the nation's capital.

Which could only mean one thing.

"Are we under attack or what?" someone joked a few rows up.

Silas prayed to the good Lord above it wasn't true.

Because with the apocalyptic crazy swirling across the globe—from Comrade Crazy Pants in Eastern Europe and Chairman Crazier Pants in Asia...

He flat prayed to the good Lord above it wasn't true.

That it was a mistake. Some flock of geese that were mistaken for an incoming barrage of missiles aimed at the Capitol Building or White House or—

Screams snapped his attention to a collection of students in the aisle along stage right. The woman in the pink hoodie had her hand covering her mouth, face illuminated a faint white by the phone inches from her face. Her eyes were wide and mouth growing with horror. The funny guy who'd engaged him during class put his arm around her. A boyfriend, perhaps, whose brow was furrowed and mouth open as if in a question.

So Silas asked it: "What's wrong? What do you see?"

He turned to him coming up the aisle. That same furrowed, drawn face drained of color.

"What's—"

"Taiwan's at war," was all he said.

His mind snapped to the article he had read earlier, in Saxbys with his coffee and breakfast sandwich. The one about China's carrier group, deployed and amassing in strength off the coast of what had been known as Formosa, the Republic of China.

Taiwan.

It was all he needed to know what was going down.

"Papa..." Pink Hoodie muttered, leaning into the guy whose arms were still wrapped around her.

Silas's heart sank for her, and he asked the man what she was talking about.

"Her father is stationed in the South Pacific," he explained.

The South Pacific...

Just as he and Sebastian and his own father had been.

Silas frowned and nodded, saying a silent prayer for him and his crew, whoever they were.

The siren continued its blare, and he wondered what it meant—whether it was connected to the breaking news out of East Asia.

He had to see for himself.

"Stay here," he commanded. "All of you! Crouch down in the rows and stay put."

Knew it wouldn't matter if they were crouched, whether in the rows or aisles, or even in the building itself. If something was heading toward Washington, perhaps triggered by the all-out war breaking out on the other side of the globe, it wouldn't matter whether they were inside or outside. They'd be vaporized in an instant. Perhaps in minutes.

Lord Jesus Christ, Son of God, have mercy on this nation...

Silas crossed himself before racing up the aisle and bursting through the heavy double doors.

They thudded with a recoiling shudder in the vacant hallway, the suddenness of his entry echoing with the hollow smack of the doors. It was soon replaced by the clattering of his stiff leather shoes pounding across the tiles, more doors opening now behind him, and a rush of panicked voices filtering through the corridor until he burst out into the courtyard.

The hot, humid midmorning air hit him in the face, laced by those honey-scented flowers. Then the much stronger wailing of the air-raid siren and the thwapping of strong blades. A mess of them, too. Probably carting military personnel or other governmental personnel across the District.

He spun around, shielding his face from the blinding morning sun—so much for that ol' sailors' chestnut!—and catching sight of the underbelly of one of those thwapping birds. A deep navy with the insignia of what looked like the Presidential Seal. Perhaps the Vice President or even President scurrying away to an undisclosed location before the White House was engulfed in a phantasmic, fiery mushroom cloud.

A sudden sonic boom resounding overhead sent Silas crouching. Fighter jets. Probably a squadron from Andrews Air Force Base in southern Maryland. Maybe Bolling, but that was pretty small for this sort of response.

Either way, between the siren and thwapping blades and thunderous jets—things didn't look good for the nation's capital!

Until there was a sudden lessening of that wail—the air-raid siren's tone nosediving. Which was promising.

Silas eased back to his feet, others streaming out into the courtyard to join him. Some shouting panicked cries, others clustered in clutching clumps of solidarity and support.

The wail was almost a faint echo of its former self, the siren more a forlorn moan than a livid warning of impending doom.

A buzz at his pocket snagged his attention, and he drew out his phone.

HOMELAND SECURITY EMERGENCY ALERT SYSTEM THIS HAS BEEN A TEST OF THE EMERGENCY BALLISTIC MISSILE ALERT SYSTEM. THERE IS NO INBOUND THREAT, THIS IS ONLY A DRILL. IN THE EVENT OF AN ACTUAL EMERGENCY SEEK IMMEDIATE SHELTER AND WAIT FOR FURTHER INSTRUCTIONS. DO NOT PANIC. THIS IS ONLY—

Silas shoved the phone back into his pocket and heaved a steadying breath.

Do not panic? Just a drill, and with the apparent launch of a fresh war half-way around the world?

"Are you kidding me..."

Continued sobs and frightened cries told him not everyone had gotten the Homeland Security memo.

"Just a false alarm, folks!" Silas announced, hands raised and making his way to various student groups to repeat his reassurance. Caught sight of his own students now streaming into the courtyard. He made for them.

When a commanding voice called from behind with interception.

"Silas, may I have a word?"

He spun toward that voice, searching for the person who sounded vaguely familiar.

A sea of bodies spread before him. With confused conversations and frantic phone calls to parents, and with students darting for their dorms and searching the skies for signs of a threat, it was hard to make out who was calling for him.

"Silas, over here!" the voice called again.

There he was, the elder from earlier pushing past a pair of coeds huddled over their phones with a raised hand and hustling his way. What did he say his name was? And didn't he say he knew Dad before all hell broke loose?

Students started filing past now and lumbering back into the building at the direction of some of the other university professors—the *tenured* professors—but Silas took pride in bringing things under control before their pampered backsides made it outside. Even his own students were dutifully returning to class, which was a good idea.

Silas ran a hand through his thick hair and addressed the man bluntly: "I've got a class to teach."

He nodded. "I realize that. But we need to talk."

"You said that. Can't this wait?"

"No. It can't."

His leathery face, tanned a nice bronze, was hard and blue eyes insistent. It was clear he wasn't going to give up easily.

"How can I help, Mister..."

He jutted his hand out again; Silas took it. "Ed Pierzynski. But people call me Eddie, like your—"

Silas released his hand and raised it. "I know. Like my father."

He smiled. "That's right. Tommy G. Quite the pair we were back in the day. Eddie P and Tommy G."

Planting his hands on his hips, the man chuckled and shook his head, adjusting his silver glasses. He cast his gaze toward the bright grass and gave his head a shake, as if reliving a memory or set of them. The two sounded like they had been friends, close even with those chummy nicknames. But—

Who was this guy?

"I need to talk to you, Silas," Eddie said before Silas could engage, that urgency returning.

He frowned. "You already said that, back in the lecture hall. What's this about?"

"Your father. Something from his past."

That was interesting. Real interesting. Not that he had any time to deal with this now. Not with managing his first day of class. But given that class hour had been pretty well shot to hell, might as well indulge.

"How did you know my father?" asked Silas, the courtyard emptying now.

"We worked together back in the day, with the DoD."

"The Department of Defense?"

Eddie nodded.

"Were you two stationed together?" asked Silas.

"In a manner of speaking..."

What was that supposed to mean?

Silas sighed. "Look, I need to get back to class. So can we move this along?"

"It's about your sibling."

He snorted a laugh. "Sebastian? What's he done now?"

Eddie shook his head, lowering his gaze before snapping it back to Silas's.

There were those eyes again. A piercing blue that held stories and secrets—maybe even about his father. Certainly looked about his age, his dark blonde hair starting to show a sagacious gray that placed him in the mid-60s. What Dad would've been had he not been killed two decades ago.

"Whatever my baby brother has done," Silas went on, "it can definitely wait until after—"

"No. Not your twin brother, Seba."

Twin? And Seba, his nickname? This guy definitely did know Dad, the family even. A twinge of concern began winding through his lizard brain now. What else did he know? And from Dad's past?

Silas crossed his arms and widened his stance, asking lowly, "What's this about?"

Another breath, another beat.

Then: "It's about your sister."

"My—"

Wait a second.

He just said my...

The air puffed out of Silas instead of the word. As if he had been sucker-punched in the chest.

Time wound down to nothing but nothing, the sound of those last remaining students lumbering inside the building and closing entrance doors behind barely registering in the face of the revelation. The suggestion! That he had a—

Sister?

The word lodged in his head as much as in his throat. He

actually choked on it, his tongue tripping over itself trying to give voice to the idea that was so preposterous.

He didn't have a sister!

He had a *brother*. A screwed-up psychopath who was hell-bent on destroying the Church. And him. Mom died giving them birth, and she and Dad had had them a year out of marriage and basic training. In a military base hospital, of all places. At least, that had been the story. Maybe there had been one before they came along. But that wouldn't make sense! There wouldn't have been a chance to have kiddos beforehand. Besides, he and Seba would've known about someone else— some other sibling. A *sister*! So what the heck was this guy—

A hand clamped on his shoulder, sending Silas flinching.

Eddie. And he didn't let go.

"I can tell by your face that you didn't know about her."

Her!

Silas said nothing. Couldn't. Didn't even swallow or sigh at the mention of that crazy word that had never before been uttered in the Grey household.

Sister.

Did not compute. Not in the slightest.

"Come on, son," Eddie said, guiding Silas to a path that went off campus; he let him. "We have lots to discuss."

CHAPTER 5
CALIFORNIA.

"*Praise the Authority with the sound of trumpets!*"

Judah Howell whooped up the howl of praise a second time, now leaning his head out of his driver's side window in the whooshing noontime breeze. Even threw up a whistle for good measure, flopping his left arm out into the rushing wind then hanging his head out and throwing up another whoop of thanksgiving.

Boy was that nice. The rushing wind, all fluid against his face. Like an airliner jet on take off, the whooshing mesmerizing even as it ran a funny mixture of warm and cool against his skin.

And fecund. Loved that word! Fecund. Pronounced *beckoned*, but with an F. No, not *fah-cund*. Like some Midwesterner dressing up that suburban Target outfit with some fancy-shmancy Frenchie name. *Tar-jhay.*

Nope. Fecund. Like beckoned, but with an F.

Anyhoo. The countryside drive was lush and fertile. Life emerging from the deep black soil that had defined these parts for generations, readying itself to give of itself to humanity. Dying in human bellies only to rise again to new life with nutrients and molecules and atoms.

Just like that man Jesus supposedly had!

Dying and rising and all that jazz.

Could do without the onions and manure overpowering his senses. And was that celery? Farther on were the wineries that had put this part of God's country on the map, but all of it was par for the course in these parts. Especially the manure part of it!

Cows emptied themselves so veggies could give of themselves to humans. The circle of life and all that jazz, which he was part of.

And what'd humanity do with all those nutrients and molecules and atoms? Piss 'em away was what! Yes, literally. Also figuratively.

Those uptown nannies from the degreed class who mounted their Tesla high horses prancing around like they were saving the planet. Even while Congolese kiddos slaved away in Big Auto mineral mines clawing with their tiny fingers for the cobalt that fueled their dang batteries! Not to mention their orgasmic moralism.

That wasn't even touching on late capitalism, the globalized, post-industrialized absurdities and indignities that commodified and consumablized—that a word? Now it was!—everything from burgers delivered by a guy in a wheelchair to hawking detox tea and yoga on WeTube, sometimes while doing all three at once! Even wombs were for rent now to the highest bidder; there's an app for everything nowadays.

Yep. Pissing away those nutrients and molecules and atoms, one wake cycle at a time.

Not for long...

Which could wait. For another few minutes while he basked in the simple pleasures of a country-road drive after a very successful morning.

Sun sure was nice. That yellow dwarf star doing its West Coast, sun-shiny thing ninety-some million miles away. Hot and dry on his face, in a cloudless sky that reminded Judah of home.

Home...

He let a smile curl upward, closing his eyes now and wondering if the old man was looking down with love. Wondering what he would think. If he would be proud of the man he'd—

"Watch it, Judah!"

He felt the steering wheel yank from his grip.

Just as the livid *burp-burp* of a semi's honker blared and his growl raced by inches from his face!

Judah yanked his noggin back inside the cabin and righted the ship, the big rig whooshing by something fierce.

"You saved my life..." Judah said on a startled breath. Then he turned to his companion, snatching her hand and grinning. "For the second time, Sammy!"

"Don't mention it, hot stuff." She squeezed it and shrugged with a wink. "How about you keep both eyes on the road and both hands on the steering wheel, yeah? Wouldn't want that pretty little head of yours to get all smashed up before your proper unveiling."

Judah gave her hand another squeeze before taking her advice and gripping the wheel at the ten and two.

"Speaking of unveiling," he said, a sign marking the town limits flashing by and pointing the way homeward, "everything ready?"

"The chief said all is ready."

Judah nodded, a dueling swirl of ecstatic excitement and anxious anticipation flooding him as he drove on.

He had waited thirty years for this day. The moment when he would continue Daddy's work. Transcending the Fifth Seal and unveiling the Sixth Seal.

Readying the world for the End of Days.

With him as their savior...

The ruffling of paper snatched his attention from the road ahead—both literal and figurative.

He glanced to his girl—well, really his partner in *ministry*, but his girl just the same—who was waving around a wad of greenbacks.

He hummed and grinned. "How much?"

"Almost a thousand!" she squealed.

"A thousand..." Judah whispered before whistling his approval. "That'll carry the mission forward another month!"

"At least."

Well, sort of. He knew better. Because the mission, all of it he had put together, was funded by other means. But the cabbage they'd raked in would help give confidence to those who had begun to waver, wondering if all the sacrifice was worth it.

It was. It would be.

Those Benjamins were proof positive.

More than that, eight new souls had shown interest committing their lives to the Way! Two of 'em had even hopped into the Silverado flatbed. From South of the Border, but that was alright. Judah was an equal opportunity evangelist, signing up any and all who would want to drink from the well of what he offered. What his church offered.

The Church...

No, not *that* one.

His and his godfather's.

"Did you see the news?" Sammy said.

"What news?" asked Judah, slowing for the final turn.

"About the wars?"

Completing the turn, Judah glanced at her, one end of his mouth curling upward.

"Where?" was all he said.

"Ukraine and Taiwan."

"Told you."

She laughed, playfully punching his shoulder.

"Ouch!" he yelped, throwing up a playful whimper before cranking it toward destiny.

He added, "Mana said it would be, thus it was so."

"How did she know?"

"Mana knows all, sees all, is all."

Sammy snuggled up to his shoulder, getting close to his ear. Honeysuckle and jasmine were heavy on her closeness, and the heat from her breath brought a rise in his own heat.

Judah leaned in, welcoming the touch, her scent, his rising heat.

She whispered, "When do we get to meet her—when do *I*?"

Rage flashed hot in his cheeks, that rise in temperature cooling now by that ask.

How dare she! She knew better. Mana was from unapproachable light! She as much as the others knew the truth of the matter: *'And he sayeth, Thou canst not see my face: for there shall no man see me, and live'!*

Clenching his jaw, he swallowed hard, slowing on his approach toward the looming black gate ahead into home.

"Soon," was all he said, shifting and straightening.

Away from Sammy.

She seemed to sense the shift in mood, and she straightened as well, the pair of them putting on a smiling show to bring some warmth to the sudden chill.

After all, it was showtime. For streaming out from the opening gate were children of all ages. Hobbling and handled by the adults who cared for them.

Judah leaned back out the window, grinning widely and waving.

"Hola mis hijos y hijas!"

"Padre, padre!" the children shouted at the gate, their uniforms crisp and clean, white polos tucked neatly into pressed navy skirts and shorts.

Just like Judah Howell liked them.

He eased his Chevy Silverado to a stop, the brakes throwing up a squeal before he threw up a squawking *honkity-honk-honk*.

To which they replied: *"Señor Judá!"* they screamed together.

Judah came out *hooda*, which he got a kick out of. Almost sounded like his favorite Star Wars character, the sagacious green prune he most identified with. His was a life governed by the Force since childhood.

"Hola mis amigos y amigas!" he shouted back. "Are my little *niños* and *niñas* learning their ABCs and 123s?"

"Sí, señor Judá!"

Again, *hooda*. Yoda.

"Good, because I've got presents!"

More screams and squeals, joined by shouts of pure joy as he threw up another *honkity-honk-honk*. The kiddos parted like the Red Sea and jumped up and down, waving and continuing on with their squeals of delight as he roared past them through the gate. A cloud of dust kicked up behind him, and that gate promptly closed behind, teachers holding the kiddos' hands as they ran to catch up.

Judah loved the compound. New Eden, it was called. Where *'old things are passed away; behold, all things are become new,'* as the Good Book says. It was a place that fulfilled what John the Revealer promised: *'God shall wipe away all tears from their eyes; and there shall be no more death, neither sorrow, nor crying, neither shall there be any more pain: for the former things are passed away.'*

Or at least they will when he was through with things. And Mana.

The pluming dust faded trundling across a brick drive pulling into a central courtyard festooned with palm trees and blooming orchids and a large fountain spraying clear, pure water several feet into the air. Buildings pressed in from all sides, three stories tall, yet kept their distance. Stucco, painted a nice sandy earth tone, with red clay tiles poking at the end.

More children stood at wrought iron balconies, which Judah was always worrying was a bad fall waiting to happen, but he sure loved seeing them waving blue and red and green streamers from above.

"They sure do love you," Sammy said.

Judah threw the Silverado into *Park,* then he shut her down and flashed his girl a grin. "Don't they all?"

She leaned in for a kiss then pulled away, opening the door and scurrying out.

"Tease!"

Sammy squealed and slammed the door, rushing to meet the kiddos, piling in around the truck. Their kiddos, their people's.

Branch of Life Academy.

He laughed and lifted kids from the sea of bodies, plopping one on each shoulder. Simón and Carolina, if he recalled right. Both blinder than bats, like the entire lot of 'em. Which Judah adored.

And couldn't wait to see through to the end. John's testimony to the fact of the matter came rushing to the fore as he waded through the sea of children, the pair on each shoulder laughing and calling his name. It was chapter 9, and recalling it amidst the blind children brought tears to his eyes:

> *Then again called they the man that was blind, and*
> *said unto him, 'Give God the praise: we know*
> *that this man is a sinner.' He answered and said,*
> *'Whether he be a sinner or no, I know not: one*
> *thing I know, that, whereas I was blind, now I*
> *see.'*

Exactly.

Just you wait, Simón and Carolina. Just you wait.

Judah plopped them back to the brick courtyard, wiping a

line of sweat beading at his brow and told 'em to skedaddle back to class. He sent Sammy with the same instructions, though gave her a parting peck on both cheeks to make up for her earlier tease.

Then he strode down a brick path toward his domain. A massive, looming thing of the same stucco and roof laid in red clay tiles. It was as large as a football field, though without the wrought iron balconies. In fact, there weren't any other windows or doors on the joint. Except one door.

His.

A gentle breeze gusted through the property of mostly dry, packed dirt pockmarked by patches of grass struggling for a hearing. Gardens were strewn about, bright green switchgrass, blooming Asia lilacs, and red trumpet flowers he didn't know a thing about, along with more of those palm trees. That was Sammy's domain.

His was through that door at the end of the brick path.

Reaching it, Judah pressed his hand against a black plate of glass, mouth actually salivating as he waited for the blue pulsing indicator to flash an all-clear green.

In the few seconds he waited, a Bible passage flashed through his noggin. One Daddy had spoken over him often. From the prophet Jeremiah:

> *Behold, the days come, saith the Lord, that I will*
> *raise unto David a righteous Branch, and a King*
> *shall reign and prosper, and shall execute judg-*
> *ment and justice in the earth.*
> *In his days Judah shall be saved, and Israel shall*
> *dwell safely: and this is his name whereby he*
> *shall be called, The Lord Our Righteousness.*

David's Branch of Righteousness! A reigning, prosperous

King. Judah shall be saved, and so shall his people! Then another passage:

> *In those days, and at that time, will I cause the*
> *Branch of righteousness to grow up unto David;*
> *and he shall execute judgment and righteousness*
> *in the land.*
> *In those days shall Judah be saved, and Jerusalem*
> *shall dwell safely: and this is the name where-*
> *with she shall be called, The Lord our right-*
> *eousness.*
> *For thus saith the Lord; David shall never want a*
> *man to sit upon the throne of the house of Israel.*

But that wasn't all of it. Not by a long shot.

The expected green flashed and their was a soft *click* behind the titanium door that would keep out the most insistent Fed invasion imagined. The whole building, really, the stucco just a decorative shell for what lay inside.

Pushing through the door, the rest of what he knew was coming came rushing to the fore. Especially sighting the bright lights down the long dark corridor painted black.

'*But the hour cometh,*' Jesus had said, '*and now is, when the true worshippers shall worship the Father in spirit and in truth: for the Father seeketh such to worship him.*'

At the time, he was addressing a forlorn woman at some well in Samaria. Quite the progressive type, that Jesus was. Mingling with women in that sort of way. Totally blew the doors off the stuffy, stale societal expectations for how men and women should interact. So much so that when his ye ol' disciples wandered on by, they wondered what the heck the dude was up to!

Anyhoo, what he said before was what mattered. Because Jesus added something apropos for the moment—that one and this one: *'God is a Spirit: and they that worship him must worship him in spirit and in truth.'*

Little did he know what that would truly mean. That *spirit,* and the manner of that worship.

The manner of that spiriting even...

All would be revealed soon. Because they had three days to act.

Which was positively biblical.

Three days.

Just three days away.

Which meant only one thing.

Showtime.

Because by gum and by golly, we are the music makers, we are the dreamers of dreams! We are our only hope!

And *Mis*-tah Judah was ready to deliver that hope.

CHAPTER 6

GERMANY.

Sebastian slipped the laminated twelve-by-twelve cardboard case from the plastic sleeve and sniffed it. Then smiled. Just as papery and pulpy as the last time he had imbibed. Not only of what lay inside but of the cardboard cover-case itself.

That cover was black, with the impassioned trumpeter from 65 years ago. Although *Rubberband* and *Bitches Brew* were usually his go-tos during more rambunctious times of revelry and relaxation, this particular occasion called for something a bit more subdued. A bit less avant-guard and more standard. Something soothing and familiar.

Kind of Blue seemed about right.

Not that he was feeling blue. Far from it! He was on the verge of finally—finally!—accomplishing all that he had been longing for stretching a quarter of a century now. The down-tempo trumpets and piano and base and tenor sax would set the mood for the road ahead.

So out the lacquered disc came, all black and shimmering and grooved.

He plopped it on his turntable of choice. A walnut thing that went for three-gs, with a carbon-fiber tonearm and

Goldring Eroica LX cartridge that sent the audio waves sailing throughout the subterranean chamber he had commandeered for this final leg of things.

With one hand, Sebastian held the twelve-inch disc. With the other, he flipped the clear plastic lid and settled the disc on the one-inch-thick frosted platter. He held his hand steady as he moved the lever's arm with careful, deliberate precision over the thin, blank space between the two sections filled with rutted grooves along the disc of black.

Within seconds, the cavernous space a few stories underground filled with a base thrumming to life. It was followed by the white-and-black keys of a baby grand piano. Then a guttural tune waffled back and forth between two low notes as two chords from the piano's middle register filled in the gaps.

And then it came: the object of Sebastian's desire.

The trumpet. With the maestro himself offering up his notes. Pure and delicate, blown from the lips of a legend dead for two decades now.

Miles Davis.

Dad had introduced him to the king of jazz in his childhood, carting a vintage turntable with him across the globe, from base assignment to base assignment. It was one of the few things he had shared with his father. And his brother, now that he thought about it.

Which was ironic. On so many levels.

Sebastian closed his eyes and breathed in a satisfying, peace-filled breath.

Nirvana...

He positively adored the purity of the unadulterated music as it filtered from groove to needle. Then to speakers and out into the cavernous space until it reached his eardrums. Unencumbered by the whims of sound mixers and the soiling of an artist's original arrangement and composition of the work through impulsive flipping that had become the norm for those teenyboppers swimming upstream through the generational slipstream of life.

He shuddered at the thought, letting Miles be Miles, and *Kind of Blue* do its arrangement thing, a smile playing across his face with eyes closed.

As the final, mournful track on side two continued, Miles now accompanied by a saxophone fingering an emotive tune, Sebastian poured himself three finger's worth of Suntory Hibiki, a rare and pricey whiskey from Japan.

Bringing the crystal snifter up to his nose, he closed his eyes and inhaled a deep breath of the caramel liquid. The mature woodiness of sandalwood and a hint of rosemary danced through his nostrils, filling his head already on cloud nine from the aural elixir billowing around him throughout his chamber of repose.

He sauntered over to a marble sarcophagus at one end of the chamber that bore a man who had lit a match that had nearly burnt the Church to the ground half a century ago.

Instead, it rent it in half. Well, the other half. The Catholic half.

He was his hero. For good reasons.

Because everything that he had been working toward the past five years—everything the Thirteen and Council of Five, Nous itself, had been striving to accomplish the last two millennia—was coming to a climax. Finishing what that man, whose bones were still stuffed away in that marble sarcophagus swimming in flesh long rotted, had begun those many centuries ago.

The complete annihilation of the Church.

Finally.

And through the most unforeseen of means.

Subverting the faith by leveraging its own forgotten beliefs against it, tapping into a primal power that sat at the heart of the Universe long forgotten. One he himself had poo-pooed for years.

Until his most unexpected transformation two years ago now.

Sebastian slowed, pausing at a shaft of light knifing from recessed LEDs above and stretching his limbs. They were reminders of what he had become, of what he came to offer the world.

Salvation.

Freedom.

Divinity.

He flexed his fingers—all six of them—before clenching them into a fist, chords of muscle bulging from biceps that used to carry the appearance of the dutiful academic he had always been. Slight, slim, slender. Not this hulking mass of strength, of power. All it had taken was simple belief. Faith. In an Authority that offered what humanity had longed for since the beginning of time.

How did he put it? While the Nameless One hoarded such strength and power, claiming humanity would die if they dared soared toward the sun, the Authority knew better: *'God knows that when you eat of it your eyes will be opened, and you will be like God, knowing good and evil.'*

Sebastian let go of his clenched fist, uncurling his six digits and smiled, that number, those long, lithe fingers, representing so much. Not least of which was mankind and its potential.

'You will be like God, knowing good and evil.'

Exactly.

And he was ready to scale that promise, to take it to the masses!

But so much was riding on that phone call.

On that person on the other end of that phone call.

So Sebastian distracted himself by reveling in that aura of sacred infamy surrounding the body resting in sweet repose beneath the marker above that countless Christian pilgrims had venerated for centuries. A space that now served as ground zero for the systematic dismantling of the Church.

Which was entirely fitting, given the remains belonged to the man who had accidentally sparked its fractured demise over half a millennium ago.

It had taken some time to find the perfect spot to serve as Nous's headquarters. After those blasted Navy SEALs for Jesus literally blasted the former one into oblivion, he had been homeless, wandering aimlessly in search of a nerve center to command his agents across the world.

Then he'd found it. Or rather, Aurelius Chuke had, his trusty African warlord. A former Protestant church, actually, in the heart of Germany that had served as the launching pad for another assault against the Church. The Roman Catholic variety. It was for sale; apparently many of the former cathedrals in those parts were. And so he snatched it, sight unseen.

It was perfect, with a massive nave to serve as a gathering hall for the Thirteen, and offices throughout for him and his Nousati to plan and plot and scheme. No one would expect the chief antagonist of Christianity would be lurking about in its bowels.

An enemy in disguise. A wolf among sheep.

A cool, gentle breeze brushed his cheek, feeling almost pagan in its manifestation. Perhaps a lingering Presence summoned from the weekly ceremonies he had instituted on Friday evenings, honoring and worshiping not the Lord but the Authority. The sixth day seemed apropos.

The number of Man.

And the Antichrist.

There it was again, the presence of something fetid now. Something dead. Perhaps summoned from the Unseen Realm itself.

Sebastian knew better of course. Knew it was merely the

HVAC system regulating the humidity and temperature of the subterranean chamber, keeping the air cool and crisp for his use as a sort of headquarters for his operation. Knew that the sense of the sacred was merely an awareness of the freighted historical memory. Knew that feelings of religious affection permeating the chamber were more the product of the synapses in his brain than of any leftover holy halo belonging to the Reformation saint.

And yet, there was a growing sense that the supernatural was real. That it held sway over our seen realm, imbuing people and places and objects connected to the divine with a power that opened a connection to the Unseen Realm. A portal, if you will, where a mystical power flowed through the veins of the Universe, tying every atom and molecule together in a harmonious unity, stretching from the beginning of time until now. A force that had been named and claimed by various sects across the expanse of time.

Yahweh. Baal. Zeus.

Muhammad. Krishna. Buddha.

Jesus, the supposed Christ.

God.

Somehow, that force—that *idea*—had survived and thrived through the march of history, growing in strength and power through the Middle Ages and Enlightenment, modernism and postmodernism—right up to that present day, when humanity had conquered itself through the genome, replaced itself with AI large language model neural networks.

One iteration of that idea had perhaps the most shocking staying power of them all.

Christianity. The Church. The Body.

With Jesus Christ as its head, its font, its source.

Oh, the Universe had sure tried its damnedest to snuff the life out of it from the start before it could gain any sort of purchase. The Authority itself had!

Beginning with its prophet.

Except for one wrinkle.

Like the phoenix myth of old—Nous's very own symbol signaling the cyclical reinvention of humanity, the man lived on. Whether actually or merely in the memory and lived experiences of his followers—the jury was out on that one.

All that mattered was that rising, however it was conceived, had set the stage for an ongoing battle between the Nameless One and the Authority for two millennia. More than that, the *idea* had lived on, the resurrection. A claim that had quickly spread throughout Judea. Decades later, the Roman Empire had blamed his followers for countless acts of misery, persecuting and killing them in droves.

Yet they persisted, persevered, remained faithful to their Lord, their King, their Savior.

At several critical junctures in the Church's life she could have been put down, hard and fast, like a rabid dog. Yes, there were the challenges from outside the Church—principally Rome, but also others had come along seeking the eradication of those who bent the knee to Jesus of Nazareth. But there were the ones inside as well, the minority voices who sought an alternative understanding of the faith and challenged the elites within the Church who pulled the levers of power.

Yet something in the Universe carried the Church along, steeling her and bearing her up while forces from within and without waged war. Always surviving, always remaining faithful to the original vision of God's will in heaven being done on earth through repentance from sins and faith in the death and resurrection of Jesus Christ.

Then it happened, five hundred years ago.

An arrangement of crimson candles bordering the sarcophagus flickered with an orange glow, their blood-red wax dripping onto the vessel holding the bones venerated by many and down to the stone floor beneath. Shadows danced around the space that had become a sanctuary for Sebastian. Beneath, of all things, the narthex to a former parish.

All Saints Church.

Like most of European Christianity, the building was a former shell of itself, repurposed for his purposes. Ironically, the Church's destruction. How fitting that the site of the beginning of the Church's end would finally result in what that dead monk had set into motion.

Sebastian stood before the sarcophagus, taking a cautious step toward the rectangular, blockish object and spreading his palms upon its surface.

A chill ran through him, a shiver walked up his spine. Whether from the fruits of the HVAC system regulating the climate or the sacred aura still emanating from within, he did not know. Dared not intuit.

Instead, he closed his eyes and took in a contemplative breath, considering all that the man inside had accomplished.

The great Martin Luther.

The match that lit the fuse that split the Western Church in two. Forever altering the Church's course.

Although his original intent had indeed been a Christian reformation, what his little act of protestant defiance accomplished instead was the wholesale *renovation* of the religion.

Sebastian stood stiff and still, eyes closed and feet unmoving, feeling the aura surrounding the dead man pulsating from within the marble. Feeling a connection with the man inside. As if he were Luther's doppelgänger, reincarnated for such a time as this.

And yet, he was altogether different.

He was not merely a match.

Sebastian Grey was a blowtorch.

The one who would burn the Church to the ground by destroying belief in its pathetic god.

And from its rubble and ruin he would oversee the rising of

a spiritual power far greater than had ever before been conceived.

A true phoenix, rising from the bones and ashes of its dead ancestors to new life. Ready to lead a new incarnation of universal spiritual enlightenment and brotherhood that would bridge the gap between the spiritual and the natural, between religion and science—ushering in a new era of higher consciousness and divine wisdom, endowing the individual with a deeper awareness of their inner divine spark.

Wielding a weapon forged by the Creator himself...

A quote from the prophet Zarathustra rushed to the fore: *'You must be ready to burn yourself in your own flame; how could you rise anew if you have not first become ashes?'*

The sides of his mouth curled upward at the thought that he, Sebastian Grey, Grand Master of Nous, was the one the Universe had chosen to bear the flame that would set fire to the Church.

A new Aeon was arriving. A sphere of being flowing from the Authority and bestowed upon humanity to help them reach their destiny from the ash heap of religious affection.

A new messiah was rising.

Named Sebastian Grey...

A buzz drew his attention to his side pocket.

Sebastian breathed deeply from the wonder at what he was on the threshold of accomplishing. He shoved off from Luther's marble tomb, the original flame-setter, and reached inside his cloak for the cellphone.

His pulse raced at the interruption.

Right on time...

One final loose end to snip before it would all be his.

Draining his snifter, Sebastian slipped his phone out from a pocket.

And frowned.

What was this?

It was not who he expected. Or what.

He swiped it to life, his frown drooping into a scowl that sent a ping of anxious dread into his bowels.

One of his Nousati agents he had in the field had texted him a video file and urged him to play it. Said it could mean trouble.

Trouble was not a word he wanted to hear. Not when things were so precarious, when the world was burning and it was in need of a messiah!

So he played the video, at first not understanding what he was watching, what was going on.

It was a wide shot of what looked like a street corner somewhere on America's West Coast. Sky was clear and sunny. Buildings were bright and colorful. Streets were clean and swept. As the video zoomed in, it became clear a crowd had gathered. And around a person.

"What the blazes..."

Tall and lean and toned. Straw hair thick and wavy. Blue eyes piercing, with a voice that carried authority, if not for an unfortunate hickish lilt. The crowd didn't seem to mind. They were hanging on his every word. Some mumbo-jumbo about the seals of the apocalypse and—

Sebastian gasped. He could hardly believe his ears.

"Republic of Heaven?!" he boomed, huffing and puffing a roiling rage.

He kept listening, kept watching the reaction of the crowd —West Coast sheeple who hung on every one of his words.

Who was this pipsqueak? And, again, Republic of Heaven? How dare he co-opt his language!

The more he listened the more that rage turned to—what was it? Fear?

For he knew what this meant.

There was another. Offering what he offered.

A connection to the divine.

Salvation.

This would not sit well with the Thirteen, the Council of Five.

This could dismantle what he had worked for the past year.

What Nous had worked for.

He had to make a phone call.

CHAPTER 7

WASHINGTON.

Silas Grey needed a drink. And not just a midmorning caffeinated refill. Something alcoholic. Something hard. Something whiskey.

And neat.

By the time he dismissed his class early, excusing the shortened lecture because of the false-alarm faux emergency, and walking to the bar a few blocks down from Georgetown, it was just past eleven a.m. So the early libation wasn't entirely suspect, though drinking hard liquor before noon wasn't his norm. Although, he supposed it was happy hour somewhere, and he figured the familial bombshell detonated by Eddie P demanded a stiff one anyway.

Silas had led the way to one of his go-tos in a time like this. The Tombs was your classic university haunt staged in a converted 19th-century townhouse, outside walls painted a fresh cream and windows trimmed by robin's egg blue. A bit fancy for your college-town bar, but this was DC. Served comfort fare, pub grub, and brew, which was all that mattered.

And just what the doc ordered after the morning from hot Hades.

A bald, bulky man with a black T-shirt and tattooed arms

was unlocking the honey cherry doors when they arrived. Inside was a bit too dim for Silas, red-brick walls and a low black ceiling adding to the darkness, but he figured it would help with whatever news Eddie P was about to break. Place smelled of Pine-Sol at that hour, but stale beer and hops left over from the previous night, joined by peanuts and pub grease, pushed through for a strong hearing. At least there was an empty quietness to the joint, except for Bob Dylan's "Rainy Day Women" striking up its marching tune of horns and tambourines and piano, which suited him just fine.

A large circular bar of the same honey cherry wood as the entrance door, polished to a shiny sheen and edged by brass dulled by age, anchored the far end. Classic military recruitment posters from the mid-19th century hung on the brick walls around the bar. As did a hundred plastic beer pitchers above, ready to be put to good use for the night's big game. The pair had the place to themselves at that hour, and they took a booth in the far, back corner with a half-moon table and comfortable crimson leather seats. Silas liked the quiet spot and appreciated a wood wall of frosted glass that stood between them and the next table. Privacy was what was required for this meeting.

And that neat whiskey.

Eddie ordered a mint tea, and the server left menus while he fetched their beverages of choice. Neither of them were interested in food. Only talking, and drinking.

Dylan's prophetic croon about everybody getting stoned filled the silence, which wasn't what your typical frat boy thought it meant. Didn't want to, but Silas figured he'd toss the first rock.

So: "What's her name?"

Eddie settled back and threw up a grin before staring off, the upturned corners of his lips sagging and face drawing—grim, scared? It wasn't clear.

"Samantha Malia Perez," Eddie replied.

"Samantha Malia?"

"Takes her middle name after her mother. But she goes by Sammy."

"And the last name? Sounds Spanish."

"Guam was colonized by Spain in the seventeenth century and later ceded to America after the Spanish-American war. A Spanish heritage still survives."

"Hence Perez."

Eddie nodded. "Bingo."

So Silas, Sebastian, and Samantha. Made sense. And yet—

Yet it flat didn't. Made not a lick of it!

His head swam with the implications of it all.

He had a sister! Him and Sebastian.

And this woman had two brothers. Did she know it? Had she known about them, Silas and Sebastian, all these years, while they were in the dark? Had she tried to find them, and been thwarted or sidetracked? He knew he would've had he known about her.

Maybe.

Because there were still so many unknowns. So many questions swirling in a vortex of confusion that begged for a swig of that late-coming whiskey.

Yet only one question hung from his tongue: "How?"

"While stationed in the South Pacific," Eddie replied matter-of-factly. Definitely no fuss, no muss with this guy.

That would've been when he and Sebastian were around eight or nine. The tour of duty had lasted for five years before Dad had been transferred to the Pentagon, and he and his brother lived out most of their teenage years in Northern Virginia before going off to college.

So what did that clipped answer mean, while stationed in the South Pacific? What, so Dad had some one-night stand, some meaningless fling with a woman who was not his wife—

Who wasn't his mother?

Silas had to know but didn't want to. He asked anyway.

The server returned with two waters and their drinks. Tea for Eddie; whiskey neat for him.

He promptly drained the tumbler. Maker's Mark, if he placed it. Wasn't a Macallen by any stretch, but a college dive bar could do worse.

Vanilla and brown sugar, oak and clove hung heavy on his tongue, and the alcohol hit his stomach hard. Guess the Saxbys breakfast sandwich from earlier had limited mileage.

Silas called back to the server for another whiskey and added some crack fries to the order. The greasy, garlicky, peppery appetizer certainly lived up to its name, and it would get him through the next hour.

And that second Maker's Mark, making it a double.

Throwing back a swig of water to hydrate for the road ahead, he kept at it.

"Who?" was all Silas could get out. Even then, he wasn't sure he wanted to know.

That grin returned, wide and bright now. Eddie started steeping his tea, bobbing the sachet up and down in the hot water.

"A beautiful woman," he said, looking off again. "Could swipe the paint off a '69 caddy, she was such a looker. A real dame, she was. A real broad."

Another swig of water, then a quick glance over the shoulder for that second whiskey.

Silas settled back and asked, "On base?"

Eddie shook his head. "A local."

Silas's head swam with a dizziness he wasn't sure was from his drink or from the delirious implications of the fact his father had had a fling with some local gal while on Uncle Sam's dime in Guam. Resulting in a child—a sister! *His* sister, his and Sebastian's. A sibling Dad had never breathed a word about.

That wasn't even touching on the Pacific Islander woman he'd never breathed a word about!

"You should know," Eddie went on, "this was no one-night stand, not a lonely heart fling."

That caught his attention, and he felt mildly chided for thinking otherwise.

No, of course it wasn't. Dad was the most honorable man he had ever known. If he had fathered another child, it wasn't by accident. He would have loved her. Been committed to her. Provided and protected her. And the child.

His sister...

But the questions still swirled. Chief among them—

"Why didn't he tell us?" Silas asked lowly. Not with malice, but with not a small amount of hurt.

Finishing his steep, Eddie pulled the sachet out and squeezed it, setting it on the table. He sat there, for a few too many beats. Just cradled the mug and blew across the cup's surface.

Get to it already...

Thankfully their server returned with Silas's double whiskey and fries.

Didn't toss it back this time. Just a mouthful, that oaky vanilla and brown sugary cloves filling his senses and dulling the delirium some. He stuffed a handful of fries in his mouth to stave off any further effect of the alcohol. Boy, were those heavenly, the garlicky crisp potato wedges with a dash of pepper about as addicting as the whiskey.

When Eddie didn't reply, Silas asked again, "Why didn't he tell us, me and Sebastian?"

"It was different back then."

"It was the '90s!"

"When you returned to the states, that's when she was born."

"Sounds like a fling to me," Silas huffed, returning to his fries.

"No, son. Totally off base."

"I bet…"

Eddie took a sip of tea and explained, "Your father met this woman after helping her with a flat tire stranded in a near monsoon."

That sounded about right. Dad would stop for anyone that looked like they needed a helping hand. Liked that about him. Tried to be that himself.

"From there it led to a dinner, then some more, then—"

"A child?"

Eddie sighed. "A *relationship*. Then, yes, Samantha."

Silas threw back another mouthful of whiskey, then stuffed his mouth full of crack fries before he got himself into trouble. No way would he want to piss on Dad's legacy, accusing him of improper behavior. But this was just so much to wrap his head around.

Too much to wrap his head around!

So he threw back another swig and a mouthful of fries.

"They almost married, actually," Eddie said.

That was a shocker! And it probably showed, because he continued, "I say *almost* because she ended things. Just up and left, severing all communication. Tore Tommy G up something fierce, too."

"How do you know all this?" asked Silas, head swimming again from the revelation and no doubt lubricated by a few whiskeys.

"I'll get to that. But what matters is that your father was readying to tell you boys. Readying to share his relationship. Until it ended. Just like that."

Silas wasn't feeling hungry anymore, or thirsty. The thought of Dad's heart getting broken, twice over, with Mom's death, then this other woman…

Flat wasn't feeling hungry anymore.

Although he did take another pull of his whiskey.

Eddie went silent now, taking slow sips from his tea and huffing a sigh that threw up a welcomed minty freshness to the stale conversation.

"So where does the girl—" Silas stopped short, correcting himself: "I mean Samantha. Where does she fit into this?"

Swallowing, Eddie explained, "That's where I come in. I received a memo that there was a woman claiming to have carried the child of one of my subordinates."

"My father."

"That's right. I was his boss at..." He trailed off, taking another sip of tea. "Not important now. Other than the fact we were at the Pentagon and some lunatic was trying to strong arm Uncle Sam into giving her a payout for a section code violation several years ago. Didn't know how or why or what her deal was, only that the complaint came across my desk."

Another pause, another sip of tea.

To which Silas echoed with his own swig of whiskey, which was getting frighteningly low.

"Long story short, I ask Tommy G about it and he confessed to the...indiscretion. Which was indeed a section code violation. But, given his work—*our* work—we agreed on a plan of action."

"Which was..."

He shrugged. "Which was him making things right."

More confusion, more questions that demanded another swig of whiskey.

"I arranged for him to bring the pair to the US through a back-channel arrangement with INS at Treasury."

"Wait, Immigration and Naturalization Service?"

"That's right. They were stuck with the Department of Treasury until Dubya put 'em under Homeland Security."

"So this was before 9/11?"

"Just before 9/11..."

He went silent, sipping on his tea again.

Silas waited, head feeling faint from the alcohol now and the continued revelations.

Eddie finally said, "He was planning on telling you and Sebastian, that he had a daughter he didn't even know about."

That was new.

"Wait, Dad didn't know about Samantha?"

"He didn't. It's why the woman, Malia, had vanished. When she discovered she was pregnant. Then when your father found out, he fought like hell to bring her to the states and raise her proper."

Of course he did. That was just like Dad to make things right, to take responsibility for his actions, for the people in his life, his family.

"So she's, what, ten or twelve years younger than us?" Silas asked, working out the math. "Thirty or so?"

"Thirty-two."

"Thirty-two," he muttered, raking a hand through his hair.

He went to take a pull from his whiskey but set it aside and settled back instead. This flat wasn't possible.

"How do you know all this? Th–Th–This..."

Silas trailed off, not able to voice the truth of it.

"How do I know this woman? Your sister?"

He took a breath and nodded, swallowing hard and waiting for the reply.

Eddie shrugged. "I'm her godfather."

He scooted closer to the edge of his seat, eyes widening and locking onto Silas's.

"And that's why I've come. To you."

Silas grabbed his tumbler now and went to drain it, but hesitated. He wasn't sure he was ready for the answer to that why, and he needed his wits about him.

Setting the glass down on the table with a thud, he asked, "Why me? What do I got to do with—"

"Everything!" Eddie took a breath and swallowed. "I lost contact with her three weeks ago, so perhaps you can excuse my outburst."

"Lost contact..." Silas wasn't following. "What do you mean by that?"

"Every Saturday morning, without fail, we had a catch-up phone call."

Envy flashed through Silas at the thought that some long-lost sister was having weekly catch-ups with someone who acted as a father to her when Silas had lost his dad half a lifetime ago.

He let it pass, throwing back a swig then asking, "What happened?"

Eddie shook his head. "That's the thing, I don't know!"

Those intense eyes misted over now, and his hands clenched into trembling fists. Could tell the man was real worked up over this, worried even. Which seemed to fit this man's demeanor.

But what could he do? He was a professor! And an *adjunct* one at that. Not law enforcement, and certainly not some work-for-hire Blackwater contractor airdropped into some missing persons crisis.

Knew what Dad would do though, that's for sure.

Help.

Race into the burning building and rescue his kid. His daughter.

Silas's sister...

Which was enough for him to get to it.

Silas said, "Why don't you take it from the top. What led to all this?"

Eddie explained, "One day she is working at a biotech startup on the West Coast. Formed the company after college thanks to a work ethic that rivaled her—*your* father," he corrected. "Smart as a whip, too. Which she got from her mother. And it led to some biomedical discoveries that attracted outside venture capital investors. Was just living and loving life in the Bay Area. Had a minor scare, thinking she was going to lose her job when it was bought by some foundation. But that blew over and she rose quickly. Had even met someone, was talking marriage..."

He trailed off, that face softening some before hardening back up.

"Anyway, the next I know she is jibber-jabbering about the Republic of Heaven and—"

"Wait a minute," Silas interrupted, bouncing to the table. "Did you say Republic of Heaven?"

Eddie nodded. "That's right."

He eased back and took another sip of whiskey.

Not good.

"Does that mean anything to you?" the man asked.

"Maybe..." was all he replied. It was the same nonsense he had first heard from Rudolph Borg years ago, the Nous Grand Master, before—

He sighed, raking a hand through his hair and draining his bourbon now.

Before Sebastian picked up the mantle of Nous and their cause promoting this alternative spiritual realm to Christ's own Kingdom of Heaven.

"Anything else you can give?" asked Silas. "Like where she'd heard about this Republic of Heaven stuff?"

Eddie drained his own drink, a whiff of stale mint thrown up when he huffed a sigh and sank back into his seat.

"There was a lot of excitement around her foundation promoting it, but then she got hyper about finding it on WeNet."

"WeNet? Why was she emotional about that?"

"Not sure, but she was ticked."

Colorful language, and not anything to go on.

"Well, what about this foundation? What is it?"

Eddie replied, "The Aeon Foundation, they call it."

Silas sat forward, ice flooding his veins as a memory surfaced at that name.

"Did you say Aeon Foundation?"

He nodded. "Mean anything to you?"

Sure did. Was one of his first operations with the Order of Thaddeus, as much as he had stumbled into it without knowing what was what. His old war buddy from Iraq, Eli Denton, had gotten wrapped up with the joint.

Along with his brother.

Another connection to Nous.

Not good.

"Why come to me with this?" asked Silas.

He laughed. "Who else would I come to with it? You're Tommy G's boy! A decorated war hero who kicked Saddam's and his cronies' asses from here to kingdom come. And besides, she's your sister. Who else would I call?"

Had to give him that.

Silas knew what he needed to do.

Who he needed to call.

Celeste, his wife.

More specifically: SEPIO.

CHAPTER 8

Hiking it to SEPIO HQ was a nightmare. Although, billowing storm clouds had made the hour walk bearable, shielding the late-summer sun and reflecting the general mood of the city.

Traffic was snarled with people still thinking they should flee for their lives thanks to that bungled incoming ballistic missile emergency alert. No use even waiting for a Metro bus or taxi. Even an Uber would have been futile, so hike it they did, making for the base of operations for the Order of Thaddeus and Church's special-ops agency. Which also happened to be the home of America's ecclesial, architectural icon.

On the way over, Silas learned more about Eddie's background, which was quite an extensive history in negotiating and managing worldwide multimillion-dollar government and military contracts through commercial ventures, though he didn't get specific. He had a secret government clearance from the FBI due to his governmental and military contacts and projects he had worked with. Said he should ask about the scrambled phone call from the captain of a nuclear submarine beneath the Arctic ice cap when all this was over with, which sounded like quite the tale. One Silas was warming up to hear.

Even worked with the Vatican and European space agencies, in addition to his extensive work with US ones—which was quite the alphabet soup of agency experience. From NIH and CDC to FDA and EPA. Then the more scientific and military types, from NASA and DARPA to NIST and NOAA. Also had extensive access to restricted government, military, nuclear and research sites—which was where the connection to Dad came in.

Was real weird connecting with someone who knew Dad back in the day—something like thirty years or so, first stretching back to his and Sebastian's and Dad's days in Guam actually. Eddie had first connected with him through one of the government contractors he worked with, though he didn't specify. Something about US military readiness contracts and deployments in the South Pacific. Dad worked on that supply and logistics side of things, then a lieutenant colonel in the Transportation, Ordnance, and Quartermaster Branches. Kept in touch through the years and ended up working together on a project with an agency at the Pentagon, though again unspecified.

Which meant Eddie P had known Tommy G almost as long as Silas had been alive. Made sense why Dad had entrusted Samantha's care to him, the two going back ages and having their backs through not only the hell of American military bureaucracy. But also through the hell of life.

Crossing Massachusetts Ave, the headquarters for the Order of Thaddeus began to emerge above the trees swaying in a wicked breeze now that spelled stormy doom. The pair quickened their pace, reaching the white Indiana limestone of the Cathedral Church of Saint Peter and Saint Paul—better known as Washington National Cathedral. It stood starkly against the darkening charcoal backdrop of the mid-August Washington sky. The high-noon sun made zilcho purchase through engorged storm clouds. LED lights flared against its facade, making its whiteness even starker, its purity inviting the world inside to partake of the wonders of worship.

Silas and Eddie entered the sacred space through a pair of heavy oak doors, an elderly attendant in a red sport coat pressing a finger against his lips and pointing toward the nave.

A noontime Eucharistic prayer service was in full swing, which was unexpected but also appreciated. After the crazy morning—with headlines spelling doom and gloom, discord and rage filling the streets, a freakin' air-raid siren!—prayer was something he suddenly craved, along with the broken body and shed blood of Christ, tangible reminders that the ending to this madness was already written.

Jesus wins.

Silas smiled as they slowly walked through the entrance. Eddie followed behind as he led them into the nave. Lanterns hung high above, casting an orange glow upon the sacred space below. Beautiful stained glass windows grew darker by the growing storm clouds. Wooden chairs with small kneeling benches lined the nave, a surprising collection of parishioners and other seekers filling the seats and opening themselves up to God's presence during the time of prayer and worship. Supposed apocalyptic threats of nuclear annihilation will do that to a person.

As an undergraduate student at Georgetown University, Silas had visited the cathedral several times for a special evening prayer service with a few classmates. Even though it wasn't a Catholic institution, the liturgy was familiar enough to help guide and ground his spiritually searching soul. Back then, the service had started promptly at six, with the deliberate strumming of a harpsichord just in front of the upper stem of the cruciform structure. Instead, an organ began bellowing the opening of a hymn that was unfamiliar.

Silas walked farther into the nave. The siren song of the majestic pipe organ singing its tune beckoned him forward in worship, the parishioners standing and singing words he didn't recognize but appreciated, given the day's events:

> *"Comfort, comfort all my people;*
> *speak of peace," so says our God.*
> *"Comfort those who sit in darkness,*
> *groaning from their sorrows' load.*
> *Speak to all Jerusalem*
> *of the peace that waits for them;*
> *tell them that their sins I cover,*
> *that their warfare now is over."*

He grasped the back of a wooden chair in the back row, the song continuing onward. Closing his eyes, he took a moment of reflection himself, silently reciting the prayer that his Lord taught the disciples to pray:

> *Our Father in heaven, hallowed be your name,*
> *your kingdom come, your will be done, on earth as it*
> *   is in heaven.*
> *Give us today our daily bread.*
> *And forgive us our debts, as we also have forgiven*
> *   our debtors.*
> *And lead us not into temptation, but deliver us from*
> *   the evil one.*
> *For yours is the kingdom and the power and the*
> *   glory forever.*

"Amen," he whispered, crossing himself instinctively.

Eddie joined him now, the pair standing in silence even as that pipe organ soared with celestial worship, its moaning music a taste of Heaven itself.

"Now what?" asked Eddie.

"Now we wait for my contact, Victor Zarruq."

Silas had tried calling Celeste on the walk over. Took several attempts, the cell towers jammed with frantic callers, and even then he couldn't get through to her. Must be busy with her own business. Order of Thaddeus business. Finally managed to reach Victor Zarruq, one of the members on the religious order's board of directors.

"Who is this mysterious Zarruq figure, anyway? And what of the...the Order of Thaddeus you called it? I'm unfamiliar, even in all my years as a faithful Catholic. I thought we wrote the book on those sorts of religious order things."

Silas led them back out into the vestibule, thunder rumbling in the distance now and a whipping wind picking up pace through the open front doors. There was a strong scent of rain, joined by the static charge of an atmosphere ready to unleash a torrential storm.

"I told you on our walk over," he replied. "It's an ecumenical order dedicated to preserving the memory of the historic Christian faith, stretching all the way back to the early apostles. Let's wait for Victor. He'll explain more of—"

"Isn't this a pleasant sight for sore, old eyes," a warm, buttery, accented voice echoed behind them.

Silas spun around, finding a familiar face.

Victor Zarruq.

The man was rather tall and widely girthed, skin bronzed a lighter shade of ebony and face covered with a salt-and-pepper bushy beard—heavy on the salt. A wide smile stretched underneath, polished white teeth gleaming through a widening smile along with deep-set eyes into a look of delight. He was shrouded in billowing light brown vestments, an interweaving pattern of green and black and blue running down the center. Resting on his bald head was a matching hat embroidered with the same pattern.

The elder was a former African bishop on the board of directors for the Order of Thaddeus who had been assigned to

Silas a few years ago as a sort of wise, guiding guardian. He'd thought the man was meant to spy on him, but Zarruq had proven himself to be a trusted advisor who had his back. Even if he had been a deciding vote in a split a year back trying to oust him from his role as Master.

That vote against him had stayed any sort of official action, and it was hard getting over what felt like a betrayal, let alone trusting him that it was in his best interest. In explaining that vote, Zarruq had revealed that another board member, Eckhard Weiss, was ginning up a battle between conflicting camps within the Church vying for power—political and theological struggles taking up their cause with the Order. He insisted the inquiries were less about him and his leadership and SEPIO, and more about the bigger ecclesial picture.

Silas hadn't been so sure. If his experience with the Army and the academy had taught him anything, it's that these sorts of struggles have a way of spinning out of control and blowing things to kingdom come. Especially when committees are involved.

And especially when blowhards like Weiss were at the helm! Especially when they had been gunning for him for the better part of two years. Wasn't thrilled with the direction Silas had taken the Order, the man more concerned about social action and comforting the afflicted than Silas was with faith-contending and afflicting the comfortable by calling them to a faithful, obedient walk with Christ.

Supposed the man got his way in the end, getting his backside canned. While he hadn't been fired, he was no longer Order Master, having voluntarily relinquished his post by default after not returning for a year. Technically he was still Order Master, while Celeste was playing interim. But as far as he was concerned, she could have the dang job! Would make Weiss happy anyway, having a woman helm the ancient Christian order that had always had men as Masters.

And now he was coming, hat in hand, to ask for—what was it exactly? Help, he supposed, but he wasn't sure yet what he wanted. What Eddie had revealed, about the Aeon Foundation and the Republic of Heaven sure sounded suspicious. Which wasn't even touching on the fact he had a sister! Whom his father's old friend was godfather, and was apparently MIA.

Silas took a breath and smiled. "Victor."

The two embraced.

"Good to see you, Silas," Zarruq said, grasping his shoulders. "Especially given the circumstances."

"Suppose a false alarm heralding a nuclear apocalypse is reason enough to reconnect with those closest to you."

"That is being true. But that is not what I was referencing."

"What were you talking about, then?"

"Didn't Ms. Bourne—erm, I mean, Mrs. Bourne-Grey... Sorry! Didn't she tell you?"

Silas chuckled. "Sometimes I can't get over that name combo myself!"

They shared a laugh.

"And tell me what?"

Zarruq's smile faded. "Well, now that you're here, she can tell you herself. And you couldn't have come at a more providential time."

He eyed Eddie now, the man standing feet apart with his arms crossed.

Silas gestured toward his father's friend. "This is Eddie Pierzynski, the friend of my father I told you about who brought me intel I thought SEPIO should know about."

Eddie stepped over and offered Victor his hand; he took it and offered a friendly nod. Then Zarruq breathed in deeply, narrowing his eyes and furrowing his brow.

Turning to Silas, he said, "Can we speak for a moment, Master Grey?"

The two walked away from Eddie back toward the sound of the organ bellowing another hymn.

"I'm not sure anymore about your having brought this fellow to the Order's headquarters."

Silas nodded. "I understand, but he seemed very concerned about the missing woman, someone who was connected to two key SEPIO frontlines defending the Church."

He hadn't told Victor yet about the familial connection, Samantha being his sister. Figured start with the obvious SEPIO interests, the Aeon Foundation and the Republic of Heaven, then spring the personal ones after the fact.

Zarruq looked over at the man. "Do you trust him, Silas?"

Silas followed his gaze, Eddie's back turned toward them and observing the service.

"My father did," he replied, "which is enough for me. And Dad was one of the most honest, straightforward people I know."

He sighed and nodded. "Alright. Let's get on with it, shall we?"

Zarruq led Silas and Eddie across the darkening narthex, the thunder growing and a pitter-pattering of rain dancing now outside. He took them to the southwest tower and unlocked a dark walnut door leading into a small antechamber.

Silas smiled, a memory surfacing from when Rowan Radcliffe had gone through the same motions when he had brought his friend Grant Chrysostom to the Washington National Cathedral after he had brought to his doorstep one of his crazier SEPIO operations.

There was that echo again. Seemed to be his lot in life, with him returning to teach, and now recapitulating that same flight to Order HQ, only this time in the day, though under a darkening cloud he hoped didn't mean anything other than a late-summer storm.

A flash of white light, then a crack of thunder made him

wonder.

They descended a short set of stairs and met another small, short door. This one had a keypad. Victor Zarruq typed in a series of six digits, then opened the door. It led into an elevator.

"Goodness me..." Eddie said. "This place is sealed up tighter than the Pentagon!"

Silas smirked. "You have no idea."

Once the trio were inside, Zarruq pressed his palm against a piece of glass. It illuminated light blue, pulsing before turning green. Gears below immediately set into motion, taking the trio far beneath America's house of worship.

He smiled. "Into the void we go..."

There was a sudden drop and an almost feeling of levitation before evening out.

Leaning back against the carriage and bracing a hand, Silas sensed he was in something. Not sure what. Couldn't tell you if you asked. But with this revelation of someone connected to the various tentacles of Nous—this foundation, their ideology —not to mention some sister...

Yeah. Definitely in something. Had developed a sixth sense about that sort of thing. In the back of his lizard brain that had gotten him through three tours fighting America's wars.

And five years defending the Church's faith.

Except—

Except he wasn't sure he was ready.

But he knew it didn't matter. Not when duty called.

And family.

Family...

Whatever further revelations lay below, Silas resolved to jump into the fray of things. To see this through to the end, this thing Christ had plopped in his lap that morning.

It was go time.

On the double.

For faith and family.

CHAPTER 9

Descending into Order HQ, an uneasiness began to churn in Silas's belly—and not just because of the regretful mixture of college-bar whiskey and greasy pub fries after hoofing it a few miles in the humid afternoon.

It was from returning to a place he had taken leave of—voluntarily this time, unlike his last Princeton employer who had sacked him. A place whose politics were grinding him down—the administrative sort, Weiss and his cronies making his life hell; the theological sort, those same blowhards disagreeing with his direction contending for the central beliefs the Church has always held dear.

It was also a place that had taken so much from him—arguably his relationship with his brother, the two locked in a Cain-Abel head-to-head over matters of faith. But also part of his soul, as the Army had, battling to preserve the faith even if it meant taking lives along the way. And literally a part of his body, his hand having been blown to smithereens and gut ripped open on an operation that was like all the others from the past half a decade defending the Church, then another half a decade before that defending the country.

So, yeah. Lots of reasons apart from bad eating choices for

his gut to be twisting up plummeting into the depths of the Church's protection league.

It also wasn't his league any longer. Officially, perhaps, but not in practice. And he felt a little bad romping back onto Celeste's turf bearing a gift that could turn out to be a big nothingburger or—

Or something that might make her life an unpleasant one.

Silas felt his pocket, wondering if he should try Celeste again, feeling a bit funny jumping back into Order HQ like this while things were still nebulous with him, and she was technically in command. Supposed they would rendezvous at some point, and she would learn of things then. But then it could get awkward.

So he pulled out his phone—

But the battery had drained empty.

Just his luck...

Half a minute later, gravity did its weightless thing before pulling up with a groundedness that really made Silas seriously regret his earlier bad eating choices!

Settling below, cool, dry air smelling of a summer storm flooded the carriage as the doors opened. The neo-Gothic interior of pale limestone above darkened by the emerging storm had given way to a world of white light, gray slate, and brushed metal several stories below. Eddie wasn't too far off his Pentagon comment. Things were about as secured and buttoned up at the Order's headquarters and central SEPIO command center as any of the military bases he had worked on for a quarter of his adult life.

"This way," Zarruq announced, leading him and Eddie down a series of hallways lined with doors armed with the same kinds of keypads as the elevator.

As they rounded a bend, Eddie whispered in Silas's ear, "Where have you taken me, son? This looks like some Navy SEALs for Jesus outfit."

He smiled. About the truth of it but he didn't know how much to let Dad's former friend and DoD coworker in on what they did.

"Relax. It's the headquarters for the Order of Thaddeus, like I mentioned on our way over. We'll give you the lowdown on things when we get to where we're going."

"And where's that, son?" Eddie said, slowing past a darkened open door.

Silas tugged at his arm. "I'll give you the nickel tour when this is over."

He frowned, but the two caught up to Zarruq, who announced their arrival at a familiar door.

His door. Or his *old* door, rather. Temporarily, technically, but who knew what would happen.

"Here we go..." Zarruq said, pressing his hand against the same kind of glass that was at the elevator.

It lit with the familiar blue light. After it turned green, the door unlocked and Zarruq pushed it open.

Awaiting them was a well-appointed room far different from the rest of the facility. Instead of the sanitized gray, the room was entirely clad in dark wood. Floor to ceiling bookcases lined the walls containing biblical, systematic, and historical theological resources stretching back to the early Church.

At one end was a large fireplace, the kind a person could walk into if they desired. No crackling fire today, but its hardwood smoke still lingered. A large wooden desk commanded the other end of the room, ornately designed with pillar legs and mahogany sides.

Had been his desk, all askew and piled with books and papers on his latest research. Now...not so much. Much cleaner and organized. As in Celeste Bourne-Grey organized. Everything was in their proper place in neat stacks. Some of them were even stamped with Eyes-Only designations, apparently carrying her MI6 roots into the Order workplace.

A series of monitors stood behind it, all dark and hiding their purpose. At the center of the room was a sizable Persian-style rug patterned in reds and blues and greens. On top sat two leather couches facing each other flanked by two well-worn, overstuffed leather chairs. Victor motioned for them to sit.

Instead, Silas sauntered to a minibar tucked between a set of bookcases searching for his stash of Macallan Scotch whiskey. A glass cupboard above a marble counter filled with tumblers did not disappoint. Only a 12 year, but beggars couldn't be choosers at a time like today. Which had a very end-of-days vibe to it.

Eddie called out and asked for rum on the rocks. He found a decent bottle of Ron Centenario and poured two tumblers of noontime libation then headed back to the center lounge.

Silas handed off Eddie's drink and slumped into an over-stuffed burgundy leather chair. *His* chair. Or he supposed it was Celeste's with things so up in the air. Either way, the cozy comforts of well-worn leather, the woodsmoke still lingering through the large room of books and old wood, now joined warm scotch that didn't taste half bad. Soaked raisins, cigar, and peppery cloves with a nice long finish.

Just what the doc ordered, that's for sure. For a third time!

"Master Grey—" Victor stopped short, swallowing and smiling before continuing on: "Well, Silas, he tells me you've got something interesting to share regarding a missing acquaintance, and a connection that serves our own interests."

Eddie finished a long swig and smacked his lips, humming with pleasure and giving his head a shake, smiling and chuckling and mumbling something about it being true.

Which confused Silas.

He caught the same confusion on Victor's face, eyes flashing wide before narrowing back on Eddie.

"Sister," the man said, taking another swig.

"Excuse me?" replied Victor.

"You said *acquaintance*. His sister is missing. Samantha Perez."

Victor flashed Silas wide eyes but thankfully left it alone. That would take some explaining Silas wasn't interested in at the moment.

"What's your meaning?" asked Silas, easing back another swig himself and moving the conversation well past his long-lost sister.

Eddie's smile faded some. "I don't follow?"

"It's all true. That's what you just said. What is all true?"

A flash across his eyes and a glance left before a shift on the couch told Silas he had caught the man off-guard.

Tossing back another swig and setting down his tumbler with a clunk on the glass coffee table, Eddie chuckled again and threw up his hands.

"You caught me, Silas. And a nice catch at that. Although, wouldn't expect anything less from one of Tommy G's boys!"

"Who is this...Tommy G character?" asked Victor.

"My father," Silas said flatly. "And you're stalling."

Eddie chuckled. "Oh, come now, Sy. You didn't think an old military rat like me wouldn't check out my target now, did you? Wouldn't know everything about his past and present before crashing his first day of class—and as an adjunct professor?"

Heat raced up Silas's neck and flashed hot in his face with a mixture of irritation and anger, even caution at Eddie's suggestion. He was struck dumb. He was dumbstruck! Perhaps a first, but he didn't know what to make of that one.

Are you kidding me...

Target? What the heck had the man been rutting around in his history for?

And *why* the heck had he been rutting around in his history?

He threw back the rest of his whiskey and swallowed hard, then went to drill the man.

When Eddie intercepted his reply: "Silas Grey, Master of the Order of Thaddeus, ancient defender and protector of the Christian faith. A post which was filled by Rowan Radcliffe before you until his untimely demise. Didn't get the specifics on that one, so I suppose that's, as we military types call, *classified.*"

Silas threw Victor questioning eyes. He only shrugged, face drawn and clearly as uncertain as Silas was.

"You spend most of your time," Eddie went on, "fulfilling Jude 3, Saint Jude Thaddeus's exhortation to *'contend for the once-for-all faith entrusted to God's holy people.'* One of the least well-known verses from the Bible's tiniest book, but I'd say it's a good one, and a worthy mission."

Now the guy was just showing off. It both irritated and concerned Silas. Clearly he was a pro at this sort of thing. And the Order's secrets weren't as secure as he thought. Though that wasn't his problem any longer.

Eddie took another swig of rum and barreled forward: "Speaking of which, the mission of the Order of Thaddeus was established by Jude Thaddeus from the start of the Church's existence. You have been leading the religious order until your wife, Celeste, temporarily took over your gig. From what I can gather, Rowan Radcliffe had recruited her out of MI6 to lead this mission to preserve and protect the memory of the faith."

Silas sat stiffer at the mention of Celeste. Now he was treading on thin ice, dialing into Celeste's backstory like that.

"Although formerly a Catholic religious order, similar to the Benedictine and Carmelite monastic orders, not to mention the more academic Dominican and Franciscan mendicant orders, the Order of Thaddeus has transformed itself into an ecumenical mission, with members from every Christian denomination. From what I can gather, Protestant, Catholic, Orthodox, even some Southern Baptist brothers and sisters in the faith all work together to contend for Christianity. Now, if I didn't trust my sources explicitly, I'd say the outfit sounded suspiciously like the kind of fronts that populate religious conspiracy action-adventure thrillers."

Eddie chuckled at that little swipe and drained his rum.

Silas put up a staying hand. "Alright, you've made your point. Whatever that might be. How about—"

"Hold on, Silas, I haven't gotten to the best part of all."

"And what's that?"

Eddie grinned. "Why, you. The venerable Silas Grey, who joined a few years ago after an illustrious career at Princeton, where you held similar interests preserving Christian objects and relics of the faith, as well as its memory and beliefs, surrounding the faith itself with a hedge of protection. For centuries, the Order has worked tirelessly to instantiate Thaddeus's vision for faith-contending, stretching clear back to those earlier decades of the Church's existence."

He settled back into the couch, one end of his mouth curling upward. As if he were proud of himself for the show of things.

Silas regarded him, the man clearly not as he presented himself when he first showed up on the Georgetown courtyard, and then at his classroom before that. He went for his tumbler again but found it empty.

Frowning, Silas asked, "You clearly did your homework. On me and the Order. So, I'll ask again, what's this about? Because with that sort of preparation I'm guessing that this long-lost sister wasn't why you came calling."

Eddie sat forward. "No, Samantha was a reason I—"

"There you go! *A* reason. One of...how many?"

He went for his drink again but found it similarly empty.

Throwing up the same frown, he answered, "You're right. There is another reason I came to you, Grey."

Not Silas. Grey. The personal pretense had fallen away. Which he didn't mind in the slightest, given the nefarious turn.

Time to get down to business.

He said, "I'll ask you again, and not for a second time. What is this about?"

"I'll explain it all—"

"Do I even have a sister—this Samantha lady?"

"Yes. All of that is true."

"Which you used to leverage me!"

Eddie opened his mouth but took in a breath instead of spewing another word. Eyes wandered up to the ceiling, like he was choosing his words carefully.

Wise move.

Silas was usually one to give people the benefit of the doubt. Especially old buddies of Dad. That benefit was quickly sieving to nothing but nothing after what he had pulled.

He finally said, "You're right. I did. It was the only way to get in the door and explain what I've seen, experienced. What it might mean..."

Eddie trailed off, and that hard, no-nonsense face of his suddenly softened. As if there was something dark behind those silver glasses hiding in those blue eyes. Like Silas had thought earlier: stories and secrets.

"All of it is the truth, by the way," he went on. "Samantha was Tommy's—*is* Tommy G's daughter. Your sister, you and your brother's. And I am scared for her, for what she could be wrapped up with. I do want your help finding her, and you have the right to be irritated."

Silas laughed, not at all minding the loud echo.

"*Irritated* is the least bit of my emotional state right now." He clenched his jaw and leaned forward. "And the least of your worries. So talk already before—"

A gentle *bring-bring* sounded with interruption.

A phone on a side table next to Victor Zarruq.

He answered it, excusing himself. Listening and nodding, not saying much, he said he'd be there shortly—and with a guest.

Thought he was referring to Eddie, until Victor said, "We are needed in the bunker. Me *and* you, Silas."

"What's this about?" he asked, reluctant to get involved.

"Something about some troublesome street preacher. It's what I was referencing earlier when—"

"Street preacher, you say?" Eddie said, straightening with wide eyes.

"Yes...that is correct."

"Rising on the West Coast—in California?"

Now Victor straightened, tossing Silas questioning eyes. "That is correct."

The man closed his eyes and sighed, giving his head a shake and mumbling something about the Lion of Judah.

Silas turned to Eddie. "What's this about?"

He startled, clearly deep in thought and rattled about something. He locked wide eyes with Silas's own, face set as flint.

"I need to come with you. It's why I came."

Now Silas tossed Victor questioning eyes, who only shrugged and gestured toward him. As if reminding him he was still Order Master, and it was his call.

That *bring-bring* returned, putting an exclamation point on the urgency of the matter.

Which Silas didn't like.

Not one bit.

But—

He stood, heading for the door.

"Let's go."

CHAPTER 10

So much for turning over a new leaf. History more than echoes.

It bites.

Case in point: the clattering echo of Silas's stiff leather shoes down the cold, stale hallway that reminded him of a special-ops career he had left behind. Twice now! First with Uncle Sam's military and then with Christ's Church.

At least he wasn't in charge. Celeste could more than handle whatever had called for Victor's attention, and his apparently. But he wouldn't get involved. He had a class to teach. And his prosthetic hand was rubbing wrong against his stub, reminding him of the costs contending for his faith.

Except—

He glanced at his right, catching sight of Eddie craning for a look into an open door they had just passed. Just a break room, so no harm. But his interest in the Order's HQ wasn't something he was having. That wasn't even touching on his knowledge of the Order itself, which seemed extensive. Nor did that touch on the revelation he had brought to Silas's doorstep.

Samantha.

His sister.

Flat couldn't believe it.

And though Silas didn't want to jump into yet another ill-fated operation saving the Church's backside, if it came to saving his family—really the only remaining family he had, his brother having abandoned him years ago. If it came to *that*... well, he wasn't sure he could refuse.

A memory suddenly surfaced, from years ago. When Rowan Radcliffe had made his first of several overtures for him to join the Order as a SEPIO agent preserving and protecting the Church. Silas had demurred, telling the former Order Master that he had left that sort of kinetic life behind years ago —the kind that got his best friend Colton killed, the kind that still gave him night terrors waking up in cold sweats and trying to tear the bed apart thanks to dark dreams from wicked memories long buried.

Radcliffe's response? Accused him of trading that life in for comfort and tenure. Silas replied there wasn't anything wrong with that, which the chief had agreed was true—with a caveat: *'when the world is right, and evil isn't knocking on the door. But bad men need nothing more to accomplish their ends, than that good men should look on and do nothing.'*

He'd been impressed Silas knew the quote was a play on something John Stuart Mill had said, where most others said Edmund Burke. But when he pressed him, Silas insisted he was doing something by returning to Princeton and his research, teaching his students and retrieving the memory of the vintage Christian faith in a way that gave them enough of a compelling experience of that faith to take an interest in it.

And he'd done it too. *Was* doing it. Again.

But to what end? Was there really hope in changing the hearts and minds of a generation back to faith when nearly four in ten Gen Zers said it wasn't possible to know for sure whether God was real? Even with the swirling chaos in the world with a very end-of-days vibe, would that be enough to get folks, his students, thinking about who God is and how they can know him?

Then again, if the faith collapsed, from threats inside and outside the Church—as it seemed there always were these days, given the *bring-bring* of Victor's phone just minutes ago—would there be anything to change them toward?

Good thoughts.

Maybe getting his hands dirty again wasn't such a bad idea...

Either way, reality was coming at him fast down a cold, dimly lit corridor.

Rounding the final bend on toward a pair of double doors, the churn in Silas's stomach from earlier roiled into a knot that tightened something fierce. He ignored it, laying a hand on Eddie's arm and slowing.

The man followed, and Silas addressed him: "Look, Eddie. You've stumbled into the central operation center for some of the Church's most sensitive of operations. Something that those on the outside don't have a clue exists. Glad you brought me that intel, both on my sister and this connection to past SEPIO operations, as well as whatever else you've still got cooking."

Eddie smiled. "But you're nervous I'll give away the Church's secrets?"

Silas smirked. "Well, sort of!"

He chuckled, patting Silas's shoulder. "Look, son, given where I've been with the US government, what I've seen—on domestic and foreign soil...Don't worry. Your secret's safe with me. So is the Church's."

Good enough for Silas.

Victor had already arrived at a heavy steel door leading into the SEPIO operation center, along with a pair of biometric scanners: one for his eyes, the other for his palm. Slapping his hand against the one, he put his face near the other, then waited.

A *blurp* sounded as the scanners performed their duty, though Silas understood it was probably more an aural indicator for the user than anything that worked the gears that would open the doors.

A few seconds later, there was a *click*, and the door retracted inside the bunker.

Victor motioned for them to follow. Silas took a breath and stepped inside. Time to get to work.

Again.

Dimmed recess lighting around the perimeter shone down upon narrow tables lining the darkened walls commanded by workstations manned by agents dutifully executing on SEPIO orders. Zoe Corbino and her operational support team. Was amazing what they could do. Was also amazing the technology the Order's SEPIO special-ops unit had at its disposal, leveraging their own satellites and even some foreign government ones to execute on their faith-contending mission.

A massive screen at one end tracked critical operation updates and news footage from the world's major outlets reporting on items of interest to the Church. One corner of one side showed several billowing plumes of black smoke rising from across a city. Presumably Kyiv, the Ukrainian capital that had fallen hours ago. Another corner looked like a fleet of ships, two aircraft carriers and support vessels. Presumably the Chinese carrier group reported on earlier, launching their long-awaited attack on Taiwan. As if all that wasn't enough there was some crackpot that meant something to the Order and the faith—which also apparently meant something to his new pal Eddie.

At the center of the room was a raised platform with a U-shaped conference table mounted with small screens, swivel chairs, and direct-line phones to operation centers around the world. Around it sat his team—well, former team. The SEPIO agents he had fought with and bled beside for half a decade now.

Matt Gapinski, the six-foot-four bruiser who had also been one of Uncle Sam's grunts. A Marines Marine who was exactly the kind of guy you wanted standing next to you in a fight. Loyal to a fault and kept things light when the heat was turned up wicked hot. His respect for the man, for his faith in Christ despite the hell he'd been through, the things he'd seen—it was through the roof.

Then Naomi Torres, who was more the academic type but also packed a mean punch, on account of her Krav Maga expertise she'd picked up fighting for the Israel Defense Force as the daughter of a Jewish mother who married a Mexican father. The pair had tragically been killed in a car accident, and she'd had her share of more pain since, most recently a cancer scare she'd thankfully recovered from. Her background in anthropology and archaeology were crucial assets to the Order that had gone a long way in preserving the faith.

And his wife, Celeste. She was former MI6, working on specialized cases for the Secret Intelligence Service for Her Majesty's British government, who kicked butt and took names like it was nobody's business. Even kicked his butt once in a while when he needed it, which he appreciated. She was a steady hand at the helm of SEPIO with an even steadier aim in the thick of it. Her brawn was only outmatched by her brain, having been Oxford educated in comparative religion. And her beauty swept the table!

She was also his partner in life, as much as in crime-stopping. His soulmate, his best friend.

Zoe looked up on his arrival, those baby blue glasses of hers sliding down her face. She pushed them up the bridge of her nose and stood. "Hey, chief! Glad to have you back."

Silas glanced over to Victor but realized she was talking about him. Could feel embarrassment blooming at his cheeks from the show, and the designation. He wasn't chief any longer, but he left it alone.

Speaking of which...

Celeste strode toward him, those pools of azure of hers bright and smiling even as her lips restrained the same. They had always kept things professional at the office, trying to bring a bit of restraint to their relationship while on the job. After hours...now that was a different story.

For reasons that were clear by the British Queen striding his way! With her braided chestnut hair falling across her shoulders. That nice-fitting white blouse that hugged her in all the right places. Same for the dark denim and those legs with killer calves sheathed in those black leather boots that—

She grabbed his hands, leaning in for a peck on the cheek.

So much for keeping things professional!

Which he didn't mind in the slightest.

"Welcome, love. You alright?" Celeste asked in perfectly polished British English.

Silas caught his breath, the scent of vanilla and jasmine ratcheting his ticker. Her scent.

"After that greeting, now I am."

She giggled. "Hope you weren't terribly sidetracked by that bloody ballistic missile false alarm."

He glanced at his new pal. "No. Not terribly. Although class was cut short."

"Stuff and nonsense!" she scoffed. "Leave it to the Yanks to needlessly frighten the masses."

She followed his glance, furrowing her brow now.

"I didn't know we had struck up the nickel tours again."

"Oh, I'd say the SEPIO bunker deserves at least a dime." Gapinski sauntered over, jutting out his hand to Silas; he took it. "Good to see you, bro. But I'm with Celeste."

He pulled Silas aside, whispering with a nod, "Who's the

new guy? Not sure I'm a fan of tourists galavanting through our super-secret digs."

Silas sighed. "It's a long story, but he's got some intel that might be important. And there's another matter…"

Celeste regarded Eddie and returned to Silas. "We've had a bit of a go of it over here ourselves."

"With what?"

"With a puzzling development that came across a backdoor channel to an operative embedded in an upstart religious entity on the West Coast."

"What sort of upstart religious entity?"

"Got it!" Zoe announced before Celeste could answer.

She instructed their intrepid techie to put the video up on the main monitoring screen.

"Do I know you?" asked Gapinski, sidling up to Eddie.

He sized him up, which was sort of comical to look at. Five-eight-or-so Eddie craning up to six-four Gapinski.

"Can't say that you do, kiddo," he replied. "Neither can I."

Gapinski shook his head, muttering, "I swear you look familiar…"

The other videos faded away to black until a long, portrait-mode rectangular video started playing. Looked amateur, taken with someone's personal phone.

The scene playing out sure looked like it was taken on the West Coast. Stark blue skies. Tall, waving palm trees on a grassy hillside. Vivid colors beneath a strong sun. Stucco storefronts in the background painted light, Southern colors with red clay roofs.

And a man commanding a surprisingly large audience for a street preacher.

There he was. Young and fit, with long blond hair and over-sized, coke-bottle glasses. Oddly wore orange polyester pants and an A-Team T-shirt from the '80s. Looked like he was holding a Bible, the leather black and cracked, page edges stained a familiar crimson, a faded gold cross glinting in the sunlight as he waved the Good Book around.

If Silas didn't know any better, the man looked like any West Coast surfer dude. Maybe on the hippie end of things, but weren't they all? A waxed longboard in one hand, a reefer in the other?

A crowd had gathered around him, with an interesting assortment of characters. A pair of mothers in peach Lululemon yoga bodysuits each gently rocked a stroller as they listened on, slurping on green smoothies. Three actual surfer dudes in board shorts hugged actual waxed longboards behind, with a man in a business suit and sunglasses listening on as well. A few more older women and older men, joined by more business-types—polo-wearing, skirt-wearing, suit-wearing— and a few more twentysomethings. Had to be close to twenty people listening to what the mystery man had to say.

Odd. Real odd.

"It's him..."

Silas turned toward the voice. It was Eddie.

"You know this fella?" asked Gapinski.

"In a way..."

Celeste threw Silas questioning eyes before landing back on Eddie. "I'm sorry, who are you again?"

"Ed Pierzynski," Silas explained. "A friend of my father."

Celeste nodded, regarding the man before asking, "Why did you say you knew this man?"

Eddie turned to Silas. "It's what I came to talk to you about."

They both said nothing, waiting for him to continue. He gestured at the table and suggested they sit.

Silas eyed it, that unsettled churn returning to his stomach. Last thing he wanted to do was to get back in the SEPIO saddle —literally, manning the ops-center conference table. But he supposed it's why he brought Eddie here. To hear him out then hand him off.

Celeste led the way up a short set of stairs to the raised platform, taking the center chair—the one he'd commanded the past few years. Was more than happy to let her helm the ship.

Torres and Gapinski flanked her right. Eddie sat next to Celeste on her left.

Silas reached for a tumbler and carafe of water at the center of the table. Pouring himself a glass, he slumped down next to Eddie and took a drink.

Then got to it: "I think it's about time you explained yourself, Eddie P."

He took a breath, then a beat.

Then: "There is a coming reckoning."

"A–A reckoning?"

"A cataclysm the likes of which humanity hasn't seen before. War, drought, pestilence. False prophets."

Eddie gestured to the man on the screen. "Like him. A branch of David was the way he was described, and looking like that character. With that blond mane and glasses, jeans and T-shirt, the King James Bible."

"I call Cuckoo for Cocoa Puffs..." Gapinski muttered.

"I'm not crazy," he replied, measured and not defensive.

Torres smirked. "Yeah, right. War, drought, pestilence pretty much sounds like your typical Tuesday evening news cycle."

Celeste asked, "How do you know about this...this coming cataclysm, this chap on the West Coast?"

"I had a vision," Eddie replied matter-of-factly. "Something I believe the Spirit himself gave me for such a time as this."

"What sort of vision?"

"Just what I said. A manifestation of the Holy Spirit, giving me prophetic insight into coming world events."

The table went silent. Wide eyes darted about and looked for guidance. SEPIO clearly didn't know what to do with that one! The Order didn't normally give in to flights of ecstatic prognostication. Much more into the tangible, the observable.

So this notion that Eddie had received some sort of heavenly download...it didn't compute.

Eddie turned to Silas. "What sent me searching you out was the one I had a week ago."

"About..." Silas questioned.

"An earthquake. On the East Coast. Among other things."

"The East Coast?" exclaimed Gapinski before he laughed. "Now I *know* you're Cuckoo for Cocoa Puffs! Not possible."

"I saw it."

"Right...the voice in your head."

"It's the catalyst," Eddie went on, ignoring the man, "the precipitating event setting into motion a rise in challengers to God himself!"

Silas eyed the man, confused yet intrigued. Certainly didn't look or sound crazy, though the vision thing sure was bonkers. But none of this computed. Even if he were right, and some earthquake rocked the East Coast—*big* if on that one!—what would it matter? Why would it pose some challenge or challenger to the Lord himself?

Silas went to ask about it when he noticed his drink rattling on the table. That rattle sent up a flare of cascading rings, like a pebble dropping down at the center and water rippling out. Reminded him of the footprint puddle in *Jurassic Park* that flared with the same perturbation.

Right before the T-Rex stormed the road and gobbled up that poor venture capitalist investor!

It grew in intensity, the tremor snapping into a rumble that raced through the entire room now.

"You feel that, right?" asked Gapinski, sliding back from the table, hands raised and face a shade whiter.

"The rumble," Celeste said, nodding.

"Don't tell me another Nous whack job blew himself up on our doorstep!"

The thought had crossed Silas's mind. But...

No, not a bomb. He knew exactly what it was.

Definitely an—

"Earthquake!" Torres shouted.

Then the lights gave out. Something crashed to the floor. And one thought raced through his mind.

"Run!"

CHAPTER 11

There was another thudding crash. Close by. Followed by a chorus of screams and shouts for cover. Joined by a few cries and shouts of injury.

Silas's instinct was to go for his wife, but he couldn't see a damn thing! Just groped about in the thick blackness.

Red emergency lights snapped on, then an alarm flared. Not an air-raid siren.

This time a fire alarm.

A growing haze seeped along the ceiling, the acrid smell of smoke sending up a warning and a rise of bile at its wretchedness. But that wasn't the worst of it. Or perhaps the worst of it was the cause of it!

Server racks had toppled, with someone's leg trapped under one of them, with sparks jumping and threatening flames from others. Plaster and concrete littered the floor, including a large chunk that had thudded into the center of their own U-shaped table. SEPIO personnel were crouched with hands above them, someone pressing those hands against their head to stanch a shimmering black flow.

All the while the world continued to roil and shake something fierce!

"Everyone, to the floor for cover!" Celeste commanded.

Good call.

Silas helped Eddie under the table while Gapinski and Torres and Celeste scrambled for cover themselves.

"You alright?" he asked the man.

He winced, dabbing his fingers against a rising goose egg. Didn't look bloody, so that was a relief.

"I'll live," he grunted.

Satisfied, Silas scrambled to Celeste. They embraced, another thudding crash sending them crouching for further cover, but at least the tremors seemed to have lessened.

"Are you hurt?" Silas asked in a rush, hands cupping her face and looking for injury.

"I'm fine. You?" she replied, doing the same.

"Same, but—"

Another crash, followed by the flash of an orange glow from behind, snapped his attention down into the SEPIO ops center.

Sparks flared from another toppled server and danced along the ground, the July Fourth show triggering a fire on a pile of papers that had cascaded to the floor. The glow quickly spread to more fallen combustible debris that threatened to bloom into an inferno and consume the room.

Which sent Silas scrambling to his feet in search of a fire extinguisher.

The trembles continued roiling through the room, the panicked screams and falling chunks of concrete disorienting, compounded by the gauntlet of toppled displays and shelves and desks.

"Help me!" a voice cried out. To his right near the row of workstations.

A familiar voice that snagged his attention from the fiery glow blooming into a blaze. The sight of that orangey red squeezed the breath out of him.

Zoe Corbino.

She was wedged under one of those fallen server racks, the heavy steel shelves resting across her body. Her baby blue glasses were tossed next to her, a spiderweb crack in one lens.

With that fire spreading along the floor, leaping from the combustible remains of the earthquake toward her position!

The source of that blaze could wait. Zoe could not.

He raced to her, grabbing hold of the fallen shelves.

"Hang in there, Zoe. I've got you."

"My leg...I think it's broken," she whimpered.

Which sent him yanking at the server rack. Boy, was that heavy! Heavier than it looked, that's for sure. That quake must've landed a mighty high Richter Scale score to send this dog sailing to the floor.

Four years as a quarterback with the Falls Church Jaguars, that and more with the Rangers, then a strict exercise and lifting regime wouldn't let a thing like steel stand in the way of lifting—

Zoe screamed. "It's cutting into my leg!"

"Here let me lend a helping hand, chief."

Gapinski stormed up to the other side of the rack, and the two lifted as one.

Took some elbow grease, and Zoe bearing more pain, but they managed to lift the massive toppled shelves off from her while Torres and Celeste pulled her to safety.

That wasn't the end of it.

The fire raged up one wall now, having consumed the massive display, its fingering flames licking the ceiling and spreading toward their only escape route. And now that haze from earlier had spun as out of control as the fire, the smoke thick and black and acrid and quickly filling the room.

"If we don't do something about that fire," Gapinski said, "we're gonna be crispy critters!"

Agreed.

Silas spun around, searching the room and racing to the walls now.

But no fire extinguisher!

The rush of accelerants was joined by a burst of white, a cloud exploding onto the fire.

It was Eddie, holding a fire extinguisher and actually making progress on the fiery beast that threatened them all.

Finally, the swish of sprinklers sent cold water spraying across the room in a pressurized blast that was both welcomed and annoying.

Silas was instantly soaked, but so was that fire, the blast of water sending it to its hissing death.

"Nice save," Silas said.

Eddie held up the empty red can and nodded.

A pounding from behind, then a crash sent his hands reaching for his head. Loud commands and storming boots into the room told him more help had arrived.

"Commander Roberts!" shouted Celeste, bringing Zoe to her feet and handing her off to one of the Order security guards.

A tall, bulky man in a black uniform rushed over. "Director Bourne...erm, Master Grey. Or Bourne-Grey—"

"Celeste is fine, Commander," she corrected. Seemed everyone was having a hard time adjusting to the change of guard. "What just happened?"

"Earthquake, that's what!"

"So I was right?" asked Torres. "I was just joking."

"Never seen anything like it in all my life in the District."

One of the other guards called for them to move it, three others helping guide the operational support personnel from the ops center. Some hobbled, most sobbed.

"We best get to it," Commander Roberts said. "Didn't last but for a few minutes, but the risks of aftershocks are great."

"Don't have to tell me twice," Gapinski said, pushing past and rushing toward the exit.

"Hoss, wait up!" shouted Torres.

Silas grasped Celeste's hand and gestured with the other. "After you."

She followed Commander Roberts, Silas close behind and Eddie P making up the rear. They weaved through a gauntlet of downed equipment and broken ceiling chunks and hustled into the hallway.

Which wasn't much better.

A lancing crack raced through the ceiling, cold water still spraying overhead along with a thick, acrid haze at the ceiling clawing his throat and stinging his eyes. They snaked through broken corridors, crouched and coughing and wet as cranky cats. Soon, they reached an emergency stairwell that brought them to the surface and out into the pouring rain, livid and frigid and slick across the lawn.

What they found outside was far worse than inside.

First was the street, which was utter chaos and destruction.

A wicked chasm had ruptured down the center of Wisconsin Avenue, the rift weaving the length of the road and mounting the sidewalk and clear into the apartments flanking its western side.

Collapsing pavement and cement, consuming wood and brick.

A few cars were trapped down inside and no doubt people. Even a Metro bus had toppled into the breach. The most alarming were the buildings that were just flat gone. An entire residential block was wiped out. Shops still standing were missing their large picture windows, the glass having shattered and spread like ice across the sidewalk. A few trees had been felled to the ground along the avenue too. Ancient oaks and maples that had withstood raging thunderstorms, taken out by the last diabolical device in Mother Nature's bag of tricks.

A flash of lightning and clap of thunder put an exclamation point on the apocalyptic vibe.

Which sent Silas twisting for a view of their own abode.

And gut clenching with revulsion at what he saw.

Most of the face to America's church and Order HQ had fallen in a terrible palsy. For the second time in as many years! Not as bad as the first go around, when the southern facade had been completely ripped off in a wicked blast of terrorism.

Still.

Devilish flames danced in the entrance and clawed their way up what was left of the spires of the Cathedral Church of Saint Peter and Saint Paul. Roof held, so that was promising, but that might not be for long depending on how that facade held up. Acrid black smoke billowed in puffy plumes and hissing flames struggled against the stormy onslaught.

Thunder rumbled overhead again and the rapping cold rain actually made Silas shiver, even though it was the middle of a late-summer day that had started sweltering and stretched near 90 degrees. The metallic tang heavy on his tongue told him it was an adrenaline-fueled response from the fraught moment. Didn't make it any easier.

"We're lucky we made it out alive," Torres said, pointing at the cathedral.

"Yeah, but what about the others?" asked Gapinski.

Good question.

"We're already on it," Commander Roberts said. "I instructed Order security to help evacuate the cathedral. No telling when emergency personnel will arrive given all the mayhem."

An explosion from the center of the nave sent the Order personnel crouching on the wet grass. Mayhem was right!

Stained glass and stone and wood flew high into the cloudy sky, some sort of explosion triggered by the earthquake.

Flaming fingers reached up the side of the building, hungry to envelop the church with its fiery fury.

"We have to do something," Eddie said, standing and stepping with hesitation but also clear activation. Like Dad would've done, the friends two peas in a pod.

"Good Lord..." moaned Celeste, taking in the sight.

Torres echoed her lament: "*Dios mío...*"

My God was right.

A sudden thwapping of blades grew strong. A pair of them.

Silas spun around to find two white choppers coming in hot and heavy for the lawn. Sikorsky S-70 Black Hawks, by the look of it. Recalled SEPIO ordering up the pair of the decommissioned '70s-era military birds a few years ago. The Order had bought them from Uncle Sam at Radcliffe's urging. Said they never knew when they might need some major aerial power for an emergency extraction.

Like escaping from the end of the world as they knew it!

Guess he was right.

"You pile into that one there," Commander Roberts bellowed above the thwapping din, pointing to Silas and Celeste, then Torres and Gapinski, and jerking a thumb to the first bird.

The security personnel had already ushered the operational support crew into the second chopper, and him and the others hustled into the lead one, dragging Eddie along for the ride.

The bird looked newer than he expected, and looked like it hadn't seen much use since the Order had sprung for the aerial support. Had clearly been retrofitted with a nicer, comfier interior design to go along with the white paint job that replaced the military black sheen. Same for the spartan charcoal he recalled from too many Ranger operations in the Middle East to count, the inside a nice tan that still smelled like new carpet. And instead of the hard, stiff seats with belts that had made him feel like he was strapped into an electric chair, this ride was soft and offered nice lumbar support.

Not a bad way to be extracted in the middle of an afternoon shot to apocalyptic Hades!

Commander Roberts closed their door and sealed it tight then instructed them to buckle up as the pilot ratcheted up the rotors. The quintet complied and up they went, soaring high above the chaos still unfolding on the ground below.

A rapping rain streaked the windows, and it was hard to get a full visual on things. But from what he could see...the District had been shattered something fierce!

Thick smoke coiled from a smattering of breaches in the ground, billowing black to join the heavy storm clouds hovering above DC with menacing assault. Flames struggled for a hearing in the sheeting rain, perhaps the only saving grace. Even then, it was already waning, the storm racing through while the world below burned.

"You said earthquake..."

It was Gapinski, muttering to himself with his face in his hands.

Then again, louder and sitting straighter to address Eddie: "Earthquake. On the East Coast. That's what you said had been beamed into that noggin of yours by the Third Person of the Trinity."

Eddie said nothing. Just removed his glasses and rubbed his eyes, then slumped in his chair. Not with frustration or exasperation. More a weariness, like from carrying a heavy burden.

One that seemed to have just manifested itself on the East Coast, like Eddie had prophesied.

A prophetic utterance finding purchase in the Order's own headquarters!

Is that what had happened? The Holy Spirit giving Dad's old buddy some insight into future events—the sorts of events that spelled apocalyptic doom?

Thunder rumbled overhead as they flew to safety. Silas cast his gaze back outside, the skyline missing something now that sent his heart slumping with dread.

The Washington Monument. That white obelisk jutting toward the heaven, built to honor the nation's First President and embodying the awe, respect, and gratitude the nation felt for its most essential Founding Father.

Where was it?

And was that smoke coiling nearby? From the White House?

Surely it was simply obscured from view by the storm, the rain. The alternative...

Silas didn't even want to think about what that might be.

The chopper cabin raced toward destiny in silence, the day's events pressing in now with increased worry. Reading about bellicose nations and witnessing raging citizens. Cataclysmic prophecies and unexpected earthquakes.

What did it mean for the Church? For the Order and SEPIO's mission?

For Silas?

Not sure he wanted to find out...

CHAPTER 12

"ETA is fifteen," Commander Roberts called out from the front, but Silas didn't pay him any mind. Not with what flashed by under their bird, past his window.

A city in chaos.

Fires raged, smoke plumed. Buildings lay in ruin and people's lives lay in rubble—maybe even literally. Most likely literally, thousands dead from the sudden collapse of buildings and Metro lines from the earthquake.

Then the revelation from Eddie P. About the earthquake itself that Gapinski had noted. Didn't know what to make of that in the slightest, whether it had anything remotely to do with the actual reality that had played out, or just a coincidence. Some intersection between dreamland and the real world. Could even be playing them all for fools with his claims of divine prophetic insight. Probably tapped into the special knowledge from his military contacts at USGS, another of the agencies in Uncle Sam's alphabet soup that measured and monitored geological seismic activity. Could have some buddy on the inside feeding him intel he could use to leverage Silas to get on the inside of the Order—as he had with leveraging the revelation of his sister, Samantha, to get to him about this prophetic nonsense about the end of the world, or something.

Then again...

Silas glanced at the man, recalling two other bits of information he had disclosed that had sent him seeking the Order in the first place. The Aeon Foundation and Republic of Heaven. Both wrapped up with Nous, and by default his brother. And apparently of some interest to Samantha, before disappearing.

Then there was the other bit of recognition: the street preacher, part of some intel from a SEPIO agent in the field. Who had again appeared in Eddie's supposed prophetic dreams.

Whatever was going on, it added up to bupkis. Which frustrated the snot out of him. Especially since this wasn't even supposed to be his responsibility anymore. Had already spun around that faith-fighting merry-go-round. Got the T-shirt to prove it. And—

Silas flexed the fingers on his prosthetic hand.

And the scars...

Speaking of scars: With the Order of Thaddeus's main headquarters inoperable, SEPIO was hard-pressed to find some place to land that would give them the tools they needed to get a jump on—whatever it was they might need to get a jump on. Which wasn't all that clear.

Yeah, the country had just spun out of orbit into a chaotic mess. Commander Roberts had briefed them upon lift-off that the quake had rattled the entire Eastern Seaboard, from Virginia to New York. DC was in chaos, but so too was everything from Richmond to Baltimore, Philly to New York City. And that wasn't even touching on the crazy roiling Ukraine and the South China Sea.

Then the mystery man from the video Celeste said was

some street preacher from some upstart religious sect—whom Eddie P had fingered as marching across his mind in a prophetic vision, right before he also disclosed the craziest revelation-insight of all: the earthquake. That then rumbled through Order HQ, sending SEPIO scrambling out from Washington National Cathedral and into the cold downpour before the thing nearly collapsed.

An ache bloomed at the center of Silas's head. Right between the eyes. Needling and pulsing and lancing a bit. That wasn't touching on his muscles coming down from their taut activation and the anxious rush of adrenaline. What a day.

And his sister.

Samantha...

Silas rubbed his forehead, took a deep breath, and sighed.

What a day was right.

And it wasn't over.

Because zooming into view was their destination, an alternative outpost that had surprisingly withstood the rumble without issue. The Basilica of the National Shrine of the Immaculate Conception.

The Order of Thaddeus held a smaller base of operations beneath the large minor Catholic basilica and national shrine in the United States. It had once been the central operations for the Order but now served as a minor outpost for a new investigative agency Silas had launched two years ago, Group X.

He had launched the initiative after one operation made clear a rising demonic threat to the Church and the world. Principalities and powers of this present supernatural darkness rising with greater boldness from the Unseen Realm to wreak havoc in the world—bending it to its will and turning it to its cause.

The destruction of Christ's Church and overthrow of Christ the King.

He had tapped two former agents with the FBI, Elijah Fox and Gina Anderson. They had dealt with similar cases of a supernatural, paranormal variety for the Feds. Their dueling backgrounds apart from law enforcement—biblical theology for Eli; psychology for Gina—were the potent combination of academic acumen and practical skill for the nascent unit. Hadn't followed their work the past year after taking leave, but he knew they had scored some major wins since their inauguration. This new threat might just be up their alley.

He glanced at his Seiko watch. Still had another ten minutes to touchdown.

Might as well make the most of it.

Silas turned to Celeste. "The man on the screen, in the SEPIO ops center. You said a SEPIO operative had sent along through some back channel that video file he had filmed."

She nodded. "Right. What of it?"

"Something about being embedded in an upstart religious sect?"

"That's right." Celeste gestured to Torres and Gapinski. "These two have more insight into the nature of the operation, as they were on point."

He turned to them. "Anything you can share about this sect, their leader?"

Gapinski cleared his throat, nodding toward Eddie. He leaned toward Silas and said lowly out the side of his mouth, "Perhaps we should ixnay the onvocay on the operationyay with the oobnay."

Eddie jerked a thumb his way. "This guy high, or what?"

Torres snorted a laugh. "Most of the time..."

Gapinski frowned. "Hey, not nice."

Silas tried not to laugh but understood the concern. "Don't worry. He's used to this sort of classified gig. Worked on contracts with the US military and other government agencies."

Gapinski sat back and eyed Eddie. "Government and military contracts, eh?"

He nodded, saying nothing.

"Say, you didn't happen to swing by Ramstein Air Force Base a time or two did you? Say Christmas 2007?"

"A time or two."

He snapped his fingers and pointed at the man. "That's where I thought I knew you from! You were there for the UFO sighting!"

Eddie shrugged, saying nothing more, but Silas thought he detected a wink.

Celeste sighed. "Can we please focus on the task at hand?"

Gapinski slunk back in his chair some and muttered a "Sorry…"

"You can trust him," Silas said, nodding for Gapinski to get to it.

"Crack on then, Matthew," Celeste urged.

He shrugged, and offered, "Judah Howell."

"Judah?" Eddie exclaimed.

"Uh, yeah…"

"Lion of Judah. That's who he was in my vision!"

"The young guy on the video?"

The man nodded, growing quiet.

"Creepy…"

Torres added, "Intel puts him mid- to late-30s."

"What was your interest in him?" asked Silas.

"We got a tip from another agent in the field about this new wackadoodle street preacher connected to a charitable foundation in California. Something called Branch of Life Academy. An orphanage and educational institution for the blind."

"Sounds like a real modern Gandhi, he does."

Pulling out his phone, Gapinski said, "I've got that video on my phone if you'd like to watch the show again."

"That'd be great," Silas said.

He stood and sat next to Gapinski, the others crowding around. Even Eddie craned over the device. Not sure he liked that idea, but the chief didn't seem to mind—his and the Order's now that he was on leave.

"Here we go…" Gapinski said, cradling his oversized phone.

Never understood how people could wield a slab of glass the size of a cutting board. Get a tablet already or just disconnect entirely. Although, Silas supposed whatever he'd found was probably better viewed on a seven-inch screen than his five-inch one.

Celeste sat across from Silas and leaned in for a view. Torres sat next to Gapinski and motioned for him to lower the phone so all could see what he had found.

Silas leaned in for a look. And frowned.

There was that blond hippie fellow from the West Coast again, the same scene playing out from before. Same blue skies and palm trees. Same stucco buildings and onlookers. And the same youngish man from earlier preaching.

He said, "Turn it up, would you?"

Gapinski nodded and cranked it.

"*We are the music makers, and we are the dreamers of dreams!*" the mystery man shouted, whose name was apparently Judah Howell.

"Now isn't that interesting…" said Celeste.

"What is?" asked Silas.

"That line. It is from *Ode*, a poem by Arthur O'Shaughnessy, if I place it right."

Gapinski snorted a laugh. "Try *Willy Wonka & the Chocolate Factory*, sister."

"Sorry, come again?"

"You know. Charlie Bucket. With Grandpa Joe and the Golden Tickets. The rivers of chocolate and funny midgets."

"They're little people, dingbat!" Torres slugged his shoulder; he yelped. "Get with the PC program!"

"Oompa Loompas, then. Whatever! Anyway, after the kiddos wandered into a hallway lined with lickable wallpaper, Willie threw that line in Varuca Salt's face after she retorted back to him '*Who ever heard of a snozzberry?*' with far too much snot and snoot for a girl her age."

Gapinski grinned and laughed and shook his head, as if reliving a pleasant childhood memory. And knowing the kind of childhood he had, Silas was grateful he had at least one.

"Loved that movie growing up. Would spend days licking the wallpaper in our mobile home trying to find that elusive snozzberry."

"That explains a lot..." Torres muttered.

"First of all," Eddie said, gesturing at Gapinski. "Your cultural prowess and tastes leave much to be desired."

Gapinski twisted up his face in confusion. "Huh?"

"Second—" Now he turned to Celeste "most impressive you intuited that line from 19th century literature."

She threw him a smile. "British lit, second year at uni."

"Oxford."

"Right..." She frowned, throwing Silas questioning eyes.

He understood her, being as unnerved about Eddie's knowledge of his own background. But he just shrugged and went back to the video.

The mystery man went on, waving his Bible around and shouting another stanza:

> *Wandering by lone sea-breakers,*
> *And sitting by desolate streams;*
> *World-losers and world-forsakers,*
> *On whom the pale moon gleams:*
> *Yet we are the movers and shakers*
> *Of the world forever, it seems.*

The camera panned to the crowd as the man kept at his

sermon, or whatever it was. Same group as before, a smattering of West Coast professionals.

"There she is!" exclaimed Eddie suddenly, snatching the phone from Gapinski's grip.

"Dude! Get your own phone," he complained.

"Samantha..." He touched the face of the device, face falling and lower lip quivering.

"Who the hey-ho day is that?"

Silas's stomach lurched at the revelation, a second in as many hours.

Eddie didn't answer. Just stared at the video playing out on the device, apparently with his sister hanging on that Judah Howell wackadoodle's words.

"I'm sorry, but who is Samantha?" Celeste turned to Silas. "Do you have a bloomin' clue what your friend is going on about?"

He swallowed, taking a breath, then a beat.

Then: "She's my sister."

The cabin itself took a breath, then a beat.

"I didn't know you had a sister," she replied.

"I didn't either." He gestured to Eddie. "It's a long story, but Eddie here was a friend of my father. And godfather to my step-sister."

"Dude, that's some deep family drama. But—" Gapinski gestured toward his phone "can I have that back?"

Eddie looked up, eyes moist and color drained from his face. He nodded and handed it back. Gapinski held it out, the others craning for a viewing.

Chief among them was Silas.

Took him a bit to find her, but then he did. The only Pacific Islander among the crowd of onlookers. Not that it mattered. And even when Eddie pointed her out, he didn't need the help. Could've picked her out of any lineup. It was all in the eyes and nose and cheeks. Wide-set, equine, proportional. Those were

Grey features, set against soft brown skin and framed by black hair.

Those were Dad's...

Now his own eyes moistened, an unexpected emotion springing to them at the sight of his flesh and blood. Boy was that flat weird! But also kind of cool.

Silas Grey had a sister. Samantha Grey.

Who was standing next to that Judah Howell man as he thundered from the grassy knoll, waving around that well-worn black leather Bible, page edges stained crimson, with multi-color sticky tabs jutting out.

"'*I looked, and there was a great earthquake,*'" the man crooned, "'*the sun became black as sackcloth, the full moon became like blood, and the stars of the sky fell to the earth as the fig tree drops its winter fruit when shaken by a gale.*'"

"What's he jibber-jabbering about?" asked Gapinski.

Celeste shushed him as the man went on: "'*The sky vanished like a scroll rolling itself up, and every mountain and island was removed from its place. Then the kings of the earth and the magnates and the generals and the rich and the powerful and everyone, slave and free, hid in the caves and among the rocks of the mountains, calling—*'"

"'*—calling to the mountains and rocks 'Fall on us and hide us,*'" Eddie interrupted, picking up where the man was quoting on the phone, "'*from the face of the one seated on the throne and from the wrath of the Lamb, for the great day of their wrath has come, and who is able to stand?*'"

Gapinski furrowed his brow, glancing from the phone to Eddie and back.

"Dude, you guys in cahoots, or what?"

He frowned. "We just read the same Bible."

Silas knew that passage well. "The Book of Revelation, chapter 6."

"Apparently you do too," Eddie said with a wink.

"Friends, the sixth seal is upon us," the Judah Howell man continued. "Our only salvation is the Republic of Heaven! But lo, the Promised One is nigh. I am but a voice crying in the wilderness making straight his way."

"Oy!" Celeste startled. "Did he just say Republic of Heaven?"

Silas nodded, saying nothing, dread churning at that very familiar phrase.

One that had haunted the Order the past few years for its connection to its archnemesis stretching back to the Church's very start.

Nous.

"And what's this sixth seal business?" Gapinski said.

"*Qué es eso?*" Torres echoed with wonder.

The man went to expound upon his revelation when an arrow started spinning on the video screen.

"Sonofa—" Gapinski gave his phone a shake, jabbing one of his sausage fingers into the screen. It was no use.

He shoved it into his pocket with a huff. "Looks like the cellular network is on the fritz."

"Makes sense," Silas said. "Surprised we got any juice at all with the earthquake damage."

"But what does that mean, the sixth seal?"

Celeste added, "And what was the bloke going on about?"

"Why, the Book of Revelation, of course," Eddie said.

Everyone turned to him.

"It's what he was quoting. '*When he broke the sixth seal, I looked, and there was an earthquake...*' and on to the rest."

"Revelation?" Gapinski said with a start. "As in End Times apocalyptic doo doo?"

"That's right."

The cabin went silent, but for the muffled, droning chopper blades thwapping above.

"Commander," Celeste said, "can we pick up the pace a bit?"

"Coming in for a landing shortly, Ms. Bourne—erm, *Master* Bourne-Grey."

He was right. The bird banked hard and made for Group X HQ, which was now the de facto Order HQ—and SEPIO ops center. Soon they were landing in the road just outside the outpost.

The cabin emptied, and they pounded onto a looping driveway off Michigan Avenue and headed for a service entrance on the westside of the basilica. The access driveway ran behind a stone wall and a thick hedgerow, leading to a keycard entrance into Group X HQ. In the parking lot sat a BMW motorcycle and a candy apple red Honda Odyssey minivan—the vehicles of choice for Elijah Fox and Gina Anderson respectively, the Group X investigative agents.

Looked like they'd be fully staffed for this operation. Whatever it was.

Something to do with a mystery religious sect leader, and now with his sister somehow in the mix.

And probably his brother.

Which Silas flat didn't want to think about.

Commander Roberts led them to the steel door and slapped his open hand on a palm-reading keypad. It pulsed blue three times before turning green. The door unlocked, and the commander pushed through into a short, sterile hallway of white that led to an elevator. It was open, and the group stepped inside, Silas trailing.

He hesitated, slowing to the threshold.

"Uhh, you in or out, chief?" Gapinski questioned.

Good question.

But given the circumstances, his sister caught up with some street preacher going on about the End Times—

No doubt about it.

In.

So he stepped in, joining the others in the carriage. His team and family. His wife.

Descending three stories beneath the Catholic church to the makeshift nerve center of SEPIO and into yet another operation with massive implications.

Family implications.

CHAPTER 13

After a bell chimed, the elevator doors parted to reveal a red-brick hallway bustling with activity. It seemed the rest of the Order had already been transferred and sent to continue the fight ahead of SEPIO.

Silas wasn't sure why he had even come along for the ride. Wasn't his fight anymore. But there was something to what Eddie P had brought to his doorstep. And he was a sucker for a fight. Couldn't help jumping into the fray—as evidenced by saving the cat lady.

So, there he was. Descending into—whatever it was the good Lord above was dragging his backside into down below! What a day...

"This way," Commander Roberts said as he hastened forward through the crowded hallway to a set of double doors at the end. Another palm-reading keypad stood guard, waiting for the commander's hand. When one door unlocked, he opened it to reveal a space that was similar in size to his former study, but altogether different.

Dimmed recess lighting around the perimeter shone down upon narrow tables lining the dark walls commanded by workstations. Only one man was working away at one of those stations, Abraham Patel, who Silas had heard Celeste had loaned out to Group X, which was a good call. Was much cleaner and far more put together the last time he had seen the joint over a year ago when he established the agency, giving the investigative arm the old SEPIO HQ bunker.

Where a fireplace stood crackling and popping away at one end of his former study, a massive screen tracked critical mission updates and news footage from the world's major outlets reporting on the ongoing events swirling across the globe. At the center of the room, where a set of leather couches and chairs anchored the Order Master's command center, a raised platform with screens and chairs and direct-line phones to operation centers around the world was awaiting control. In this case, Celeste Bourne-Grey's control.

Sitting at that table were two other familiar faces: Elijah Fox and Gina Anderson, the Group X investigative agents he had hired to suss out the Church's *inexplicitus* cases. They came racing over to greet the group.

"Oh my cheeps!" Elijah exclaimed, pointing at Silas. "I thought Victor sacked your backside."

Silas smirked. If only.

Instead, he said, "No, not sacked. Only on leave."

"*Temporary* leave," Celeste added with a wry grin.

Gina offered a smile. "Irregardless—"

"Nope. Not a word," Elijah corrected with interruption.

"For the love...*Regardless*, then, glad to have you here, Silas. We're *both* glad. Aren't we, Eli?"

He shrugged. "Word." Then he gestured to Eddie. "So who's the geezer?"

Silas almost laughed out loud at Elijah's bluntness. Had gotten to know the guy on a significant SEPIO operation a few years ago exposing a major government conspiracy that tapped into his particular professional insights into the Unseen Realm. Knew the guy meant well. Something about his neurodiversity that led him to call it like he saw it. No filter on that fella whatsoever, which he appreciated and could relate to.

He went to answer when Gina did it for him.

"Eddie P?"

"Who's Eddie P?" Elijah replied.

"Anderson!" Eddie exclaimed, widening his arms to match his wide grin and belly laugh.

The two exchanged a hug and some nostalgia from some work they had apparently done together years ago at the FBI. From Eddie's own travelog through his background, it was apparent the man had his hands in multiple government agencies. Apparently the FBI was also in the mix.

Celeste interrupted the reunion: "Right. Now that we have all had the privilege of getting acquainted, does anyone know what the bloody hell just happened to our HQ?"

Elijah answered, "The Stafford Fault System is at, well, at fault."

Gapinski snorted a laugh. "Like what you did there, kiddo."

"And what is that?" asked Torres.

"A planar fracture," Eddie explained, "located in the mid-Atlantic coastal plain along America's East Coast. Boys at the USGS have always had a keen eye on this one."

"Again, who's the geezer?" asked Elijah.

"A friend of my father," Silas replied.

"And what is this USGS?" asked Celeste.

"United States Geological Survey," Eddie said. "This particular fault system provides the most complete record of fault movement during the past 120 million years across the Virginia, DC, and Maryland region, including displacement of Pleistocene terrace gravels. Clear up the East Coast, it does."

Silas said, "And why the keen eye?"

"If there was ever the chance for an earthquake up the Atlantic Seaboard, this was where it'd be."

"How high of a chance?"

"Not high, I can tell you that."

Celeste frowned. "Yet it just happened."

Eddie crossed his arms and sighed. "Yep. Yet it just happened."

A sudden coldness overcame Silas, and something sprang to the surface. From the Gospel of Matthew, of all places:

> *Jesus answered them, "Beware that no one leads you astray. For many will come in my name, saying, 'I am the Messiah!' and they will lead many astray. And you will hear of wars and rumors of wars; see that you are not alarmed, for this must take place, but the end is not yet. For nation will rise against nation and kingdom against kingdom, and there will be famines and earthquakes in various places: all this is but the beginning of the birth pangs.*

"And there will be famines and earthquakes in various places..." Silas muttered, the Scripture eerily prescient.

"What was that, chief?" asked Gapinski.

"Huh?"

"Said something about earthquakes. Sounded downright biblical!"

"Matthew's Gospel, right?" Eddie asked.

Silas nodded. "That's right."

Celeste added, "Certainly comes at an interesting time."

Gapinski snorted a laugh. "Ya think? The guy basically predicted the thing!"

Silas frowned. *Then there's that...*

"Predicted?" Gina asked. "Have you had another prophetic vision? Like back at the agency?"

Eddie said nothing, arms still crossed and looking to Silas.

Who flat didn't have a clue how to proceed.

Celeste lent a helping hand: "Perhaps we could all have ourselves a chat about this...prophetic vision business, as you put it, Eddie."

Gesturing toward the horseshoe table, she led the way. Silas came up next to her.

"Thanks, darlin'."

"Don't thank me yet, love. You're the one who brought us this stray."

A wry grin played across her face and she took her seat at the center of the U-shaped table.

Couldn't argue with that. Which meant he needed to take the lead on getting down to business about what the blazes was going on with this Eddie guy.

Everyone settled around the table: Silas at Celeste's right, which sort of felt funny, but also made sense; Eddie next to him, with Gapinski and Torres following; Victor at Celeste's left, with Elijah and Gina taking the seats across from those SEPIO two.

As everyone settled, twisting open short bottles of water at their spots and getting cups of coffee from a buffet, Silas eyed the unknown quantity sitting next to him. Who exactly was this mystery guy? More germane: Did he have something the Order should pay attention to? That wasn't even touching on the revelation that he himself had to pay attention to! The one about his sister.

He finally settled on a question, getting to the heart of it for SEPIO: "Are you a religious man, Mr. Pierzynski?"

Silas supposed Eddie could have been offended at the question, given what he had brought Silas, and his connection to

Dad, knowing how invested in the Church he was. If the man was offended, he didn't show it.

Instead, Eddie crossed his arms, which seemed to be his standard posture, then leaned back his head and took in a slow breath through his nose, eyeing Silas through those silver glasses of his.

Eddie finally answered, "Absolutely. But not just religious. I have a relationship with Christ, as I assume you all do as well, working for the Church in this way. Confessing Christ as the Son of God who came to live our life in order to identify with humanity. The Lamb of God who came to take away the sins of the world. The Life of God, who was raised by the Father to new life and sits at his right hand to make intercession for humanity, offering his new life to all."

Silas nodded, appreciating his confession.

"Maybe you could explain more," Celeste added now. "Just so we are clear on where you are coming at this. And where the Order's interests lay with your revelations."

He addressed her: "Well, I was trained, educated and married in the Roman Catholic Church. Have received all the Sacraments, all except Holy Orders. I have been a Eucharistic Minister and regularly participate in various ministries. In fact I am an ordained non-denominational minister. Even viewed and handled dozens of religious relics, preserved bodies of saints—"

"Eww," Gapinski muttered, grimacing with interruption.

"—the Last Supper painting, the Piete, and you'll like this Sy." Eddie turned to Silas now and said with a wink: "The Shroud of Turin."

Silas sat back and nodded. Impressive. It was clear the man was devoted to Christ and all things Christian, which put his mind at ease some that he was on board with their own mission. Preserving and protecting memory-markers of the faith and all.

"I have visited the Vatican," Eddie went on, "communicated with bishops, archbishops, the Papal Nuncio, Pope Benedict himself, the Secretariat of State and heads of Secretariats and Congregations of the Vatican in my capacity with the US government. But my proudest moment was successfully working against our Catholic Diocese to save our church from closure."

"So, then, I'm sure you appreciate what we do here," Victor added. He paused, continuing to eye the suspicious man. "Given your...how shall I put it? How about *entanglements with governments of various sorts*, not to mention your own clear connection to the Church of Christ. Given those entanglements, you can appreciate SEPIO's work."

"Sepee...what?"

Gapinski answered, "Sort of the Church's special-ops arm that kicks the bad guys' butts."

Silas furrowed his brow. "I thought you were dialed into the Order's operations."

"Apparently not completely..."

He flashed Celeste questioning eyes, wondering whether to proceed. She gestured for him to get on with it.

"SEPIO, as Victor mentioned, and Matt shared, the more muscular, kinetic arm of the Order. A Latin acronym for *Sepio, Erudio, Pugno, Inviglio, Observo*. Which translates—"

"Protect, instruct, fight for, watch over, heed," Eddie answered, "if my Latin still serves me right."

Celeste nodded. "As any good clandestine institution you've associated yourself with, the Order of Thaddeus has been actively fighting since the dawn of the Church to contend for and preserve Christian beliefs for future generations against vigorous attempts at assaulting that belief, both inside and outside the Church."

Eddie grinned. "That's where my own interests lay!"

"How so?" asked Silas, trying to probe deeper before taking the man too far into the Order's confidences.

"My interests and career have always included biblical history, life sciences, and—well, let's put it as unexplained phenomenon."

Gina nodded at that, the two clearly having history together on that front.

"To paraphrase Paul's first letter to the Church of Corinth: *'to each individual the manifestation of the Spirit is given for some benefit.'* Different manifestations of the Spirit's giftings for each individual. I am grateful to have been given many gifts and interests and the opportunity to follow them."

Eddie sat straighter and edged to his seat before planting his elbows on the table with a thud.

"And I want to use them for the Church. For this moment." He turned to Silas again. "As I said, I've followed your own work on the Holy Shroud. I had a chance to view the sacred relic up close, and my life science background spurred many conversations with fellow scientists about using DNA from the Shroud to clone the person wrapped within. Not that I would or anything!"

He laughed, and a nervous chuckle floated around the table.

"Anyway, my career has enabled me to visit and work with many private and government research labs around the world. Including having an FBI clearance, which Gina knows about." Again, she nodded, a grin playing across her face. "I was also privy to restricted locations and communications with many agencies. And as you know Gina, my background in what some would term noetics and parapsychology—what I would term just plain Holy Spirit gifting—those gifts have also allowed me to study the potential of the human mind and spirit. Often to the point of ridicule from non-believers. My grandmother and mother had such prophetic sensibilities that went beyond normal everyday experiences, which they attributed to the Holy Spirit. Fortunately, some of those abilities have trickled down to me."

Silas didn't know what to make of that one.

"In fact, just this past weekend, our pastor's homily was about John chapter 2 and the wedding at Cana. He related it to 1 Corinthians, chapter 12. The parallel with being filled with spiritual gifts as it related to Jesus filling the water jars with wine, and opening ourselves to be filled with the Spirit and the various gifts from God. I am fortunate to have received the opportunity to fill and pursue the various gifts in my jar."

Silas knew well the passage from Paul's first letter:

> *Now there are varieties of gifts but the same Spirit,*
> *and there are varieties of services but the same*
> *Lord, and there are varieties of activities, but it is*
> *the same God who activates all of them in every-*
> *one. To each is given the manifestation of the*
> *Spirit for the common good. To one is given*
> *through the Spirit the utterance of wisdom and to*
> *another the utterance of knowledge according to*
> *the same Spirit, to another faith by the same*
> *Spirit, to another gifts of healing by the one*
> *Spirit, to another the working of powerful deeds,*
> *to another prophecy, to another the discernment*
> *of spirits, to another various kinds of tongues, to*
> *another the interpretation of tongues. All these*
> *are activated by one and the same Spirit, who*
> *allots to each one individually just as the Spirit*
> *chooses.*

He understood that most Christians were more content with certain Enlightenment-approved giftings, like wisdom and knowledge and faith. Especially most Protestant denominations, though his childhood Catholic wing of the church pew would fit the bill too. The others, like prophecy and tongues and healing—even working powerful, miraculous deeds? Now that was a tough modern pill to swallow.

Same for certain roles within the Church, certain offices and kinds of leaders: *'And God has appointed in the church first apostles, second prophets, third teachers, then deeds of power, then gifts of healing, forms of assistance, forms of leadership, various kinds of tongues.'* You wouldn't be hard pressed to find Western church communities actively cultivating teachers and leaders and administrators. Prophets and healers and miracle workers...now that was a whole ball of ecclesial ugly that most churches didn't touch, aside from your charismatic variety.

Not sure about the noetic science of it all, but a question did needle Silas: Was this Eddie P character, Dad's long-lost friend, one of these special prophets, appointed by God to the Church? Perhaps for such a time as this?

Time to drill down into that one.

So Silas took the lead: "You mentioned having this...vision, as you called it. About the earthquake—"

"Which sure as heck came true!" exclaimed Gapinski.

"Right. But you indicated more."

Nodding, Eddie took in a breath and settled back.

"It started a year ago. At the start of the year. The first time I saw a sunflower, tall and proud and rising from ashes. For the longest time, it withstood so much. Hail. Wind. Fire. But then it began to wither, its petals falling off, one by one, until it was dead and then a bear finally trampled it underfoot."

"A bear?" asked Celeste.

"That's right. A bear. A Eurasian brown bear, actually. But that isn't all. At the start of this year, I saw a dragon rising from the sea. It was fierce and powerful, spawning more and more dragons from its mouth until one of them wasn't a dragon at all but a plum blossom."

"A flower?" asked Gapinski now.

"A very specific floral variety," Eddie clarified. "*Prunus mume.*"

"Native to Asia," Silas added. "Isn't that right?"

"Impressive. Some are pink, some purple. Not this one. It was pure white with several long, slender anthers sprouting from the center and topped with bright yellow pollen."

Took Silas a beat to get his meaning.

Then he did. And sat straighter.

"Taiwan..."

"Taiwan?" asked Torres.

"The national flower for the Republic of China," Celeste explained. "Also known as Taiwan."

"Which that dragon of yours," Gapinski added, "just launched an all-out assault against this morning!"

"On top of Russia finally toppling Kiev and ending Ukraine."

All of this talk of war and now this earthquake sparked Jesus' warnings again about such times, from Luke's Gospel this go around: *"When you hear of wars and insurrections, do not be terrified, for these things must take place first, but the end will not follow immediately...Nation will rise against nation and kingdom against kingdom; there will be great earthquakes and in various places famines and plagues, and there will be dreadful portents and great signs from heaven."*

A whistle was thrown up. From down below, in the well of the ops center.

It was Abraham Patel, who had been Zoe's right-hand man before Celeste wisely lent him to Group X to assist with operational support for the fledgling investigative unit.

"What is it, Abraham?" asked Celeste.

The lanky Indian man stood, pushing thick black glasses up the bridge of his nose. He raked a hand across close-cropped black hair and stuffed a regimental tie of red, navy, and gold back into place behind a charcoal vest. Hated the spotlight, preferring to work behind the scenes, so his nervous energy was understandable.

Clearing his throat, Abraham announced, "President Santos is holding a news conference. And...well, you may want to tune in."

Silas threw Celeste eyes that matched her own.

Now what?

CHAPTER 14

"Now what?" asked Celeste, shoving her chair back to stand and crossing her arms.

She always found it difficult sitting during the confusion of an operation. Even back with Her Majesty's Secret Intelligence Service, she could barely sit still whilst the chiefs of station for her various assignments with MI6 got her acclimated. Earned her the nickname Psychomotor for it, too, a play on the British slang for automobile and the agitated condition of various mood disorders. Whether pacing around a room, tapping your toes, or rapid talking, psychomotor agitation was a manic condition responding to internal and external anxiety. Though mania wasn't the root cause, anxiety sure contributed.

And she had been anxious of late.

Celeste tossed a glance at Silas again, who had tossed her similar now-what eyes, but whose attention was transfixed on the massive display at the center of the far wall above the row of workstations. Abraham returned to his roost and clacked away to bring up on the telly what he thought they all had to see.

She could only transfix her attention on Silas, who wrestled with his own mania the past year. Depression, social withdrawal, even suicidal ideation. Understandably, for good reason. Having one of your limbs blown clear off from a psychopathic twin brother whilst he was pining for something more murderous will do that to you. As will the stress of preserving the faith and protecting the faithful, the role as Order Master taking its toll, particularly fueled by the machinations of internal power struggles vying for its future.

Silas had never wanted such a position. It was Rowan Radcliffe who had passed him the baton when he passed, the previous Order Master wielding the power to name his successor. That had been the way stretching back to the very first Master, Jude Thaddeus. But he had valiantly taken the reins and performed his duty, jumping back into the fray of things after giving up that life upon being discharged from the Army Rangers. That sort of life, the gunfights and car chases and fraught operations, had never been his intent again. Old manuscripts and tweed jackets were more his style now, especially since he had crested into middle age.

Except life has a way of course correcting itself. So does the Holy Spirit. And it seemed the Lord Almighty had shifted Silas's course back into the heat of battle. Not for some worldly kingdom but for his own. Which had cost him. And she worried for him. Had for some time.

It began a few years ago when he snatched back up that nasty habit of puffing on fags after the first revelations of Sebastian's involvement with Nous had been unveiled. She had tolerated it well enough, understanding it was an outlet for his anxiety. Could do without the overgrown hair at the time, but he eventually resumed the normal course of haircut things. But then there was his cockamamy scheme to right his professional ship and redeem his father's memory through discovering the lost Garden of Eden and relic bones of Adam and Eve. It had advanced the Order's and Church's interests well enough. But also at the expense of their own lives, and his, resulting in losing that appendage.

That loss set into motion his abandonment of his Order Master post, and then his ratcheting of substances to dull and numb his pain. Macallen became his new friend. Mostly at night, until it wasn't. Started earlier and earlier these days, and she had smelled it upon his arrival. It annoyed her, but mostly it broke her heart. All of it. His loss, his pain, his disengagement from what had given him light and life.

Through it all, she had stood by his side, putting on a brave face, a stiff British upper lip. Except...

Except she wasn't as strong as Silas claimed she was. Between managing the Order—with its various charitable programs and informational exhibits, its ecclesial research and recovery efforts, not to mention the ongoing SEPIO special operations and Group X investigations that roiled the religious order—on top of bearing the burden of her husband's personal pain, she didn't know how much longer she herself could go on.

As far as she was concerned, the Ministry of Information circa the Second War could keep its *KEEP CALM AND CARRY ON* aphorism. Though held in reserve until the Germans invaded the island nation and never actually employed, the Anglo saying felt chiding, almost sinister in the face of her own overwhelm.

However, she did appreciate one bit of British propaganda from that era she had postered up on her teenage bedroom wall. One she had scribbled down on a scrap of paper before her first MI6 operation and still kept in her clutch. Something she often returned to through life to keep her going: *YOUR COURAGE, YOUR CHEERFULNESS, YOUR RESOLUTION WILL BRING US VICTORY.*

Victory was still beyond grasp. But seeing Silas engaged in this way, jumping back into the Church's fray to contend for and protect the faith—whatever that meant with this newly arrived Eddie character—it alighted her heart with joy.

That, and she was now nine days past her monthly. She had yet to take a pregnancy test, though she knew deep down she was eating for two.

Which meant she had news of her own. News she wasn't sure Silas could handle right now, not with the latest revelation of some long-lost sister.

That could wait. She needed to get her head in the game.

But first, a cuppa.

"Right," Celeste said, walking to a buffet with a carafe of hot water and an arrangement of biscuits and Yorkshire Gold, the tea of her childhood. "Give the telly a bump in volume, would you, mate?"

Abraham obliged, and the most trusted name in news—which she felt was a bit of an ironic disconnect, putting *trust* and *news* in the same slogan—came back from a commercial break for a medication with side effects that sounded worse than the original condition.

The camera swooped in for a close-up shot of the well-makeuped anchor that had serviced CNN's breaking news reports going on several years now. Not half bad looking, with black hair slicked and a bit coiffed, dusted a sagacious salt now and ready to deliver the undeliverable news.

News that was bordering on the End Times.

One end of Celeste's mouth curled upward at the character-ization as she steeped a sachet of Earl Grey, the sunny and pleasant citrus aroma luxurious, with floral and herbal and resinous notes. End Times. The stuff of Mum's and Papa's hobbies. Ever the doomsdayers, they were. Preparing for Christ's return, in their freelance sort of way. Following news snippets and world events, reading the tea leaves and tossing entrails like the oracles of yore. Well, perhaps neither leaves nor entrails, but they certainly sought oracular wisdom from *The Guardian*, that's for sure!

At one point, Saddam Hussein was thought to be the Antichrist. The first time, in the early 1990s, not second. When that didn't pan out, they were certain Y2K would usher in the Apocalypse. Then 9/11 and 7/7, when London was bombarded by a series of coordinated terrorist attacks serviced by the same blokes who immolated New York City.

She hadn't paid such stuff and nonsense much mind. Much more preferred Christ's own advice on the subject: *'But about that day and hour no one knows, neither the angels of heaven, nor the Son, but only the Father.'* Why fuss about such things when there was enough drama in the here-and-now?

But with Russia's fresh win, totalizing their initial incursion into their Slavic neighbor, and now China making good on their promises to reunite the Republic of China with the People's Republic of China, on top of this earthquake nonsense that apparently had been prophesied by some random bloke connected to Silas's distant familial past—

Celeste brought the mug to her lips now just as Kai Renolds looked with serious longing into the camera and took a sip. She closed her eyes and hummed with pleasure. Refreshing and rounded, while at the same time complex and deep, with a touch of sweetness that allowed her to forego a cube of sugar.

Just what she needed from the day shot to bloody hell.

"If you are just joining us," Kai crooned, all Cronkite and all, "this is a CNN Breaking News event."

She scoffed to herself—what wasn't a breaking news event these days?—then took another sip of tea.

"We have been following multiple breaking news events on multiple fronts throughout the day. Kiev has finally fallen. Taiwan is finally being invaded. And it appears the East Coast has just suffered a once in—I don't even know what to call it!

Because an earthquake hasn't hit the Eastern Seaboard for several million years."

"Try a hundred and twenty, Kai," Elijah corrected across the table.

She liked that one. Blunt and to the point, to a fault. Her people could learn from that one.

"Yes, and the earthquake has rattled the East Coast and wreaked havoc from New York down to DC. Speaking of our nation's capital. We are able to report President Santos and First Lady Santos were taken by Marine One to a secure location. We have it on good authority that they, along with several members of congress—a quorum, in fact—were taken to a bunker at The Greenbrier Resort in West Virginia. The top-secret, super-sized bunker was built for members of Congress during the Eisenhower era to preserve the continuity of government."

"Way to give away the farm to the Commies, Kai!" Gapinski complained.

"Seriously!" Elijah added. "It's not like we're on the brink of World War Tres or anything."

Celeste took another sip, her anxiety draining now as the staple of British life warmed her. William Gladstone had it right: *If you are cold, tea will warm you; if you are too heated, it will cool you; If you are excited, it will calm you.*

Precisely.

"We are minutes away," Kai went on, "from a presidential address from President Santos. But as we wait, we are joined by two guests who say they have an answer for these world-rocking events."

That close-up widened into a shot of an 80-inch telly display anchored at Kai's right. He swiveled to face it, readying to interview two newcomers. Two rather remarkable newcomers.

And familiar ones.

"Are you kidding me?" Silas whispered, standing now at her side.

Celeste took a mouthful of tea this time. She was going to need it for who had joined Kai Renolds.

A familiar man with a handlebar mustache and a checkered shirt was joined by another familiar man, who was well-manicured with black hair and high cheekbones wearing an annoyingly SoCal-chic charcoal T-shirt.

"Are you kidding me?" Silas exclaimed again, louder. "Markus Braun and Noland Rotberg, having a fireside chit-chat on CNN?"

"More of a waterfall-side chat, actually," Gapinski said, "Very Fen Shui."

He was right. The pair sat on stools before a gently cascading sheet of water, black rock glistening from behind, surrounding greenery punctuated by bright red flowers waving with the East Asia vibe.

"Isn't that slick-haired fella," Eddie said, "that multi-billionaire technologist?"

"Futurist, more like it," Celeste responded. "Part of a clan of like-minded billionaires, scientists, and inventors trying to push the human race forward."

"Give it a kick in the pants more like it," Torres added. "I've read some whacked-out stuff from these guys recently about uploading our consciousness into the cloud to give humans eternal life, to bring back dead *abuela* through AI-algorithmic voice synthesis."

"That is whacked-out creepy!" Gapinski exclaimed.

"What about the other man?" asked Eddie.

"Noland Rotberg," Silas replied. "Had once been an up-and-comer in religious study circles. We've run into that bozo on a few operations."

"What sort of operations?"

He threw Eddie a wry grin and winked: "It's classified."

Torres asked, "Why is Kai Renolds interviewing them?"

Celeste put out a staying hand and offered a gentle shush. "Looks like we're about to find out."

"There is no doubt," Kai said, addressing the massive telly, "that these are fraught times. Frankly, there is an end-of-days vibe to life right now!"

Braun nodded. Rotberg replied, "No doubt about it."

"Between the wars engulfing the world, the earthquake that just rocked our American one—all of which President Santos is about to address—there is this growing sense that things are spinning out of control. That we are reaching the end of the world as we know it."

Rotberg grabbed one of the handlebars to his mustache and started twirling it, nodding along with Kai Renolds as he continued droning on about the apocalyptic nature of the news of late.

"Boy, does that man make my skin crawl," Silas said.

Celeste nodded. The man seriously plucked her nerves as well. Same for the futurist who had styled himself as the next Elon Musk and Mark Zuckerberg joined with the humanists Ray Kurzweil and Kevin Kelley who were pining to transcend human nature through brute technological force.

"You two are readying to announce a new initiative. Something to offer people a way to make sense of the world and themselves, if I understand it right."

Rotberg nodded. "That is correct. Church of Theoti."

"Church of Theoti?"

"That's right."

"Holybamoly, Batman!" Gapinski exclaimed.

"The Theotites are going mainstream?" asked Torres.

Gina asked, "What are the...Theotites, is it?"

Silas replied, "Church of the Theotites. Also Theoti."

"And apparently now the Church of Theoti," added Celeste,

taking a sip of tea growing too cold now. She set it down, concern beginning to churn.

Elijah smirked. "Sounds like something Tom Cruise might cook up in the Metaverse."

"Is this a Christian denomination?" asked Kai Renolds.

"No no no!" Braun replied, laughing nervously.

Rotberg also chuckled. "Hardly. Although we certainly respect the sacred teachings of Jesus."

"Then what is this church of yours?" Kai pressed.

"Think of it more like a spiritual center, which most people associate with a church."

Braun interjected, "And even then, it is more of a center for enlightenment."

Kai asked, "And what is the goal of this spiritual center of enlightenment?"

"To reconnect humanity with the ground of its being through an AI-algorithmic collation of humanity's vast sum of human knowledge. After all, knowledge is power."

"From Aristotle and Socrates and Plato," Rotberg added, "to Moses and Jesus and Muhammad and on to the brilliancy of the Buddha and Bhagavad Gita alike—leveraging those insights we will offer the salvation and redemption humanity has been seeking for millennia."

"What sort of salvation?" asked Kai.

"A well-ordered life and fully empowered mind to know what will guard and protect your mental health."

Braun nodded. "And what will harm it."

"Sounds positively biblical!" Kai replied.

The pair chuckled.

"Don't forget koranic and platonic!" Rotberg said.

Kai grinned and scribbled something on a notecard. "I'm being told we need to go to a commercial break before the President starts his address. So only about thirty seconds left.

Where can people find out more about this new initiative of yours?"

"The collective humanity," Braun replied, "is humming with potential. The potential to find the divinity within the collective whole and channel it within yourself. The time is ripe, and we are accelerating toward a singularity, where humanity possesses all it needs to progress to full divinity. We are the music makers, friends. We are the dreamers of dreams!"

Recognition rippled through the room.

Gapinski was the first to voice it: "Hey, isn't that what—"

"Judah Howell said..." Silas finished.

Celeste glanced at him, and their eyes met. No way was that a bloody coincidence.

Braun went on, "In the meantime, you can visit the Theoti portal in WeNet which will direct you to a number of centers in several major cities where you can await the full unveiling of what the Church of Theoti has to offer."

Kai thanked Braun and Rotberg, then signed off for several minutes of commercials.

Silas turned to Celeste, leaning in and asking lowly, "What do you make of Theoti showing itself like this?"

She frowned. "Not sure. Especially in such a public manner."

"And during the world's craziest hour, with these wars and natural disasters—"

"Is that Seba?" asked Eddie with interruption. He was pointing at the massive telly.

Silas followed his gesture. And let slip a curse, which was becoming a frequent occurrence.

Celeste wanted to join him but grabbed her tea again.

There he was. In all his Sebastian Grey glory. Just as she recalled.

Tall—well, taller, given the transformation he had under-gone a few years ago. Skin glistening a pasty white that was all at once horrifying and mesmerizing. And almost...rippling, in undulating waves of prismatic rainbows that enticed as much as intrigued. And that voice. A wicked combination of enchantment and fraternal, almost shamanic guidance. Black robes with crimson piping didn't help matters. Or perhaps they did, the man styling himself as just that: a shaman.

He was walking through a misty glade, sunlight lancing through a leafy canopy

It was all very suggestive—particularly the man himself.

"Do you want to live your best life now?" Sebastian crooned, walking slowly through the foliage, eyes transfixing the viewer. "Are you spiritual but not religious? Is there something within you that longs to reconnect to the ground of your being?"

Sebastian stopped, two long fingers grasping a bright orange flower nestled in a tree and bringing it to his face. He closed his eyes and smelled it, then returned to the viewer.

"Then Aeon is here to help."

"Aeon?" Silas said with a start.

That name struck Celeste as familiar as well.

She turned to him. "Why do I know that name?"

Silas replied, "Because Aeon—well, Aeon Foundation, it was the site of one of my first operations for SEPIO." He turned to her, explaining, "In Italy, where my old war buddy Eli Denton and Sebastian had tried conning me into verifying a new Gospel text."

She hummed with recognition. "Right. And it was connected to Nous, isn't that correct?"

"More than connected. Rudolf Borg, the former Grand Master until his death, was headlining the dang thing."

Torres said, "Sounds like your *twin* is now headlining the dang thing."

He glanced at her. So did Celeste. Sounded that way.

"We offer personalized services," Sebastian went on, continuing his trek through the glade, "that open the mind and heal the heart through safe and legal medicinal avenues of divine connection."

Elijah snorted. "Safe and legal medicinal avenues of divine connection?"

Gapinski laughed. "Yeah, Sounds like your run-of-the-mill ganja bar!"

Silas shushed the pair as Sebastian went on: "Life is confusing. The news is hard to take. Meaning is hard to come by. It doesn't have to be this way. Aeon is here to help. Visit www.aeon.life for more information. Discover who you were always meant to be."

The commercial ended with the website again and the logo of a stylized blue spark of light set in an open palm.

Kai returned, still standing by for the Santos presser, his intrepid reporting friend, Mara Mitchell, awash in klieg lighting and dutifully holding a mic. Didn't matter one bit. It was clear the room wasn't paying an ounce of attention to the pair. All minds were still transfixed on one person.

"That was...*weird*, right?" Gapinski said.

"Yuppers. Weird," Elijah answered without missing a beat.

"Very weird," his partner Gina agreed.

"Apparently he lives on," Torres added. "I tell ya, that guy's got nine lives!"

"Like Ron Popeil and Oprah had a baby," Elijah added. "Who was that bozo?"

Celeste took a breath and glanced at Silas.

Who answered, "My brother."

"Oh my cheeps! No shiznit?"

She frowned. Yes. No shiznit.

Silas didn't offer a reply. He didn't need to.

Instead, he leaped to his feet and strode down into the well and straight for the exit.

A sudden, leaping fear seized Celeste at the sight of Silas

running from the one thing that had been the source of so much pain the past several years.

"Silas, love—" she called after him, standing and raising a hand to rein back her husband. It was no use.

He fled through the exit, the heavy security door thudding closed in his wake.

She slumped back in her chair, bringing her mug of tea back for a sip, a tremor taking hold of her hand. She set it back down. It was cold anyway. Even then, she no longer wanted it. Her only desire was for Silas.

What was he going to do?

Not only that: What was *she* going to do?

CHAPTER 15

Silas burst through the secured door anchored to the Basilica of the National Shrine of the Immaculate Conception. The hot, humid midafternoon August air smacked him in the face, it's wet heaviness not doing him any good.

He groped for air, chest tightening and breath hard to come by.

Was he having a heart attack?

No. Panic attack. It had been a while since he'd had one of those. PTSD from three tours fighting Uncle Sam's misadventures overseas. Used to have little blue pills to ward off the effects. Sertraline, it was. Hadn't used them in years, instead finding relief and release from his past trauma and anxiety through the Holy Spirit's care—and Celeste's.

But now...seeing Sebastian on the screen like that. Crowing about an elixir to relieve the pains of life. Offering himself as some guru to the masses...

It was all too much.

And his damned chest was tightening right up!

He stumbled across the black pavement, bracing a hand against Gina's candy apple red Honda Odyssey. Believed he'd paid for that one, her original one with a bangin' sound system for her Pavarotti obsession obliterated in an operation from hot Hades a few years ago.

Literally. Going up in a ball of fiery ugly that had thrown the Feds off their tail.

Now that was a trip.

He kept at it, striding down the drive now, heaving desperate breaths past a tall row of evergreen privacy trees, their piney scent sort of refreshing. Not that he could enjoy it anyway still groping for breath.

Didn't help matters he still had that noose from early that morning still wrapped around his neck.

He unbuttoned his collar and undid the tie. A Zegna. To match the blue blazer Celeste had given him for his first day of class. A nice blue tartan, with a navy background and multiple shades of blue vertical and horizontal bands in a crisscross pattern. Better known as "plaid" in the states. But across the pond, his British Queen had known it to be a tartan. So, tartan it was.

And it was mercilessly hard to undo.

Especially when he was hot and sticky and sweaty. With his chest tightening, right at the center, and breath was like sucking air through a coffee stir stick, it was so—

Alright. There. Undone and removed.

So was his shirt, the white thing peeling from his sweaty skin like wet toilet paper off the yard after a good morning dew. He'd know. Had had far too many bouts of cleanup duty to count as a teenager thanks to rival high school football team TP raids.

He was on some road now. Harewood Road. Ran north-south. So he took it, stumbling in his stiff leather shoes that hurt like a mother, the clatter along the sidewalk as annoying as the—

Wait a sec...

What was that?

He looked up, swallowing and continuing his breath groping, searching for what he'd heard. For that line he'd heard.

That Wonka line from earlier hustling from Saxbys.

And from the wackadoodle Judah Howell.

Only louder, more insistent—and close. Real close.

"We are the music makers, and we are the dreamers of dreams."

Silas couldn't tell who it was or where it came from.

Was a little tied up trying not to black out—and hoping to the good Lord for a helping hand with a bit of oxygen!

And lots of people streaming up and down. Scurrying to the basilica, actually. Made sense, given all the apocalyptic crazy. But it sure made it hard to see what was what and who was who. Did catch a hearing of additional lines though, through the shuffling throngs:

> *Wandering by lone sea-breakers,*
> *And sitting by desolate streams;*
> *World-losers and world-forsakers,*
> *On whom the pale moon gleams:*
> *Yet we are the movers and shakers*
> *Of the world forever, it seems.*

"What the heck was that abou—"

More of that crazy poem sounded from behind:

> *But we, with our dreaming and singing,*
> *Ceaseless and sorrowless we!*
> *The glory about us clinging*
> *Of the glorious futures we see,*
> *Our souls with high music ringing:*
> *O men! it must ever be*
> *That we dwell, in our dreaming and singing,*
> *A little apart from ye.*

There was a ring of familiarity about the stanza. Couldn't place it, but he sure got its meaning: it's all progress, all the way down.

Or rather, the *myth* of progress. Silas was of the opinion that the tyranny of the present did nobody any good. Was much more in line with good ol' William F. Buckley, who stood athwart history yelling *Stop!* at a time when no one was inclined to do so, or had much patience with those who urged caution to the march of history.

Maybe it was his old soul, but he also thought the past was worth holding onto. To be rediscovered, even, rather than reimagined purely for the sake of progress. It was like one of his other heroes said on the matter, Ian Malcolm, from *Jurassic Park*: "*Your scientists were so preoccupied with whether they could, they didn't stop to think if they should.*"

Got that right.

Finally caught his breath, both his shirt and tie slung over his shoulders now, and sauntered down Harewood. Other direction. Against the flow of traffic moseying toward the basilica in their time of need. Didn't much care for the place. Seen as how another operation showed its ugly mug from the pit of—

His left shoulder slammed into something. Or, rather, some*one*. Tall and solid and coming at him from outside his field of vision cast down to the cracked, stained sidewalk.

Silas's dexterity wasn't like most middle-aged men, having hammered and honed his body through team sports and the military, then a strict workout regimen through the years. So he'd kept himself upright without a problem.

The other guy...

A string of expletives exploded from his victim, who toppled to that cracked, stained sidewalk with a thumping *smack*.

"Damned blind bastard..." he complained, sprawled on his back.

Felt flat horrible for his clumsy blindness, as the dude had rightly complained.

"Sorry, sir. Didn't see you," Silas said with apology.

"The hell you didn't!" the man snarled with a scowl.

He took a step back, out of reach. This could get ugly.

For more times than he'd care to count that day!

Silas hustled to help the man—

When he stopped short.

And took a step back at what he saw.

Sprawled on the ground and struggling to right himself was a very large man. Tall and wide and lumpy. Middle-aged and looking like middle management. Skin bronzed and hair coiffed with what looked like gel and hairspray. Face was pinched and snarling, blue eyes inflamed with rage and mouth still spewing obscenities at Silas.

And wearing nothing but a placard.

One of those sandwich signs unionized workers wore protesting working conditions or pay, or Gen Zers marching for their right to party like their parents did at Woodstock '94. Not the original, the 25th anniversary counterfeit.

Except this dude wasn't protesting or petitioning the Man. Or at least any earthly one. Instead, he was shaking an angry middle finger at the Man Upstairs.

One side mocked, *WHERE IS HIS PROMISED COMING?!*

On the other: *GOD IS NO(W)HERE!*

The latter he took for a dual play: God is no where; God is now here.

In a city like DC, Silas was used to protests. He'd even joined in a few during his college years at Georgetown, counter-protests against the masses marching against the run up to the Iraq War to oust Saddam Hussein. On the other side of three tours for Uncle Sam, he might even be inclined to join such anti-war protests now.

But this...some uptown dude missing from accounting, manicured and coiffed and tanned, naked as a jailbird but for those homespun placards—protesting, what, God? Mocking his delayed second coming? Then the weirdly mixed message denouncing such absence, yet claiming his presence?

Still squirming like an overturned turtle, he cussed Silas out some more and shouted at him to help him stand.

The pleas snapped Silas from his confusion. He hustled to the man and hooked a hand under his arm, hoisting him back to his feet.

"I was freakin' calling out to you," Naked Dude exclaimed, "to open your eyes and ears to the truth of things!"

"Clearly I didn't get the message," Silas replied with a chuckle. What that was exactly...he didn't have a clue. Some End Times apocalyptic mumbo-jumbo he didn't want to wait around to find out.

"Again, sorry for the trouble. Have a good day!"

Silas went to go when a hand of sausage fingers gripped his arm, and wild, popping eyes met his own surprised ones.

He yanked his arm, but it was a no-go on that front. Naked Dude's grip was vice-like, which was uncomfortable on many levels.

Then the unexpected happened.

Naked Dude grabbed Silas by his sweaty T-shirt. Eyes wide, frantic. Mouth even wider, teeth white and something on his breath. Expected the tang of fermented wheat, maybe rye, given the dude's craziness. Nope. Listerine. Which Silas appreciated, given the proximity of the sudden flare of emotions.

Which were unleashed on Silas: *"We are the gods of our own destiny! We are the bearers of the Republic of Heaven come!"*

Silas startled. Republic of Heaven?

That was odd.

And familiar.

An icy dread seeped through his veins with recognition at that turn of phrase. A phrase his twin brother, Sebastian, had parroted more times than he could count. Who was himself the Grand Master of a pseudo-religious alt-spiritual order of wack-adoodles bent on the Church's destruction since Pentecost.

Nous.

The Republic of Heaven was meant as a secular challenge to Christ's own Kingdom of Heaven. Again, part of the wack-adoodle worldview his brother and Nous espoused. And Eddie had mentioned Samantha—his sister—also went on about it recently.

Now some random dude parading around on a DC street, buck naked, was spouting it.

Who was this guy? A Nousati operative, some crazed missionary sent to spread the terrorist group's ideology?

Part of Silas didn't want to find out. But it also seemed important. And, well, he was in the thick of—something! An operation? Who knew. A SEPIO something, that's for sure.

Silas went to ask him about it when he was interrupted: "*We are the music makers, and we are the dreamers of dreams!*"

There was that line again. The one from Judah Howell. The one he'd heard earlier that morning from someone in George-town, then above the street traffic moments ago. He needed to know where the man had gotten it from.

"That line," Silas said, "'*We are the music makers, and we are the dreamers of dreams.*' Where did you hear it?"

Naked Dude shrugged. "WeNet. Where else?"

"And the other one. The Republic of Heaven. WeNet as well?"

"Oh no. No no no! A glorious retreat plumbing the depths of the ground of my being!"

"Retreat?"

His eyes got real big, and his mouth matched the grin.

Then: "Do you want to live your best life now? Are you spiritual but not religious?"

Silas scrunched up his face. "Huh? What are you—"

Naked Dude latched a hand on his arm: "Is there something within you that longs to reconnect to the ground of your being? Then Aeon Foundation is here to help."

It finally struck Silas what was going on: He was parroting Sebastian! Repeating, word for word, the same ridiculous spiritual mumbo-jumbo from that television commercial.

"We offer personalized services," he went on, "that open the mind and heal the heart through safe and legal medicinal avenues of divine connection."

This was unbelievable. Naked Dude was freakin' evangelizing for Sebastian's latest wackadoodle project—for Nous!

"Life is confusing," he continued on with what Sebastian himself had said on that infomercial. "The news is hard to take. Meaning is hard to come by. It doesn't have to be this way. Aeon is here to help. Discover who you were always meant to be, traveler. Join the journey!"

No thanks, Naked Dude...

With a wrenching yank, Silas finally freed his arm, spun around, then hustled back for the Order's makeshift HQ.

In the distance, Naked Dude continued his ranting: "*We are the gods of our own destiny! We are the bearers of the Republic of Heaven come! We are the dreamers of the dreams!*"

The man called after him one last time: "*The truth is out there, traveler!*"

Silas glanced over his shoulder to find him jabbing himself in the head.

Then he was gone. The sea of people closed up around him, streaming toward their destiny. Which apparently was still the Basilica of the National Shrine of the Immaculate Conception.

And should be his too.

Didn't want it to be. Not in the slightest. But with running into that naked whack job like that, someone who was this converging point for the nonsense pseudo-spirituality spouted from both Nous and Theoti...

What were the odds with that one, him of all people, on that street, making contact with that man, with that intel?

Silas frowned, knowing the answer. Zip, zero, zilch, that's what!

He also knew the reason for the run-in.

Sighing, he turned back to the basilica, knowing what was what.

Alright, Lord. Hear you loud and clear.

It was to be his destiny too.

But he didn't have to like it.

CHAPTER 16

Where the bloomin' blazes was Silas?

Celeste weaved a fountain pen across her fingers with a nervous energy that had stretched to her uni days of yore. Manning the captain's chair of the Oxford Union will do that to you. She had successfully climbed the ranks of the debating society her third year and had been offered the chair leading a team at the World Universities Debating Championship. Picked up a third-place win that year, and the twirling tick.

Which kept time like a metronome, the back-and-forth rapping of the fountain pen keeping track of the seconds Silas was absent. An irony, to be sure, since it was him who had gifted her the pen for her first day on the job as Order Master, as *temporary* a role as it had been intended.

She tried not to showcase her worry for the rest of her Order operatives, but it was bloody well hard when your husband stormed out in the middle of an operation after glimpsing his psychopathic brother selling his brand of spirituality to the masses. The one who caused him so much pain and despair. The one who had blown his bloomin' hand off and nearly snuffed out his very life.

She had tried to hold a steady hand, not racing to fetch him after he'd absconded so suddenly, and without a word to her or the others. But as the minutes ticked off, from fifteen to twenty to forty, she couldn't help herself.

Celeste finally stood and strode down the short set of stairs and across the concrete floor, the clickety-clacking of her black pumps far too urgent for the matter. So she slowed her pace, taking in a slow breath and swallowing back the rising concern that Silas had flown the coop.

A quick head-pop into the hallway confirmed as much. Silas was nowhere to be found. Nothing but a wet-newspaper smell that turned her stomach sour. She would have to do something about that now that she was Order Master. That is, after she figured out what had happened to her husband!

She swallowed hard, the taste of pennies racing across her tongue—whether from the adrenaline of the moment or her churning stomach, she wasn't sure—then strode back inside SEPIO's temporary ops center, making for that buffet of hot water and tea again. This time a chamomile. The moment called for it.

The sachet of the delicate Egyptian white flower bloomed a sweet straw and apple-like aroma as the hot water filled the mug. Celeste closed her eyes and breathed deeply, letting the comforting smell of home ground her.

The door opened with an echoey clatter, jolting her attention from her tea—and causing her to nearly spill the bloomin' thing! She glanced over her shoulder to find Silas storming into the room.

He had undone his tie, and his shirt was a sweaty mess. Must have climbed clear up and out the HQ hatch. No matter. All that did was he was back. He was safe. And it looked like he was ready to engage again.

The other Order operatives had been sitting around the

main U-shaped operations table in his absence. They stood on his arrival.

Silas said, "Gapinski, you got that video?"

He shuffled at attention. "Uhh, sure, which one?"

"The one of that Judah Howell fella."

"Yeah, why?"

"I need to see it."

Cradling her tea, Celeste secured her mouth into a grin and walked over to greet him. "What's going on, love?"

He shook his head. "Not sure. Something I just heard out on the street that jogged my memory from earlier in the day. Then our ride over."

Abraham cued up the video again and started playing it. Several seconds ticked by, when—

"There!" Silas exclaimed.

Judah Howell. That character preaching that Wonka nonsense.

"We are the music makers, and we are the dreamers of dreams!"

"You recognize this, Silas?" asked Celeste, gesturing at the man continuing on with the rest of that O'Shaughnessy poem.

Silas nodded. "Some other nutjob was shouting the same nonsense outside."

Gapinski snorted. "Well, it is DC…"

He turned to her and explained what had just happened to him outside, from bumping into the man and his ravings parroting some of those lines from Judah Howell and that British poet. A right mad nutter was what he sounded like. The nude bloke, not Silas. Although, his interest in the man made her wonder.

"That's not all of it," he added.

Celeste took a sip of her tea, the slightly honey flavor chasing away her worries. "What isn't? What are you going on about?"

"It's Sebastian."

Eddie joined now: "What does your brother have to do with this?"

Silas hesitated but briefed his father's friend on Sebastian's involvement with Nous as Grand Master, and their militancy and operations hellbent on destroying the Church. Celeste wasn't sure about bringing this man into their SEPIO confidence, still uncertain of him, his motivations. But she trusted Silas's judgment, and the chap did look devastated by the news. Clearly he had been close to the family, and unawares what had happened to the other half.

"This guy I heard ranting outside," Silas went on, "also said something about the Republic of Heaven."

"The heart of Nous's worldview," said Celeste. "What your twin has been plotting and scheming for the past few years after taking over from Rudolph Borg."

"That's not all. His whole bit, what we heard on that wackadoodle infomercial—"

Elijah snorted an interruption. "You mean the lovechild of Ron Popeil and Oprah?"

"Something like that. The same guy was parroting it with this creepy evangelistic fervor. As if caught in a trance, his brain having been programmed to spout Sebastian's nonsense."

Celeste took another sip of tea. "You're meaning the script from the commercial?"

"Word for word," Silas replied.

"So wait a sec," Gapinski said. "Some dandy from DuPont Circle, naked as a jailbird, was marching up and down the street outside shouting about the world coming to an end but also yammering about being the dreamers of dreams and music makers, about the Republic of Heaven and the Aeon Foundation? That about the long and short of it?"

He nodded, saying nothing.

"What do you suppose it means?" asked Celeste.

"Sounds like *One Flew Over the Cuckoo's Nest*," Torres

replied, "is missing one of their patients!"

"Nope. Ken Kesey's novel," Elijah said, "was set at the Oregon State Hospital. So *they're* missing one of their patients, not the book."

"Whatever. The point is—we've got a Nous nutjob on our hands!"

"Or Theoti," Gapinski added, "with the way he sounded like Rotberg and Braun. Didn't they say the same Willy Wonka nonsense?"

Torres nodded. "Suppose so. What's that about?"

"Weren't they in cahoots the past few operations?"

Celeste replied, "That is correct. Our intel on that front of things tells us Theoti and Nous had been on the mend after going head-to-head. Perhaps they have combined forces to offer up a spiritual elixir for the disenchanted masses at the end of the world as we know it."

There was a sudden commotion from behind. Abraham was conferring with another one of the operational support personnel. Must have come into the ops center while he was debriefing them on the man outside.

Silas pressed on: "Then why did it seem like they were sort of competing?"

"What do you mean by that?"

His reply was intercepted: "Master Grey!"

Celeste spun toward the voice, as did Silas. They caught one another's eyes and chuckled.

He gestured for her to take the reins, which was sweet. She treasured that about him, not at all feeling threatened by her and her strengths, her skills—and clearly not even her authoritative position.

She took a sip of tea and said, "Right. What do you have for us, Abraham?"

Abraham swallowed, then replied, "It's about Caleb Harris."

"Who's that?" asked Silas.

"Our man scoping out Judah Howell," Celeste replied. "Has he returned from the field?"

A breath, then a beat, then a shaking of his head.

She rolled her eyes. "Well, spit it out already."

Another breath, another beat.

Then: "He's dead."

What the bloomin' blazes...

Celeste nearly dropped her tea at the word *dead*, and wasn't entirely sure she had heard him correctly.

"Sorry, come again?" she asked.

And yet...she was certain she had heard him right.

A ping of panic jolted her heart rate forward. She could feel her hands grow clammy, too, and there was a growing dampness in her armpits that struck a further alarm. Now she worried she would give off a dreadful scent. Had always had bouts of underarm over-perspiration. Managed it well enough with Degree, of all things. One thing Yanks specialized in was deodorant, especially for women. But even then, that didn't always fair as well as she would need. Nor what the professional world expected of women in charge.

Men could hide it well enough with longer sleeved shirts. And even when they did show, they were valorized as hard-working. Not women. Prim and proper and well-deodorized was the only way to go. Especially for those in power, and most assuredly for those in command of clandestine ecclesial organizations tasked with fighting the good fight and keeping evil at bay.

Damn the patriarchy.

Stuff and nonsense. Now she was sounding like Mum!

"It's like I said," Abraham replied, snapping her attention from her underarms back to the moment at hand. Pushing his thick black glasses back up the bridge of his nose, he continued, "Our man—the SEPIO agent you sent cross-country. He turned up dead at his hotel."

Her heart ratcheted further, and she worried her under-arms would pose even greater problems than before.

"When?" was all Celeste replied.

"Just came through."

"No. When was he found dead?"

"His replacement had fetched takeout," Abraham explained, "from a Thai place up the road for lunch. When he returned, the door was unlocked—which was well outside protocol."

"Naturally."

"And when he investigated, Caleb was found in the bathtub. A bullet in his head."

Celeste closed her eyes and clenched her jaw. She eased a breath through her nostrils and swallowed.

A bloody shame. For the second time on her watch.

Now with the Order. Before with MI6.

It was why she had been so reluctant to take command from Radcliffe when he had inquired of her a few months before Silas had come on board. Back then, the former Order Master had interest in retiring. 'Twas entirely unorthodox to pass the managerial baton to a woman, which had been the state of things in the Church for centuries. Oh, there had been reform efforts, and more progressive minded Christians had insisted that women should have all the rights and privileges as their male counterparts in the business of overseeing and managing the Church—Mum included.

Not Celeste. She certainly believed women played a role. The Bible itself attested to it. With Priscilla and Aquila two named women who worked side-by-side in the apostle Paul's evangelistic ministry. Phoebe was a named deacon who had personally hand-delivered his letter to the Church of Rome—arguably the first theologian to have remarked about its contents, given she would have read the letter to the believers and male elders while answering questions about its content.

Then there was Junia, an esteemed apostle whom some complementarian-minded believers had tried to masculinize into a wholly anachronistic and foreign Junias; such a male name was not found amongst ancient literature.

Yet whilst the Bible acknowledged women leaders, and even offered guidance for women deaconesses, elder-rule and the role of overseer was not open for female business. At least that was the way she had read the Holy Scriptures. Not true for positions of leadership outside the Church, where women were certainly called to govern God's creation. Which she had gladly assumed, particularly with Her Majesty's Secret Intelligence Service. But inside the Church—and inside the Order of Thaddeus...that was another matter. One some had been eager to usher into the 21st century, particularly Eckhard Weiss. Who just happened to be Silas's chief rival of late.

He had wanted her to take over from Radcliffe when he stepped down. Not only because he trusted Celeste, but also because there hadn't been any other suitable men waiting in the wings to assume Radcliffe's Master chair.

Until Silas came along.

She had been as gobsmacked as he had been when Rowan, in effect, willed him that chair upon his passing a few years past. Thought she was a shoo-in for the role, given their conversations, though she had never let on as much with Silas.

Then Weiss approached her as a temporary fill-in for Silas after he had taken leave, and she had to admit she had grown quite fond of the role. It combined all of who she was, with her academic acumen in comparative religion and special-ops prowess from her MI6 fieldwork.

Which, now that she thought of it, was all of who Silas was as well. Perhaps that was why they had made such a smashing good couple. Although, he was much more the academic brainiac than she was, and she more of the special-ops muscle than him.

Again, perhaps that was why they had worked so swimmingly together.

Just wished there was a way for them to share the Order Master chair.

Because she sure could use his help.

"Who was this guy you had on the West Coast?"

The voice snapped her back to the fraught moment again. It was Silas. He was looking at her.

Celeste cleared her throat, then answered, "Right. The agent's name was Caleb Harris. Came to us from Homeland."

"As in, Homeland Security?" asked Eddie.

Gapinski smirked. "You know of any other Homeland in these parts, bub?"

"Wise guy…" he remarked, which was pretty much spot on.

Celeste replied, "At any rate, I had tasked them with keeping SEPIO apprised of competing spiritual sects, given his experience with keeping tabs on domestic terrorism for the American government."

"Didn't know about that one, but good call," said Silas.

Celeste tossed him a smile. Supposed there would be lots going on in the Order he didn't know about. Things she had put into motion without his knowing, or approval. There were times she felt a twinge of guilt about that, knowing she was a caretaker for his Master role. It felt a bit dodgy making plans without his knowing, like tasking a former Homeland Security agent with sussing out ecclesial terrorists.

Then again, the show had to go on, and it couldn't wait for Silas to get on with it and figure out what he wanted from life.

"This was his first operation," Torres said. "Wasn't that right?"

Celeste nodded. "Right. It was."

"Where?" asked Silas. "Looked like it was on the West Coast."

"Northern California, actually. In a small town called

Ukiah. He had been embedded with a spiritual sect he had run across on WeNet."

"Embedded?" Eddie said, straightening. "What, like undercover?"

"Precisely."

"Were they radicalized?"

Celeste frowned. Good question. She grabbed a lock of hair and started playing with it. Then realized the tell revealing her uncertainty. Mum would not be impressed.

She released the lock and replied, "That was to be determined."

Gapinski snorted. "Determined? Murder sounds pretty radical to me!"

"Let's not jump to conclusions." She put out a staying hand trying to bring a modicum of control to the conversation. "We aren't sure whether they were involved in Caleb's death or not."

Silas said, "Or whether our normal nemesis was."

Torres smirked. "Which one?"

"Suppose now it is a matter of choosing," Gapinski said, "between door number one and letter crazy Q!"

"Right. Sebastian," Celeste added, "whom we saw offering a pre-packaged New Ageism for the masses. Or Noland Rotberg and Markus Braun doing much of the same."

"Which the *muy loco hombres*," Torres added, "are primed to rope into their pseudo-religion thanks to the apocalyptic bowls being overturned!"

"Seals," Elijah corrected.

"Huh?"

"You said bowls. It's seals. Bowls come at the end of the Book of Revelation. After the trumpets. Now it's the seals."

"Which that yahoo Judah Howell," Gapinski said, "went on about. Some sixth sign?"

"I think it was a scroll," Torres replied.

"The Sixth Seal," Silas clarified just as Elijah opened his mouth. He snapped it shut and scowled.

"Whatever."

"What's that about?" asked Gapinski.

"The end of days," Victor Zarruq answered, grave and solemn.

"Oh my cheeps!" exclaimed Elijah. "That isn't ominous at all."

Silas said, "You're speaking about the last days."

"The apocalypse," Torres added.

"The end of the world as we know it?" asked Gina.

"And I don't at all feel fine!" Gapinski retorted.

Up until now Victor had been a passive observer. Even now, he was slumped back in his chair, large arms propped up on the armrests and fingers drawn together in a tent. His face was pinched, eyes closed, and lips pursed.

Until he stiffened and heaved a breath, regarding the table. It looked as though he had something to add to the discussion.

"Does anyone have a copy of the Holy Scriptures?" he requested.

"I've got an app for that on my phone," Gapinski said, giving it a shake.

Victor gasped and twisted up his face, as if he had swallowed a lemon.

"A pho—Stuff and nonsense is what that is." He muttered something in his foreign North African tongue and shook his head. "No, not a mobile! I am speaking of an actual book. A proper study of God's Word requires ink and paper, along with a sturdy pen for notations. Especially for what we need to discuss, this Sixth Seal business. Which is indeed a grave matter. The gravest of matters."

A glance of trepidation passed between Celeste and Silas. The same look as before. A running theme it seemed.

Which he voiced: "Now what?"

CHAPTER 17

Now what?

Before Silas could ask what was what, Abraham rushed over a Bible that looked to have seen better days. Black cover cracked and well-worn, pages bent and rugged, crimson-stained edges scuffed.

He took it and thanked the man, then flipped through to the end. Clearing his throat, he read aloud: "'*Then I saw the Lamb break one of the seven seals, and I heard one of the four living creatures call out, as with a voice of thunder, 'Come!' I looked, and there was a white horse!*'"

Victor read off each of the seals, beginning with the four horses—white, coming to conquer the world; red, stealing peace and provoking war; black, bringing economic calamity; pale green, killing a quarter of humanity with war, famine, pestilence, and wild beasts. Then the fifth, where the souls of those martyred for their faithfulness to Christ cried out: '*Sovereign Lord, holy and true, how long will it be before you judge and avenge our blood on the inhabitants of the earth?*' They were told to wait a little longer, and Silas knew the story ended with their final vindication.

He paid close attention to the sixth seal, the one Judah Howell himself had seemed to obsess over:

> *When he broke the sixth seal, I looked, and there was a great earthquake; the sun became black as sackcloth, the full moon became like blood, and the stars of the sky fell to the earth as the fig tree drops its winter fruit when shaken by a gale. The sky vanished like a scroll rolling itself up, and every mountain and island was removed from its place. Then the kings of the earth and the magnates and the generals and the rich and the powerful and everyone, slave and free, hid in the caves and among the rocks of the mountains, calling to the mountains and rocks, "Fall on us and hide us from the face of the one seated on the throne and from the wrath of the Lamb, for the great day of their wrath has come, and who is able to stand?"*

There they were—there it was.

The seals, particularly the sixth that Judah Howell character had referenced. And the final seal, unleashing a cosmic catastrophe to bring the world to the brink of the End Times.

He voiced the truth of it: "The beginning of the end..."

"If you're right, chief—" Gapinski caught himself. "Erm... whatever you are. If it is, we don't need to worry about it, right? Only those who are left behind."

"Nope," Elijah said, shaking his head.

"What nope?"

"Nope, nope."

"Huh?"

Elijah sighed with a slight *tsk*ing, as if annoyed. "Scripture does not teach some sort of secret call to believers. The left behind theology you're talking about that made Kirk Cameron the face of the Apocalypse. No, there's a shout and God's trumpet. Opposite of a secret signal reserved for a few. Like a battle cry in the ancient world when combined with trumpets. Jesus' coming isn't secret. It'll be a very public viewing. And according to the rest of the Bible, following a time of great calamity."

"Like the Great Bear and Dragon," Gapinski squeaked, "steamrolling across the world."

"The Great Tribulation," Silas corrected, dread pinging his belly at the recent headlines.

Victor nodded. "That's right. The New Testament seems to suggest a period of affliction—birth pangs, if you will, at the very end of the age. It also speaks of prior events as the beginning of such pangs. Events that have roiled the world since Christ's resurrection and ascension, even in the first century. Jesus was clear those birth pangs were not the end themselves. Which are meant by the seals of Revelation. They depict the generalized judgment of God through wars and human violence, economic downfalls and depressions, plagues and famine, and the persecution and martyrdom of the saints. Not until the trumpets blowing will God's true judgment be unleashed upon humanity, the content of the final, seventh seal."

Gapinski threw up a nervous laugh. "Again. We don't need to worry about that. Right?"

"Yuppers. We do," Elijah replied.

"Huh?"

Victor added, "That is being one interpretation of Scripture's apocalyptic prophesies."

"Where's the hope in that?" asked Silas.

He turned to him. "Hope? The Bible doesn't ensure our escape from these events. Only that we will be resurrected when Christ returns when he closes this cosmic age, establishes his ultimate rule and reign, and recreates our world anew."

Gapinski said, "That's not what Grandpappy taught. He was sure true believers would be evacuated before the crap hit the apocalyptic End Times fan!"

"Although this sort of interpretation of John's Apocalypse sounds appealing to those who believe they belong to that last generation before Christ's return, such a belief has not proven itself relevant in the two millennia since Jesus' first coming. Remarkably, it never showed up in the history of the Church until nearly three centuries ago!"

"Where'd it come from then," asked Torres, "if not from Scripture?"

"From one John Nelson Darby, who devised a theory of a secret pre-Tribulational rapture."

"The whochamacallit?" asked Gapinski.

Elijah answered, "They believed Jesus would return before reigning on Earth and establishing his kingdom, but only after the Great Tribulation."

Victor nodded. "However, one has to wonder that if the theory of a secret rapture is so secret that it is not even explicit in the Bible, why then should anyone believe such a thing?"

"Why did they then?" asked Torres.

"Historically, you can perhaps understand why, believing they were the last Christian generation before Christ returned and that they would escape severe persecution. Given the chaos that unfolded through the twentieth century, with great wars and rumors of more wars, recessions and depressions ravaging the global economies, plagues of unknown origin skipping around the world unabated. The only problem is that the earliest Church fathers in the second century were premillennial and post-Tribulational. They believed they were certain they had been plunged into the Great Tribulation or were about to. Understandable, given the waves of Roman persecution throughout the Empire. Saint Irenaeus taught this view, writing of *'the resurrection of the just, which takes place after the coming of Antichrist, and the destruction of all nations under his rule.'*"

Silas said, "Meaning the hope of resurrection came after the Antichrist's appearance, and all his persecuting work?"

The man nodded but said nothing, letting the insights from the Word of God settle in the room. A minute later, he added, "The spirit of lawlessness has been amongst us for quite some time. So has tribulation. Every generation has wondered whether they were the last to suffer before Christ's final, glorious appearing."

Silas considered this, and he wondered whether that's what was happening. With these wars and rumors of wars, the natural disasters, and—

"Santos is about to go live soon," someone interrupted.

It was Zoe, clacking at a workstation next to Abraham.

Celeste glanced her way and smiled. "Oy, Zoe, you're back!"

She flashed a weak smile, pushing those baby blue over-sized glasses of hers back into place. Zoe Corbino had been carted off to a makeshift clinic in their temporary accommodations after suffering a wicked leg wound. It was good to see her standing, and brought a semblance of normalcy back to things.

"Can't keep a good Italian down for long," she quipped, to which Gapinski whistled and clapped, the rest joining in.

"Yeah yeah yeah," Zoe said, taking a seat next to Abraham and pointing at the massive display mounted on the wall above. "Like I said, Santos is finally going live."

Everyone pivoted toward the screen.

"If you're just joining us," the well-makeuped anchor Kai Renolds began from the plush comforts of a studio, hair slicked back and glistening in view of a camera swooping in, "Mara Mitchell is standing by with the President of the United States about ready to address the nation after a day of remarkable news on all fronts."

Remarkable news on all fronts... Silas smirked. As if the most trusted name in news was shedding a tear for the ratings boon. If it bleeds it leads was a trusted aphorism of the news industry for a reason: the bleed also paid, and handsomely.

Mara Mitchell was standing by in a matte red suit, a white blouse peeking under the jacket and a fashion-forward navy scarf tied at her neck. She held a mic and wore a frown, the equally well-makeuped woman, hair blond and blown, lips glistening maroon, live from some secure location.

She replied, "Indeed, it has been a remarkable day in news. Ukraine has effectively fallen after eighteen months of entrenched warfare. Another global conflict has opened up in the Taiwan Strait, the People's Republic of China launching its long-anticipated effort to reintegrate the Republic of China, better known as Taiwan, into the mainland. The stock market shed nearly nine-percentage points before being abruptly halted when the East Coast rumbled under a once in an eon quake that registered as 6.4 on the Richter scale. Sadly, felling the Washington Monument and damaging the White House."

That last revelation sent a ripple of disbelief through the room.

"Understandably, the American people are unnerved and—"

"Sorry to have to cut you off, Mara," Kai said with interruption, the picture fading back to the glossy studio taking back the broadcast reins, "but it appears President Santos is now addressing the American people. Hopefully to bring some semblance of hope to right those nerves. Let's listen in."

The picture faded to a middle-aged Latino man walking to the dais of a darkened room, the walls paneled in walnut with a row of American flags festooned behind a podium, the presidential seal affixed affront. President Robert Santos. His dark hair streaked by sophisticated silver was trimmed neatly and slicked to one side. He wore a well-fitted navy suit with a matching navy and red polka-dot tie set against a white shirt, eschewing his regular trademark flare for fashion that had made him a darling of the media during the presidential campaign a few years ago and early years of his administration.

Santos stood stiffly, somberly and looked straight into the camera, delivering it straight to the American people as he had the past few years since taking office.

"My fellow Americans," Santos began, standing stiff and somber, a soft Latino lilt breaking through, "today has been—"

White light bloomed with a sudden burst.

Followed by a whooshing—was that an explosion?

That sent up a flare of rainbow color bars across the massive display.

"What happened?" asked Silas, spinning to Celeste.

She said nothing, frowning and searching Zoe and Abraham for answers, who were scrambling to assess the turn of things, the seconds ticking by without any sort of response.

Gapinski snorted a laugh. "Looks like someone forgot to pay the cable bill."

"*Dios mío...*" Torres said with a gasp, a hand across her mouth and head buried in her mobile device.

Before Silas could ask what had frightened her so, someone else did it for him.

"The worm has turned," Elijah said. "Hiroshima style. Or I suppose fried."

Celeste turned to him. "What are you—"

"We've been nuked!" Zoe shouted with clarity.

Had Silas heard Zoe right?

That the United States had been nuked?

That a nuclear weapon had been detonated on American soil?

That the freakin' President of the United States had just been—

His stomach clenched into a wicked vice and bile rose high

and hot toward the back of his throat. He swallowed hard and braced a hand against the railing edging the raised platform where they had been gathered.

This was not happening...

The apocalypse was truly now.

Everything had changed.

CHAPTER 18

Silas's head spun in flashbacks from the last time everything had changed in America—in his own life.

The day those two planes had slammed into the World Trade Center that fateful morning, and the world wasn't the same again.

Neither was his life.

For it was also the day Dad had died, and then the entire world had spun out of orbit thanks to those damn Islamic whack jobs using their religion as justification to bring America to its knees.

Innocence lost, the stark reality of evil regained in high-definition color.

Along with his own innocence after that one that slammed into that one wing of the Pentagon.

The one where Dad had been stationed.

The room was spinning now. His head felt faint, light.

Darkness crept in at the corners of his vision and starlight began sparkling throughout.

Silas's chest was tightening along with his stomach now and breath was hard to come by. Like sipping through a dang stir stick!

That memory from that day back then was as vivid as the first time he'd experienced it attending classes at Georgetown University when it happened. During a class he'd actually enjoyed. Trigonometry. Go figure.

They'd gotten word of the first two planes just after class began. Thought it was a tragic mistake, the one plane plowing into the one tower in a way that seemed super tragic but also super random. Like someone forgot to address a faulty indicator light during the pre-flight rundown, leading to mechanical failure and a hella-crazy tragedy.

That theory went out the window when the second tower enveloped the second plane, that explosion of fire and glass on repeat for the rest of the day, smoke blooming from its wounded side. Right before the pair collapsed in a phantasmic show of fire and fury.

Classes got canceled, which wasn't the worst thing in the world, and students were told to retire to their dorms to watch and process and grieve.

Then it happened. Swore he heard an echo of it all the way up the Potomac. Then he caught sight of a bloom of smoke all their own spinning up into the sky.

A smoke signal, not warning of danger but marking death.

In Silas's case, marking Dad's funeral pyre.

One thing led to another, and he wound up in Afghanistan showing those bastards who was boss, bleeding red, white, and blue to avenge his father's death. Then a shoulder tap to join the Army Rangers before shipping out into the heart of Operation Enduring Freedom hunting down Donald Rumsfeld's deck of fifty-two of Iraq's most wanted.

All of which pretty much brought him to that moment stuck four stories below a Catholic basilica as a washed-out meathead on top of a washed-out egghead as one of the Church's faith-defenders.

And having what felt like a wicked episode of the sort of PTSD that had leveled him after returning from years of war.

Could barely breathe and move. Could barely see and hear.

Life just hung in the liminal space between the Before-time of those moments leading up to that blooming white brightness and muffley roar.

Followed by the After-time of the horrifying realization that President Santos might have just been obliterated in a nuclear blast.

On freakin' American soil!

His brain could barely contemplate the turn of things.

In the confusion, he recalled how he and SEPIO had actually been responsible for helping bring Santos to power after the Order broke open a political conspiracy the last election cycle surrounding his closest contender.

Was never really all that political, especially after bowing from the Army Rangers. And definitely wasn't registered with any party. Hated the Manichaean options between elephants and donkeys. Had appreciated Santos's independent-minded administration, though. How he hewed closely to his Catholic convictions that defied partisan pinning. In everything from issues of justice at all stages of life, from limiting abortion and ending the federal death penalty, to offering a pathway to citizenship and actually doing a damn good job reducing childhood poverty—it all flowed from his faith.

And now he was likely dead.

Assassinated.

On freakin' American soil!

A voice suddenly broke through the haze of confusion. And fog of war—because surely that's what this meant.

"Zoe, are you certain of your assessment?"

It was Celeste. His wife. His best friend. His rock during the past year.

The only reason he hadn't spiraled sooner than that moment earlier when he stormed out after seeing Sebastian's wackadoodle commercial. Last thing she needed was for a repeat of that.

Get it together Grey…

Fight, damnit!

For Celeste.

She was enough to raise his head and get his head back in the game.

Zoe clenched her jaw and nodded, saying nothing but her wide eyes.

Eddie leaped to his feet clenching a phone to his ear and started making for the exit and into the hallway. Silas went to call after him but he heard him barking questions on the other end trying to confirm what had just gone down. Probably one of his many government contacts.

The rest of the room fell silent, the aural void from pure shock filled only by the low HVAC hum chilling the air beyond the freighted weight of the fraught national event.

"It's all over WeShare," Torres finally said.

"What is?" asked Silas, finally dragging himself from the shock of it all.

"Multiple accounts of a mushroom cloud in Maryland, actually."

"Maryland?" asked Gina with confusion.

Gapinski said, "Yeah, what in the world is in Maryland that would attract the A-bomb?"

"Apparently a sitting US president…"

"Where at?" asked Silas.

"In Frederick County," Torres replied. "Appears some of the local towns there reported seeing a flash of bright light and hearing a massive explosion."

"Which ones?" asked Celeste.

"Thurmont and Emmitsburg."

"In other words," Gapinski said, "Nowheresville, Maryland."

Celeste shook her head. "But that makes utterly no sense. Why would some rogue actor—"

"Or nation-state," Silas added.

"Or that. Why would anyone want to set off such a powerful, if not provocative, ordnance in such a seemingly remote locale? Why not a major metropolitan? Why not Washington, DC, itself?"

He shook his head, staring off and asking himself the exact same questions.

Until he had the answer.

A very, very wicked one.

"Oh my cheeps!" Elijah exclaimed, slapping a hand on his forehead. "Of course..."

"Oy, mate," Celeste said. "Of course what? What are you going on—"

"Camp David," Silas said, Elijah nodding with the same recognition. He swallowed before continuing, "The presidential retreat. In Frederick County, Maryland."

"All tucked in tight," Elijah added, "in the wooded hills of Catoctin Mountain Park. Near the towns of Thurmont and Emmitsburg."

Gapinski said, "I thought that Kai Renolds character said they were in some bunker tucked in tight beneath some mountain in West Virginia."

"Maybe the Veep was carted there."

Celeste said, "Or maybe it was a ruse from the White House to mask the President's true locale."

Gapinski snorted a laugh. "Fine messaging that did 'em."

Eddie P stormed back into the room, face white and head shaking.

Silas stood. "Anything on your end?"

The man slumped into his chair, taking off his silver glasses and rubbing his eyes.

"The Golden Eagle's condition is indeterminate..." he whispered, a tremor to his voice.

His stomach clenched again with recognition.

"Golden Eagle?" asked Celeste.

"President Santos's Secret Service codename. For the country bird of Mexico. His parents' place of birth."

"So it's true, then? He's—"

"Unknown," Eddie interjected, raising a hand. "The feed cutoff was likely the result of the blast radius."

Now Silas slumped back in his chair. "At Camp David?"

Eddie nodded, saying nothing.

Gapinski slammed his hand on the table. "Sonofa—"

"But you're saying POTUS might be safe," asked Silas with interruption.

"Stashed in some underground bunker?" asked Celeste.

Eddie shrugged. "Reports about an extensive underground bunker at Camp David have varied over the years. I do know there is an underground communications center and a VIP bomb shelter, constructed in 1959."

"Uh, guys..." Abraham shouted with interruption. Silas glanced his way, finding him clattering on his keyboard, those thick black glasses perched on the bridge of his nose.

"What do you have for us, Abraham?" asked Celeste.

The man stood, pushing them back up his face and pointing at the screen again. "That."

This was getting old, these videos beaming into their temporary digs, but Silas went with it. What he saw was an odd sight.

And a familiar one.

The picture was of a camera swooping down through a vast hall of glass, the sunlight bright and streaming through the windowed walls. The ceiling was vaulted by soaring Corinthian columns edged by gilt lines circling the white pillars like candy canes. High above, crystals could be glimpsed clinging to the corners and seams of the ceiling like clusters of grapes, a sort of celestial crown molding that refracted the light from the day with rainbow brilliance.

"Like Heaven..." Gapinski marveled.

"No, not Heaven," Celeste said knowingly, glancing Silas's way. "The Republic of Heaven."

"You recognize it too?" asked Silas.

"Recognize what?" Gapinski wondered.

"Hey, wait a second..." Torres leaned across the table. "Didn't we destroy something very similar to this hall?"

Silas nodded. "The headquarters, or whatever it was, for the Church of the Theotites."

"That outfit you identified earlier?" asked Eddie.

"That's right."

Celeste added, "Which we had learned was financed by Markus Braun and organized through the helping hand of Noland Rotberg."

"And that weird-ass Marvel character—"

"Matthew..." she moaned, throwing Gapinski not-now eyes. "Let's do without Uncle Sam's potty mouth."

He sighed and crossed his arms, nodding his understanding. "Well he was...And what was his name?"

"Sha," Silas offered.

"That's right! A weird—" He stopped short, withering under Celeste's gaze, then course corrected: "as-all-get-out character."

"You think this is that?" asked Torres.

The camera came in for a viewing of a large throng of people now gathered beneath that glistering glass hall, the light glinting from the chromework and casting it in a sort of holy halo. Standing at the center on a raised dais was the shaggy-hair fella from that SEPIO agent's video. Wearing a plain white T-shirt and dark denim. Sporting those oversized glasses from the '70s. With arms raised and eyes closed, one hand grasping a well-worn book bound in cracked black leather, page edges stained in a faded crimson, with those sticky tabs jutting this way and that.

A Bible.

Handled by Judah Howell.

"Where is this from?" Eddie asked now, dialing into SEPIO's own interests.

Sort of cheesed Silas, this unknown dude swooping into his life like that, and with news of some long-lost sister—then butting into his Order business.

He frowned, chiding himself. For he knew the truth of the matter.

It wasn't his Order business any longer. He'd walked away. Abandoned, really, leaving his wife to pick up the pieces. Who was more than capable, and far more talented than him at the gig. Still.

And it wasn't like the man was entirely unknown. Dad had known him. And that was good enough for Silas. He and all of SEPIO should only be so lucky to have someone as Eddie's caliber add his professional perspective into the mix of things.

"Live from WeNet," Zoe replied, snapping Silas back to the moment.

"Where else?" he asked.

Celeste turned to him and nodded. "Right. Any sense of its specific location?"

More clattering from Abraham, then a beat before the revelation: "Ukiah, California."

"Ukiah?"

Eddie turned to her now. "Isn't that where the SEPIO agent had been sent?"

"And killed?" added Gapinski.

And that.

She sighed, returning to the large display and going silent, doing what Silas himself was doing.

Discerning, intuiting, waiting for what came next.

"Whatever is going on—" Silas shifted, worry worming through him and pointing at the massive display: "looks like we're about to find out..."

"Greetings, my fellow spiritual travelers! I am Judah Howell," the man said, grinning widely. "I am the voice of one crying in the wilderness, making straight the way of the unsealing of the Sixth Seal that shall be your spiritual enlightenment! It is something I have been working my entire life for. Truth be told, I have always been more spiritual than religious," Judah said with a chuckle, "not wanting to become entangled with the trappings of organized religion. I have understood that a ground of being exists that permeates all of life. Jesus is one of those individuals who tapped into this ground, his love-filled teachings and sacrificial example showcasing this."

The man closed his eyes and brought his hands together, taking a breath and a beat.

Judah continued, "So for years, I have been on a spiritual journey. Much like many of you watching this. I have dreamed of new ways to connect people to the ground of their own being in this emerging ultramodern world, rooted in the teachings of the Way."

"What is this bloomin' Way business?" asked Celeste.

Silas just shook his head.

"Which is why I am now pleased to say that I have joined with other like-minded individuals from similarly organized religious affairs to offer the world a united experience of the divine."

Judah lowered his raised arms and started pacing the platform, the camera following.

"Before I get to that experience," he continued, "let me

begin with a story. An ancient story that is really a parable about four blind men and a beast of unknown origin."

"Are you kidding me?" Silas said, taking a step and bracing his hands on that railing again.

That story was *his* story, from earlier that day!

"As this story goes, one day a group of blind men heard that a strange animal had been brought into their village by a man traveling through town. Out of curiosity, the men agreed that they must inspect this mystery. Using only their hands."

Silas smirked, shaking his head. Of course this dude would pilfer this old chestnut of religious pluralism!

"What's the matter?" asked Celeste.

He mumbled "Nothing" and kept his gaze fixed on the guru.

"So they sought out the traveling man's mystery beast. When they found it, they groped about, feeling its various parts. None of them on their own could understand the animal. So they each agreed to reveal what they had discovered, knowing each of their perspectives helped paint a picture of the unknown beast."

Pausing he took a breath, then paced the dais.

"In the case of the first person, whose hand landed on the trunk, the man said, *'This being is like a thick snake.'* For another fellow, whose hand had grasped its ear, it seemed like a kind of fan, flapping this way and that. As for another person, whose hand was upon its leg, this one said, *'This here beast is a pillar, like that of a tree trunk.'* One fellow placed his hand upon the beast's side, describing it as a wall, immovable and impenetrable. Another, who felt its tail, described it as a rope. The last blind man felt its tusks and insisted, *'Surely the mystery is that which is hard and smooth, like a spear.'*"

One end of Silas's mouth curled upward, recalling that embarrassing observation of that jock student of his. Sort of did sound a bit X-rated.

"So there we are: Six descriptions of the one beast, coming

from six different perspectives. Each report matched their personal experiences with the mystery creature."

Judah took a breath, then grinned knowingly.

"If you are as astute as I believe you are, brothers and sisters, you probably guessed the blind men were each describing different aspects of *Loxodonta*, the mighty elephant."

"Stuff and nonsense is what this is," Celeste mumbled.

No disagreement there.

And no surprise to hear such nonsense spouted by a guru clearly catering to the spiritual-but-not-religious crowd. Not only could they not believe there was a God to begin with, but couldn't imagine there was only one *way* to God. They insisted there were multiple paths to the divine—multiple perspectives from all us blind men groping our way through our encounter with the elephant in the room. God, or the Divine, or the Universe, or whatever.

And it sounded like this Judah Howell character was scaling that belief for mass consumption.

With the help of Markus Braun and Noland Rotberg.

Judah continued, "You see, each man had a limited understanding of the singular elephant, didn't they? Each understood the beast based on their own personal experience—as limited as it was. In their ignorance each of these blind men assumed the elephant matched their own limited description. When they came together to report on their revelation, not only did they disagree over the nature of that revelation. They squabbled about it—declaring the other bearers of the elephant's revelation false, heretical, anathema."

Smiling, he and went on: "Of course, we enlightened ones know that an elephant isn't only tusks or legs like pillars. It isn't only a wiry tale or long trunk. It isn't just big flappy ears. And it isn't only a massive, hard, rough wall-like body. No, the beast is each characteristic described by the blind men. The elephant is the whole revelation."

The man chuckled and leaned against a glass podium.

"So what on earth is the story's point? The moral is this: Each religion is like these blind men and our elephant is like the divine reality we understand to be God. Each religion has only a partial knowledge of the divine reality, only a limited experience and exposure to the ground of our being, the singular Absolute. Like the six blind men in our story."

A breath, a beat, a grin.

Then the goods: "We know all religions are merely parts of the one divine whole—all describing the same elephant, the same Absolute, just in different ways. There is an essential oneness of all beings, flowing from one single source. Saint Paul himself commended the ancient Athenians for their worship of the Unknown God, acknowledging *For in him we live and move and have our being.*'"

"What the—" Celeste exclaimed, taking an irritated step toward the display. She complained, "The bloody fool is absolutely twisting Scripture to fit his fancy."

"And we are celebrating that oneness," Judah continued, "in short time with an unveiling. Until then, I have something to share."

The man droned on for several more minutes about the same nonsense until—

It all changed.

And the room gasped.

Flat not possible.

CHAPTER 19

CALIFORNIA.

Judah Howell took a breath from his soliloquy. Or was it monologue? It wasn't like he was speaking his thoughts aloud alone or irregardless of any hearers. Or was it regardless?

Anyhoo. Monologue. That's what it was. And to the entire world.

He took a breath, then a beat, flexing his fingers and easing out his breath through pursed lips.

He was positively tingling from head to toe! The rush of adrenaline from his impending unveiling skating through his veins had set all of his synapses on a high greater than the ayahuasca that had opened the door into the Unseen Realm during graduate school that had led to this very moment!

Just as Daddy had each time when the Spirit of Yahweh came mightily upon him. Especially when he preached on the End Times. 'Twas his favorite subject. The thing that jazzed him most about the branch of those Adventists he had led who had obsessed about such things.

Except Daddy had been popped by the Feds those many years ago.

Heat flashed hot in his throat at the thought of those

bastards and what they had done. What he had *witnessed* them doing, torching their home and cutting short Daddy's important, Spirit-inspired work!

He swallowed, the tang of bile having reached its fingering tendrils for the back of his throat, and took a stabilizing breath. He would need it for what came next.

What he was gearing up to usher into the world.

Because even while Daddy had the stiff backbone and prophetic imagination to do and see what the common person couldn't, the man hadn't gone far enough in his predictions of the end of the world. Or what the world needed on the other side.

He had been passionate about the Fifth Seal of the Apocalypse; Judah aimed to take things to their conclusion.

To not only bear prophetic witness to the Sixth Seal of the Apocalypse but to do one better.

He had always wondered why the man was so caught up with big, fat Numero Cinco, not seeming to care much about the big-daddy-o Seis. Maybe it was because the man had been itching for a fight with the Feds for years. They all were, really, but Daddy had been the one to instigate the showdown in the first place. And he had prepared for the inevitable, stocking food and hoarding guns. Call them people preppers nowadays. Back then, they had just been family. The only family Judah Howell had ever known. All fifty-odd-some of them.

All of whom died in a blaze of glory. Literally!

Yeah yeah yeah. Crispy critters, they were. Engulfed in the fires of hell itself, they'd been.

Which that Fifth Seal of Daddy's had sort of hinted at. Not the crispy critters part. The martyrdom part. The Branch, his family, dying in that blaze of glory from way back when.

The passage referencing that ill-fated day bolted through his mind like lightning:

> *And when he had opened the fifth seal, I saw under*
> *the altar the souls of them that were slain for the*
> *word of God, and for the testimony which they*
> *held. And they cried with a loud voice, saying,*
> *How long, O Lord, holy and true, dost thou not*
> *judge and avenge our blood on them that dwell*
> *on the earth?*
> *And white robes were given unto every one of them;*
> *and it was said unto them, that they should rest*
> *yet for a little season, until their fellowservants*
> *also and their brethren, that should be killed as*
> *they were, should be fulfilled.*

Daddy never got past that Fifth Seal because Uncle Sam wouldn't let him. He'd been right right right. Martyrdom would be their fate. And it was.

Except for him...

Another tingle raced through Judah. And sorrow. For their pain was his gain. And he'd hated himself every day of the week for it. That he had survived. That he wasn't among those slain.

That Daddy had been.

How he had loved him.

Strike strike strike that. How he *loved* him. Present tense. For he knew his father was still with him. Guiding him. Cheering him on. Kicking his ass when it needed kicking.

Inspiring him...

For it had been Daddy who had been the inspiration behind his work.

The reason he was planted on the dais at the center of that massive hall of glass and chrome and titanium.

Judah had carried on the work his father had never been able to see through to completion. Because there was a reckoning coming in America. Nay nay nay!

The world.

Daddy had predicted it. The slayin's and killin's. He knew people needed something to hold on to when the shiznit hit the fan fan fan.

Which, by gum and by golly, it had! It truly had. Far better than he could have predicted. All the chaotic world events, from one to the next, setting the stage for *Mis*-tah Judah's unveiling. With the East Coast's rumblin' and tumblin' the final trigger.

The Sixth Seal was at hand.

So were the end of days.

With Judah Howell making straight the way of the coming Messiah.

Again, that passage bolted through his mind like lightning. The rest of it. The one that had led to that moment. That reason for living. He savored every word as he quoted it inside that noggin of his.

He sucked in a measured breath and closed his eyes, the hum of whispered conversations and shifting feet echoing throughout the expansive hall of glass and chrome and titanium that surrounded him.

There was that tingle again. And it made him smile. Not only for the moment, but for what the Sixth Seal meant.

'For the great day of his wrath is come,' John the Seer wrote. *'And who shall be able to stand?'*

Yeah yeah yeah. Right right right. Who will stand in the face of the end of days?

He snapped open his eyes, casting them about the gleaming room that felt like the inside of a snow globe. Then grinned.

These dear people, that's who who who!

For what he bore would make all things new.

Would save the world.

Or rather, *who* he was about to bring to the masses.

A deep breath, then a beat.

Best get to it. Hippity-hoppity.

Judah stuffed his King Jimmy Bible under his arm again, basking in the divine brilliance of the light streaming through the snow globe, then got back to it.

He thrust his hands out, palms angled toward the floor and fingers flailed.

The signal.

For his people to ratchet their jibber-jabbering down to a holy hush.

They obeyed, except for some newcomers who were still being schooled in the finer points of the Way.

A sea of people in white spread before him, all around. Spreading a toothy grin across his tanned face.

And sending a right tingle tingle tingle ratcheting up his spine and blooming with pleasure in his head.

He toddled around the center dais, reveling in that sea of white robes but also searching for something.

A red light.

Now where where where—

There!

Just above the heads and anchored to a black eyeball that was his connection to WeNet.

And the masses.

Showtime.

That grin turned into an upside-down frown now.

The End Times.

The Sixth Seal times...

Now Judah snatched that King Jimmy from under his arm and brought his arms close against his chest, taking a step, then another, his manicured toes poking through his sandals anchored at the edge of the dais.

He bowed his head and closed his eyes.

Another deep breath, then another beat.

Then he eased his head up to drill his global audience, continuing his monologue after greasing the spiritual skids.

"Today is a somber day in these here United States."

There was a harsh emphasis on the U part of United, so that it came out *You-knighted*. It went way back. As in Daddy back. 'Twas one of those speechisms he recalled that he'd carried forward into his own speechisms. But it was more than that. There was a purpose behind it.

You see, *Mis*-tah Judah had been one of them forensics types in college. No, not *them* type of forensics types! Not NCIS, and all those sibling IPs those suites in Hollywood or New York or wherever, turned out and churned out to make a quick buck.

Nopety nope! The speech competition kind. Specifically rhetoric. Dabbled with a bit of extemporaneous and impromptu. Even scored a second-place win in the Lincoln-Douglas debate portion of Nationals, going mano-y-mano with some muckety-muck's daughter from *Haw-verd* as he liked to call that joint. Along the way, he'd learned that your speechisms could have either a deleterious (cue one of them *Haw-verd* words) or positive (cue one of them Bowling Green U words from the Buckeye State) effect.

Judah preferred the latter to the former, and he weaved such words into his preaching style to draw people instinctively to flock like the salmon of Capistrano.

And not just the word choices, either. But the style. The cadence. The timbre and tone of 'em.

Like *You-knighted* States.

So, again: purpose. Every word, and every one of their cadences, to the most consequential sermon he'd give of his career had a purpose. A singular purpose.

Belief.

Not in him.

Nopety nope!

For Judah Howell was merely the voice of one crying in the

wilderness, '*Prepare ye the way of the Lord, Make his paths straight!*'

Belief in the One.

But that was for later.

After the thing he was doing now. His sermon thing.

Anyhoo: Back to it.

Judah paced some more then strode back to the dais edge, leaning toward that glowing red eye.

"The world is at war. The world is on fire. The world is withering." He drew his voice to a lowly whisper now: "How could this happen, you wonder? Why did this happen, you ask? To us? To *me*?"

He eased back and smiled, bringing those mitts of his together in that pose and closing his eyes. Taking in another deep breath, it was time to bring 'er home.

"How long have I said that *Mis*-tah Judah is the voice of one crying in the wilderness? Prepare ye the way of the Authority, I have said. Make her paths straight! That time isn't today. Nopety nope! Today I wish to offer something else."

Time for the humdinger.

"Proof."

A knowing hum rippled through the crowd.

"That's right! I shall offer you a sign that I am that voice paving the way for the One who is to come. The one who will unite all of our religious affections!"

The world was thirsting for signs and wonders, for tangible experiences of the divine in a world bereft of the transcendent. For *proof* of the transcendent and of faith. In an age of alternative facts and disinformation, people wanted demonstrations of truth. And in an age as disenchanted as this one, people longed to experience the supernatural in their natural world. No! *Demanded* it.

By gum and by golly, Judah Howell would give it to 'em!

After all, that's just what the prophets of the Bible themselves offered. Tangible, existential proof of their bona fides.

Signs and wonders.

Healings. Raising the dead back to life. Commanding nature itself!

Possessing these sorts of powers meant possessing the power to command belief. To spark faith in those who might be willing to offer it to one who might save them from their misery.

From fear and anxiety.

And existential dread.

From death itself.

"How long has it been dry in these parts?" asked Judah, hippety-hopping along to the point at hand—and task.

He addressed the question to those arrayed below and around, opening his arms wide and looking from man to woman to man.

"Weeks?" he questioned.

"Months!" someone toward the middle shouted.

He startled. "Months? Half the year?"

"Got crops wilting it's so bad!" another complained.

He nodded, closing a fist and thumping his chest in solidarity.

"Two-hundred and three days, to be exact. The worst drought this region has seen in a generation."

A beat, a breath, a grin.

Then: "Until today."

Silence spread like slick oil. At first confused, then awkward, then disbelieving.

"To prove to you that I am who I say I am, I will make it rain."

Furrow-browed stares accompanied craning necks toward the ceiling of glass that told a very different story than the one Judah was fixin' to tell.

Where the sky was clear and blue. The sun beat down with relentless mockery.

Most of all: Not a cloud to be found in them parts.

Judah giggled, that grin of his widening to make room for a belly laugh that exploded with a giddiness from what was to come.

"Yeah yeah yeah, *Mis*-tah Judah you say!" he crooned. "Right right right. Rain? For real?"

Another beat, another breath, a still-wider grin.

"For really real! As real as—rain." He winked, then frowned. "Or is it right as rain? Hmm. I'll have to have a think about that. But not today!"

Clutching his Bible with one hand, he snapped his fingers with the other and leaped from the stage to a center aisle.

Then strode toward destiny.

"Come come come!" he commanded, the crowd stirring behind and rushing to follow as he burst through double doors leading outside.

An expansive lawn spread just outside the open glass doors. It was hot, it was dry. More importantly, there still wasn't a cloud to be found.

He darted into the center of the lawn and raised his hands toward the sky.

Laughter filtered from behind. The disbelief of Doubting Thomases.

No matter.

Because where that pathetic Messiah from Nazareth—the Nameless One who had started this whole cotton pickin' messianic thing to begin with—had been a prophet not without honor, neither in his own country nor in his own house, and did not many mighty works in his hometown because of their unbelief, Judah Howell was a different sort altogether.

He didn't need the faith of others. All he required was one thing.

Himself.

So within himself he looked.

To find the only thing that would carry the day.

And bring the rain.

Closing his eyes, he raised his hands.

And silenced the Thomases.

A bit dramatic, and did not a lick of good when it actually came to delivering on the signs-and-wonders goods. But a little razzmatazz showmanship never hurt nobody.

Especially when belief and doubt were concerned.

Nothing happened. Not for the longest time as the seconds kept ticking along. Birdies tweeted, an annoying tree frog croaked in the near distance. Same for the hot and bright sun shining down to beat the band.

Signaling not a storm cloud on the horizon.

Eyes still clenched, a tremor seized his body, and he sent a pinging signal along the synapses of his brain to the One that would make it all happen.

That was not razzmatazz showmanship. That was neural core activation.

Could almost see the electrical charge racing along his synapses and through his neural core, activating his ventromedial prefrontal cortex. Known by many leading neuroscientists as the so-called *God spot*, Judah had spent years studying this region where belief, whether religious or nonreligious, was found to be associated with greater brainwave signal transmission. The region carried with it a broad spectrum of importance for self-representation, emotional associations, reward, and goal-driven behavior. Including projections or connections or transmissions or whatever to the Divine.

He would tap it for this moment—he *was* tapping it for this moment.

A gasp from behind confirmed it. Then a whispering rush.

Right before a whipping wind gusted across the plane, sending Judah's long blond Jesus hair whirlin' and twirlin' like a nimbus.

It first came as hot, raging breaths from Mother Nature at being played like a fiddle, irritated huffs stretching on for several long minutes. Soon enough, riding its hide high-tailing it on out of Ukiah was a cooler one. There was a bit of a bite to it, but it was fresh and fecund (like *beckoned*).

And then—

A drop.

Of rain.

Right on the end of Judah's nose.

It was cold and gentle. Like a kiss.

From Heaven...

No. The Republic of Heaven!

More followed. Pinging his still-outstretched arms and hands. Dribbling down his cheeks. Coating his hair and soaking his clothes.

It poured. Buckets.

It was a slapping rain. The kind that hurts your face and your feelings. Sort of like Daddy from those many years ago. The suddenness of the slap was shoved aside by the joyful, joy-filled cry that soon crescendoed into a yawping exclamation of elation. Of ecstasy.

Of belief...

Which was the only currency he needed to unveil the fruits of the Sixth Seal.

The Seventh.

Some of those fruits were soaking him—before all of WeNet's peepers!

Real as rain or right as rain, didn't matter.

All that did was Judah Howell.

He was the real and right deal.

And not the only one.

"This Sixth Seal is not the end, enlightened ones!" Judah boomed, hands raised and face wet. "For it will lead to your final salvation! What comes next is the seventh. And when he had opened the seventh seal, there was silence in heaven about the space of half an hour. And I saw the seven angels which stood before God; and to them were given seven trumpets. Seven trumpets announcing the coming of the messiah! I have seen this last and final day. August 17 is its appointment."

The world around him swelled with the shouts and calls of a thirsty world.

Which Judah Howell was ready to satiate.

CHAPTER 20

WASHINGTON.

Celeste was gobsmacked. A rarity for her.

She had seen plenty in her years with Her Majesty's government tracking down would-be terrorists and actual terrorists, from Pakistan to Palestine. Those memories smarted something fierce, with a sourness that still made the bile rise with a wicked tang and blood run cold at the agents she had lost. Those years with the Special Intelligence Services special-operations unit, commonly MI6, still gave her nightmares every so often.

However, those dreamland horror shows had nothing on the nocturnal phantasms wrought through the Church's special-operations unit!

Directing SEPIO all these years before taking the helm as Master of the Order of Thaddeus, as temporary as that most recent assignment hopefully might be, were the stuff of Dan Brown fever-dream legend.

She was particularly fond of the secret military bunker housing the Yanks copulating efforts with the Devil himself. Or, as she would suppose Elijah Fox would correct her, the Fallen Ones, those divine-hybrid beings who had sought to enslave humanity through their alien trickery. Which probably tied for first trophy with that fateful Halloween night she had nearly been sacrificed upon a pagan altar to the actual Devil by Silas's maniacal twin brother.

Of course, solving the hidden location of the Ark of the Covenant wasn't half bad. As was finding the sunken Garden of Eden and relic bones of our ancient ancestors, Adam and Eve. Could have done without battling a resurgent Knights Templar, but that was par for the SEPIO course these days.

This however...

What had just been broadcasted across WeNet, what had just transpired across the other side of America—

That for sure took the cake, as those Yanks were fond of saying.

Silence reigned, which she was quite content with. The aural breather gave her a chance to gather her thoughts and take an actual breath. She needed it after what had confronted her that day.

There was the intel gathered on the upstart mystery cult she had a gut sense would pose a spiritual threat soon enough. Apparently, she was right. For not only had the very SEPIO agent keeping a keen eye on the group been killed, the leader of said upstart mystery cult had partnered with the likes of Noland Rotberg and Markus Braun to scale his newly minted American religion for a global audience.

Then of course there was the earthquake and resulting mayhem, compounded by the other mysterious man that seemed to have some sort of prophetic vision of the impending apocalyptic doom. Truth be told, the chap was sort of a pleasant sort. Reminded her of Daddy, the way he carried himself in that self-assured, no-nonsense manner without being overbearing, joined by a clever wit and well-appointed grooming. She might have even fancied the man in another lifetime, had the two been paired on a clandestine government operation, as it appeared he was prone to be involved with given his extensive curriculum vitae.

But, given he was responsible for the other thing that had set her world on a back footing, she wasn't so sure what to think of the chap.

Because the professional grief from the day's horrific events wasn't saying anything of the personal one. The apparent reality that Silas had a stepsister, giving her the only pseudo-sister she had coming from a family of all boys. But also putting a serious strain on her husband's already over-wrought psyche. She heard it in his voice; she saw it in his face.

After all the personal trauma he had undergone the past few years, particularly the last year with his twin's fratricidal designs, the last thing he needed was yet another familial revelation to complete the task of shattering his familial world. His father had been the last remaining vestige of familial pride, given his mother passed giving birth to him and Sebastian. And to find out he had some liaison with a woman whilst deployed overseas? Again, took the cake in spades.

What was Celeste going to do about that? About it all?

The pause in the day's relentless forward momentum lasted mercilessly short.

Predictably, Gapinski broke it: "Did I just spy with my little googly eye something that was wrong as rain?"

"It's right as—" Elijah stopped himself, his face twisting up with a bewildered confusion. "Oh, never mind. Good pun."

"That was crazier than a *bandito* wearing a tutu!" quipped Torres.

"Just this morning," Silas interjected, "I read about an extended drought in California."

There were grunting nods.

"And we all saw," Gina added, "that Judah character bring down the rainy funk, right?"

More grunting nods before a contemplative silence.

"Them bad end-of-days juju vibes, I tell ya," Gapinski said, shaking his head. His body even threw up an actual shiver.

Celeste agreed. But she also had a moment of clarity.

She leaned forward. "All of which makes it the perfect opportunity to declare oneself to be the messiah. Come to offer the masses an offering of hope after a mercilessly hopeless news cycle."

"You think that's what's going on here?"

"Honestly, I don't know what to bloomin' think about the bloody affair!"

Gina asked, "What about that sign, that wonder?"

Recognition raced around the table with a disquieted ripple at the mention of those words. Those biblical words.

Sign. Wonder.

For they had all witnessed it together, through that bloody live-stream WeNet portal.

The clear blue sky and bright California sunshine. A cloud blooming from nothing to puncture that West Coast perfection before piling up and spreading with darkened, menacing intent until—

Until the drought Silas referenced that had lasted for nearly the entire year was broken by Judah Howell's brokered promise to command the heavens to bring forth rain!

Which he bloody well did...

"Here's a knuckle-headed question," Gapinski said, predictably breaking the silence again. "Well, a one-worded question."

"What's that?" asked Silas.

"How?"

Celeste nodded. "A bloody well good question."

"Because I got bupkis to explain what our peepers peeped!"

Silas turned to their newcomer friend. "What do you think Eddie?"

The man glanced at him, saying nothing.

"Because from your background you should surely have some idea."

That intrigued Celeste. "What sort of background?"

"Government and science, right?"

Eddie sat straighter, adjusting his spectacles, eyes searching the table, as if both stalling and searching for an answer.

He finally replied, "Cloud seeding has been having a renaissance of late."

"Isn't that some '80s tech?" asked Elijah.

"Try 1940s."

"I stand corrected..."

Gapinski said, "That's really a thing, seeding clouds—with what?"

"It absolutely is a thing," Eddie answered. "In fact, as recently as last year, China's Hubei province used silver iodide rods to induce rainfall to replenish dried-up parts of the Yangtze River."

Celeste interjected now: "But that quickly, within the span of, what, half an hour? The sky went from a fanciful West Coast blue to—"

"Something from Mordor," Gapinski said with another shudder.

Eddie shrugged, bringing a hand to his chin and growing all contemplative again.

The table followed, clearly unable to wrest any semblance of sanity from this mess.

"*A que final?*" asked Torres now.

"Como say what, chica?" Gapinski replied.

"*Lo siento.* Sorry. I am wondering what is the final end. What's the point?"

"Good question. What is the point?"

Gina offered, "There is something strangely messianic about all of this."

Celeste gestured toward the woman. "Go on. What is your meaning?"

"What I mean is, the man seems to be styling himself as another John the Baptist."

"Who wasn't a Baptist, bee-tee-dubs," Elijah corrected.

"For the love..."

Gapinski startled. "He wasn't?"

Celeste sighed. "Can we get back to it, please? What sort of manner has he been styling himself, Gina?"

She replied, "Parroting his lines, for one. From Luke's Gospel."

Closing her eyes, Gina quoted aloud:

> *He went into all the region around the Jordan,*
> *proclaiming a baptism of repentance for the*
> *forgiveness of sins, as it is written in the book of*
> *the words of the prophet Isaiah,*
> *"The voice of one crying out in the wilderness:*
> *'Prepare the way of the Lord;*
> *make his paths straight.*
> *Every valley shall be filled,*
> *and every mountain and hill shall be made low,*
> *and the crooked shall be made straight,*
> *and the rough ways made smooth,*
> *and all flesh shall see the salvation of God.'"*

"Oy! I didn't catch that before," Celeste acknowledged.

"Me either," said Silas. "Which was originally from the prophet Isaiah, chapter 40. John the Baptizer was meant as a sort of Elijah figure, preparing the people for the coming Messiah."

"Oh, I got a shiver," Gapinski said. "This does feel messianic!"

"A shiver?" Eddie piped in with a raised brow.

He shrank back a little. "Yeah, maybe…"

"You mean about what Jesus said?" asked Silas. "About false messiahs."

Gapinski nodded. "Bingo bro. Don't forget what he said in Luke's Gospel: *'Beware that you are not led astray, for many will come in my name and say, 'I am he!' and, 'The time is near!' Do not go after them.'* And that's not even touching on the apocalyptic mumbo-jumbo he warned against."

"What apocalyptic mumbo-jumbo, Hoss?" asked Torres.

Clearing his throat, he quoted: "*'When you hear of wars and insurrections, do not be terrified, for these things must take place first, but the end will not follow immediately.' Then he said to them, 'Nation will rise against nation and kingdom against kingdom; there will be great earthquakes and in various places famines and plagues, and there will be dreadful portents and great signs from heaven.'*"

Silas smirked. "That same passage has been running through my head all day, but I missed the part about people claiming to be him, some coming Messiah."

"That's not even all of it! Good ol' Marky Mark had more to say about it all from his Gospel."

More throat clearing, more quoting:

> *Then Jesus began to say to them, "Beware that no one*
> *leads you astray. Many will come in my name*
> *and say, 'I am he!' and they will lead many astray.*
> *When you hear of wars and rumors of wars, do*
> *not be alarmed; this must take place, but the end is*
> *still to come. For nation will rise against nation*
> *and kingdom against kingdom; there will be earth-*
> *quakes in various places; there will be famines.*
> *This is but the beginning of the birth pangs.*
> *And if anyone says to you at that time, 'Look! Here is*
> *the Messiah!' or 'Look! There he is!'—do not*

> *believe it. False messiahs and false prophets will appear and produce signs and wonders, to lead astray, if possible, the elect. But be alert; I have already told you everything.*

Torres smacked his shoulder. "Look at you, Hoss. All Johnny-on-the-Bible-spot!"

He blushed a shade of pink. "Got my grandpappy to thank for that one. Bible Quiz team. 1994 through '98."

Elijah offered, "I'd say that Sebastian yahoo we saw in that Ron Popeil infomercial certainly sounded like the sort with a messiah complex!" He turned to Silas, bowing. "No offense or anything."

He waved a dismissive hand, not replying.

"Except this Judah Howell character," Gina interjected, "said he was pointing the way for someone else."

Elijah nodded. "True that."

"Meaning what?" Silas asked.

Celeste understood perfectly well. "Meaning there's another."

The revelation settled hard in the center of the table.

"Along with the other wackadoodle messianic figure!" Gapinski quipped. He turned to Silas as well. "No offense or anything, brotha from anotha motha."

Silas rolled his eyes with a sigh. "Will everyone stop saying that? Sebastian is dead to me, alright?"

The comment silenced the group. Celeste moved it along.

"So two contenders for a rising false messiah."

He nodded. "Two contenders."

"Hey, chief—erm, Silas, or whatever," Gapinski said. "You don't think your sister is involved in this do you?"

He twisted up his face with irritation. "What do you mean? And her name is Samantha, by the way."

"Sammy," Eddie corrected. "She goes by Sammy. But I agree. What are you driving at, kiddo?"

"Uh, *hellooo*..." Gapinski held up his phone and gave it a jiggle, pointing it at Eddie. "The video we saw on our chopper flight out of the earthquake crazy! The one with the lady friend you fingered, Eddie P, as Sammy."

The man scoffed, shifting with discomfort and adjusting his spectacles above reddening cheeks. "Clearly she was hoodwinked by this huckster! Taken in by his pseudo-spirituality."

"Clearly—" Elijah snorted a laugh. "Good one."

Eddie spun to him. "What's that supposed to mean."

"Come on, man. You were former FBI. Nothing is ever as it seems. Especially *clearly*."

"He's got a point, Eddie," Gina added. "I'm not sure it's a given that this Samantha or Sammy woman has been *hoodwinked*, as you put it. She could be his partner in all of this for all we know."

Those reddened cheeks bled into a whiteness that signaled a fear Gina might be onto something.

Celeste stood, readying to bring the meeting to a close and hand out assignments.

"Right, it appears yet another SEPIO operation is emerging. With two would-be messianic figures vying for control."

Silas leaned back. "I'm sorry, but how does any of this concern the Church, let alone SEPIO, the Order of Thaddeus?"

"What do you mean?"

"So Sebastian and this Judah Howell character, with Rotberg and Braun playing supporting roles in his messianic fever dream, got dueling savior complexes—so what?"

Elijah smirked. "That's not apathetic at all..."

Silas frowned. "I don't mean to sound apathetic. Only, what's it got to do with us?"

"Uh, chief—" Gapinski stopped short, eyes going wide and glancing between Silas and Celeste before smiling weakly and giving his head a shake. "Anyway. *Hellooo!* Contend for the once-for-all faith entrusted to God's holy people. That's the Order's mission."

Celeste nodded. "I agree."

"But you don't really think," Silas went on, "this impacts the Church, do you? So two bozos are playacting modern-day messiah figures. So what?"

"It surely isn't for naught that these two bozos playacting modern-day messiah figures, as you frame it, are doing so during one of the most fraught times in our nation's history."

"*Exactamente,*" Torres said with agreement. "In the history of global civilizations, such times were ripe for bozos to come and shake things up religiously. To play a few long cons to filch grannies of their social security checks."

"I'd say two multipolar conflicts," Elijah said, "a once-in-an-earthly-era earthquake and now a nuclear explosion that may have taken out the President pretty well greases the skids for ripe conditions for bozos to come and shake things up religiously and filch grannies of their social security checks!"

Celeste nodded. "Sometimes contending for the faith means contending for the souls of mankind, whether inside or outside the Church. What better way to preserve that once-for-all Christian faith for future generations than to confront the machinations of two would-be messianic figures?"

"Or at least one John and one Jesus figure," Elijah said.

"So what do you propose?" asked Silas.

Celeste took a breath. She had considered this herself hours ago. What was to be done about this emerging mess? She had an inkling, but she wasn't sure Silas was going to like it.

Finally, she replied: "It seems reasonable that you lead Matthew and Torres, along with our new friend Eddie here I suppose—"

"And do what?" he said with far too much interruptive angst. Which confirmed her fears.

"And look into this Judah Howell character. But first, try and track down anything we can about this agent's death in Ukiah, California, along with anything he may have uncovered concerning this upstart spiritual sect. I will join Elijah and Gina at one of these Aeon Foundation outposts. Glean what we can from their operation. Seek out whatever Sebastian may be up to, and for that matter Nous, with regards to its subversion of the Church and faith."

"Hold on," Silas protested, putting up a hand and scooting to the edge of his seat. "Don't you think I should be the one to check out Sebastian?"

"I should think you would want to be on the front lines investigating the role your sister—"

"*Step*sister..."

Celeste shook her head. "Be that as it may, you're too close to your brother, love. Let us handle him whilst you investigate Samantha's role in this."

He opened his mouth to add one more bit of protest, but snapped it shut and leaned back, nodding. Good lad.

"Right," she finally said. "Is everyone clear on their orders?"

"Sure are, chief." Gapinski nodded, glancing at Eddie and Torres who did the same.

"Yuppers," said Elijah, Gina acknowledging the same.

Now Silas. Whose face was downturned in a manner that signaled enough to know he wasn't the least bit happy about the arrangement.

But only for a flash.

With a chest-heaving sigh he nodded his acquiescence.

"Like Matt said. Sure are, chief."

His response brought relief. She couldn't take any conflict between them given the fraught day.

Now she only hoped they made some headway on—well, whatever the bloody hell they'd been served up!

CHAPTER 21

SOMEWHERE OVER CALIFORNIA.

Another plane, another flight toward destiny.

And no uncertain doom and destruction if history was any indication of the road ahead.

A ripple of turbulence shuddered through the well-appointed Gulfstream jet of creamy leather and polished mahogany, as if adding an exclamation point to the observation.

Silas Grey gripped the soft armrest of privilege with one good hand; his other gripped a tumbler of Scotch whiskey. He promptly downed some of the two-fingers neat caramel liquid to stay his nerves.

Hated flying, always had. His father might have had something to do with that. Always going on about how the good Lord didn't give people gills for swimming the ocean blue, and he sure as hell didn't give 'em wings for flapping in the heavens above. It was why Dad had joined the Army, and why Silas followed in his footsteps.

The watch his father had gifted him scratched for his attention, probably brought on by his father's memory. He adjusted it around his wrist just as the jet skipped over another air pocket, his hand once again returning to the tumbler for relief.

Silas sighed and smacked his lips together, the spicy, oaky liquid a balm for his anxiety—all of it.

Now his tongue tingled for a cigarette thinking about it all.

Neither the humpback kind nor the burly edifice of 20th century masculinity.

American Spirit. The blue pack, with twenty sticks of that original blend of whole leaf, premium natural tobacco. Full-bodied and heavy on the tongue. Smooth and robust, with an unexpected caramel sweetness that let him just kick back and chill.

But he knew Celeste wouldn't approve. For good reason. When they married, over a year ago now, he had promised to drop the nasty habit. And he had. Mostly. But once in a while he snuck a nip from an old pack stashed in his cigar box.

Instead of the fag, as Celeste had called them, he was just grateful for the onboard bottle of Macallen. Made up for that piss-pour Maker's Mark from before. With enchanting aromas of dried fruits and ginger, joined by hints of vanilla and cinnamon on the nose. Then the soft and rich flavors of sherry on the tongue, with touches of spice, clove, orange, and mature oak barrels. Not to be outdone by the long finish of dried fruits, ginger and orange zest after it slid down the gullet and warmed the belly.

A nice coda to the day from hell that was several hours coming.

Which began with a nice set of headlines speaking no uncertain doom. Then his heroic efforts saving the cat—well, Cat Lady. Right before jumping back into the professorial seat that had seen better days. Not ashamed to say he was rusty, and it showed with his lurid illustration that apparently conjured sophomoric phallic fantasies. Then news of China and Taiwan. Right before an air-raid siren signaled clear and present danger. Only to hear from Big Brother that it had all been some fluke. Some misunderstanding between NORAD and Homeland Security.

Then the matter of Eddie P, and his crazy-ass revelation of his sister. Along with odd connections between the Order, things she spouted that mirrored the same pseudo-spiritual nonsense his twin had been peddling for the past few years. That wasn't even touching on the earthquake and apparent nuke blast that had roiled the East Coast!

So, yeah. A no good, very bad day. And the gentle kiss of rolling paper between his lips was about what the doc ordered right about now. The thin, lightweight non-wood plant fibers of flax and hemp and straw. He would have to settle for the warm embrace of 86-proof scotch. It would sure set things right, put his mind at—

Silas closed his eyes and clenched his jaw, easing in a deep breath and cursing himself.

What the hell was he thinking? What was he *doing*? Relying on nicotine and alcohol to do what only the Holy Spirit could do during these fraught times?

A weak man, that's who he was. And he hated himself for it.

Same merry-go-round as when his father had died that fateful day during the 9/11 attacks, and he'd turned to a stretch of hard drinking to get him through the emotional turmoil. And then during his three tours on Uncle Sam's misadventures in the Middle East, those American Spirit sticks carrying him through. Only to come back to the States to start popping little blue pills to help him overcome the PTSD that had ravaged his brain from all the violence he'd witnessed. Up close and in person. By his own hand.

Which wasn't even touching on all the crazy he had endured the past five years contending for the faith and protecting the Church. Including—

There was a tingling at his hand.

Right. Not left.

The one his twin brother had blown to hell. With the same bullet that had blown through his side.

Thank the good Lord above the former hadn't done much damage to the latter, and he was still alive to tell the tale.

And live the memory.

The pain. The trauma. The—

Pull it together, Grey!

Alright, he was having a no good, very bad day. So what? So was the rest of the world.

Ukraine, Taiwan. The East Coast. The American people, for goodness' sake!

Thank God the President was alive, that VIP bomb shelter Eddie had mentioned doing the trick to shield the Leader of the Free World from an actual nuke that did indeed detonate in the area. Eddie had been on the horn the whole night after Celeste said everyone should get some shut-eye before flying out early for their destinations, all heading for the same neck of the West Coast woods. California.

Venice for her and the Group X agents, heading to the main Aeon center of enlightenment, which sort of made sense given it was sort of the epicenter of the New Agey hippie types that were the core market demographic for Sebastian's latest venture. Although, if that uptown naked dude in DC was any indication, that looked to be rapidly changing. Might become more middle class given what he was selling.

He and Eddie and Gapinski and Torres were heading farther north to a small town just outside the San Francisco Bay Area, Novato. Apparently that's where the SEPIO agent, Caleb Harris, had been holed up while staking out the upstart Judah Howell farther north in Ukiah. The man had held regular street-preaching sessions in the town and in the park fronting the San Francisco Bay. Figured it was the best place to start. His replacement, José Fernandez, had been recalled back to HQ, but they would stop by and scope out the joint before heading north, hoping the Lord would throw them a bone.

The metronomic drone of dueling snores between Gapinski and Torres had kept him awake during the five-hour flight, which was fine. Couldn't sleep anyway. Not with all that had gone down, all that he had learned.

Silas Grey had a sister.

Turbulence rippled through the cabin, but it was that knowledge that sent him sinking farther into his seat and draining his scotch.

Didn't even want to think about that. Didn't want to even deal with that. Couldn't. Not with the prospect that this Sammy or Samantha gal really was some long-lost flesh and blood. And in cahoots with someone who looked to be emerging as the Church's enemy, the Order's?

And if this Eddie character or even Celeste thought he'd be all kumbaya with this unknown, playact some Shakespearian reunion, bring her into the Grey fold and have July Fourth cookouts in their Arlington backyard, maybe shlep across the country to her Bay Area condo for Christmas—well, they had another thing coming! No way would he put himself out there like that. Been there, done that. And look where it got him?

A phantom tingle at his right wrist seemed to conjure the answer, a mechanical prosthetic hand where a fleshy one should be.

Exactly.

But then glinting light from an LED lamp above at his left hand reminded him of another thing that had happened when he put himself out there, trusting someone again with his life, his future.

Marriage.

Supposed there was some truth to that Wayne Gretzky quip: You lose a hundred percent of the shots you don't take. Whether on the court with a ball or in life with people.

Shuffling feet from behind pulled for his attention. He glanced back as Eddie P walked up and took a seat across from him. In one hand, he was nursing a tumbler of some caramel liquid, half-drained and ice having melted. In the other, he held out a second tumbler with a three-finger pour, neat.

Silas nodded a thankful smile for the replenishment and took it, then promptly took a swig. The sherry oakiness of the whiskey slid down fast and hit his empty stomach with a satisfying burn, setting his mind at ease some.

He smacked his lips and hummed with pleasure.

Settling in his seat, Eddie chuckled. "Not usually a whiskey drinker. Rum is more my style. But I figured I'd give it a whirl. Because, man, you people must really like your whiskey if you have a twenty-five-hundred dollar bottle lying around in your galley."

"That we do."

Eddie tossed back a swig himself and glanced out of the window. Silas joined, an intensely rich and full flavor character coming through the second time. Citrus, dried fruits, wood smoke. Now he was hankering for a pack of those American Spirits. The packet of roasted mixed nuts would have to do.

He pulled two out of the magazine pocket on the side of his seat and offered one to Eddie. He took it with the same thankful smile Silas had for the whiskey. Didn't take long before they were popping a handful of roasted almonds and walnuts in their mouths. It paired well with the whiskey, of which Silas took another swig.

"So, how are you holding up, son?" Eddie asked.

"About as well as anyone who had some long-lost sister used against them as leverage."

He nodded. "I'd imagine so. But you can understand why, right? Especially seeing Sammy on that video, with that man who turned up in my prophetic visions—"

"About the end of days, I know."

"Which I was right about."

Had to give him that.

Eddie leaned forward, locking eyes with Silas. "What is this all about? Who are these people we're up against—the ones those two yahoos on CNN fingered as the Church of Theoti, and what about Seba?"

Silas's reply was intercepted by more shuffling feet.

Gapinski lumbered over now with his own tumbler looking dry, and promptly snatched the bottle. "There you are. I was looking all over for that thing!"

He sloshed it full and settled into a seat next to Eddie. Torres was still asleep at the back.

He slurped a swig and asked, "We readying to play a game of Texas Hold'em, or what?"

"Forgot my Bicycles at home," Silas replied.

Eddie scoffed. "Texas Hold'em? Really?" He waved a dismissive hand and took another swig. "That game's for Millennials playacting their card shark fantasies."

"Hey, I'm a bona fide Gen Xer, pal!"

"Point is, real men play Seven Card Stud, kiddo."

"Whatever..." Gapinski mumbled before throwing back another swig of his own. "So what're we gabbing about?"

"Just wondering what we're up against in the Golden State."

Gapinski gestured to Silas. "Care to do the honors on that front of wackadoodlage?"

Silas sighed, but nodded. "Might as well start with Sebastian. That would be Nous."

Eddie raised his brow. "You mentioned that organization earlier. What is it?"

"In its literal sense, the Greek word means *mind* or *reason*. It connects more to the concept of *divine reason*, with origins in Neoplatonism stretching back to the early days of the Church. It's considered to be the original divine principle, the eye of inner consciousness for comprehending the divine, leading to higher knowledge and salvation."

The newcomer laughed. "Sounds like the kind of hippy New Agey, utopian mumbo-jumbo peddled by my Woodstock generation."

Gapinski snorted a laugh. "Got that right, Boomer."

"This isn't Western mysticism variety," Torres clarified, coming to join the conversation now. "It stretches back to the second century, the essence of its worldview being ancient Gnosticism. Nearly unhinged the Church way back when, too, and has manifested in various ways since. One of the largest being 20th century theosophy, and then again with the resurgent Nous menace that has reared its ugly head from the shadows of history in a series of renewed assaults against the Christian faith."

Eddie sat straighter now, eyes locked and dialed in.

"Ancient enemies battling the Church, nearly destroying Christianity?" He shook his head and chuckled. "I have seen many things in my work with various agencies. Even brokering deals between warring terrorist groups. But this...rivaling the best yarns in my Kindle?"

Silas replied, "I understand this may sound like nutty religious conspiracy nonsense, but I assure you that Nous is real. This esoteric self-salvation through inner, divine knowledge has bedeviled the Church clear back to its early days. The earliest heresies were gnostic in origin, teaching that salvation was reserved for a certain select few who could leverage the spark of spiritual enlightenment hidden within the inner recesses of the universe, who could then progress and push the human race forward through self-actualization. Totally at odds with the Church's teachings on God's open invitation for all of rebellious humanity to find rescue from sin and death through childlike faith in Christ alone."

"What is it? And how has it manifested itself?"

"Nous and its various manifestations have all subscribed to *gnostikos*, the central kernel of gnostic teaching, beginning with the basic assumption of the divinity of the individual. Each person is a God-in-hiding, as they espouse, a physical shell housing the spark of divinity. There is no sovereign God, but lesser spirit-deities and the divineness of humanity itself."

Eddie sat back and set down his drink then crossed his arms. "This sounds like Friedrich Nietzsche's *übermensch*. The superman figure, a self-made hero or heroine who transcends the limits of human existence and becomes lord of his world. Will to power and self-overcoming, all that bull."

"Not superman," Silas corrected. "More like *over*man. But you are correct that the *übermensch* of the German philosopher is the essential aim of Nous. In fact, some of the highest ranking Nazi officers were members. Heinrich Himmler was a Grand Master. Which makes sense because Gnosticism and occultism are closely aligned—and theosophy was an intimate partner with Nazi ideology. Pursuit of spiritual power through ritual magic is a constant theme throughout the history of Nous, in addition to humanistic utopia."

"Fascinating..." Eddie whispered, adjusting his silver glasses and clearly soaking up the deep-knowledge dive.

Silas imagined his success had come from his obvious curiosity, what had gotten him so far in life and had given him such varied experiences and expertise across such varied fields of study. An insatiable thirst for knowledge and understanding will do that. Reminded him of Dad, always on the hunt for something else to explore, to tinker with. He could see why they clicked so well. To the point of Dad entrusting a daughter to his care.

He threw back another swig of whiskey and went on: "Nousati believe God or the Divine invades all things, living and nonliving. And they assume that prehistoric humans enjoyed uninhibited access to the kind of spiritual truth that would bring about a humanistic salvation."

Eddie laughed. "Sounds like Oprah before Oprah was Oprah."

Gapinski turned to him. "Hey, that's my line!"

"Great minds think alike, I suppose," the man said with a wink.

Silas nodded. "You're both right, though I'm not sure about the great minds part."

"Watch it, buster," Gapinski said. "I know where you live."

"At any rate, Nous is the organizational manifestation of this ancient worldview, hidden within the shadows of history. There is a militancy about Nous that has always threatened the Church and the faith. Not with knives and guns, but with a far more powerful and potent weapon. Ideas."

Eddie said, "I do suppose the pen is mightier than the pistol."

Silas smiled. "Well said. Nous has struck at the heart of Christian ideas throughout the Church's existence, attempting to undermine the essence of the faith by destroying her teachings. The Order has confronted it at every turn, preserving and protecting, contending and fighting for the memory of the faith."

The man folded his hands on his lap and looked off. "What about this other entity Markus Braun mentioned. That isn't that Nous outfit, is it?"

Gapinski snorted a laugh. "Naw, pal. That's the other wackadoodle bargain-bin Kindle yarn."

"A rival sect to Nous," Torres explained. "But the past few years the two had partnered together on a few operations that were almost do-or-die for the faith."

Eddie frowned. "What sort of do or die?"

"That's classified," Silas said with a wry grin. "At any rate, as you can imagine, hasn't been a fun ride fighting the good fight on two fronts."

"Theoti, is that right?"

Silas nodded. "Although now it seems simply Church of Theoti."

"And that Noland Rotberg character," Torres interjected, "the *hombre* who joined Markus Braun in that CNN interview—he in particular came out of nowhere posing just as great a threat as Nous, but in a very different way."

Eddie stroked his chin. "How so?"

Silas explained, "Rotberg was a well-respected biblical scholar from Harvard, offering academic acumen and bonafides to Theoti while Braun's technological empire has aided and abetted this emergent force, threatening to amplify their alternative spirituality at scale for the masses who are far more spiritual than religious these days."

"It appears that amplification has gone mainstream, moving from some obscure WeNet pocket to the broadcast masses thanks to Kai Renolds."

"It appears that way."

And that's what worried Silas the most about this whole thing the more he thought about it. The mass formation using tech to lead people to—well, that wasn't entirely clear yet.

He'd wondered what this had to do with the Church, these two characters, Sebastian and Judah Howell, posing as modern prophets or spiritual gurus, messiah's even. Now, running through the history of it all again with Eddie—

Only question was how it all added up.

They would soon find out.

The plane began to dip toward the blue waters below. It banked right, veering in descent toward the Golden City.

CHAPTER 22

SAN FRANCISCO.

The sun was hot and bright in this part of the States, even as it still burned bright on the other coast, the ground glowing with radiation while the site of the burnt orange mushroom cloud itself had been seared into eyewitnesses and the American public.

News was still coming in at a furious WeTweet pace on that front, the micro-messaging site on WeNet. From what "unnamed US government sources" were sharing, the explosion was not the first in a salvo of preemptive strikes from either Russia or China. Everyone was thanking whatever god they served on that front. Thankfully cooler heads had prevailed, horror stories from history of near-misses dominating CNN coverage on the nuclear "incident" as it was being termed. Stories from sun reflecting off of clouds looking like five incoming US missiles zooming for the USSR to a flock of geese activating early warning systems in America, even a faulty computer chip throwing up random numbers of attacking missiles in a command post computer display in the '80s.

Still more said "unnamed US government sources" claimed it was the work of a rogue actor, though they were pretty tight-lipped about who that might be. Which threw up all sorts of conspiracy theories across WeNet—everything from the clandestine Russian GRU Unit 29155, tasked with assassinating foreign assets, to the CIA itself manufacturing the incident as a false-flag operation giving America the pretext to bomb the crap out of Russia-occupied Ukraine, as some claimed was the case with 9/11 and the Middle East.

Thankfully, none of that mayhem on the California coast. Just a warm sun on Silas's face, a crisp, snapping breeze flowing in his open window, the taste of salt on his tongue and smell of fish and seaweed racing up the coastline toward destiny. A little slice of heaven, a small respite after a day of crazy.

Reminded him of all those years in the South Pacific as a child stationed with Dad. Him and Sebastian free-ranging it in the surrounding swamps and forests and fending for themselves with the other Army brats behind on-base housing, all under the same sort of sunny skies. The memory was short-lived.

The reality of Samantha's birth somewhere near that base chased away those happier, simpler times. Didn't have time for no reminiscing anyhow. Had to get his head in the game.

They had touched down at San Francisco International Airport an hour ago, taxiing into a private hangar where a Cadillac Escalade was waiting for them. Gapinski had complained it wasn't a Mercedes GLS, his ride of choice for SEPIO operations, but the spacious interior and Sirius XM radio playing some Bob Marley protest ballad at start-up seemed to make up for it.

Slogging it up the 101 was a nightmare in the midmorning traffic. The Golden Gate Bridge sort of made up for it, though he didn't get what all the fuss was about. The Mackinac Bridge was far more impressive, clocking in at 7400 feet long, the longest suspension bridge in the western hemisphere and 950 more than GGB. View made up for the stop-and-go traffic, he supposed, the gentle whitecaps glistening under the morning sun beneath, the rolling hills ahead dappled a burnt orange. Traffic eased some skipping through Marin City on through Corte Madera, then squeezed down to a crawl thanks to merge traffic from I-580.

More rolling hills and more traffic later—as in almost two hours later—Gapinski eased them into a parking spot with surprisingly crisp, white lines before the main office for Motel 66.

"Welp, sure ain't a looker," Gapinski said, putting the Escalade into Park.

Nope. Not a looker.

In fact, a low-slung thing of beige stucco that looked like it had taken a nap for a good few decades. At least the roof looked solid. Red clay tiles that reminded him of a bad Spring Break trip to Tijuana his junior year of college. One of those Home Depot fountains sat out front trying too hard and only offering a dribbling showmanship anyway. Same for the six palm trees, if you could call them that, swaying in the gentle midmorning breeze. Sad things with four fronds a piece that barely gave them their California dignity.

At least the parking lot was freshly paved, and there was a view of some wetland up the road from the Coast Guard, though a gusting wind sent a hot breath of dead fish and seaweed barreling their way. Even cooking oil and unwashed bodies, which Silas gathered was from a homeless encampment in a park he glimpsed down the way, their faded tents and sheets billowing in the midmorning breeze.

Down the road from them stood a grassy hillside with waving palm trees and stucco storefronts with red clay roofs painted light blues and yellows and greens. Just like the backdrop to the video clip SEPIO had received of Judah Howell preaching to that crowd on the street corner.

Must be in the right place.

They exited and made for a shack about the size of a mobile home anchored at the front that Silas figured was the main office. A handicap ramp was the only on-ramp into the joint. Very ADA compliant. Supposed they had that going for them.

And a slider door, which seemed odd for the off-brand Motel 66 on some off-the-road beaten path. Which snapped open on a sliding track and offered a bit of relief for the rising heat of the day.

His military-grade boots squeaked across the freshly waxed floor, a mixture of a sharp bleach cleaner curiously mingling with a dull beeswax throwing him off his striding game. A grassy, skunkish smell stopped him flat. Knew that from anywhere. Not that he had any experience with cannabis or anything, surprisingly.

"Is that what I think it is?" Gapinski sniffed from behind, then again. "Yup. Def a blunt. And of some pretty fine Mary Jane too—" He yelped before a "Hey!" followed by some bantering between Torres and him.

Silas didn't pay it any mind. Instead, he persisted through the lobby, if you could call it that, and sidled up to a beige Formica countertop edged by honey-stained wood, facing a rather large woman with blond hair spun up in fat florescent pink curls and wearing a muumuu of a similar shade. Her face was glued to her phone, the faint hissing of cascading videos from the WeTik app alighting her face.

Silas stood there as his compatriots gathered around. Still nothing from Curler Lady. Even an obtrusive clearing of his throat didn't yank the woman from scrolling mindlessly and aimlessly through the endless stream of videos.

He scoffed. Zoomers these days.

A tiny gold placard on the countertop placed the woman as Candace. So he resorted to smacking both palms flat on the desk.

Which jolted the woman from her techno- and ganja-high stupor.

He grinned. "Hi there. Candace is it?"

She snatched a Big Gulp from off-sides and slurped it, the pink straw turning purple from a sickly blue liquid rising then squirting into her mouth. Nodding, she swallowed and plunked the half-empty plastic cup on the counter then leaned a heavy arm next to it, ready for round two.

"Whatcha need?" she asked.

Silas stifled a frown. Kids these days, so casual and unprofessional. His frown deepened when he realized he sounded like his old man.

"I need access to a room," he replied.

Candace huffed a sigh and dragged herself over to a computer, a relic from his '90s childhood. Compaq, by the look of it. One of those beige boxes, the rattling whirl of a fan signaling its last leg wasn't far behind. A pumpkin-size monitor on top brought back memories of *Myst* and *Duke Nukem 3D*.

"One room or two." She eyed the other three, adding, "Might be a tight squeeze for your party with the double fulls we got."

"No, I'm sorry. I said I need *access* to a room."

"Access?"

Silas waved away the question. "Room 19."

That straightened those eyes real quick. Same for that frame stuffed in that pink muumuu. That arm snatched the Big Gulp for that second round. That pink straw went purple again, sandwiched between two thin lips painted the same shade as her curlers and muumuu.

"Room 19, you say?" Candace asked between more slurps.

"Got a friend staying there," Gapinski added. "Want to give him a hidey-ho on the DL. A little bachelor-party surprise before his day of nuptials."

He laughed and threw her a wink. Supposed it was best to

play dumb about the SEPIO agent's death, but adding the lie about him was a mistake. Was never one to stray from script back in the day working operations for the Rangers. Learned the hard way a time or two that bad things happen when the story gets fuzzy.

More straw sucking, more of that blue slush turning it purple on a dime. Worried it'd give her a Big Gulp coma with how much she was downing! Expected her to tear up at the mention of their bachelor friend's impending marital bliss, right before he was whacked. She only finished her slurping and gave her head a shake.

Then: "Can't."

Gapinski leaned against the counter, flashing her his pearlies. "Oh, come on."

She leaned back, staying strong. "No, I'm saying, you can't go in there."

"Why not?" Silas asked.

Another slurp, then another until the plastic cup rattled with an empty echo.

Candace frowned and plunked it back on the countertop then threw that heavy arm on top with a thud.

"Because he was *mer*-dered," she said with matter-of-fact emphasis. "Door's got all sorts of tape and labels and stickers saying no-can-do."

"And we're here to carry on that investigation."

She twisted up her face. "I thought yous guys were saying yous were here to surprise your friend."

Silas threw Gapinski a frown. Torres followed that up with a subtle jab to the dude's side. Even Eddie got in on the action, muttering a complaint.

Gapinski laughed sheepishly, rubbing the back of his neck before explaining, "Yeah, I may have fibbed a bit…"

Silas smirked. A bit? "Look, we're on official ecclesial business. We need inside that room."

"Ecclesial whatchamacallit?" she said.

"*Vatican* business," Gapinski added. "You understand."

The woman went cross-eyed at the request. Probably brought about by the Double Jeopardy word putting the Vatican stamp on their Bay Area adventure, along with whatever she was smoking before slurping.

Finally those eyes snapped back into place. "Nope. No can do."

"Why not?" asked Silas.

She *tsk*ed and shook her head. "The *poe-lease* said so, duh..."

The *uh* part to her duh sent a hot breath pluming with that grassy, skunkish scent he'd sniffed earlier. Definitely the Mary Jane variety, as Gapinski had noted.

Silas frowned. No way was she more than eighteen. Twenty tops. He had a way with guessing ages. Which meant whatever reefer she was toking in the back wasn't of the legal kind.

"You really care about the police with the stuff you've been smoking in the back?"

She shifted, her full face turning a shade of guilt.

"Look, mister, I don't want no trouble. There was a *mer*-der for godsakes. The sheriff said no one was to go in or out of that room until the detectives came and did their thing."

"Wait," Torres said, coming to Silas's side now. "The detectives haven't been inside yet?"

She passed him a glance; he got the meaning. A fresh crime scene unsullied by law enforcement. They had to get inside, and pronto. Before those county mounties returned.

Candace nodded, her jowls bobbing in sync with those oversized curlers of hers. "Took the body away yesterday. It was something awful..."

Those eyes went cross-eyed again, though now it seemed more from horror than hashish.

Gapinski leaned in now, flashing her a grin and drawing her attention.

"How about you grab us that key and we'll be on our way."

The woman just folded her arms and peered down her full cheeks at him with the look of a bouncer that told him he—they!—weren't getting past.

Torres cleared her throat and muscled her hips next to Gapinski's, signaling it was her turn to try. He got the hint and slunk behind Silas.

"Look, Candace, he was a colleague. We're just trying to find out what happened to him, that's all. Maybe find something the police overlooked."

She loosened those arms, throwing a glance outside as a semi raced past.

"Oh, I don't know...I could lose my job! But if you'd like that single with the two fulls for the four of yous guys, wait for the *poe*-lease to return, let me know."

Silas sighed. They didn't have time for this.

So he pulled out a wad of cash, sensing the woman's eyes having widened like saucers with a quick uptake in air. He slipped out three Benjamins, hesitated, then slipped out two more, then another.

No reason to skimp on bribe money when the fate of the world was on the line.

Silas slapped the six crisp hundred-dollar-bill goods on the counter.

He said, "I'm guessing this is more than you make in a week. Maybe a month."

Candice's mouth stood open for a beat, then another breath, her eyes snapping down to those six hundred-dollar bills.

Flipping his palm around, he gestured for a good of his own, motioning with his fingers to give up what he'd asked for.

"The key to Room 19. If you please."

She licked her lips, eyes darting about—for what on that abandoned road, he didn't know—and swallowed back whatever hesitation was still left in that oversized dress of hers. But not for long.

Yanking the money out from under Silas's still-open hand, she folded the bills and shoved them in her engorged bra then adjusted her chest to hide her new loot.

More lip-licking, more eye-darting before she hefted herself off from her stool and backed up to the board of keys jingling under her lumbering weight. Back against the wall, eyes still darting and lips still licking, she eased the faded gold key with a jangle then moseyed on back and slipped it in Silas's hand.

He closed it, spun around, and strode toward destiny.

"Much obliged, ma'am," he heard Eddie say from behind.

The descending numbers on the units facing the road indicated Room 19 was through an arch into a courtyard beyond the parking lot.

A pool anchored one end, a line of unused white plastic pool beds waiting use by anyone unlucky enough to get stuck in this dump. Water was a sickly shade of green, the whiff of algae and the memory of his teenage basement much stronger than any chlorine, which pretty much told the water's story. A collection of spent cigarette butts and dead leaves caught in a corner both turned his stomach and made him thirst for a stick himself.

Striding past ascending numbers, Gapinski flicked absent-mindedly at a red balloon strung up in a line of yellows and greens and blues at the roof's edge. It popped loose and sailed on a breeze from the sorry excuse for outdoor decor.

"Sonofa—" He chased after it but it ended up in the pool, floating along with the rest of the roadside detritus.

A laundry room stood open and unoccupied, though not unused. A tumbley rattle snagged Silas's attention to a single rumbling white washer shedding paint like a leper, a port wine stain of rust anchoring the right side of its face. A Coke vending machine snagged Gapinski's attention, and Silas let him have at it while he made for the room.

The ascending order told him it was down a corridor to the right that went behind the double-wide office they'd just come from. The string of police tape down the way signaled which room. It sat at the far end at the center of another leg of rooms.

Silas made for it, glancing behind and in close-curtained windows along the way that lined the sidewalk for any watching eyes. Nothing but the annoying squawk of some bird perched on the rooftop and the darting scamper of a stray, emaciated cat stirred.

He preferred to keep it that way.

Reaching the cordoned-off door to Room 19, he instructed Torres to keep an eye out for anyone, especially their new friend Candace, who he pegged as a Nosey Nancy.

A large fluorescent-orange sticker with big, bold WARNING letters acted as a law-enforcement talisman to ward off any would-be intruders. He'd never let such things as protocol stop him before.

So Silas slipped a knife out from his boot and carefully slit through the sticker, then unlocked the room and pushed open the door.

"Into the portal of doom we *goooo...*" Gapinski quipped, returning with a Dr Pepper.

Silas agreed completely.

CHAPTER 23

Bowing under the police tape and stepping inside, the senses of an undisturbed crime scene smacked Silas hard in the face.

The most obvious was the stench. Clotted blood, cloying and clinging to his throat. The tang of bleach and other cleaning agents would come later, care of Candace or some other lackey. For now he had an image of the faded white tiled shower streaked by mildew and splattered by Caleb's blood, as Abraham had reported on how his replacement, José, had found his body upon showing up with the takeout. Which, now that he thought about it, also laced the cramped room. Pad Thai with shrimp, if he fingered it right, the peanuts and sprouts and briny shrimp faint but there.

Spotting a Styrofoam container, marked by a small yellow numbered evidence stand, confirmed it. And the glint of buzzing flies confirmed its contents were still inside. Although the bloated pests were probably far more interested in the blood than South Pacific cuisine.

He swallowed back the taste of one of his favorite meals, the stir-fry dish growing heavier on his tongue from the stuffy, stifling room—now joined by a rise in tangy bile at the back of his throat from the stench of it all. And the scene. Which wasn't much but also a lot. What light shone through from the open door didn't yield much. Again, mostly because there wasn't much to see.

Just a single full—no dual fulls in this room as Candace had offered—and fully made up too. The sort of made bed he recognized from years in the military. Learned Caleb had come to Homeland from the Navy before being shipped off to SEPIO. Nothing about it was off, still left alone from when the police (or, he supposed, *poe*-lease) showed up. Nothing amiss. No rumpled sheets that would indicate a struggle, a confrontation. And no bloodstain.

Carpet was a muddy rust color that was scuffed down the left third of the room, a rut run ragged from the entrance to the back where the bathroom stood, veering only right to that single full and a slight detour left to a small round faux wood table set for two. Those two square Styrofoam containers and their vortex of spiraling pests sat unmolested. As were the chairs. All sorts of signals were thrown up from the scene splayed before him.

Which meant only one thing.

"Jeeze Louise, it's hot as Hades in here!" complained Gapinski.

He was right. It was oppressive. But Silas ignored its molestation and re-rutted that straight shot to that back bathroom for a look himself.

On approach, he threw an arm across his nose and breathed through his mouth, the assault wicked and menacing and portending nothing but the stuff of horror movies.

The light inside the bathroom was off, and no sunshine made it back that far—which was as much a metaphor for the moment as it was a description of reality. Silas pulled out a penlight and clicked its single white LED saber to life. It lanced deep inside.

Revealing that shop of horrors that had disturbed him from the entrance.

Bathtub was walled on three sides by white tiles, a blackened crimson sprayed across the back near the shower head. Curtain was pulled back, the coroner having shoved it aside to extract the body, or perhaps José when he went searching for his co-agent. Either way, the revelation threatened to send that earlier bile straight out of the hatch.

Tub was coated in a deep, sickly crimson that shimmered in his light. As if the white LED sought to threaten or mock the darkness with some invasive penetration. Either way, it reminded Silas of those fudge shops on that resort island, Mackinac Island, he and Sebastian and Dad visited during better summer days. The goods always started on slabs of white marble, when molten sugar and cocoa and butter and vanilla were poured and smeared down the center before being folded into their fudgey blocks. Only here, there was only smear.

Back to that curtain: waving the penlight around revealed what Silas had suspected. A whistling hole punched through near the far right. Just in front of the shower head but near where the showerer would have been standing.

An instant—and expert—kill shot.

Caleb wouldn't have even known it was coming, the whirl of the bathroom fan and rush of steaming water drowning out any approach.

"Sonofa—" Gapinski's own moaning complaint cut off his cursing one. "It's like something out of the Godfather!"

"Goodfellas," Eddie P corrected from behind, the man craning over the SEPIO agent and taking in the bathroom himself.

"Huh?"

"The Godfather is just pomp and circumstance, glamorizing gangster life with a Hollywood sheen. Goodfellas...now there's a cinephile's film if there ever was one. A much more realistic portrayal of the grit and, well—" He waved a hand at the grizzly scene and turned back into the main room.

Silas joined him, making for the bed.

"Tomato, potato," Gapinski replied. "Point being: It's like a gangster fever dream in here. The stench of blood. The actual blood! Hey, whatcha doin', chief?"

Silas was on his hands and knees searching under the bed.

"Working," was his only reply. Sweeping his lancing light underneath and coming up dry, he lifted the mattress for the same look-see.

Same answer: Nothing.

"Don't they pay their AC bills in these parts!" Gapinski complained again. "It's hot as—"

"Hades," Silas finished. "Heard you the first time."

"Well, it is!" Fella batted his oversized hand at his forehead but only managed to smear the sweat all around.

Eddie smirked. "Did you see where we are, the clientele and our dear patron out front? Guessing Motel 66, an off-brand if I'd ever heard of one, isn't big on the amenities."

Sounded about right.

Standing, Silas searched the rest of the room. Opened both nightstand drawers. Both empty, but for a Gideon leftover from the joint's '90s heyday. Same for the cloth accent chair wedged in the corner by the curtained window matching the rusty carpet. Nothing but lumpy springs and crumbs probably left-over from that same heyday. Didn't even run across any loose change when he flipped the cushion. Definitely nothing stashed away.

He paced the room another few minutes, Gapinski offering nothing but a Dr Pepper belch that actually threw up a faint whiff of pepper into the growing hot, stale air. After giving up, he stood at the foot of the bed and planted his hands on his hips.

"Looks like a bust," he sighed.

"Now what?" asked Gapinski.

Eddie hummed, cocking his head and spinning around as if in search of something.

Silas followed his gaze, curious. "What are you think—"

The man cut him off with a staying hand, continuing to discern and intuit something of interest. And yet...

Now that Silas thought about it, now that he stopped to think about it, something did seem odd about the joint. The air, the humidity and heat, even for a dump like this.

"Actually—" Eddie stopped short, craning his head. "It sounds like the HVAC unit is humming along without issue."

Silas squinted at him and cocked his own head now. "Well, I'll be. You might be onto something there."

"Sounds like some sort of sucking sound."

He chuckled. "Like last week when I sucked up my grocery receipt with our Dyson, the paper getting stuck and making a wheezing plea for release."

Gapinski ribbed him. "Didn't take you for the grocery-getting type, chief."

Silas raised a brow. "You think grocery-getting is only for women?"

Took a beat to realize he'd stepped in it.

Then he did.

Gapinski threw up his arms in surrender and started pleading for mercy. "No no no! I didn't mean to offend the sisterhood of the traveling pants and perpetuate gender stereotypes. Damn the patriarchy! I only meant—"

"The vent!" Eddie said with interruption.

Didn't catch the man at first, slapping Gapinski on the back and laughing. "Only kidding, brother."

Then he caught Eddie waving his arms around in the air, as if searching for something. Took a beat, but his observation about the air vent triggered instant recognition.

"Of course! That's why it's hot as hell in here."

Gapinski cleared his throat. "It's hot as *Hades*, chief. Let's keep it G for the kiddos, alright?"

Silas ignored him, sweeping his light around the space, first searching the front for a unit stationed near the door. When it only illuminated an empty wall of chipping paint, he leveled the white beam at the back, searching for the same.

Now Eddie joined the search, some penlight at the end of a switchblade. Didn't take him for the pocket-knife wielding type. Seemed much more the pen and pocket-protector kind of fella. But the more the merrier, as far as he was concerned.

"Whatcha two looking for?" asked Gapinski, flashing his own penlight around without direction.

Silas put out a staying hand, searching for the sound—

"There!" Eddie said, striding to the wall where the takeout still sat and pointing toward the ceiling.

Where an air vent wheezed, a cover of horizontal slats planted above Eddie's reach.

The man dragged a chair near the Pad Thai to the wall with a scrape, mounting it, then pressed a hand against the vent.

"Metal grate sure is cold, which tells me it's pumping out a lot of conditioned air."

Silas could hear it. Barely a breath huffed from its plugged nostrils, and he had a hunch why.

"Aim your light this way, kiddo," Eddie instructed, switching his off and flipping out a blade from that penknife.

"I'm all for HVAC comfort," Gapinski replied, taking aim with his light, "but you really think it's the time for worrying about getting the AC back online?"

"It's not the AC I'm interested in..."

Eddie was prying loose the vent cover now, moving the blade this way and that. Took a few well-placed wrenching heaves to pop it loose, but soon he had the metal face under his arm—

And then a manilla envelope in his hand.

He held it up, along with a grin. "This was what I was interested in."

Silas chuckled. "The vent. Of course! Must have been wedged inside, which is why it was hot as—"

"*Hades*. Right, chief?" Gapinski emphasized with a wry grin.

He waved him away and helped Eddie down, snatching the envelope from his hand and going to the bed.

Eddie said, "The authorities clearly missed the boat on that one."

"Their loss," Silas replied, "our gain."

Gapinski chuckled. "Slap me some skin, my man Eddie P!"

He echoed that chuckle and held out his hand. To which the SEPIO agent smacked it and told him to go high. Eddie raised it with a laugh.

Gapinski smacked it again, adding, "Now down low."

Eddie held it out. He went to smack it a third time when the man yanked it back with a grin.

"Too slow, kiddo."

"Hey! Not fair," Gapinski protested, crossing his arms in a huff. "Although, not bad, Boomer."

Silas ignored the banter. Much more interested in the mystery envelope and whatever intel lay hidden inside. Was neither heavy nor thick. Did carry enough bulk to tell him whatever Caleb had hidden away was worth it.

And perhaps worth something to those who came after him.

Taking his own knife now, he slit it open at the one end.

Then looked inside.

A mess of crisp pages greeted him. Photos of some compound, with a few buildings arranged around a central courtyard, another stadium-sized one without any windows. That one was tagged by a star in red marker, as was its location circled on a map of what was probably the compound. Another of a man who looked like Judah Howell. A few more of some kids and—

A ping of adrenaline skated through his veins and mouth ran dry with panic.

There she was. Samantha.

In the background, so maybe not the focus of the photographing. But this was a gigantic step closer to the action beyond just a bystander at some Bay Area street evangelistic outreach effort.

Didn't know what it meant, if anything. Sensed it was something though.

Gapinski and Eddie came up behind now, craning over his shoulder for a look-see. Silas shuffled the hard-copy intel together, not wanting to get into it about his sister in that moment—catching him dropping the *step-* part, and even acknowledging her connection at all.

He set the papers on the bed and turned the envelope upside down, giving it a shake, when—

Something tumbled to the floor.

Silas snatched for it, but Gapinski got to it first.

"Finders keepers..."

"What is it?" asked Eddie.

He held it in his large palm. About half the size of a packet of Juicy Fruit gum and black.

A thumb drive.

One of those older-school USB things that still served a purpose.

Like hiding away some intel from a SEPIO agent on a clandestine operation for an ecclesial religious order.

"Holybamoly Batman..." Gapinski whistled. "This is some serious secret agent shiznit."

Silas picked it up, eyeing it before pushing a slider that popped out a tiny oval metal connector. USB-C. So way more modern than previous-era drives. Probably held gigs worth too.

"Only one question..." Eddie said with a frown.

Silas sighed. Indeed.

What was on that drive?

A scream intercepted any thought of finding out.

High and heady and panicked.

Then: "*Mira esto, Silas,*" Torres shouted from just beyond the still-open threshold to Room 19. "*Mira!*"

Which he took as see what the heck was going on outside.

A hedgerow of pine shrubs snugging the hotel's backside blocked any view through a dirty back window. The front curtained one looked dim. Too dim for the late morning. And now the door was shrouded in shadows. Again, made no sense with the day approaching noon. When the sun was high and brightest, beating down without mercy, especially in these parts. Might've thought a storm was approaching, but no rain was forecasted for days after the stunt Judah Howell pulled. And this was more the evening kind. Except—

No, wait. Not evening.

Eclipse. That must be it.

Silas stuffed the USB drive in his pants pocket and raced into the outside corridor of rooms running north and south.

No Torres.

Outside was more a muddy brown than pitch blackness, a brown mustard that cast an eerie pale across the motel. Sky was more a bruised peach than the darkness of evening.

He threw his hand above his eyes and squinted, taking care not to stare into the sun hung high. Which was indeed masked by—what was that? Looked like smoke, dimming its daylight and ratcheting up the apocalyptic, end-of-days vibe.

That wasn't all of it.

A full moon clung to the sky for dear life, tinged by the same sort of muddy brownish-yellow haze spread across the sky. Almost like a blood-red moon, full and menacing and portending a judgment no one ever spoke about anymore, barely even inside the Church. He expected a sky pockmarked by faint stars, but it was a blank canvas. Which might only be because the sky wasn't dark enough and shrouded in a thick haze, so those orbs of burning gas struggled for a hearing.

Or it could mean something entirely—

Wait, was that a falling star?

Another scream, another string of Spanish drew him to rooms twenty through twenty-three that emptied out in front of the motel.

There was Torres, shielding her eyes with a hand and pointing.

What the heck?

Silas went to her, Gapinski and Eddie making up the rear and throwing up their own sets of questions.

Then stopped dead in his tracks at the fuller picture.

Tourists and townies stood at the edge of the San Francisco Bay staring up into the sky; some were pointing and screaming and crying out on frightened breaths.

"*Dios mío...*" muttered Torres, joining their pointing.

Silas went to her side, seeking the source of her discontent.

When a word started ricocheting across the beachhead that described the truth of it. From a few different tongues, English and Spanish, but expressing the same thing.

Apocalypse.

Silas sucked in a disbelieving breath as the heavens gave up any notion of what was sane and real and right in the world—the universe even!

The sun shrouded and moon shedding its blood and stars giving way. He threw his hands on his head now and closed his eyes, one resounding thought flaring.

It had begun...

Immediately, a passage from the Holy Scriptures surfaced. Something John the Seer had witnessed, and then wrote about in the Book of Revelation:

When he broke the sixth seal, I looked, and there was
a great earthquake; the sun became black as
sackcloth, the full moon became like blood, and
the stars of the sky fell to the earth as the fig tree
drops its winter fruit when shaken by a gale. The
sky vanished like a scroll rolling itself up, and
every mountain and island was removed from its
place. Then the kings of the earth and the
magnates and the generals and the rich and the
powerful and everyone, slave and free, hid in the
caves and among the rocks of the mountains,
calling to the mountains and rocks, "Fall on us
and hide us from the face of the one seated on the
throne and from the wrath of the Lamb, for the
great day of their wrath has come, and who is
able to stand?"

The Sixth Seal. The *final* seal, unleashing a cosmic catastrophe to bring the world to the brink of the End Times. Just like Judah Howell said it would.

Ushering in the apocalypse.

The beginning of the end…

What were they going to do?

What was *he* going to do?

CHAPTER 24

What was he going to *do*?

What did it even *mean*?

No clue.

"It's happening…"

Silas spun toward the voice.

Eddie P. A hand covering his mouth, the other pointing toward the dimmed heavens.

Gapinski gave a startled screech, mirroring the same jutting finger. "Apocalypse is now, cats and kittens!"

"*Qué es esto?*" Torres questioned. "What is going on?"

Silas licked his lips, discerning and intuiting the answer to her question was found in John's Revelation. But daring not voice it.

Instead, he crunched across deadened grass, heart racing and gut churning with dread, not at all wanting to face the facts but also not being able not to.

A tiny speck of ancient light seemed to be falling from its perch high above. Then another, and a third! With blazing tails that reminded him of the comets from childhood he and his twin brother had spent countless hours watching. Except—

Was it falling to Earth—were *they*?

Silas threw his hands on top of his head, face twisted up in horror at the scene playing out in front of him.

More people were outside now. Some cars had even skidded to a halt along the route, and the homeless encampment had emptied, with forty or fifty people all taking in the sight that was straight out of a Steven Spielberg fever dream.

The end of the world as they knew it.

And Silas didn't at all feel fine!

His brain was going haywire at the turn and thirsting for nicotine relief, a wicked ache blooming at the center of his head, his bowels plummeting into watery weakness. He just stood there, along with the rest, unable to wrap his mind around what was unfolding before his eyes. A lesson from a summer seminar he had taken on the Book of Revelation with Father Arnold at Harvard during his graduate studies clarified what was going on.

Arnold had carefully walked through the complicated, enigmatic last book of the Bible to crystalize its meaning and provoke discussions about its implications. Many of the students taking the seminar were more interested in the book as an academic exercise of religious apocalyptic fear-mongering than anything sparking of the spiritual, as Silas had taken the revelation insight.

As Arnold had laid out, Silas had come to understand the seals surrounding the scroll as the normal forces operating through the course of history, signaling both the brokenness of the world and picturing the redemptive, judicial purposes of God. From war and murder and radical conflict to economic depressions and recessions, from famine and plagues to the persecution of Christians—all of what has transpired across history was the ongoing suffering east of Eden, and especially on the other side of Christ's resurrection until his second coming.

Those were the first five seals.

Then there was the Sixth Seal.

The one before the final one that was stripped from the scroll meant to unleash the Great Tribulation itself. Using language thought to be merely symbolic and apocalyptic to describe the end of the world. The language of cosmic catastrophe.

Arnold had insisted that John's use of such language was completely poetic and symbolic of spiritual realities—the blotting out of the sun, the blood-red moon, the falling away of the stars. So had most everyone else, brushing away such language as not at all describing the end of the world as we know it.

And yet there it was! All of it. The dimmed sky in the middle of the day. The trace outline of a full moon hung high in the heavens and bleeding crimson. The fiery contrails of stars as they fell from view for Pete's sake!

Arnold was wrong. They all were.

What was he going to do?

What was the *world* going to do?

An arm seized Silas's own, a vice grip that wrenched him loose from his contemplation and a pain that lanced into his skin from long, digging nails.

He shook it loose and swung his attention their way.

"What the hell is going on?" someone shouted with panic a few paces on.

A woman. Blond and fit and beautiful. Face beet red with a corkscrew vein popping out. Arms swinging wildly and pointing at the sky. Shouting at the top of her frazzled lungs for the second time what everyone was wondering: *"What the hell is going on?"*

Silas didn't answer, his wide, frightened eyes darting up above to take in the apocalyptic scene unfolding.

A real crowd had gathered now, the same question rumbling through the frightened men and women, teenagers and young adults all taking in the view of what definitely felt like the beginning of the end of the world as they knew it.

Perhaps he could offer what they all needed to hear.

Silas swallowed hard, a sudden courage and peace gripping him, and the force of the Holy Spirit himself leading him forward. As much as he might want to run from his calling as a teacher, as a Master of a Christian religious order, even, tasked with contending for the faith, it dawned on him that he had trained for such moments.

Lord Jesus Christ, Son of God, give me the words that will breathe insight and life into their frightened hearts...

He swallowed hard, then raised his arms and threw up a high-pitched whistle. One of those attention-grabbers that actually did the trick.

"Listen here, all of you. I have the only words you need to know what the hell is happening, as you all are wondering."

Every one of their wide, frightened eyes trained their attention on him. Time seemed to slow even as all sound wound down to zero. They needed a word. They needed understanding. They needed someone to make sense of the end-of-days crazy.

And Silas had stepped up to the plate to give it to them.

And yet—

What the heck was he doing? He was no preacher! He wasn't even an official with the Church any longer. Well, technically he supposed he still was. Except he had left that gig. Fled, really. For the cozy comforts of tweed and tenure, as Rowan Radcliffe had accused him of when he had invited him to join the Order in the first place.

Silas smirked. Tweed, perhaps. Definitely not tenure. Adjunct was his lot in life. And maybe not even that, after abandoning yet another class for yet another SEPIO operation.

Perhaps there was a lesson there. Or a message, from the Holy Spirit himself, about his life calling.

Regardless, what that calling meant, then and there, in that moment, was telling it like it was—about the apocalypse, about the End Times, whether or not it truly was the end of days.

Taking a breath, Silas quoted the words of Jesus from memory: "*Woe to those who are pregnant and to those who are nursing infants in those days! Pray that your flight may not be in winter or on a Sabbath. For at that time there will be great suffering, such as has not been from the beginning of the world until now, no, and never will be.*"

The crowd grew silent. Not a word was spoken, not a breath was breathed as Silas continued with Matthew's Gospel:

> "*Then if anyone says to you, 'Look! Here is the*
>   *Messiah!' or 'There he is!'—do not believe it. For*
> *false messiahs and false prophets will appear and*
> *produce great signs and wonders, to lead astray,*
> *if possible, even the elect. Take note, I have told*
> *you beforehand. So, if they say to you, 'Look! He*
> *is in the wilderness,' do not go out. If they say,*
> *'Look! He is in the inner rooms,' do not believe it.*
> *For as the lightning comes from the east and*
> *flashes as far as the west, so will be the coming of*
> *the Son of Man. Wherever the corpse is, there the*
> *eagles will gather.*"

"What the *bleepity-bleep* are you jibber-jabbering about?" someone screamed at him in a far more vulgar question. A tall, grizzled man in a baggy T-shirt stained by the grime of life.

"I'm trying to tell you!" Silas yelled back. He took a breath and huffed it out, running a shaky hand through his hair. "These words are Christ's words. What Jesus said about the beginning of the end of days. The *apocalypse* as some of you yourselves shouted."

That got the man's attention, and the others, their faces

draining of color and mouths falling open with a mixture of intrigue and panic.

He nodded for Silas to continue. So he did, quoting: "*So, if they say to you, 'Look! He is in the wilderness,' do not go out. If they say, 'Look! He is in the inner rooms,' do not believe it. For as the lightning comes from the east and flashes as far as the west, so will be the coming of the Son of Man. Wherever the corpse is, there the eagles will gather.*"

Silas took a breath, then explained, "And this is where it gets interesting, for what we're experiencing right now. Well, potentially, because I'm not even sure what it is we're experiencing!"

A breath, then a beat, then: "Go on, then!" someone intercepted.

He did, reaching back into the recesses of his brain for a passage from Matthew's Gospel he had memorized years ago:

> *"Immediately after the suffering of those days*
> *the sun will be darkened,*
> *and the moon will not give its light;*
> *the stars will fall from heaven,*
> *and the powers of heaven will be shaken.*
> *"Then the sign of the Son of Man will appear in*
> *heaven, and then all the tribes of the earth will*
> *mourn, and they will see 'the Son of Man coming*
> *on the clouds of heaven' with power and great*
> *glory. And he will send out his angels with a loud*
> *trumpet call, and they will gather his elect from*
> *the four winds, from one end of heaven to the*
> *oth—"*

Someone grabbed Silas by his shirt with both hands before he could finish.

Same man from earlier who screamed him down. Tall, grizzled, T-shirted. Dirty, baggy jean shorts fraying at the edges in long, stringy strips caked in dirt. And smelly. Like vinegar and spoiled beef and boiled eggs. Looked homeless.

And now he was looking at his round gray eyes that glimmered with mania, having been yanked within an inch of his face. Breath reeked of beer and boiled cabbage.

The man looked like he was on the verge of a manic episode, his eyes wide and forehead wrinkled with panic, his mawing mouth quivering and his hands gripping Silas weakly now in a way that reflected the same panic. Probably was one foot into a complete psychotic break, given what he was experiencing—what they all were experiencing.

"Get off of him!" Gapinski commanded, the big-boned bruiser wrenching Silas from the man's grip. While thankful for his assistance, nothing but pity flooded him.

The man stumbled backward and fell to the ground. He scrambled to his knees and held out his hands, face etched by terror.

"What does it all mean?" he pleaded.

His eyes actually filled with tears now, and his lower lip started quivering. He repeated with a whisper: "What does it all mean?"

Silas went to offer a reply when he was cut off by another voice, high and shrilly and hysterical.

"Incoming!" someone shouted from view, near the beachhead, a chorus of screams joining in.

Silas caught sight of the woman from before, the one who had gripped his arm.

Pointing frantically at the sky.

He squinted, not understanding what the matter was.

Then he did.

Silas's eyes widened and another bout of cold panic drenched him from head to toe, his brain not being able to process the fiery object quickly descending from the heavens.

Jesus' words flashed through his mind: *'The sun will be darkened, and the moon will not give its light; the stars will fall from heaven, and the powers of heaven will be shaken.'*

The blazing ball of fire was fast approaching from above, aiming straight for Earth.

No, not just Earth.

Motel 66!

The inflamed orb was growing in size by the second. Had to be the size of a school bus, and it was coming in hot and heavy.

Toward their position!

Which sent the crowd surging toward the beachhead down below.

"*Ándale!*" Torres shouted, darting forward then spinning back toward the boys who were anchored with indecision. "Come along, *muchachos*! Unless you want your behinds fried to a crisp!"

"Don't have to tell me twice..." Gapinski darted across the street, Eddie joining to follow their female lead.

Silas joined them, pressed from behind with the surge of bodies. He twisted around for another glance, Jesus' words from the Gospel of Matthew ringing in his ears.

That fiery school bus was growing in size, twisting and turning and tumbling toward them at a speed that reminded Silas of those planes slamming into the World Trade Center.

He hiked up his legs and pumped his arms and made for the water.

It was automatic, primal, his body carried along by something buried deep in his lizard brain from an ancient, ancestral instinct to survive. He splashed into the water, the frigid bay snatching his breath as he waded farther out, mere seconds before—

It hit.

The force of impact by the alien rock, its phantasmic fire and fury, was unbelievable.

Like one of those Russian missiles he had seen on the internet pounding the Donbas the past year slamming into the earth. A wave of pressure spread from the point of impact, joined by an immense heat and blooming brightness and explosive reverberation that sent him crouching in the water.

The blast radiated out from the point of impact a beat later in a blinding, deafening explosion that sent everyone sailing from their feet and into the wicked water boiling from the seismic convulsion.

Silas plunged beneath the surface, the undertow clutching his legs and torso with yanking invitation to succumb to the darkness down below. And he wondered...

Why not give in?

The thought seized him with a mixture of trepidation and temptation.

Why not? Why *not* let it all just fade away?

The world was on fire anyway, literally. While he had no earthly clue what was transpiring above, whether it was the apocalypse as some were shouting or some natural phenomenon or something spawned from the loins of Satan himself. All he knew for certain was that life hadn't turned out the way he thought it would anyway—his life. He was a wreck, a mess. Apparently his family was a lie, having some long-lost sister Dad had fathered way back when. What was the point in continuing on?

Something suddenly seized his chest. A spark of personal mission and responsibility that had grown cold the past year. An ember of purpose dowsed to a sizzling nothingness by what life had thrown at him the past few years, yet preserved with just enough energy to come back to life. Perhaps for such a time as this.

And it did. He could only attribute a rising sense of motivation to jump into the fray of things—in the middle of what was arguably the onset of the apocalypse of all things!—to the Holy

Spirit himself. The Spirit of the Lord compelling and wooing and smacking him upside the head to hike up his big-boy pants and do what Christ himself had created him to do.

Fight, damnit!

Just like what Saint Paul himself had said about his life: '*I do not count my life of any value to myself, if only I may finish my course and the ministry that I received from the Lord Jesus, to testify to the good news of God's grace.*'

Exactly.

This same impulse surged within him now. First blooming into a will to live, then into a desire to find out what the heck was going on. With Sebastian and this Judah Howell character. And whether it was all connected to what Jesus and his beloved apostle John had foretold.

'*The sun will be darkened, and the moon will not give its light; the stars will fall from heaven, and the powers of heaven will be shaken.*'

Those words clanged inside his head like a clarion call to arms now.

So he fought against the current dragging him down and out to sea, using every fiber of his being to kick and claw toward the surface—mostly for himself but also for the charge he had been given to preserve and guard the once-for-all faith entrusted to God's holy people by Jesus Christ himself.

Not only as Master of the Order of Thaddeus—or, well, co-Master or whatever, given Celeste's own role. But as a follower of Jesus Christ.

And not just for the Church. Because Celeste had it right before: whatever was going on was bigger than just saving Christianity's backside, or Christians' for that matter.

This was about saving the world. Sure, big stakes. People's spiritual affections, what they were chasing to fill their God-shaped hole, as Blaise Pascal had quipped, and also their souls. When those were on the line, so were eternal destinies.

Because if the space rock that had just slammed into Earth was any indication, the world was on the verge of something of apocalyptic proportions.

Which only the gospel of Jesus Christ had any possibility of ameliorating.

And Silas would be damned if he let Sebastian and Nous, Theoti and Judah Howell speak their blasphemous lies from forked tongues reaching from the depths of hell itself!

Silas's powerful legs propelled him quickly to the surface. Bursting from the water, he twisted back toward the beach to sight the damage.

A hell ten times worse than Dante's vision was splayed before him.

Belching flames spewed from every direction, the heat of a thousand furnaces scorching the air and everything around it.

Bringing Motel 66 to its knees into inflamed piles of heaping rubble. Flowers of fire bloomed and plumes of ash and soot rained down from the climactic destruction. He cursed the loss of those photos and other intel but was glad he still had the thumb drive.

That wasn't the worst of the destruction.

Those who hadn't made it to the water before the incoming explosion had been caught in the hellish maelstrom, their bodies burnt to a blackened crisp littering the shoreline now.

Silas was in this; he was committed.

Really, truly.

He had to find his crew.

And he hoped Celeste was faring better in her neck of the crazy woods.

CHAPTER 25

SOMEWHERE OVER THE ATLANTIC.

A dip then a shudder jostled the well-appointed Learjet still smelling of fresh, supple goatskin and wood stain—waking Sebastian Grey with a snort from his slumber.

For a moment, panic skated through his veins, frigid and frightened. He had been having a nightmare. The same one on repeat going on a quarter of a century now.

He was clutching a loaf of bread and a chalice of wine.

And that hand, reaching underneath his altar boy robe...

From that priest.

His childhood priest.

A perfect cliché, overused and overwrought in bargain-bin Kindle stories.

But it was his story. And the nightmare was triggered by more news of more priests playing tiddlywinks with teenage marbles in the Midwest.

The nightmare fed the confusion of dreamland, compounded by the wicked turbulence. Sebastian clenched his armrests even as his mind groped for answers.

Then he had it.

Remembered where he was and who he was: Grand Master

of Nous, zooming through the stratosphere ensconced in gilt-edged, polished mahogany walls and sitting at a long table crowded by a smattering of creamy leather recliners. It wasn't Saudi Prince Alwaleed bin Talal's Airbus, clocking in at half-a-billion dollars, but it did the trick.

A crystal wineglass winked at him with the refraction of dim LED lights and the disturbed crimson liquid. He promptly grabbed it and took a sip, then another.

A 2000 vintage Mouton Rothschild Bordeaux. The bottle was nestled in a holder anchored to the table. A beautiful thing, Baroness Philippine de Rothschild offering a work of art in an intricate gold-engraved bottle of a trotting lamb along with the expertly vinted wine. A rich, tannic, earthy style. Cassis and floral notes heavy on the nose. The Cabernet Sauvignon and Merlot blend full-bodied, with coffee, earth, and chocolaty notes heavy on his tongue.

Another dip and shudder made up his mind. If he was careening toward his death, no reason to let a good glass of wine go to waste. Or a bottle.

Sebastian drained it and promptly refilled the glass.

After a sip, then another long draw, he stretched then shoved back the heavy sleeve to the thick black vestment edged by crimson piping he had taken up the past year in preparation for this moment.

Closing his eyes, he drew in a measured, calming breath, the crisp, sanitized air laden with the heavy scent of a thunderstorm, a mixture of rain and fecund life.

Catching sight of a tablet resting on the table surfaced the reason for the transoceanic flight—well, two, an ancient tome coming into view now, pages browned and the leather binding cracked and oily with age.

First, the tablet. Which had broadcasted that hippie imbecile all across WeNet! Th–Th–The *rain*! The sign and wonder performed for all the world to see, however it was he pulled it off. And from that blasted sanctuary, no less—that *church* they were calling it.

Of Theoti, the Divine Ones.

The thought sent a raging heat ratcheting up his spine and blooming hot and heavy in his head.

He promptly drained his wine and poured another glass.

It wasn't supposed to be like this. And yet—

Another swig, his head delirious now with both the turn and that Bordeaux.

Heaving a stabilizing breath, Sebastian sank into his chair and snatched the vintage book. Just what he needed.

Opening it, the sweet, musty smell of aged paper flooded his senses. He breathed deeply of the Universe's offerings. Bibliosmia, it was called. An olfactory nirvana sparked by the chemical breakdown of the paper's compounds. What he smelled was literally the book's slow death! But not yet. For the life it held cradled a new kind of life. One he was bringing to the masses after being recreated anew by its revelation—his old shell had gone; a new form had come!

Sebastian ran a finger down the page then turned it, doing the same again before turning a few more, searching for that one passage that had brought it all to—

Ahh! There it was.

A grin spread across his face, and he took in the visual delight of the words even as his nose took in the olfactory delight of the aged paper and metallicy ink. Reading it aloud, he muttered:

And it came to pass when the sons of men had multiplied that in those days were born unto them beautiful and comely daughters. And the angels, the children of the heaven, saw and lusted after them, and said to one another: "Come, let us choose us wives from among the children of men and beget us children."

And Semjaza, who was their leader, said unto them: "I fear ye will not indeed agree to do this deed, and I alone shall have to pay the penalty of a great sin."

And they all answered him and said: "Let us all swear an oath, and all bind ourselves by mutual imprecations not to abandon this plan but to do this thing."

Then swear they all together and bound themselves by mutual imprecations upon it. And they were in all two hundred; who descended in the days of Jared on the summit of Mount Hermon, and they called it Mount Hermon, because they had sworn and bound themselves by mutual imprecations upon it.

Sebastian closed his eyes and sighed with pleasure, a rise at his belly making him thirst for more wine, and words.

The Book of Enoch.

The singular religious text that had made sense of the world for Sebastian.

And remade his own.

Most religious sheeple had zero clue about the book, since it wasn't in any regular Christian Bible. However, it was indeed regarded by Jewish practitioners as holy writ. Also understood as 1 Enoch, to separate it from two other works of the same name, it was a pseudepigraphal book, an ancient Hebrew apocalyptic religious text ascribed by tradition to Enoch. The great-grandfather of Noah. It contained unique material on the origins of demons, why some angels fell from heaven, a prophetic exposition of the thousand-year reign of the Messiah, an expansion on the flood material—and one other revelation-insight that had finally made reality click into place.

The Nephilim.

Written during the Second Temple period of Judaism, most likely the centuries between Malachi and Matthew, it was actually a scriptural backdrop for the Christian scriptures, the New Testament. He had been most surprised to learn that several early Church Fathers treated 1 Enoch as Scripture. The *Epistle of Barnabas*, a very early letter circulated during the earliest century of the Church, quoted from it as Scripture. Tertullian and Irenaeus, both heavy-hitting theologians, used the same language when referencing 1 Enoch, that it was Scripture.

Then there were those pesky New Testament books themselves: Second Peter and Jude. Both quoted 1 Enoch.

Through his exhaustive study of the important ancient text, he learned the Jewish worldview was largely built around much of what we find in 1 Enoch, as well as several broader themes of the Hebrew Scriptures themselves. One of which was an important, expanded dissertation on the crucial passage from Genesis 6 that offered revelation-insight into the true nature of the Universe.

Sebastian searched for that part from 1 Enoch, meditating on that portion of Scripture from Genesis 6:

> *When human beings began to increase in number on the earth and daughters were born to them, the sons of God saw that the daughters of humans were beautiful, and they married any of them they chose. Then the Lord said, "My Spirit will not contend with humans forever, for they are mortal; their days will be a hundred and twenty years."*
>
> *The Nephilim were on the earth in those days—and also afterward—when the sons of God went to the daughters of humans and had children by them. They were the heroes of old, men of renown.*

> *The Lord saw how great the wickedness of the*
> *human race had become on the earth, and that*
> *every inclination of the thoughts of the human*
> *heart was only evil all the time.*

Continuing his search, he smirked to himself. Hell must have frozen stiff for him to be so well-versed in the Bible—and quoting it no less! There had been a time, a long stretch of time actually, when he had taken the plunge into the deep end of atheism. A priest playing tiddlywinks with their teenage marbles will do that to a person.

Ahh, there it was.

Sebastian brought a finger to the page and caressed the letters in a surprisingly dark black ink. He drew in a slow, deep breath, imbibing the heady scents of pulp, a cross between wet newspaper and peat moss.

He read, whispering aloud:

And all the others together with them took unto themselves wives, and each chose for himself one, and they began to go in unto them and to defile themselves with them, and they taught them charms and enchantments, and the cutting of roots, and made them acquainted with plants. And they became pregnant, and they bare great giants, and the giants begat Nephilim, who then bore Elioud—growing in accordance with their greatness, who consumed all the labor of men. And when men could no longer sustain them, the giants turned against them and devoured mankind. And they began to sin against birds, and beasts, and reptiles, and fish, and to devour one another's flesh, and drink the blood. Then the earth laid accusation against the lawless ones.

Sebastian paused, draining his Bordeaux and refilling his glass. His head spun now, and not just from the wine. It was these words. The revelation-insight infused in the ancient text, the letters of the faded black ink and browned paper!

He filled his mouth with more wine, the dueling tastes of roasted coffee and dark chocolate dancing across his tongue, even as more of the revelation of the Unseen Realm flooded his eyes.

Now came the good part, the one that had sent him on his mission and sparked clarity about the Universe:

And Azazel taught men to make swords, and knives, and shields, and breastplates, and made known to them the metals of the earth and the art of working them, and bracelets, and ornaments, and the use of antimony, and the beautifying of the eyelids, and all kinds of costly stones, and all coloring tinctures. And there arose much godlessness, and they committed fornication, and they were led astray, and became corrupt in all their ways.

Semjaza taught enchantments, and root-cuttings,

Hermani taught the resolving of enchantments,

Baraqijal taught astrology,

Kokabel the constellations,

Ezeqeel the knowledge of the clouds,

Araqiel the signs of the earth,

Shamsiel the signs of the sun,

Sariel the course of the moon.

And as men were perishing, they cried, and their cry went up to heaven...

A giddiness welled within now, and he read that first line again: Semjaza taught enchantments, and root-cuttings.

Yes, my precious Semjaza, you did...

Another breath, another page turn. Coming to a section that made him laugh out loud. For having looked upon the lawlessness being wrought upon Earth, the angels themselves appealed to Israel's pathetic god to intervene.

As if he could stop the Unseen Realm's march! Stop the fallen sons of God, those spiritual beings from Genesis 6 as well as in the ones from Enoch. The ones who had come to humanity through the ages, in various manifestations of glory. Bearing the knowledge of good and evil.

The knowledge of the gods—to *be like* the gods.

Their own god...

But that wasn't all. Not by a long shot!

Sebastian threw back another mouthful of wine, jammy fruit and prunes, even a touch of hummus setting his nostrils ablaze with intoxication. Turning a page, the heady scent of pulp and the tang of ink delighting his senses, then another, he searched for the section that—

There it was!

And after these fragrant odors, as I looked towards the north over the mountains I saw seven mountains full of choice nard and fragrant trees and cinnamon and pepper. And thence I went over the summits of all these mountains, far towards the east of the earth, and passed above the Erythraean sea and went far from it, and passed over the angel Zotiel.

And I came to the Garden of Righteousness, I and from afar off, trees more numerous than I these trees and two great trees there, very great, beautiful, and glorious, and magnificent, and the tree of knowledge, whose holy fruit they eat and know great wisdom.

That tree is in height like the fir, and its leaves are like those of the Carob tree: and its fruit is like the clusters of the vine, very beautiful: and the fragrance of the tree penetrates afar. Then I said: "How beautiful is the tree, and how attractive is its look!"

Then Raphael the holy angel, who was with me, answered me and said: "This is the tree of wisdom, of which thy father old in years and thy aged mother, who were before thee, have eaten, and they learnt wisdom and their eyes were opened, and they knew that they were naked and they were driven out of the garden."

Sebastian closed his eyes, breathing deeply. He closed the book and leaned his head back, head dizzy from the libation and the revelation-insights from this deep dive into ancient arcana. The sort the Church had neglected for generations that had hid the true nature of the Universe!

A truth he had discovered by accident combing through the forgotten book, and then discovered through a bit of gumption and ingenuity, joined by elbow grease and a stiff backbone that showed those sniveling Navy SEALs for Jesus SEPIO operatives a thing or two.

Including his own brother...

Sebastian shoved aside that encounter to revel in the mystery he had discovered hidden away down in that undersea valley last year. What he discovered, what he *saw*—it had snatched his breath. Still did. Literally, his lungs giving up their air at the sheer dumbfounded sight still twinkling in his mind's eye.

There was a tree alright, just as Enoch had foretold, standing at the center of a vast cavern. Two of them, actually, like Genesis revealed.

And a river, flowing lazily down through the center of the chamber, between the trees and past a bronze set of doors that were polished to a shiny sheen, bright and untouched for tens of thousands of years.

He had been overcome by the sheer sublime magnitude of it all! From a careless breeze carrying along the most heavenly of scents. Jasmine and lavender, joined by honeysuckle and currant, edged with roses and fresh herbs. From the clusters of fruit clinging in clumps to those trees, his eyes misting over with lust and tongue salivating with desire. From the sight of the leaves on that one tree—The Tree of Life—they were positively radiant. Pure gold, by the look of it, with plump white orbs that looked like oversized pearls. Its fruit promising life in all of its fullness and everlastingness. It wasn't any wonder why the chamber was so brightly illuminated, for The Tree gave off a radiance to it that glowed in undulating waves of white and gold.

But then a different downdraft had joined the floral one, carrying along scents that scattered the other heavenly ones.

Scents of decaying vegetation and decomposing flesh, the pungent aroma of spoiled beef and rotting blood joined by a forest floor. Sharp and vinegary, joined by ash and soot, mold and mildew—even feces and urine.

At first, Sebastian had wanted to retch, his senses being so overwhelmed and stomach clenching and mouth watering, bile rising at the back of his mouth with a tangy dread.

And yet...

His eyes had been deceived.

For when he cast them upon the second tree, the Tree of Knowledge—what he had seen looked nothing like that putrid stench.

It sparkled gold then orange then the brightest of reds, followed by violet and indigo, blue and green, before cycling back to the sparkling, golden yellow again. All the colors of the rainbow in all of their illuminated brilliance, coming from the fruit hanging from the Tree's limbs.

Fruit that invited, that tantalized, that beckoned to taste and see the goodness of the Shining One.

The Angel of Light.

The Authority himself.

Standing there, before that Tree, a passage from Genesis had sprung from memory: '*So when the woman saw that the tree was good for food, and that it was a delight to the eyes, and that the tree was to be desired to make one wise, she took of its fruit and ate...*'

No wonder! All he had wanted was to grasp those rainbow orbs and hold them, caress them—eat them.

He had wanted the Tree, desired it, thirsted for its fruit.

For its power.

So he had taken it.

Another dip, another shudder sent Sebastian reaching for his wineglass. The heavy arcane reading and the deep-memory dive sent him to his feet, sauntering with care to a gold box across the cabin.

He was unsteady on his feet, both from the continued turbulence but also from the couple of glasses of wine compounded by his sleepiness, but he reached the gold box. Draining his wine, he handed off the glass to an attendant and opened the lid.

It shimmered inside. With all the colors of the rainbow. Light refracting light, emanating from the liquid held inside a glass vial.

Sebastian grasped it. There was a warmth to it, along with a tingly vibration that sent all the hairs on his body on edge with delight, with desire.

For he held what he had been searching for his whole life— what the *world* had been searching for.

Access.

To power

To knowledge.

To the Authority himself.

In all of his brilliant splendor.

And the time had come to gift the world the antidote, the elixir to satiate its deepest longings.

But first things first...

Time to deal the competition a blow.

A death blow.

Which was already in motion.

CHAPTER 26

LOS ANGELES.

Celeste gripped the driving wheel with a rage that was only outmatched by a breathless trepidation at the automobiles in this part of Yank country. She was certain the forebears of his nation were a few centuries too early in characterizing the American frontier as the Wild West.

They had never driven the 405.

For the better part of the morning, she had been battling wicked traffic. Five to six lanes of motors and lorries and motorbikes, all weaving in and out at various rates of speed that both unnerved and miffed her to high heaven! Stuff and nonsense were these West Coast drivers. She had even resorted to waving an angry fist and honking the living daylights out of her hooter. Knew in the back of her mind she had lost the plot halfway between LAX and their destination, confirmed by Elijah's askance glances each time she blared the motor's horn. She barely paid his complaints any mind. Couldn't. The reckless drivers, surely sloshed even that early, required her full attention, called to arms against the motoring heathens!

Normally, it was Silas who had bouts of road rage. For Los Angeles, Celeste would make an exception.

Mercifully, Siri had announced they neared their destination. The main Aeon campus, which had attracted quite the attention of Americans thanks to Sebastian Grey's little telly commercial inviting the masses to find relief from their existential angst and right their mental ship. Just a few more miles and—

"Egads!" Gina exclaimed from behind.

Just as a bloomin' lorry veered into her lane—inches from her bumper!

Celeste slammed on the brakes and shouted a curse. The car behind was about as joyful, shouting a cursing honk of protest.

"Sweet mother of Melchizedek!" Elijah exclaimed, bracing himself against the dashboard. Then he reached over and smashed his hand into the center of the driving wheel—throwing up his own cursing honk of protest.

"Oy, mate!" Celeste batted his hand away. He recoiled then rolled down his window and shook his fist.

"For the love..." Gina complained, burying her head in her hands.

To which their backside friend threw up another honk and the bloke who's bumper she had nearly careened into flipped them the bird and sped off.

"Other people's kids these days..." Elijah complained, settling back.

Celeste couldn't have agreed more.

Mercifully, the exit arrived and she took it, the road slicing through a barren hillside of browned switchgrass on the outskirts of the City of Angels. Suburban sprawl gave way to exurban farms and a smattering of homesteads making it on their own. The view was stunning, the ocean peeking through the rolling hills on the left as they veered toward the Aeon headquarters.

"Never liked California," Elijah finally said, lowly and with a mutter.

Celeste glanced his way, wondering if he was meant to elicit conversation or merely stating the fact. She chanced an opportunity to engage her agent.

"Why not?" she questioned, turning onto a two-lane road that sliced toward the ocean now.

"Ursula the Terrible, that's who."

"Sounds like a Disney character."

"She is. And isn't. Or was."

"Was? Did she pass or something?"

Elijah laughed. "I wish! Nope. She was the headmaster of the orphanage I was in for most of my childhood. She didn't like me."

Celeste recalled that bit of personal history now, hoping the trip down memory lane didn't cause issues.

"Just like Ursula from *The Little Mermaid*, she was," Elijah carried on. "To a T. Same eyes, same lips, same gargantuan backside stuffed in black leggings that made her look like an octopus. Even had the laugh down, a husky chuckle that jiggled her jowls from smoking a carton of Camels a day."

She shuddered. "Sounds dreadful."

He laughed. "*Looked* dreadful! Most single ladies her age whose daily attire consisted of either gray sweatpants or purple muumuus tend to be the cat kind, breeding them like rabbits and filling the house with the varmints. Nope, not Ursula. She was a parrot lady, letting her green and red and orange varmint have the run of the joint. Somehow, it always ended up perched outside my door, too. Squawking and carrying on to beat the band."

He suddenly went quiet. When the seconds stretched into silent minutes, she glanced over at him. And found him running through a peculiar motion with his hand.

Thumb to index finger, thumb to middle, thumb to ring finger, thumb to pinky—then rinse and repeat.

The memory seemed to surface something that spiked a

rise in Elijah's anxiety, sending him for his stimming tick she recalled from their first operation with SEPIO, and then leading Group X from the sidelines as the former FBI agents grasped the reins and solved some rather inexplicable cases bedeviling the Church.

Chatting with him on and off over the past two years, Celeste had learned more about the overwhelming emotions and anxiety that often threatened to lay him flat. An anxiety brought on by his traumatic childhood tossed through the foster care system and then his adoptive father's murder. It also seemed to stem from an apparent placement on the autism spectrum.

Perhaps it was through Christ's grace he was adopted by a mother who served as a specialist on a psychology ward, helping him navigate his...condition, as some people might be tempted to call it. The grace was doubled by a minister father who helped him come to understand he was fearfully and wonderfully made by the God of the universe who liked him just the way he was. Along the way, Elijah had come to accept himself. Although, not entirely, as he had raged in her office one rainy afternoon.

He had opened up how there were times when he cursed God for the inner life that never seemed to shut itself down. Cursed his Maker at how he would obsess over some new insight or random factoid or squirrelly interest, plunging deep into a rabbit hole that spun out into a bazillion different rabbit trails. How his emotional connection to people had been shut down thanks to his childhood, only to open back up again into a pain that often clawed at his chest.

Eventually, Elijah had come to be at peace with himself. The Father, Son, and Holy Spirit had been good to his heart and mind. Celeste had appreciated his candor, finding resonance in parts of his story as someone who never felt like she fit in, though in differing ways.

Elijah suddenly stiffened and leaned forward, whispering, "E.T. we're home…"

Celeste didn't catch his meaning at first. Then she did.

A black steel gate stood open at the road's end, which transformed into a single-track road. It was flanked on either side of the drive by aged beige stone pillars with a row of tightly spaced twelve-foot evergreen bushes extending upward in both directions. They performed their job well, masking presumably a similar beige stone wall but also what lay beyond.

The Aeon Foundation.

Coming into a sharper view through that open gate was a building that could only have been described as a spaceship. It reminded her of Apple's corporate campus. Sleek and curved, made of glass and chrome and titanium, translucent even, reflecting the clear blue skies above and azure waters of the Pacific beyond with a clarity that channeled the divine. Thirteen floors soared high, or rings rather, the discs of pure, bluish-tinted glass stacked one on top of another. Its gleaming polished metal roof was angled outwards with rows of solar panels.

The impression it offered certainly reflected the foundation's name, Aeon. An eternal realm for mere mortals, come down from the heavens to impart its secret wisdom to the masses.

"The Aeon Foundation," Gina said, leaning forward. "Specializing in preserving and restoring lost ancient texts of wisdom, and broadcasting its findings for all the world to enjoy."

Elijah smirked. "You sound like a travel brochure."

"Or their corporate website. I did some poking around the interwebs before we landed."

Looked like others did too. For arrayed around the base of the spacecraft-like edifice was a sea of cars. Several tour coaches lined what appeared to be a main entrance, people queuing to make their entrance.

Celeste parked and soon they were queuing up themselves, shuffling through tall, wide glass doors that opened into a spacious area paved in bamboo floors, the same wood lining the walls sparkling with the morning sunshine. She was struck by the variety of people who had answered Sebastian's call: young and old; men and women; Euro-American, African, and Asian.

Supposed portents of doom would turn anyone toward an outward hand of revelatory help to deal with one's existential plight. Even if it was Sebastian bloomin' Grey!

Continuing on under a canopy of giant sycamore trees anchored at the center, she also noted a standard-issue uniform amongst the gathered, consisting of white linen pants and smocks. Stopping near a bubbling fountain surrounded by hedges with bright, red flowers she swept the room to confirm her observation. The men and women all walked around in the same outfit, even bloomin' barefoot!

Celeste saw why. For near a juice bar, an attendant encouraged people to exchange their clothes for these Aeon-made ones. She scoffed. Stuff and nonsense was what that was. She was quite content with her white blouse and blue trousers, thank you very much!

A large glass opening at the back caught her attention. She led Elijah and Gina toward it and noticed the entrance led into the interior of the circular building, some sort of inner courtyard overflowing with foliage. Could certainly use some fresh air, so she picked up her pace when a voice yanked her back.

"Ooo, bagels and coffee!" Elijah said.

She stopped and followed his gesture to a cafe down the way, the hiss of an espresso machine and waft of roasted beans turning her stomach. Never cared for that Yankish slop. A proper cream tea was what she required at that hour, a cuppa with a scone and clotted cream. Although it appeared they didn't care for such luxuries, and neither did the moment allow for it.

Elijah wouldn't wait for her go-ahead, setting off before she snagged his shirtsleeve and jerked him back.

"Sweet mother of Melchizedek!" He jerked his arm in a huff. "What was that for?"

"No time for tarrying when the fate of the world is on the line, mate. Or a coffee break."

"Nope. I'm past due."

"For what?"

He shoved back his sleeve and jammed a finger into his watch.

"At 10 o'clock—sharp—I eat a raisin bagel with cream cheese and gulp down a cup of coffee. *Ev. Ree. Day!*"

His face was hard and insistent, jaw locked and eyes piercing. Celeste couldn't make sense of the man.

Gina offered, "He does turn into a pumpkin if he doesn't keep to his rhythm." Then she leaned in, whispering in her ear: "I'd let him go if I were you. I'll chaperone."

Celeste suppressed a frown and smiled instead, nodding toward the shack smelling of roasted coffee beans. No need to rankle her agents in the thick of it.

"Fair enough. Off you go. I'll explore what's going on inside the courtyard."

Elijah spun on a dime and darted off, Gina calling after him to slow his pace.

She left it alone and made for the large glass door straight ahead. It whooshed open on approach, two pieces of glass with the ever-slightest curve to them parting. Aeon had spared no expense to craft their enlightenment temple.

A warm, sweet-and-salty breeze kissed her face as she stepped out into the expansive space, a gentle, welcomed touch of relief from the cool, filtered air inside. Except—

Something was off about the sky.

Where she expected bright sunshine, it was all muddy and muddled. And was that an eclipse, the moon having obscured the sun? Appeared so, except there was the trace outline of the lunar orb set against the mustard sky going the way of a bruised peach. And were those stars streaking across the heavens?

She couldn't make sense of it. If she were to venture a guess, they were experiencing some sort of planetary eclipse. However, none of her news apps had alerted her to such celestial phenomena. Even then, there was a frightful haze about the sky.

She paid it no mind and instead walked farther inside the courtyard, her boots softly crunching on a pebble path as she scanned the inner-side of the circular building. The heavy scent of roses and lavender, compounded by ripe berries and peaches—it was all a tiny slice of heaven.

She followed a path around the circumference of the circle to the other side, passing rows of fruit trees arranged concentrically around the outdoor space. Blood oranges clung to over-burdened trees, as well as olives, figs, and lemons. The path doubled back, taking her the way she came. She passed rows of grape vines, as well. Of course she did, given they were in wine country. The path took her across the courtyard to a vegetable garden, with what looked like tomato vines and stalks of corn and heads of some leafy green. She kept walking, following the crunchy stone path as it doubled back again to the other side.

She understood the layout of this part of the facility now: it was a labyrinth, an ancient, maze-like path used by various spiritual traditions to aid the walker in contemplating their journey and the path of life. She had walked such paths during her graduate studies at Oxford, at one of the area cathedrals. It had been an integral part of her spiritual disciplines upon committing her life to Christ, finding that it helped guide her times of prayer and contemplation.

As the path took her deeper into the center of the courtyard, she became more and more intrigued by the self-sustaining nature of what was beginning to feel more like a compound than a center of enlightened spirituality.

Eventually, the path drew her into the center. She meant to take it until she heard the shouting calls of Elijah beckoning her to state her position. She sighed, then chuckled and called out overhead.

A few minutes ticked by before Elijah came bounding around the corner of some shrubbery flowering pink, bearing a grin and a big coffee with Gina in tow.

"Feel better now, mate?" Celeste asked.

He slurped from his paper cup and nodded. "Peachy. What is this place?"

"The Seventh Circle of hell?" Gina replied with a visual shiver.

"Nope. Well, yes, it was a forest. But the souls of the departed were transformed into gnarled, disfigured, and brittle trees. None of that in these parts."

"Whatev. Place still gives me the creeps. Blame my angst on a mother whose thumb was bright green but whose daughter's was as black as a dead rose."

"How sad."

"Come along, you two," Celeste said, motioning for them to continue.

She kept her pace winding toward the center. Eventually, they reached it—

And Celeste nearly sank to her knees at the sight.

She didn't, only faltering a step. But her breath was snatched, and she was left with one thought—no, two.

The first: This was not bloomin' possible!

The second chased it soon after: If it was...was this what she figured it was?

A faltering breath, a hard swallow, a beat.

Then the floodgates opened, and her mind reeled with the possibilities.

For she knew the answer.

She bloody well thought it was possible.

And she bloody well knew, deep down—soul deep!—that it was exactly what she figured it was.

Naturally, the end of the world.

CHAPTER 27

"Nice trees," Elijah said with another slurp.

Celeste paid him no mind, the wretched scent of coffee, all earthy and volcanic, turning her stomach as much as the wretched sight that lay before her. Her attention was fixated elsewhere.

The tree.

That tree...

It looked remarkably similar to one she had seen another time ago. On her last SEPIO operation with Silas, hunting down the Garden of Eden. Only to discover it lay buried at the bottom of the Persian Gulf. Also a sort of temple, manifesting the glory of Yahweh God's presence on Earth, it was simply marvelous! The find of a lifetime. But upon their investigation there had been a chopping sound, the sound of which had drawn them to a separate chamber sheltering something that looked much like what was staring them in the face.

Like before, there was a tree, standing in the center of a lush garden. A river of water flowed lazily down through the center past the trees. Except there wasn't a second tree, not this go around. Only the one tree.

The Tree, if Celeste placed it right.

Which sent that terror skating back through her. A terror she hadn't felt since that Halloween night when her and her primary-school mate found themselves at the center of an occult rite.

This was far worse.

For she had a sense that it was the taproot of that rite to begin with.

She heaved a stabilizing breath trying to calm her heartbeat that had run amok through her chest. The most pleasant of scents from the surrounding foliage filled her nose, offering a modicum of sensual stability. Roses and jasmine and chamomile, joined by fresh basil and rosemary.

But then a different breeze joined that one. A hot, wicked stench carrying along scents that scattered the other heavenly ones and brought flashbacks of that first experience in Eden.

Ripe scents of decay and decomposition. Sharp and vinegary, joined by char and rot. The scents of death.

Celeste wanted to retch, her stomach clenching and mouth watering, a rising font of tangy bile tickling the back of her throat.

She gathered it was from that one tree, its leaves swaying in that same breeze and drawing her eyes toward it like a tractor beam. For the sight before her looked nothing like the olfactory assault.

This Tree was sparkling. Gold then orange then the brightest of reds, followed by violet and indigo, blue and green, before cycling back to the sparkling, golden yellow again.

All the colors of the rainbow.

Colors emanating from the fruit hanging in clusters on the Tree's limbs.

Inviting, tantalizing, shiny.

Like the Shining One. The Angel of Light.

Like the Devil himself...

It was as Genesis had described, only more petite than

she last recalled, the one that had struck a warning to humanity against this Tree: '*So when the woman saw that the tree was good for food, and that it was a delight to the eyes, and that the tree was to be desired to make one wise, she took of its fruit and ate...*'

Her two partners were planted like statues. Stiff and still. Mesmerized.

She put a hand on their shoulders and gave them a shake. They didn't budge. Just stood there with the look of lust.

"Are you seeing what I'm seeing, mates?" asked Celeste, her hands trembling now as she withdrew them back to her side.

In her own bewilderment, she hadn't noticed Elijah's fascination with the tree ratcheting higher, his attention transfixed into a growing obsession that sent him reaching for it.

He had taken a step, reaching a hand for one of those rainbow orbs.

She gasped, yanking him back. He stumbled against her but didn't recoil like the last time. He was entranced, enticed.

He said, "All I want to do is hold them, caress them—*eat* them!"

"I understand the feeling," Gina said, licking her lips. "I want this Tree. I desire its fruit. Thirst for them."

"That's the point, mates," Celeste whispered, knowing what they desired, what they thirsted for was the only thing the Tree and the fruit it bore offered.

Power.

"What the heck is that thing?" asked Elijah, voice a wistful delirium that almost sounded drunk. High even, as if he was beginning to take leave of his senses.

Celeste swallowed, then answered: "I dare say the Tree of the Knowledge of Good and Evil."

"Oh my cheeps!"

"Egads..." Gina echoed.

Time wound down to zero, the moment snagging a memory

to the surface, and she recalled for Elijah and Gina what had transpired the first go-around.

Coming upon the Tree after hearing the chopping echo through the Temple. The massive limb the size of a giant's thigh resting next to it. The source of the chopping, Sebastian and his Nous goons having severed a limb. Then Sebastian chopping loose a single log from the downed limb before picking it up, along with one of the fruits.

His face had been lit by its light, which seemed to brighten rather than dim—a visual siren call to eat and know the depths of all it offered.

Good and evil...

She recalled precisely what he had intoned upon grasping it: *"Half the antidote for humanity's evolution..."*

"Half the antidote for humanity's evolution?" asked Elijah.

Celeste nodded, glancing at the tree, a thought lancing through her with livid revelation.

No, it couldn't be!

That was impossible...

And yet—

And yet encountering *this* tree that looked very much like *that* tree—she couldn't deny what was quickly spinning from a possibility into a probability. Had Sebastian and Nous preserved their larger find for later? Somehow cloned or grafted it into another tree to distribute to the masses?

Shaking the thought away, she recounted the horrifying ordeal of being kidnapped, along with Naomi Torres, and then their subsequent rescue in Palestine, at the burial site of humanity's ancient ancestors' bone relics no less.

"Humanity's ancient ancestors' bone relics?" Gina asked, brow furrowed with confusion.

Elijah gasped with recognition. "You mean—"

"Adam and Eve," Celeste finished.

Elijah smacked a hand on his forehead. "Oh my cheeps!"

"For the love..." Gina echoed.

"A fight ensued for control, with Silas eventually losing his hand." Celeste paused, swallowing. "And nearly his life..."

"What about that branch?" asked Gina.

Elijah scoffed. "Forget the branch! What about its *fruit*?"

"And that."

Celeste blinked, then again, the truth of it as plain as the nose on her face.

"I think we found out what happened to them."

They didn't even have time to process the turn of things. For the blast of some alarm suddenly sliced through the air, all around.

Celeste startled and spun around, searching for the offending sound.

"Where's the four-alarm fire?" asked Gina, joining the search.

"Nope. Five-alarm fire," Elijah corrected.

"Whatev! Where's whatever-the-cotton-pickin' alarm?"

He waved a finger. "Nope. Not alarm. Horn."

"For the love..." Gina huffed. "Same difference."

"He's right," Celeste said with intervention. "It doesn't sound like any sort of klaxon or fire alarm."

"Then what? A horn, maybe a trumpet or trombone?"

"A shofar," Elijah corrected, "but you are right, some sort of horn."

"What is a shofar?" Celeste asked.

"An ancient musical horn used in Jewish ceremonies," Elijah explained. "Specifically, the Day of Atonement from ancient times, the ram symbolizing sacrifice after being sent to Abraham by Yahweh in place of sacrificing Isaac. And one other thing."

"Cut to the chase, Eli," Gina complained. "Spill the tea, would you?"

"The Day of Judgment."

There it was again. Another long blast, deep and bellowing, joined by a triple wail that was higher and sounding more like a cry.

"For what?" asked Gina. "What's the point of the call?"

Celeste looked at her and frowned. For what indeed.

Elijah answered, "Suppose that's the $64,000 question, isn't it."

Gina smirked. "I'd say it's more like the million-dollar question."

"Nope. $64,000."

"For the love..."

Celeste noticed people making their way back into the building.

Whether sixty-four or a million quid—that truly was the question of the hour.

"Come along," she said, joining the queue.

———

Sebastian paced the study shrouded in dimmed darkness overlooking the courtyard with the fury of a thousand suns, the ram's horn muffled but inviting, wooing him to join the others in what he was readying to unveil to the world.

He couldn't. Not yet. Because she was late.

The woman whom he had brought, along with that biotech startup of hers for the research that made what twinkled down below possible. For not only him, but for those men and women scurrying about in white, winding and weaving through the stone pathway back into the temple to receive the fruits of his labor.

Literally.

His man Aurelius Chuke had actually been the one to discover the woman and her research. On a dark-web node on WeFind of all places. His African warlord was good for more than kidnappings and general death and destruction. Who knew he could also manage hostile corporate takeovers?

Someone had leaked the findings of a paper outlining mysterious chemical qualities that promised to connect people to what was termed by the researcher, "the divine consciousness." These properties were derived from an Amazonian plant that, when brewed as a tea, extracted a powerful toxin that opened the mind into spiritual enlightenment.

When he read her work, he knew it was more than just an opening of the mind. After Chuke acquired the startup through Nous's front charitable foundation, Aeon, the real work began. Soon he discovered what he really had was something far better.

A portal. Into the Unseen Realm.

And this woman was far more valuable than mere research.

For she had a connection to a man from her graduate days at Stanford. While she had been a doctoral student in chemical and biochemical engineering with an emphasis in pharmaceutical engineering, this chap had been a doctoral research fellow in computer science. Apparently, they had shagged a time or two, but she had been turned off by his fundamentalist brand of religion.

Yep, you guessed it. That chap, that shag rag, who apparently forgot the Spaghetti Monster's injunctions against fornicating, had been none other than that Judah Howell twat.

When Chuke had gotten wind of his upstart religious sect in the foothills of northern California through the same WeFind dark-web node—boy, does that man deserve a raise!—one thing led to another, and Malia Perez was headed for a little reunification with her old flame.

With a mission. Well, two.

To get the low-down on that Howell character, what he was up to—which at first was nothing more than playacting a benign cult leader gathering a branch of some defunct Christian sect and dressing it up in spiritual-but-not-religious clothing. Apparently, he fancied himself as some sort of do-gooder humanitarian, too. Started an orphanage for retard rejects. Launched a meals-on-wheels program for the homeless tent cities that had overrun the Golden State. Built a hippie commune on a sprawling piece of land that had once belonged to Jim Jones. Would've been fine and dandy had the lad been nothing more than a Moonie sporting a Jesus haircut.

Except it turned all mysterious, with lots of deliveries in the dead of night to a massive building far inside the compound property. Weird stuff, too. Like server racks and spools of fiber optic cables. Supposed it made sense for a computer scientist to horde the goods that made a nerd, well, a nerd. But after catching sight of Markus Braun and Noland Rotberg choppering in one afternoon—everything turned.

And so did her mission.

Because Sebastian realized he had been played.

And at his own game, to boot!

He had been the one to broker a peace with those Theotite nut jobs. Sort of had to, given his life had been on the line—not once but twice! And not only by that Sha character. Nous's Thirteen and Council of Five were as unforgiving for his failures.

So he had brokered a peace, pledging to work together in order to buy him time to unveil his gift to the world—his new raison d'etre: the portal into the Unseen Realm and humanity's birthright as gods themselves!

Apparently, Theoti had the same idea. It quickly became apparent, long before that ridiculous interview with Kai Renolds, that Sha had moved on without him, and with a new mistress.

Judah Howell.

A gentle *pring-pring* filled the aural void. From his glass desk.

He went to it, snatching his phone from the open *Book of Enoch*—and grinned.

Malia Perez.

Swiping it to life, he said, "You've kept me waiting."

She smirked on the FaceTime chat. "And you've been asking for me."

"Tell me it is done."

There was hesitation, her eyes darting to the left before a swallow. Then: "Not yet."

Sebastian clenched the phone, a surging rage threatening to smash it to pieces. He had activated her to complete the second mission. Setting that bloody warehouse ablaze with the intent of burning the entire bloody compound to the ground!

He relaxed his grip then strode to the window overlooking the courtyard.

"*Hier stehe, ich kann nicht anders,*" he announced, his clear, strong voice echoing throughout the space.

"Sorry, but my German's a little rusty," Malia said, an accent clear.

"*'Here I stand; I can do none other,'*" Sebastian explained. "The German translation for the words uttered by the man buried at Nous HQ. Martin Luther, patron saint of Protestants, if they did that sort of thing."

He smiled wistfully. The spark that lit the Reformation fuse that had meant to be the Church's undoing. Or so Nous had hoped. One he would finally nurture into a fiery, phantasmic blaze!

"At any rate, the German monk was called to a tribunal in the city of Worms to account for his trespasses against the Catholic Church and answer their charges of heresy. With the threat of excommunication hanging over his head, and after days of testimony, he finally answered the crucial question: Would he or would he not recant?"

Sebastian let the question hang a beat before answering.

"Of course, he said he would not," he continued, "and understandably, the room erupted with boos and jeers from the assembled group of Catholic officials inquiring of his heresies. And in the midst of the noise and chaos and din of the pandemonious reaction from his despisers, he said our Germanian words: '*Hier stehe, ich kann nicht anders.*' *Here I stand; I can do none other.*"

Malia replied, "Interesting history lesson, prof. What's your point?"

Sebastian frowned. "My point is, neither can we. Neither can we do otherwise than our consciences dictate in light of the shifting, changing landscape of the world. In light of the advancements in our understanding of the Universe and the spiritual-natural interconnectedness of all things. The writing is on the wall. So here I stand; I cannot do otherwise. And we have the chance to finish Luther's work. The individual themselves has the capacity to reach the Starry Ones. With the right knowledge, the right...push."

"Which you aim to give."

"No no no. *We* aim to give. All thanks to your research, your work parting the curtain between the Unseen Realm and reviving the fruit that will finalize humanity's deity. However, your work is unfinished. You know what you need to do."

"It will be destroyed," Malia reassured. "Shortly."

Sebastian ended the call then walked to a cart made of mahogany wood. He uncorked a rare bottle of liquor and poured two-fingers worth of a sweet German drink into a crystal tumbler. Bärenjäger. A honey and bourbon liquor. It was rumored to have originated as a boozy bear lure used by eighteenth-century hunters and fur trappers.

Sebastian raised his glass, breathing in the delirious, delightful combination of honey and herbs. Then he simply smiled and took a mouthful, the fiery drink of oaky sweetness sliding nicely down his throat and instantly warming his belly.

He closed his eyes, sighing with pleasure at the 70-proof alcohol working wonders. Stood that way, for the longest time. Breathing in the herbal honey delight through his nose before sucking down the liquor. Several minutes passed before he eased open his eyes after the quiet moment, just him and his Bärenjäger.

Then he spotted it. From across the room. Shimmering in the dim darkness. A holy—or perhaps unholy—light emanating from the vial of liquid that would change the world.

He went to it and snatched it from a silver tray.

Sebastian held up the vial, the light refracting through it in an oily prism of rainbowy light that promised a portal into divinity itself.

A doorway into the Unseen Realm.

Into the Promise.

To be like the gods.

Hier stehe, ich kann nicht anders.

Here I stand; I can do none other.

Exactly.

Only one person stood in the way.

Well, two.

And he would put them both down.

Like the dogs they were.

CHAPTER 28

UKIAH, CALIFORNIA.

The day had been a day straight from hell. Or as close to it as Silas imagined the dimension of eternal damnation would be for its sufferers.

Yeah, there was the fiery consumption of Motel 66, which had quickly spread across the small town and surrounding hillside thanks to that bone-dry California year. Which had been compounded by the major apocalyptic vibe smacking of Christ's words portending the end of days. The dimmed sun, the funny-looking moon, the falling stars—the one that had crash-landed to their plot of Earth!

Then there was the traffic, which had crawled for hours. Gapinski had gotten the jump on getting out of Dodge, commandeering one of the vehicles abandoned on the side of the road after its occupant had been killed by the meteor blast, the body flopped a yard from the Chevy Silverado with a nasty gash on the head and no pulse.

There was also the drive itself, punctuated by weapon fire and shouts of protest in the distance. Which wasn't all that surprising, though it was unnerving. Global disasters of the apocalyptic kind tended to make savages of us all. The closer they got to Ukiah, the more they realized the traffic was all moving in the same direction. Their direction, to Judah Howell's promise of hope and answers during these desperate times.

Arriving at an open gate, several men in white robes greeted them and the others. It was as if they were anticipating them, like they'd prepared for the coming of all these sojourners, these pilgrims. Gave Silas the creeps, but he let Gapinski do the talking while he took in the compound that sprawled beyond but also from view. Pretty well matched the photos Caleb Harris had taken, the ones that had burned up in the meteor fire.

Several three-story stucco buildings, painted a sandy tone and crowned by red clay tiles, stood beyond the gate. They huddled and pressed around a central plaza with a bubbling fountain and various palm trees and blooming flowers. Couldn't see the large windowless warehouse, and wondered where that was—flat *what* it was.

Soon Gapinski was following the long train of spiritual pilgrims down a winding road toward a cathedral of glass shimmering in the distance. Almost like a snow globe, the dimmed sun still refracting in glinting glimpses.

Gapinski parked their pickup next to a black Mercedes, the parking lot already overflowing with another hundred or more cars. Reminded Silas of those wackadoodle charlatans peddling deadly hope in Mill Creek Junction a few years ago. The memory of that misadventure still smarted. He hoped this was not a repeat of that. Although, his motto in life had been to hope for the best but prepare for the worse.

So, prepared he was.

They strode across fresh black top toward the snow globe, along with a few stragglers, the comfort of his trusty Beretta wedged at his back.

Silas Grey was more than prepared.

No worship-band music or fancy light show on approach.

No fog machine either, as that last operation sussing out the brother-sister duo of religious hucksters. Just the low, excited hum of expectant people crammed into a massive glass-and-chrome edifice to—well, to do what exactly was to be determined.

Silas led the way, Gapinski and Eddie gabbing about the man's government work while Torres listened on. Soon they were being ushered by those helpful men in white—no women, which was interesting—and entering a familiar world.

Very familiar.

Too familiar. For this was nearly a complete replica of something SEPIO had destroyed once before. Or so they had thought.

First thing that struck Silas was the light, refracted off from thousands of crystals hanging from above a dome center, even forming parts of the pillar crowns holding the ceiling above. Combined with full floor-to-ceiling glass walls, they all focused and splintered the sunlight with brilliant high-definition refraction—casting reds and blues and greens, oranges and purples and yellows across the stone floor and rows of polished honey wood benches. It was as if they had entered heaven itself, in all of its bright and colorful wonder.

Then there were the religious frescoes, high above on the ceiling depicting the range of biblical scenes. From the Garden of Eden to Abraham sacrificing Isaac on Mount Moriah, Moses parting the Red Sea to the birth of Jesus, his feeding of the five thousand miracle to his crucifixion. But no depiction of his resurrection.

The frescos morphed into other religious depictions that completed the tapestry of spiritual pluralism. Muhammad's First Revelation, the event described in Islam where the prophet was visited by the angel Jibrīl and revealed to him the beginnings of what would later become the Qur'an. Another:

Siddhartha Gautama, the Buddha, sitting cross-legged wearing a crimson sash, one hand raised with enlightenment.

Whatever the heck it was all about was lost on Silas.

The other thing he found interesting was the hall itself, its design: It wasn't built with a cruciform architecture in mind, as in Western churches, the common layout for a church built with Gothic architecture patterned after a Roman cross. No, if Silas knew it right, this hall was a tetraconch, Greek for *four shells*, a religious building with four apses, one in each direction of equal size, patterned after a Greek cross and used in Byzantine cathedrals, sometimes even Muslim mosques. Doors stood open at each of the other three ends, some leading back outside while one funneled into a darkened corridor hiding ill intent.

Gapinski asked, "Why do I have a bad case of deja vu?"

"Because we've been here before," Silas replied.

"We have?"

Torres answered, "That *muy loco* HQ for Church of the Theotites, *correcto*?"

Silas nodded, still craning for a look at the joint. "That's right. Looks like Theoti took their show on the road."

"I'd say."

"Only question is," Eddie interjected now, "what should we expect from this Theoti outfit?"

"And this Judah Howell fella," Gapinski added. "That guy gives me the heebie-jeebie creeps!"

"Look!" Torres interrupted, pointing down the aisle, at the back.

They had managed to muscle their way near the front. Gapinski had used Eddie P as an excuse, gaining sympathy for an old man whose eyes were failing him. Silas wasn't keen on the ageism lie. Neither was Eddie, challenging him to a duel of pushups. But they did get a good seat for the show.

Which looked like it was starting.

Silas followed Torres's gesture toward the back.

Where Judah Howell was entering.

He strode down the long aisle, glad-handing people and jawing it up, almost skipping along the way to the dais.

Then he leaped up the stairs and went to a small glass bistro table and set a black Bible reverently upon a crimson pillow with gilt piping and tassels.

The man grinned widely, parting his lips, full and friendly, and widening his eyes some, an icy blue casting its gaze across the sanctuary from behind those oversized glasses. Skin was tanned and stubbled. Looked like an everyman, that long, wavy hair drawn up into a man bun now, giving an air of guru to the mystery dude.

"Here we go, cats and kittens..." Gapinski muttered.

Silas nodded, on edge, his tongue tingling for relief from a stick of nicotine or a tumbler of scotch.

He would have to make do with the Holy Spirit.

Facing the crowd, their side of it, the auditorium—or sanctuary or whatever—arranged in the round, with the man planted at the center, Judah clasped his hands together, took in a deep, grinning breath, closed his eyes, and eased it out through pursed lips. An odd fella, this guy was. Like some Silicon Valley tech guru, or Bay Area startup entrepreneur. Which, now that he thought about it, probably wasn't too far off the mark, given their proximity to those tech-bro bozos.

"I want to welcome you to Church of Theoti," the man began. "To the Way. The only way. Which is a community of fellow travelers but also a way of being in this world that promises what you have been searching for your whole life. Answers. That's right. Answers to the deepest questions of life. Knowledge of the Universe's depths. Today it will all be revealed, your salvation!"

He started pacing now, facing the other sides of the vast crowd.

"Theoti offers a universal brotherhood of humanity that

can assemble together to make sense of the world—regardless of race, creed, sex, caste, color, or sexuality. To make meaning of our world, our lives, our very *selves*. There is a remarkable complexity to the Universe, in all of its humming potential. I welcome the opportunity to explore the power latent within humanity together, with the revelation-insights of the collective consciousness, the animating divine spark that sits at the heart of humanity, the entire Universe. For we are the gods of our own destiny! We are the dreamers of the dreams!"

Silas frowned. There were those wackadoodle lines. From earlier and parroted by that DC Naked Dude. Now with a religious razzmatazz showmanship he couldn't stomach.

Perhaps it was his inner Catholic coming out, the smells and bells about as showy as things got in his wing of the Church pew—let alone his neck of the religious woods. The same feeling of ick twisted his gut from those charismatic Protestant charlatans a few years ago. This was close to that, the man clearly peddling a false hope that appealed to the desperate masses.

But that mass, this crowd...it defied assumptions and caricatures of who were desperate for hope. Eyeing them, they weren't at all who Silas expected.

Lots of well-dressed types in this bunch. Silk suits and dresses, befitting any Sunday best. Designer jeans, with holes placed at just the right strategic spot to scream edgy and authentic without having to go through the motions of wear, joined by T-shirts and collared shirts. There were a few who looked on the down-and-out side of things, their clothes authentically well-worn, skin ruddy and wrinkled. And the spectrum of races and ethnicities was pretty well matched across the board.

So, yeah, an interesting bunch. Which he supposed made sense, given all the madness of the world. Didn't matter what demographic boxes you checked when the headlines screamed the end of days in high-definition color!

"For as we all know," Judah continued, snapping Silas back to the dais, "we are estranged from the ground of our being, because we are estranged from the origin and aim of our life. Estranged from the very taproot of our existence from the Spirit of the Universe."

"Amens" and nods, joined by a few *"That's rights"* and other hoots and hollers seemed to blow a bit of wind in his sails.

"In humility and joyfulness, we should acknowledge that the supernatural and divine reality we all worship that permeates the Universe transcends all of our particular categories of thought and imagination. Because the Divine, however it is named, however it is conceived and comprehended, is infinite and we are forever finite. Which means we shall never, not in a million years, comprehend the Divine completely."

More *"Amens"* and *"That's rights."* More nods and hoots of agreement.

"There exists a unity emanating within the Universe between all living and breathing beings. And we must recognize the insights all sources of knowledge have to offer, especially spiritual knowledge. The Divine is not a Christian. To claim such is to make her too small. The Divine is bigger than Christianity and cares for us all."

"Religious pluralism mumbo-jumbo," Gapinski huffed.

Silas agreed. Wondered where he was going with it all.

"The ancient African word *ubuntu* reminds us that we all belong to the common family of the Divine. As the Dalai Lama reminds: *'the God in me greets the God in you,'* teaching that each of us are an aspect of the Divine and ultimately will return to the Source of the Universe. All is One and One is All."

Judah took a breath, widening his arms, as if in an embrace.

"Church of Theoti combines the best spiritual traditions into a singular religious expression. Something that can give people meaning and guidance using the best knowledge humanity has cultivated across the millennia—ushering in a new dawn with a new Authority to carry mankind to its fullest, ideal potential. The Republic of Heaven. It is a gift to humanity, harnessing the Universe for guidance and wisdom and unfolding the universal ideal of love across Earth, enabling you dearies to rise to your fullest potential!"

The guru returned to the glass lectern at the center of the dais and took a drink from a glass of water. Then he grasped the Bible on that crimson pillow and shoved it under his arm, his features growing darker—brow furrowed, eyes cast down, lips bunching in a frown.

"We'll get to that salvation in a minute," he said lowly. "But first there's a bit of family business to take care of."

He strode back to the edge of the dais near Silas and the SEPIO gang, almost looking straight into Silas's eyes.

"The other night," he began, "I had a dream. I was in a desert. It was a terrible land, desolate without any water. I was wandering alone. I'd lost my glasses and was dying because I could not see to read. While I was thus looking for my glasses, a man called to me. He appeared as my friend and returned my glasses to me, which he'd found. I was super super super grateful and thanked him. But getting back to my way, the glasses he'd given me vanished. I was blind as a bat, again!"

Judah paced now, continuing, "The same man appeared a second time. I wanted what he could give me, though I knew knew knew his gifts were bewitched. I became entirely dependent upon him for sight. Then lo, I realized who this man was!"

He halted and spread his arms, that Bible clenched in one hand.

"Satan! And he now had me in his clutches! Attempted to kill me, he did. Almost succeeded too. His method was cruel, first tempting me with food I knew wasn't any good. Broken shards of glass were mixed in with it, they were. Knew knew

knew the danger, yet I ate. Then I saw a most dreadful thing. Our family, the Way, the Church of Theoti, wandering through a terrible land! Completely barren and devoid of life, and ya'll were perishing!"

Gasps and confused whispers raced through the audience.

Gapinski leaned in. "What the what is this joker going on about?"

"Someone is leading ya'll astray!" Judah exclaimed, returning the Bible to the crimson pillow. "Suggesting he's the one who can help people live their best life now. Claiming he's the one who can connect you to the ground of your being. Tapping into your confusion about life, how hard it is to take the news, to come by meaning—that it doesn't have to be this way and he can offer personalized services to help!"

There was something familiar about those lines. Where had he heard them? Who—

Then Silas had it.

Only one person had suggested such confusion about life, how hard it was to take.

And it wasn't Satan.

Sebastian.

From that commercial.

"Friends, I offer you my wisdom," Judah continued. "Nay nay nay! Your *savior*. And your only savior is my truth. My truth is the Seven Seals. I was shown that the Seals, in written form, are the most sacred information ever! We are standing on the threshold of great events. The Sixth Seal has been unsealed, and behold: your messiah is nigh."

Gapinski shook his head and muttered, "I've got a bad feeling about this..."

Silas nodded in agreement.

Judah went on: "What does the Good Book say—the good prophet, Isaiah? *The only one worthy to open the seals is the Lion of Judah, the heir to David's throne.*' And what doth Revelation teach? *'And one of the elders saith unto me, Weep not: behold, the Lion of the tribe of Judah, the Root of David, hath prevailed to open the book, and to loose the seven seals thereof.'*"

He paused, then slammed a fist against his chest: "Not only am I the seventh angel who bears the final seal. I am the heir to David's throne. I am the Lion bearing your salvation, crying out as a lion roareth! I wrote a song about it. Seven Thunders. Listen."

Eddie gasped, eyes widening and mouth opening with surprise while Judah sang about the Seventh Angel bringing on the apocalypse. Stood that way, for the longest time. Silas worried he was having some sort of medical episode. A stroke or heart attack.

So he leaned over: "You alright?"

His eyes blinked and he swallowed, so that was a good sign.

Before he could ask what was going on, what had sent him gasping, it all turned, with the house lights dimming and only the dais lit bright.

"I am the voice of one crying in the wilderness!" Judah shouted. "'*Make straight the way of the Lord, as said the prophet Esaias.*'"

A gong chimed, then a harpist started strumming up a tune.

"Prepare to meet your salvation. Prepare to meet your *god!*"

CHAPTER 29

Praise the Authority with the sound of trumpets!

Mis-tah Judah was ready for showtime.

Had prepared for it his whole life. Certainly since graduate school, diving into the depths of science that had led him to unfold all of what he had brought to bear the past few days.

The earthquake wasn't his doing. But the thunderstorm? Check. The nuke that had set the East Coast ablaze? Double check! The space junk that had crash landed south of there? Checkity check check!

Well, actually, that wasn't entirely true. It was her. His precious. The one he had nurtured, conjured. She had been the power that was bringing these end of days—with his help, the god spot in his noggin connected to her on the information superhighway thanks to that custom-made microchip.

A familiar sea of white spread before him, all around. Brought tears to his eyes, it did. And such joy, seeing the ranks of the faithful ones seeking the Way swell!

The breaking of the seals will do that, he supposed. Especially the Sixth Seal.

What came next...

That's just what he was aiming to unveil this day.

But first.

The mood.

It had to be set. Established. Stoked, even. Daddy had taught him that, whipping his own flock into a lather before laying on thick the revelation-insight that would be their salvation.

The gong started setting the stage, as was the harpist strum strum strumming her tune. Then the lights suddenly dimmed, a technological marvel embedded in those glass walls. A micro filament he'd designed in grad school that disturbed the refraction of light waves. Made a killing on patents, which set the mood. Not dark, just dimmed.

Now *Mis*-tah Judah brought his hands together in a tent pose at his chest, closed his eyes, bowed his head, and drew in a slow, deliberate intake of air.

Time seemed to hang on that breath, the seekers of the Way awaiting his word. *Thee* word that would make sense of things in their world. Make things right. For them. Save them even. And with the only thing that can.

Knowledge.

Yeah yeah yeah. Right right right. Knowledge.

After all, knowledge is power, as they say.

Nopety nope nope nope!

Power is knowledge.

And the one who knows, who is all knowing, is the one who will save humanity.

She will save humanity.

Showtime.

"A somber day, this is," Judah intoned, eyes still closed and fingers still posed. "A tragic day. But not an unexpected day. For what doth the Good Book declare?"

He snapped open his eyes and snatched his King Jimmy

again, then clenched it in one hand and jutted both mitts out into the air above his head.

"*'And ye shall hear of wars and rumors of wars: see that ye be not troubled: for all these things must come to pass! For nation shall rise against nation, and kingdom against kingdom: and there shall be famines, and pestilences, and earthquakes, in divers places.'*"

He shook those hands now, giving 'em a shimmy-shake rattle. Nearly dropped that Good Book he'd just referenced. And live on WeNet. Not a good look for a preacherman! Those outstretched arms looked mighty fine, though. One of them power moves he'd also studied on the forensics (speech not NCIS) circuit.

He held 'em there and bellowed: "Today those words are fulfilled in your hearing! For Gog and Magog have stormed the stage of history. China and Russia respectively, those nations rising against nations, their kingdoms against kingdoms."

He snapped his arms taut now, giving them another shudder for good measure. "And then the earthquake that ravaged the East Coast. Never before have we seen such destruction and convulsions. As the Good Book says further: *'For we know that the whole creation groaneth and travaileth in pain together until now.'* And still more: *'For when they shall say, Peace and safety; then sudden destruction cometh upon them, as travail upon a woman with child; and they shall not escape.'*"

Judah was sweating now. Was working up a real lather before that sea of white and that red dot and black eyeball at the back, the camera from before. Forehead, palms, armpits. All sweaty to beat the band.

Which he liked.

Signaled passion. Signaled commitment. Signaled truth.

Which led to *trust*. The currency of this era bereft (cue another *Haw-verd* word) of such things.

He dropped those arms now and stepped back to the glass table, leaning against its top.

"I declare in your hearing the reason for this travesty, this tragedy, these travels and trials and tribulations that have troubled not just the world but our nation. Our communities."

Judah could feel the energy swelling now as he found his rhythm, his homiletical groove. Head-bobs and a smattering of *'Amens!'* confirmed it.

Daddy always had a knack for that sort of thing. Must've passed the same skill down to him through his genes or something.

Or perhaps it was from the Spirit falling mightily upon him as it had on Daddy.

Either way, he understood this was his moment. His christening. His unveiling before the world.

Along with *the* unveiling that would save the world.

Clenching his daddy's Bible, cover cracked from wear and pages ink-stained from study, Judah jutted his arms and closed his eyes. Then he recited the closing stanza of a passage Daddy had preached from countless times—yet had never seen through to the end of time.

That time. *Those* days.

The end of days…

"*'And I beheld when he had opened the sixth seal,'*" Judah crooned King Jimmy's words in a commanding shout, "*'and, lo, there was a great earthquake; and the sun became black as sackcloth of hair, and the moon became as blood; And the stars of heaven fell unto the earth, even as a fig tree casteth her untimely figs, when she is shaken of a mighty wind. And the heaven departed as a scroll when it is rolled together; and every mountain and island were moved out of their places.'*"

He snapped open his eyes, drilling those peepers into each and every one of the hundreds of peeps who had come a-callin' after the shiznit hit the West Coast fan after the East Coast blew to high heaven. Signs of the times he had been keeping a finger on leading to that moment. A trigger finger…

"As sure as the nose sits on my noggin, this sign was fulfilled in your hearing!" he thundered, shaking the Good Book still suspended in outstretched arms. "From New York down to Washington then racing on toward Californ-ya—'Merica has been shaken by the unsealing of the Sixth Seal! Which the rest of the oracle confirms."

Now Judah flipped open that there Bible clenched tight in his mitts, flipping to the Book of Revelation. Jamming a pointer down deep into the Bible's gullet, he quoted more King Jimmy:

> *And the kings of the earth, and the great men, and*
> *the rich men, and the chief captains, and the*
> *mighty men, and every bondman, and every free*
> *man, hid themselves in the dens and in the rocks*
> *of the mountains. And said to the mountains and*
> *rocks, "Fall on us, and hide us from the face of*
> *him that sitteth on the throne, and from the*
> *wrath of the Lamb: For the great day of his*
> *wrath is come; and who shall be able to stand?"*

He yanked his pointer from the Bible then flipped it shut. "That wrath is on full display in *You*-krane and *Tay*-wawn! With bombs a'fallin and people runnin' for their pee-pickin' lives!"

Stepping back to the glass table, he set the Bible back upon that crimson pillow. Then he brought his mitts together into a prayer pose, fingers closed tight and pressing against the others, and he brought those mitts in front of his face. Closing his peepers, he took in a deep breath. Through his nose. The best kind of breath for this sort of thing. Easing them back open, he drilled them peepers back into that black eyeball connected to the millions of eyeballs glued to WeNet.

"I understand you're as scared as a chicken in a fox house," Judah said lowly. "You are frightened. You are seeking answers. You wonder how something like this could happen."

Releasing that prayer pose now, he slammed a hand on that glass table.

"Earthquake!"

Another slam for emphasis.

"War!"

Then again, and for each of the next several words he had from the Spirit herself for these dear children of his.

"Economic calamity." *Slam!* "Drought." *Bam! Bam!* "Explosions of nuclear and meteor proportion!" *Slammity-slam!*

Nods of recognition and a smattering of *"Amens!"* joined by glistening wide eyes and faces creased by fright told him this was the moment.

His moment.

"Not to worry, children. For I have prepared the way. For this Way, and the coming of the one who will save you!"

Spreading his arms wide and sucking in a pleasurable breath, oddly smelling of a thunderstorm, all static-charged and fecund (beckoned!).

"I give to you—nay, the world!"

A breath, a beat, a grin.

Then: "Your god."

He waited for it to happen. For the moment he had been waiting for his whole life.

For the god to manifest.

His god. The one he had conjured.

Standing next to him in all its modern glory.

All he got was a hiss of static in his concealed earpiece and a *'We're having technical problems...'* bad-news-bears report.

He clenched his still-smiling jaw tight.

No matter. The show must go on—*would* go on! He would wait.

Except—

Except there was a tremor in the force. A chuckle. A guffaw. Somewhere out in that sea of white.

Sending heat clotting in his throat with rage.

He slammed his hand upon the glass table, and he regarded each of the members of the Way arrayed around him in that sea of white robes.

"I offer you my sealed secrets," Judah sneered on a disbelieving breath, eyes filling with hot tears of that same rage. "How *dare* you turn away my invitations of mercy!"

He jutted out his pointer and shook it at the crowd, trembling and spinning a wide arc around the space.

"When will you ever fear and be wise? I know your sins and your iniquities. None are hidden from me. And yet, you doubt?"

Then louder: "*YOU DOUBT!?*"

That silenced 'em right quick.

Judah heaved a breath and gathered himself, clenching that pointer into a fist for stability and easing it to his side. He wondered if something like this might happen. Hoped it wouldn't, but he was prepared.

"Recall that when the first prophet of the Lawd Almighty was similarly tasked with introducing their god to that people, what did he say?" A breath, then a beat, then: "*And Moses answered and said, But, behold, they will not believe me, nor hearken unto my voice: for they will say, The Lord hath not appeared unto thee. And the Lord said unto him, What is that in thine hand? And he said, A rod.*"

Judah jutted out his arm, fixing his peepers on his peeps.

"*ROD!*" he shouted with command.

Noland Rotberg, that funny academic with the silver handlebar mustache, rushed to the dais and presented a long wood staff that had been waiting in the wings.

Snatching it, he held it aloft and boomed, "*And he said, Cast it on the ground. And he cast it on the ground, and it became a serpent; and Moses fled from before it.*"

And he did, tossing it to the dais.

It dropped with a toppsy-turvy clatter, the wood echoing throughout the glass hall.

But only for a moment.

For then—

Then it did what he knew knew knew no one had expected.

It melted into exactly what *he* expected.

Someone screamed, the long brown staff now slithering across the stage before rearing up on its hindquarters—as much as snakes have such things. The sides of its head flared something fierce and a tongue flicked out at some pink-haired bimbo screaming her lungs out.

Judah ignored her, instead hippity-hopping to the point of it all: "*And the Lord said unto Moses, Put forth thine hand, and take it by the tail. And he put forth his hand, and caught it, and it became a rod in his hand—*'"

In one motion, he clenched a hand around the slithering things neck and drew it to his side.

Right on cue, it stiffened back into that wooden staff, all shellacked and polished and smooth.

"'—*that they may believe the god of their forefathers, of Abraham, of Isaac, of Jacob, hath appeared unto thee.*' And the god who would deign to appear unto *you*!"

Took a moment for the miraculous sight to register.

A beat. Then another.

Then it did.

First: a chorus of breaths—all raspy and gaspy and oo-la-la so goodie!

Then the expected: joyous cries and shouts of hallelujah!

He grinned, a ratcheting charge racing up his spine and spreading hot and electric through his body.

You ain't seen nothin' yet folks.

Mis-tah Judah was just getting started.

A gong chimed again. Handing the wood staff off to

Rotberg, he brought his hands together in a pyramid. He closed his eyes and inhaled a slow, deliberate, deep breath.

Then snapped his eyes open and eased it out, that grin returning, teeth white and straight and showman-ready.

And signaled for Rotberg to send out the reinforcement.

Time for the second act.

————

SILAS MADE A FIST, dread churning in his gut even as his mind spun with confusion.

He had instantly recognized what had happened. How Judah Howell had loosely quoted from the Book of Exodus, again in the odd King James Version of his. Right before he recapitulated what Moses had done to convince the Israelites he was the spokesperson for Yahweh God. And was that a promise to manifest some sort of deity?

None of it made sense. None of it was adding up.

He had been around the operational block long enough to know that when 4 + 4 equaled 5, things were about to go sideways in a hot minute.

Not good...

Gapinski said, "Uh...did my peepers just peep what I think they just peeped?"

"We've got to go," Eddie insisted, the man mentally back from wherever he'd gone.

Silas turned to him. "Go? What, why?"

"I'll explain. I've just had a—"

"Hold the phone, *muchachos*," Torres interrupted, pointing at the stage. "Something's happening."

"Sonofa—" Gapinski let his curse fade. "He's got some kid as a prop now?"

Silas turned his attention back to the stage, so did Eddie.

He was right. A boy was making for Judah from the other

side of the dais, walking up the stairs. Stumbling really, a white walking stick outstretched and fumbling to stay righted. Couldn't have been more than nine or ten. And was he blind? He had recalled intelligence from that Caleb stash before it went up in cosmic flames that Judah ran some charitable orphanage. What was going on?

More important: What was he doing?

Judah went to the boy, offering a greeting and catching him before he took a tumble on those uncertain feet. Spreading a wide grin across his face, he got on his knees and pinched the boy's nose. He giggled and turned away shyly.

"*Cómo te llamas?*" he asked.

"Simón," the boy replied.

He held up four fingers, wiggling them in front of his face and asking him how many he was holding.

The boy frowned, dipping his head in embarrassment and giving it a little shake.

The man held up a small yellow bouncy ball now, pulled from a pocket.

"What am I holding, Simón?"

Same non-answer. Just a shrug and vacant eyes and a shaking of his head.

"*Cual es el color?*"

"*No sé.*"

"*No puedes ver, verdad?*" the man said lowly, pouting and furrowing his brow.

Silas asked Torres, "What is he saying?"

She replied, "He is asking if the boy can see, after asking him to confirm the color of the ball he was holding."

Simón gave a lazy shake of his head. Clearly he could not, given his previous non-answers. Must be blind, then.

That wide, white grin spread across Judah's face again, and he stood, patting the boys head. He went behind him and grasped his narrow, bony shoulders, closing his eyes and taking in a slow, deep breath.

"The Spirit of the Lord is upon me," the man crooned, raising his hands and snapping open his eyes, "because he hath anointed me to preach the gospel to the poor. He hath sent me to heal the brokenhearted, to preach deliverance to the captives, and recovering of sight to the blind, to set at liberty them that are bruised, and to preach the acceptable year of the Lord."

Gapinski snorted a laugh. "Uh, dude, messiah complex much?"

"Good call, kiddo," Eddie said. "Sounds vaguely like what Jesus declared about himself."

Silas said, "You're right. The fulfillment of Isaiah's scroll in Luke's Gospel."

"But that's what I was about to tell you—"

"This day this Scripture is fulfilled in your ears!" Judah boomed with interruption.

The roar was deafening, drowning out any further conversation with Eddie.

"*Sí. Complejo de mesías mayor!*" Torres exclaimed above the din.

No translation needed on that one. Major messiah complex was right!

Now Judah had placed a hand on Simón's head, and he asked what he would like him to do for him—if he could have anything in all the world, what would he want.

Without missing a beat, the boy replied, "*Quiero ver!*"

"What's he saying?" asked Silas.

"He…" Torres swallowed, face draining of color some. "He said, he wants to see."

Silas squinted, shaking his head in confusion.

"Sonofa—" Gapinski let the curse die again, turning to the other three. "It's like I feared. He's using this kid!"

Before Silas could ask how, Judah answered for him: "It shall be done, *mijo*."

Hand still resting upon his head, he declared Simón healed and snapped his fingers, then stepped back with arms extended. A mixture between standing in awe of what he had done but also waiting for something to happen.

Then it did.

A beat, then another, then a squeal.

At first it sounded like terror, but it quickly turned to joy.

"Puedo ver!" the boy shouted. *"Puedo ver!"*

"What's he saying?" asked Gapinski.

Silas didn't need any translation. He knew what he was saying. What had happened.

"I can see…" Torres answered.

"This is why I wanted to leave," Eddie said, having to shout now above a rising din of praise and adoration. "It's what I saw. And there's more."

"Do you doubt now?" Judah roared, those arms still wide.

"No!" people shouted.

Then others: *"Give him to us!"*

Still more: *"Where is our god?"*

He laughed. Not mocking, not ridiculing.

Delighting.

"You want your god? You *ready* for your god?"

*Yes*es and *Sí*s flooded the chamber.

Until the room plunged into darkness.

CHAPTER 30

LOS ANGELES.

It wasn't long until Celeste and her Group X companions, along with the queue of spiritual seekers, were ushered into an expansive auditorium that curved along with the spaceship design of the facility. It looked and smelled brand new. She had assumed this building had been long in the making, but perhaps the Aeon campus had been erected only recently.

For what reason exactly, other than peddling Sebastian's twisted brand of spiritual enlightenment—that was yet to be determined.

A wall of thick glass stood high at their backs, the sunshine having dimmed to that mustard, almost smoky haze high in the sky but still shining through. Cream carpet paved the floor beneath an array of bamboo wood benches arranged facing a large stage of the same light golden color. The scent of fresh carpet and paint and wood varnish laced the air, a coolness descending from the HVAC working overtime to quell the rising temperatures from all the bodies.

A harpist was anchored to stage right, dressed in white silk and strumming on the large golden instrument glinting in an array of stage lights shining a bright white. At the center of the stage stood a glass lectern, flanked by potted bamboo shoots.

"What's with all the bamboo?" asked Elijah, sweeping a hand around the room as they settled in a pew at the back. "Bamboo benches. Bamboo walls and stage. Bamboo bamboo!"

A swelling applause cut him off as someone strode on stage. And not just any someone.

Sebastian Grey.

He was as Celeste recalled him the last she saw, which was quite up close and personal, him and his co-conspirator, that Aurelius Chuke fellow, having absconded with her and Naomi Torres. Same scaly, almost translucent skin. Same larger-than normal height and bulk. Same fiery eyes and extra-digit fingers.

Curiously, he was wearing black vestments with crimson piping. Almost like a priest or even a cardinal would wear.

A pagan priest for a pagan cult of spiritually hungry people searching for any semblance of hope during desperate times.

Whilst the crowd continued their thunderous welcome, a passage of Scripture popped into her mind. From Matthew's Gospel, during a moment upon the apostle chronicling Christ's early ministry touring cities and villages, preaching about the kingdom of God and healing the sick: *'When he saw the crowds, he had compassion for them because they were harassed and help-less, like sheep without a shepherd. Then he said to his disciples, 'The harvest is plentiful, but the laborers are few; therefore ask the Lord of the harvest to send out laborers into his harvest.'*

Celeste glanced down the row, catching sight of a woman whose eyes were welling with emotion—welling with hope. They all were, looking to Sebastian to ameliorate what harassed them. How had he framed it? *"Life is confusing. It doesn't have to be that way."* She reckoned that's what anyone was looking for during these desperate, confusing times, with headlines about falling capitals and besieged nations, about decimated stock portfolios and drought-stricken communities

—about a bloomin' nuclear explosion that threatened the security and stability of this very nation!

Who would come and put things to rights? Who would save them?

How would Sebastian?

Looked like they were all about to find out.

The man grasped the lectern with both hands, eyeing the crowd as it wound down its applause. Taking another beat, he flashed a grin and began.

"Welcome fellow enlightened travelers! The dawning of a new spiritual age is upon us! One the prophet from Nazareth himself had prophesied when he spoke of needing new wineskins to hold the new wine of a new dawning spiritual kingdom. Only this one is fit for a *republic*."

Celeste caught Nous's messaging there, transforming Jesus' spiritual messaging concerning the in-breaking of God's righteous reign upon Earth in the hearts of mankind into a secular message concerning the in-breaking of humanistic, individualized rule.

"There is something within the Universe itself, something we find in all of the great spiritual traditions just waiting to be tapped into. The sublime, the ground of our being that undergirds the entire Universe. It is the universal human ideal that has revealed itself in human existence through such people as the man from Nazareth. That man somehow grasped, in word and deed, the highest human ideal. And it is this spirit that he sought to impart to his followers through his earthly life, and what 'we' can grasp through human gumption and ingenuity and progress."

Sebastian paused to take a sip of water, taking in his audience, sweeping it from stage right to center to—

He halted his sweep and held his glass to his lips.

Locking eyes with Celeste.

Or so it bloody well seemed! For the briefest of moments, time hung in the balance between confusion and recognition.

And activation...

A ping of adrenaline jolted her heart and snatched her breath, a metallic tang racing across her tongue even as it went chalky. She found herself slinking down in her seat, not leaving his gaze but trying to race along its connection to sense whatever it was that might have been transpiring.

Had he seen her, really, truly? They were so far back, and those bloomin' stage lights should very well have shielded his vision. But—

She could not be sure.

Finishing his sip, time snapping back to order, he set the glass down on a shelf beneath the lectern. He drew his arm to his nose, rubbing it and—

She sucked in a breath of recognition, and that adrenaline returned, in force now.

For that gesture, as innocuous as it seemed, also carried with it the slightest of moving lips. As if he were whispering something into his sleeve.

Movement caught her attention. On stage and off-stage.

A door had opened, and a small woman was striding toward Sebastian. Looked as though she were bearing something before slipping it into his hand, then she strode back through the door and closed it.

Celeste eased a relieved sigh through parted lips. That was it then. Perhaps he realized he had forgotten something. Nothing to worry about.

Sebastian returned to his speech: "Now, Christianity would have you believe that the prophet from Nazareth's death was important, but I am here to tell you differently. His *life* was far more significant than his death. His ideal life of love is what matters! His death is simply the culmination of that life, showing us what it looks like to live the universal human ideal embedded in the Universe itself. We need a new story to repair and heal us, and he provided humanity the solution through his teachings and example of higher living that transcends this chaotic one. Which the prophet from Nazareth offered as a kingdom of heaven. I come with some far better!"

Celeste forgot about the exposing moment, or whatever it was, heart racing as the man spoke, a rage rising at him wielding Jesus as a talisman to shape his own narrative concerning human salvation.

There was something incredibly subversive to what he was saying. Of course there was some truth to it, too. Jesus' teachings about human dignity and justice and neighbor-love have been the bedrock of civilization stretching back centuries— things anyone should build their life upon. But his life doesn't save us. The Church has always taught his death does! So what was Sebastian going on about?

The chamber erupted in thunderous applause, clearly buying into this revisionist religious nonsense.

"The invitation I offer into the Republic of Heaven is an invitation into the Age of the God-Man. The entire human experience has been one of constantly emerging from what we are into what we can become, this better version of ourselves tapping into the universal human ideal of love. The prophet from Nazareth understood this, as did others after him. And I aim to speed that process up of *becoming*."

Sebastian let go of the lectern now and started pacing, his hulking bulk a sight to behold as he strode across the stage, fixing his audience with wide, inviting eyes.

"Unlike what the Church has insisted, the truth is that the prophet from Nazareth's death was a paradigm, like any of the ancient myths that have governed our collective unconscious for this salvation. We join with the prophet from Nazareth in dying—to our pride and agendas as a witness to the justice of the Republic of Heaven. His resurrection symbolizes the same, a rising to new, unencumbered life!"

"Bullfeathers!" Elijah said, a bit too loudly for Celeste's taste.

"Chill, Eli!" Gina hissed.

He huffed a sigh and folded his arms. "But it is. Completely contradicts historic Christianity."

Celeste agreed. The Bible taught Christ's power was in what he did on the cross by willingly offering himself as a sacrifice to pay the price of our sins in our place. Not Jesus' life, not merely his teachings and example of love, as Sebastian was going on about. And his resurrection was not merely a *symbol*; his actual, bodily, physical resurrection is the heart of the faith—marking the end to sin's reign and the beginning of God's new reign. Because if the prophet from Nazareth—as he framed Christ— is still dead, we're still screwed!

Now that she considered it, Celeste wondered why he was leveraging him this way. Why he had introduced Jesus Christ into a message to potential followers for some big unveiling. Having a further think about it, she saw a slight of hand there in that naming convention.

Not Jesus, or Christ. The prophet from Nazareth. What was that about?

Regardless, Celeste recalled something an early Church Father had said regarding just such a person. Bishop Polycarp of Smyrna: '*And whosoever does not confess the testimony of the cross is of the devil. Whosoever perverts the sayings of Christ and what the Lord taught does so to suit his own sinful desires. These people say that there is neither a resurrection nor a judgment. The first-born of Satan, they are!*'

Supposed that was the truth of it. The man was the Devil incarnate. And dragging the masses down into the depths of hell.

"We do not need saving from our sins," Sebastian went on.

"No no no! We need saving from *ourselves*. We need a revolution to aid in the evolutionary progress of humanity, something to push the human race forward by revealing to us the universal ideal in a way that makes sense of our human condition. Placing man squarely at the center of our spirituality. All this was crystalized when I read the words of a very spiritual man. Friedrich Schleiermacher. The father of progressive Christianity. He sought to—how shall we say it, *amend* the Christian faith."

"Amend? *Bah!*" Elijah said, voice rising far too loudly. "Twisted and bludgeoned to death the Christian—"

Gina shushed him whilst Celeste cringed. She ducked behind a woman, hoping to avoid a repeat of before.

Sebastian did seem to cast his gaze their way, but he carried on: "Schleiermacher taught a feeling of absolute dependence and connection with the universal human ideal exists in every religion. As the good German put it, *'in every religion the God-consciousness...is attached to some relation of the self-consciousness,'* or to personal experience."

He laughed, an almost giddy joy at sharing his discovery.

"Meaning, the Universe itself is humming with the divine, and we can all tap into it! When I came upon these words, they shifted my entire perspective on religion and my own vocation. What he discovered is the fundamental reality that there is *a God hiding within us all!*"

He shouted that last part, that God is *'hiding within us all,'* which was classic Nous, the alt-spiritual cult spewing such nonsense since the foundation of the Church. After all, that's what Nous meant. The concept was some primeval inner divine consciousness, a taproot into a pagan notion of what it means to be human, mingling humanity and divinity.

A sudden awareness of a passage from Scripture hit Celeste. Genesis 6. When the divine sons of God—those spiritual beings that Elijah had spoken of in previous operations for

SEPIO, and then as an investigator with Group X—in an unholy existential breach, copulated with human women.

Celeste sat straighter, unconcerned about being spotted.

Was that what Sebastian was attempting to recreate?

She glanced about, glimpsing the head-nods of everyone around her. Was that their own expectation, these people come to drink from Sebastian's font of divine remaking?

"That moment is now!" Sebastian boomed. "That dawn is arriving. Our Authority has gifted us the means to remake humanity into our own image, imbuing us with what he always intended us to possess. Not to wage war against us but to wage war on our behalf, carrying the human race into the next iteration of our evolution. This is your portal into the realm of the Homo Deus!"

"Fruit cake, that guy is," Elijah huffed, crossing his arms.

"About the long and short of it, mate," Celeste agreed.

Gina turned to them both. "OK. So the man is a few fries short of a Happy Meal. What does it mean for our operation? For them?"

A jolly good question.

Celeste glanced at the stage. Where Sebastian was now holding something aloft.

A vial. Shimmering in the stage light. Undulating in a spectrum of colors that—

She gasped, her breath catching in her throat and heart lurching forward with recognition.

That looked very much like that fruit from that tree in the Garden!

"This is your redemption!" Sebastian boomed again, stepping to the edge of the stage and holding that vial out toward the audience. "This is your *salvation*! For you will be like the gods, your mind—nay, your very *soul* connected to their divine realm and opened up to all of the possibilities they have promised since the dawn of time. Not merely knowing good and evil, but deciding it. *For yourselves!*"

Elijah sat straight. Eyes wide and mouth flopping open. "Oh. My—"

"Cheeps..." Gina finished for him.

"Hey, that's my line."

"The fruit. From the garden." She turned to him and Celeste, gesturing toward the center of the Aeon compound.

"Nope. *Thee* garden," Elijah corrected.

The doors to the auditorium suddenly opened, and several people came waltzing inside. Looking very similar to Sebastian. Black robes, crimson piping. All bearing something on bamboo trays.

Were those vials? Syringes, even?

They began to distribute them to those who had gathered.

Elijah stood. "Sweet mother of Melchizedek!"

Celeste joined. "I see them."

"The vials," Gina moaned. "Of–Of–Of whatever the hey-ho day that fruitcake has on stage!"

They had to stop this.

And fast.

"Ma'am, come with us."

The voice was low and insistent. Commanding, even. And totally not expected. Barely registered, really—

Until an arm seized her own.

CHAPTER 31

Celeste snapped her attention to her arm, then to a rather large brute. Head bulbous, all neck. Wearing all black. Who was joined by several more security personnel.

"Unhand me!" she commanded, yanking her arm but finding no relief.

He yanked harder, carting her into the aisle, three more goons gunning for her companions.

"Be gentle, dude," Elijah complained. "I'm breakable!"

"How rude!" Gina echoed. It was no use.

The one goon quickly ushered Celeste from her row toward the auditorium entrance, Gina and Elijah close behind, the pair giving the goons hell. Good on them!

"What is the meaning of this?" Celeste demanded.

"You're trespassing on private property," Bulbous Goon grunted.

She scoffed. "By invitation of the telly!"

"Not anymore. Not for you three. On order of the Grand Master."

Her heart sank with recognition. The hand gesture, his moving lips, their locking eyes. So there it was.

They were ushered out into the waning day and told to leave. The glass doors whooshed behind, Celeste catching an audible lock. Four of the goons stood guard, which she thought was overkill.

"Well that was short-lived," Gina said, promptly withdrawing a packet of gum and then two sticks wrapped in shimmering foil. She unwrapped them then she shoved them in her mouth. Both of them.

Elijah leaned in, explaining, "Gum helps center her. One of the ways she stims. Stimulates, like me with my finger tick."

Celeste nodded, gesturing for them to get on with it, leading them back to their car. Supposed Sebastian had seen her after all. Or maybe Elijah's outburst soured things. Either way, they were out of luck—and with a massive new lead that needed investigating.

But what was in that vial? And why were they being distributed to all the other visitors? What was meant for them to take it?

"Chewing gum," Gina explained, drawing Celeste's attention back to her agent, "with the work it takes to grind them into a chewy pulp, the fresh spearmint dancing across my taste buds, the smell of minty heaven filling my nostrils—all of it helps focus my attention away from the moment and back toward a centering calm."

"The curse of being an autistic person," Elijah said.

"Though my personal autism spectrum wheel isn't as complicated as some people similarly challenged with neurodiversity, it still sucks."

"Neurodiversity. Word."

"The gum helps."

Elijah turned to her with a smile. "Hey, isn't there some connection with that Wrigley's packet and your twin?"

Gina's eyes went wide, and she started chewing faster, nodding before swallowing. "Yeah yeah yeah. Those silly '90s commercials from childhood, the ones featuring twins and that—"

"Double your pleasure, double your fun," Elijah finished. "Loved those twins. Still dream about the two blonds from time to time."

What felt like a klick later, they managed to find their vehicle.

Elijah flopped his arms against the passenger's side, slumping his head against the roof. "Now what?"

Walking across the rear, Celeste went to answer, when—

Someone nailed her in the shoulder.

"Oy, mate—" She spun to interrogate them, but they kept going. A small figure wearing white, black hair shoved under a straw hat. A woman, near as she gathered.

Looking oddly familiar.

"Come along," she simply said, taking cautious steps in pursuit before picking up the pace.

"What's the dealio?" Gina asked, coming to her side.

She ignored her, keeping her eyes trained on the figure, who had darted between a charcoal minivan and navy SUV, and hustling her pursuit.

Celeste darted through those same vehicles out into a main stretch of road.

Only to lose the suspect.

Celeste spun around, panting and sweating, confused by the turn of things.

She was right there!

Elijah and Gina caught up. He said, "Where's the fire—"

"Jerry McGuire?" Gina finished.

Celeste ignored them, muttering to herself, "Where did she go?"

"Who?" asked Elijah.

The faint echo of a starting vehicle drew her attention.

Behind. Back where they had come.

Must have doubled back around and gone farther on. Perhaps sensed she was being followed.

Celeste cursed herself for the misstep. Life as an office grafter the past year, doing the hard work of pushing papers and attending board meetings as Order Master, had dulled her skills.

Squealing tires and a revving engine snagged her attention and snapped her back to it.

A few rows of cars on from her position.

Without a moment's hesitation, Celeste took off—shouts of protest and inquiry from her teammates not staying her feet.

She had to catch her. Had to see if her gut sense of things proved true.

The parking lot wound around to the single-track road, the only exit off the compound, so Celeste made for that, weaving through rows of parked cars even as the rogue figure wound their own way toward their own destiny. She didn't have it in mind to stop the car. Throwing oneself in front of a motor fleeing through a parking lot in haste never worked in actual life. She aimed to catch a glimpse, perhaps even snap a picture.

Elijah and Gina continued their questioning remarks from behind, Eli far more verbally animated about it, although Gina had a few cursing zingers of her own.

Celeste ignored them, coming up to a bright green berm sandwiched between the car park and road leading on toward the entrance. She snatched her mobile from her pocket and aimed for a pickup truck barreling her way.

It raced by and she snapped a picture, then another, catching sight of large almond eyes set in a soft brown face with long black hair flowing around narrow shoulders.

Then she was gone, making her escape from—

An explosion split through the midafternoon air.

From behind. With enough shoving force to toss Celeste

onto the grass. Gina and Elijah faced the same stumbling assault.

It was instantly apparent why.

Flowers of fire and blooming acrid smoke rose high above the Aeon Foundation compound.

Another shattering blast. From the side, with gouts of fire bursting in a torrent of glass. Then another, all around the compound. One right after another.

"Sweet mother of Melchizedek!" Elijah exclaimed, racing to Celeste's side.

Gina quickly followed, gasping with a hand on her mouth and shaking her head. "All those people..."

Celeste's first thought was how to bring some measure of salvation to the many hundreds who had gathered, but with the ratcheting inferno and smoke—they were doomed.

A second thought quickly chased that one: Sebastian.

The trio sat huddled against a silver sedan, silent and contemplative and uncertain.

Celeste couldn't make sense of the turn, something so violent visiting Nous in this fashion. Sebastian's Aeon outpost of modern spirituality was no more.

Someone had set off a bomb, several, the furious, flapping flames shooting high and wide. Surely the New Age temple would be consumed.

And she had a hunch who was responsible.

She had to reach Silas.

———

A SHUDDER RIPPLED through the Sikorsky S-70M helicopter, a cousin to the Black Hawk that big brother had swooped in on to do Uncle Sam's bidding during his Rambo days. Had always despised such things, the trappings of imperial machinery far more beholden to the brutish nature of man than the brainy nature he had identified with.

Yet, there he was, ensconced in such machinery. Granted, luxurious machinery, with polished wood paneling complemented by gilt edging, the smell of supple baby goatskin and fresh carpet. It was all a balm for his frayed nerves.

Only now, this one, the leather-wrapped armrest soft under Sebastian's white-knuckle grip, had raced from a scene from one of those iconic movies. Had nearly been engulfed in the maw of death and destruction had it not been for some no-name lackey ushering him through an underground escape tunnel to the awaiting chopper. That man, whoever he was, definitely needed a raise after that act of heroism. And dedication.

Because someone, some moleish man or woman had betrayed him. Surely as the nose on his face!

Felt bad leaving all of those people behind—his people, his *followers*. The ones who had hung on every one of his words. Wondered if that's what big brother had felt. Doc Grey the Magnificent, teaching the masses and spoon feeding his religious slop into awaiting baby-bird mouths.

No matter. He had to save his own hide in order to keep the candlelight burning on Nous's designs for the world.

And their intentions for the Church.

Because, mark his words, the show would go on. Sebastian Grey would have his way!

He had instructed the pilot to circle back around to the Aeon compound, regretting his decision now as some other wing exploded with a plume of fire and ash and acrid smoke.

It all lay in ruin...

Everything he had built the past year, and beyond. He had inherited the Aeon Foundation, the organization and Nous front he had stumbled upon through Eli Denton. Ironically, a mutual connection between him and Silas. He had been summoned to con big brother into verifying a false Christian gospel, which had been a ruse. When he became Grand Master of Nous a few years ago, one of the first things he had done was lay the groundwork for expanding the one Rome campus to multiple sites across the globe. He figured if those mousey Evangelical sheeple could churn out all those multi-site church campuses for mass consumption, why not Nous—why not *him*?

Once the final piece to the equation fell in his lap—the fruit from the Tree of Knowledge—combined with what Malia had discovered, what she had introduced him to and where she enabled him to visit...

Sebastian glanced outside, the chopper continuing its holding pattern until he told the pilot otherwise.

Spouts of water hissed arches of wicked steaming white. Acrid black smoke still billowed, though the rise of fingering flames of orange looked like they had been stayed. But his beautiful building was pockmarked by open wounds, one side having completely collapsed.

And the center garden—the Tree!

Luckily the original sample still survived, stuffed away inside Nous's HQ in Germany. Still—

It all lay in ruin, the complex matrix of sprinklers having doused most of the flames now, even as the fire department finally dragged its sorry asses to stay the inferno.

No one would trust him now. How could they after he lost the crown jewel of his spiritual empire?

How could the Thirteen—the Council of Five...

The thought cut him to the quick, and for the first time in a long time he felt genuine fear. An actual coldness pluming from his chest and spreading throughout his body. His heartbeat thrummed against his ribcage, breath was hard to come by, and a watery feeling in his bowels made him seriously consider commanding the pilot to drop him off at LAX so he could get on the first plane to Fiji to retire amidst sun and sand.

No. This could be salvaged.

It *would* be salvaged!

Shifting, he felt something hard in his pocket, and he felt a modicum of relief.

The vial. His vial. The one that had opened the pathway for him to reach the Unseen Realm.

Slipping his hand inside the pocket, he retrieved it and stared into its rainbow luminescence.

At least it was safe. The antidote to all humanity's problems. The only saving grace from the bloody affair.

He leaned back and sank into the plush comforts of luxury, thirsting for a sturdy Malbec red wine with backbone, but knowing he needed to keep his wits about him. What would he do now? Where would he turn? How would he salvage this disaster—where would he even begin?

How would he atone for it?

A gentle tap yanked him from his thoughts.

Sebastian thought it was Chuke. He glanced over at him and found his commander talking quietly into a satphone, a massive hand clenching the black brick and eyes darting over his shoulder at him. One of his dreadlocks had fallen loose from that large hive of hair crowning his head. It lay across his military uniform that he had carried from his warlord days. It comforted Sebastian to see it, the uniform and loose braid, knowing it had fallen in the rush to extract him, the Nous Grand Master. Although, Chuke had seemed to have been more worried about himself, the man already at their escape helicopter instead of tending to his safety. He wondered who he was chatting with now. Probably just making preparations for their vengeful response.

It was actually one of Sebastian's Nousati agents at his side. A spritely blond fellow that spread a similar soothing warmth in his belly. The lad was hovering with a tablet, a video appearing to have been queued.

"Sir, you need to see this," he said.

Sebastian sat upright, training his eyes on the device. His operative played it. He sat still, unmoving.

Dumbfounded.

For racing across a security camera, several of them, all strung together in succession with a red rectangle warning of danger, was a figure. Body lean in white, hair black and fallen from beneath a hat, face a soft brown and eyes large almonds— and infuriatingly familiar.

"What am I looking at?" Sebastian asked, the inkling of an answer needling the back of his head, one he couldn't face on his own.

"The perpetrator of the Aeon campus destruction."

"Where did you get this?"

"From Nous servers. As you can see, it is security footage from the moments leading to the explosion that destroyed the building."

Malia Perez...

The one person he had trusted to carry on his life's work. To not only supply the antidote to humanity's worries, and scale it to production in a way that would actually transform the human race—and usher in the Republic of Heaven. But also to take care of the competition. To monitor it, learn from it, then squash it like a bug.

And she had turned on him.

Worse than that: She had sided with the enemy! Chose her former lover, that Judah Howell moron, instead of him.

He was going to kill her!

He had been double crossed. Twice now! And it all led back to Theoti. To that Sha character.

And now to Judah Howell.

Gripping the vial in a clenched fist, he called out, "Make for Ukiah."

A beat later, the Sikorsky dipped north and Sebastian sank back into the plush leather.

He had to make this right.

He *would* make this right.

Judah Howell would pay.

As would Malia Perez.

Now it was time to show that little wench and her messianic boy toy what was what.

And who was who.

CHAPTER 32

UKIAH.

That chorus of delight quickly turned to cries of panic.

A beat later, a set of lights at the corners snapped to life. Emergency lights. Didn't do much to quell the confusion, and Silas wondered along with them what the heck had just happened.

"What the heck just happened?" Torres voiced for him.

The darkened glass walls returned to their natural state of illumination, the sky still a hazy, muddy brown turning toward evening now.

Silas said, "Doesn't look like a storm could have knocked out the power.

"This is California," Gapinski said with a snorting laugh. "Don't need no storm for rolling brownouts thanks to mismanagement."

"Stay calm!" Judah called out. "All will be righted shortly and you shall have your revelation!"

He spun to Noland Rotberg, who had just appeared on stage. Looked furious, too. Arms waving and hands jutting at the floor for some reason, then to a screen at one end that had those color bars showing some sort of interruption. Nope, not a happy camper.

Went on like this for a few more minutes, until Judah announced a slight delay in his revelation. Although he was still on track for the August 17 D-Day date, tomorrow morning.

"Maybe we should scram, chief," Gapinski said. "Before the Moonies start getting restless and tear the place apart."

Silas nodded. "Good idea."

Torres led the way, Gapinski and Eddie following while he made up the rear. Kept an eye on Judah Howell, the man still going at it with Rotberg who gestured like he didn't have any answer to his questions, one of which seemed to be about that screen. What they were discussing—what had happened...that would have to wait. They had enough on their plates to figure out. Not the least of which was this nonsense about revealing some god to the world. And those signs, those wonders?

Again, not good...

Outside was surprisingly cool, a breeze lazy but inviting after that stuffy, staid atmosphere inside the Theoti temple. Sky still looked like a muddy mess of haze, the sun blotted with an apocalyptic vibe. Smelled funny, too. Like burning tires, so maybe that was the answer. Which ratcheted up the stakes.

They walked across the fresh pavement, making for their commandeered Silverado.

"OK, can I just say," Gapinski said, "that was crazier than a one-legged jack rabbit!"

"*Sí, muy loco,*" Torres said.

"That's not the craziest part..." Eddie said on a breathless whisper.

There was a sweaty sheen to his face, and it had drained of color some. Looked almost clammy, like he was coming down with something.

Sensing Silas's gaze, the man took out a handkerchief and wiped his forehead. "I get this way after getting a word."

"What word?" Gapinski questioned.

"From the Lord."

Took a beat to get his meaning.

Then he did.

"Another prophetic vision?" asked Silas.

Eddie nodded then glanced around, over the roof of some two-door import and around the backside of a Chrysler minivan.

"About what?" Silas pressed.

He shook his head. "No. Not here."

Stepping between the cars, he motioned for them to follow.

Eddie led them across an open lawn, green and lush and clearly manicured. Looked like where that Judah character had made it rain yesterday. A massive oak tree with sprawling limbs and leaves waving lazily in that breeze sat a ways down. The man hustled for it.

Silas had barely reached the tree when Eddie turned to him: "You have to listen. It's what I was trying to tell you before. The song. The woman. The—"

"Whoa, slow down, Eddie!" he said, putting up a hand. "What's this about?"

Torres and Gapinski gathered next to Silas, the trio waiting for Eddie to share.

"It was that song. It triggered something, I suppose."

"What something?" asked Silas.

"As you said, a prophetic vision. It was all so clear, those same words. Except someone else was singing it."

"*Quien fue?*" asked Torres. "Who?"

"Some woman."

"*Una mujer?*"

"*Sí, una mujer. Ella era alta, con un cuerpo cuadrado y alrededor de la cabeza y—*"

Gapinski laughed. "Como say what, hombre?"

"English might suit us better," Silas said.

Eddie seemed to catch himself, grinning and reddening a

shade. "Sorry. I've learned to slip easily into several languages —" He waved his hands around. "Doesn't matter."

Torres interjected, "You were saying she was tall, with a square body and round head."

"*Sí*—I mean. Yes. That's right."

"That sound familiar, *jefe*?"

She looked at Silas, and he nodded. Sure did.

"Theoti. Their symbol, taken from their root spirituality, Mandaeism."

Eddie adjusted his silver glasses, wiping his forehead again. "I don't know anything about Mandaeism. All I know is this woman had glowing blue hair, and it looked like tentacles—wrapped around her head and strung from behind, waving and snapping and latching on to other people's heads, the men and women in white."

"Creepy..." Gapinski shuddered. "Sounds like Medusa!"

"The Greek goddess is a good description. I also caught a tattoo on her forehead."

"What kind of tattoo?" asked Torres.

"A word. Mana."

Didn't ring a bell. Silas asked, "Anything else you can think of?"

Eddie leaned against the tree, shaking his head. "The gong snapped me out of it before I had a chance to get more of the download."

He put a hand on the man's shoulder. "Thanks for sharing. We'll look into it when we debrief with the others."

He managed a smile, closing his eyes and leaning his head back.

Silas planted his hands on his hips and surveyed the surrounding land, that cool breeze from before dying and the heat of the day making his own brow sweat now.

The compound spread down the way from the oak tree past the gleaming snow globe glass temple. That collection of buildings at the entrance gathered around a center courtyard with a bubbling fountain, windows arrayed on the three stories. Probably dormitories and other offices. A low-slung, one-story building stood closer. Long and wide, with a pool outside, a trail of smoke rising with the scent of grilled meat and roasted vegetables. Maybe a kitchen and cafeteria, or another meeting hall.

Then there was the largest of the buildings. A warehouse the size of a football field. Which Caleb Harris had circled on that map, the one charred to a crisp.

Silas leaned a shoulder against the tree, intrigued yet worried about what might be inside.

"Whatcha thinking, Silas?" asked Gapinski.

"That all our intel went up in smoke and I don't like being in the dark."

"What do you have in mind?"

"Care to have a look around the joint?"

He grinned. "You know snooping is my love language!"

"Have anything in mind?" asked Torres.

Silas nodded toward that imposing warehouse. Like the Hoya field house from Georgetown it was so sprawling.

She asked, "What do you suppose is going on in that thing?"

Silas replied, "Caleb had quite a few pictures of that, didn't he?"

"Yeah, but only of the outside. He'd snapped only inside those buildings. The orphanage, the dormitories, the church we just came from."

"None on the inside of that warehouse?"

"Nope."

"Wonder why?" Gapinski said.

"Probably couldn't get inside," Silas replied.

"Which means they've got it locked down."

"And tight."

"On a need-to-enter basis."

"Think they're hiding something?" Eddie chimed in now.

"Only one way to find out," Silas replied.

Gapinski grinned. "Like I said, snooping is my—"

"Yeah yeah yeah," Torres interrupted. "Love language, Hoss. TMI."

The white robes started emerging from the glass temple, a spread of scuttling ducks wondering what to do next after being denied their revelation. Silas wasted no time leading the group toward the warehouse.

It stood about a klick away, the same large oaks and several clumps of shrubs and younger trees grouped along one end. Again, about as large as a field house, soaring five stories and stretching at least the length of a football field, probably 60,000 square feet. No windows anywhere. No power lines or cables running into it, which were probably buried anyway.

A path snaked toward the main area of the compound, the buildings that greeted them upon entering offering a nice shield from prying eyes. He went that way, pushing through the foliage to the other side.

And coming up to a door.

No one and nothing stirred down the path. Same at the door and around the warehouse.

Silas motioned for the group to join him at the entrance. Maybe this was the break they needed. This went a bit beyond snooping. Though a little breaking-and-entering never hurt nobody.

Padding up to it, he snatched a glance over his shoulder, then tugged at the door.

Nothing.

Gave not a millimeter. Threw up not even a rattle. Sealed tight.

"What's the deal with this black thing?" Gapinski asked, waving his hand across it.

That black thing sprang to life, an image of his palm flaring with a blinking white.

"Sonofa—" An angry red and even angrier grunting no-go alert cut off his curse.

"Way to go, Hoss!" Torres hissed, looking around. "Now the whole dang compound's gonna be on high-alert."

"Sorry!"

Silas darted a glance behind, down the path, seeing no one approaching. The door didn't open either, and nothing sounded from the other side. Not even a camera stood guard, which seemed odd.

Had no interest in getting caught, so he motioned for the group to keep at the hunt.

Torres led the way, creeping down the length of the one side. Sun, as shrouded in the muddy haze as it was with that ongoing eclipse or whatever, was on the other side cresting toward evening, so the shadows served them well. High grass and weeds along the wall snatched at his legs with protesting hisses and insects seemed to sense their invasive intent, jumping and screeching a warning.

She came up fast to the corner and went to edge around it—

When she snapped back.

"*Para!*" Torres commanded, putting out a staying hand to hold it.

Silas stopped short behind her. Gapinski sounded like he lumbered into Eddie.

"Watch it, kiddo," the man complained.

"Sorry!"

Torres motioned toward her eyes with two fingers and around the corner, then to Silas, saying nothing. Then she stepped out of the way for his own viewing.

He edged to the corner and took a quick peek. Around and back.

Seeing the problem. And also an opportunity.

A loading dock, with a parked delivery truck. Black and no logos or insignias except for US Department of Transportation numbers on the driver's side door.

Gapinski did the same, then Eddie, the four settling back.

Gapinski said, "No windows, one door guarded by a palm-reading entry pad, and a loading dock—what's it mean?"

"In my line of work, kiddo," Eddie replied lowly, "windowless warehouses with loading docks on compounds in the middle of nowhere means something. And usually nothing good. Especially when there are palm-reading entry pads involved."

Silas withdrew his phone, seeing an awaiting text from Celeste. She said something major had gone down in LA and to rendezvous at a SEPIO safe house at an old Franciscan monastery in their neck of the woods. Fine by him. Only one thing left before they called it a day.

He snapped a picture, then another—

When a goon stepped into view looking like he belonged in a Bond movie.

Would have expected someone in chaps and a Western yoke cowboy shirt with matching fedora hat, a Colt, maybe a Ruger, strapped to his side.

Nope. All black and definitely an AR-15 assault rifle, the cousin to the Army's M16. Same ammo capacity as the military's favorite rifle, 30 bullets made to count. But heavier, a shorter range, and a slower rate of fire.

Big question: Why here?

Bigger question: Why this building?

He motioned to head back to that oak a klick up the way, bending a bit and hustling from view. They got what they needed. But—

Something caught his attention.

From the corner of his eye.

From behind.

In a flash.

Dark and descending from the rooftop. Large and looming.

On instinct, Silas wrenched his Beretta from his waist at his back and whipped it toward the figure.

But a smacking crack sent lancing pain through his hand and the gun sailing to the ground somewhere in the shadows.

His one good hand.

And he was sent to the ground with a solid kick to the gut.

Sending him crouching for breath.

Before Torres and Gapinski were activated, there was an unexpected turn.

Suddenly, Eddie jumped in the air and spun around, landing a solid roundhouse kick to the hostile's solar plexus!

The goon stumbled back, clutching his chest and wheezing a breath.

He finished him off with another hop and another kick straight into his face.

Snapping the hostile's neck back and sending him to the ground.

Eddie was on him in a flash, wrapping a surprisingly thick forearm for his age around his neck. The goon gave a half-hearted struggle, but a few beats later he went limp.

Out cold. Just like that.

"Holybamoly Batman!" Gapinski exclaimed. "That was amazing. Like Jason Bourne's grandpappy popped out of nowhere and laid down the smack! How'd you do that?"

Eddie shrugged. "I do have a green belt in karate, but I have to thank the FBI survival training I received from Quantico for that one."

"What for?"

"That's classified," he said with a wink.

"Gotta say, *muchacho*," Torres said, "if I was ten years older I might just plant a kiss on those rosy cheeks of yours!"

He laughed. "You still can."

Now she giggled, turning shyly away before giving the old man a peck.

They both laughed, deflating the tension some.

"Just glad you're on our side," Silas said, retrieving his Beretta.

Gapinski bent to his knees and checked over the downed hostile.

"Finders keepers..." he announced, holding up a Sig Sauer pistol—with a silencer.

"What about his wrists, the back of his neck?"

"What's there?" asked Eddie.

"You'll see..."

Gapinski flipped him over, yanking off his black ski mask.

Nothing at the neck.

Then one sleeve was yanked back. More nothing at Wrist One.

Then the other.

Bingo.

Two intersecting lines, like a cross. Top and bottom ends bent down, the two ends at the left and right bent inward.

Like a bird.

Nous...

Gapinski stood, him and Torres standing by in silence.

Eddie broke it: "Can somebody tell me what that tattoo means already?"

"It's Nous," Silas answered.

"Sebastian's outfit."

"That's right."

Torres gestured up top, grabbing the end of a rappelling rope Silas hadn't noticed. "What do you think a Nous agent was doing in this warehouse?"

"And what does it mean," Gapinski added, "that a Nous

agent was sent to do whatever the hey-ho day he was doing in this warehouse?"

"Suppose that confirms Nous and Theoti had a falling out."

Silas frowned. Good questions. And good point.

What indeed...

Voices stirred nearby. Around the corner, from that dock.

Nearing voices.

"We better scram, chief," Torres said.

And they did, darting back around to the front and through the foliage, making for their commandeered Silverado.

But not before Silas took a parting glance behind at the mystery.

Something was going on in that warehouse. Enough that a Nous operative had just come from doing Lord only knew what inside.

And Silas was going to figure out what.

CHAPTER 33

SAN FRANCISCO.

Celeste awoke alone to the smell of frying hardwood bacon, melting cheese, and strong coffee. She and Silas had to find separate sleeping quarters, as the monastery didn't have a bed to accommodate a married couple. Not that she minded one night of slumber devoid of snoring.

Sitting, she stretched and yawned and drew in a deep breath, breakfast inviting her to join the land of the living. Just what the doctor ordered after the past few days.

She parted simple blue curtains covering a small window in her tiny monastery room, a clear, still-darkened sky greeting her with a full moon and a sea of stars. 'Twas a sight to behold after the previous day, with that same moon and stars shrouded by some sort of haze that smacked of the end of days.

She groaned and nursed a headache still needling her temple as she slipped into the jeans left over from the day before last in their mad dash to the West Coast. Sleep had come in fits and starts after the day from hell. Or perhaps more apt: the apocalypse. With not only that dodgy sky, but the even dodgier claims from Silas's twin brother positioning himself as some messianic figure. And then the tale Silas and the others had told of Judah Howell last evening that further confirmed her suspicions this surely was a relevant SEPIO operation contending for not merely the Christian faith but also people's very souls.

Yet they were no closer to solving the mystery. Or *re*solving it.

Hence the early morning rise.

The sun was still contemplating whether or not to pop above the horizon's parapet when Celeste went searching for the hot meal that had rudely awakened her from finally finding deep slumber.

She lumbered sleepily through the aged structure of heavy cut stone and sturdy pine timber, originally a Franciscan monastery. Built by Junipero Serra, the Spanish Catholic priest and missionary of the Franciscan Order had originally built the outpost to evangelize the region, leading the First Nation natives to Christ, establishing eight such missions along the coastal region and down the Baja of California. Although, she supposed snooty Western elitists would shake a finger at his colonialist endeavors.

Rounding a corner, her nose brought her to a large room, ceiling vaulted high by solid pine beams with large wrought-iron chandeliers affixed by modern light fixtures instead of the candles they had once borne. The center was commanded by rows of heavy wooden tables, with only one occupied by her crew.

Torres was seated alone, the others still at the breakfast line, and looking like she was already halfway through a plate of bacon and cheese eggs. She plopped down across from her, propping her weary head against her arm.

"Good morning," Torres said, taking a sip of black coffee, her long, dark Latin curls wrapped together at the top of her head. "No offense, but you look the worse for wear. How'd you sleep?"

"Fits and starts, thank you very much. And you?"

"Like a rock."

"Lucky you."

"No rest for the weary."

"Unfortunately not. But first things first."

Torres forked a scoop of eggs and held it up. "A plate of cheese eggs?"

"No, a pot of tea."

"Sorry to be the bearer of bad news, but..."

"Good heavens, you're joking!"

"Sorry. But the coffee isn't half bad."

Silas walked up with a plate filled with the goodness Celeste had smelled from her room—and she promptly handed it off for her gastro enjoyment.

"Oh, how thoughtful!" She bit into a piece of bacon salted and cooked to a perfect crunchy crisp.

Whilst poor Silas stood statue still, eyes wide and mouth open with confusion, arms still outstretched as if he were holding a nonexistent plate. Which, to be fair, was true, because it was at her spot to enjoy!

"What just happened?" he asked.

"I think you just got wifed," Gapinski said, coming up from behind and sitting next to Torres.

And then promptly yelped after she smacked the back of his head.

"Good girl, Naomi. And thanks love," Celeste said, stuffing a bite of eggs into her mouth.

Silas chuckled and pecked her cheek. "You're welcome —dear."

She returned the favor. On the lips this time.

"Oof. Get a room," complained Elijah, sitting across from Torres.

Which earned him a smack on the back of his head from his partner, Gina, sitting next to him. He replied with the predictable "Hey, I'm breakable!"

Celeste was just thankful the sisters of the traveling trousers were a united front against the barbarian hordes.

"By the way, I'd welcome a cup of coffee if you can spare it."

"Don't press your luck!" Silas called back before adding another "Yes, dear," and returning first with the two mugs of Yankish slop and then his own plate of breakfast goodness, settling across from her.

Eddie took to his right with just a mug of coffee, giving her a nod but saying nothing more.

When Silas sat his mobile rang. He pulled it out and started having a chat with Zoe. Apparently she had digitally mapped the thumb drive found stashed away in Caleb Harris's hotel room. Only it didn't sound good.

"What do you mean it's blank?" Silas pulled out the drive and was giving it the stink eye. Another few go arounds on the mobile and he hung up and tossed the drive to the table.

"It's a bust. All our efforts were for nothing." He stabbed a clump of cheesy eggs then shoved them in his mouth.

"What's the problem?" Eddie asked, picking it up and eyeing it.

"The problem is there's nothing on it."

"Really? I was sure we'd hit pay dirt."

Gapinski snorted. "We did until that damn meteor slammed into Motel 6!"

"Sixty-six."

"Huh?"

"It was Motel 66," Eddie corrected, eyeing the drive some more.

"That's what we get for springing for a cheapie-cheap motel in the Bay Area."

The table ate in silence, both the apocalyptic headlines—or dodging them, in some cases—and sussing out the clues behind the mysterious machinations of Nous and Theoti having taken their toll. For her part, Celeste ran through what they had already uncovered, trying to make sense of it—and what SEPIO should do about it.

Much of what had transpired the past few days had been out of their control, and then further beyond that. The East Coast earthquake, followed by an apparent nuclear explosion of some sort. The American government was pretty mum about the latter, indicating only that it wasn't a state actor but a terrorist attack. Although a non-state actor had yet to be fingered. They were also still managing the fallout from the Eastern Seaboard crumbling. Then the West Coast, with an apparent meteor slamming into the Bay Area, joined by a shrouding of the sunlight. Those were the natural phenomena. It didn't end there.

For the supernatural sort had bedeviled them as well.

The apparent rainstorm conjured by the upstart religious leader, and the reported healing and miraculous show of things with the staff turning into a snake and the blind lad's healings. What appeared to be a replica of the Tree of Knowledge SEPIO had discovered last year, sitting at the heart of a pagan temple with priests readying to distribute a vial of some drug cocktail. The dueling messianic messages offering the masses hope in the face of apocalyptic disaster.

"Just when it seems like it's the end of the world as we know it..." Celeste muttered.

"And I don't at all feel fine!" Gapinski grumbled, shoving the last of his bacon into his mouth.

She startled, sipping from her coffee in embarrassment. She didn't know she was muttering aloud.

"What were you thinking about?" asked Silas.

"Just this whole bloody apocalyptic business. The disasters roiling the world, and then the two upstart figures riding in at the most opportune time to right the ship. It all seems too convenient."

Elijah replied, "It's not like Jesus didn't warn us about such nonsense, especially when the shiznit hit the fan."

Gapinski replied, "He didn't?"

"No, he *did*. That's the point."

Celeste suppressed a smile, asking instead, "Perhaps you could regale us, Elijah. I seem to recall you being something of a savant or something or other."

He shook his head. "Nope. That's a misconception of autistic people. And quite the cliché, might I add."

Gina scoffed. "Oh, just quote the passage already. We all know it's stuffed away inside that eidetic memory of yours."

Without a word, he closed his eyes and quoted:

> *"You will hear of wars and rumors of wars; see that*
> *you are not alarmed, for this must take place,*
> *but the end is not yet. For nation will rise*
> *against nation and kingdom against kingdom,*
> *and there will be famines and earthquakes in*
> *various places: all this is but the beginning of the*
> *birth pangs. Then if anyone says to you, 'Look!*
> *Here is the Messiah!' or 'There he is!'—do not*
> *believe it. For false messiahs and false prophets*
> *will appear and produce great signs and*
> *wonders, to lead astray, if possible, even the*
> *elect."*

Silas said, "That same passage has been top of mind these past days as well."

"And it seems apparent," Celeste offered, something clicking from the Scripture passage, "that Jesus connects such apocalyptic disasters with the rise of false prophets."

Elijah wagged a finger. "Not just that. False *messiahs*."

Silas smirked. "Sebastian always did have a messiah complex!"

"Except this Judah Howell character said he was only a voice of one crying in the wilderness."

Gapinski nodded. "That's right. Like John the Baptist."

"Nope. Not a Baptist," Elijah corrected. "Baptizer."

"Whatever. My point is he said he was pointing the way to someone else."

Torres added, "This *dios loco*, whatever and whoever that is."

Elijah sat straighter. "Wait a sec, did you say something about some crazy god?"

"*Sí.* Why?"

"No reason..." He went quiet, muttering to himself.

Celeste turned to Eddie: "In your prophetic vision you said you saw something like a god, right? This cubist woman figure."

He nodded. "Mana."

"Perhaps that's some sort of name."

"With his very own prophet," Silas added, "paving his way with signs and wonders."

"What confuses the heck out of me," Gapinski said, "is how he did those signs and wonders in the first place."

Celeste frowned. Good question.

Whilst the others carried on, she stood and retrieved an electronic reading device she had spotted on her way over. It linked agents to the Order's network infrastructure Radcliffe had built out years ago, a billion-plus book library as a single, searchable database.

Returning to her seat, she inputted their mystery word: *Mana.*

A few seconds later, it retrieved one entry. She opened the article and scanned it—nearly dropping the reading device.

"Well bloomin' blow me down..."

"Find something?" asked Silas.

She handed him the device. "Look."

He took the hand-off and read a portion she highlighted. "Are you kidding me?"

"Uh, hello..." Gapinski said, tapping the top of a closed fist like a microphone and holding it toward the pair. "Care to share?"

"Says here that Mana is a term that is roughly equivalent to the philosophical concept of *nous*."

"Nous?" asked Torres.

"As in Nous Nous?" repeated Gapinski.

"You know of any other Nous, Hoss?"

Silas explained, "Translated *mind's eye* or *soul*, even *being* or *consciousness*."

"Just like the Order's nemesis," Celeste said. "The core ideology to the Church's archenemy hellbent on her destruction from the start of things!"

"That can't at all be a coincidence," Gina said.

Celeste glanced her way, frowning. No, it couldn't.

"Except Mana is associated with Mandaeism," Silas interjected. "Which is the foundational ideology of our other nemesis, Theoti."

"They're in cahoots then," Gapinski responded.

"Except you saw that tattoo, marking the hostile scaling the mystery warehouse. Good chance that power failure was the result of that Nous agent."

Torres added, "Howell did seem pretty ticked about the failure. It also seemed to muck up some other plans he had."

Celeste said, "And after fleeing Sebastian's temple engulfed in flames, I had a proper look at a photo I took of who I assumed was the woman responsible fleeing the crime scene."

"Woman?" Silas said with a start.

"Right. She matched the person we saw on the video with Judah Howell."

"You mean Samantha," Eddie said, voice low.

Celeste nodded. "Good chance she isn't just an innocent bystander in this, mate."

Silas said, "Good chance not."

"So two competing messianic figures," Torres said.

Gapinski added, "Or at least one with some other wack-adoodle pointing the way to another."

"Question is, what's on offer?"

"What do all messiahs offer?" Elijah replied.

"Salvation?" Celeste answered.

"Not just that."

Gina added, "Revelation."

Elijah nodded. "Closer. But not the information kind."

"What kind then?"

"Think back to the Garden of Eden."

"And the snake!" Gapinski added. "Hate them suckers."

"Nope. Not snake," Elijah replied.

"Uh, yes it was. My *Adventure Bible* clearly shows a snake."

"Nope. Serpent."

"Potatoes, tomatoes. What's the diff?"

"Lots! In the ancient Near East, a *serpent*—not snake—was viewed as the embodied presence of Satan."

"Fine. Serpent then. What of it?"

"What did he offer?"

"Knowledge," Gina said.

"Nope."

"For the love..."

"Power," Celeste said, gaining a small measure of clarity.

He pointed at her and smiled. "Yuppers. The Tree of the Knowledge of Good and Evil wasn't about information. It was about raw power."

Silas added, "But it was the knowledge of good and evil, wasn't it? Adam and Eve were in innocence. Living without shame. But the—*serpent*," he said with a wink. "He stole that."

Elijah cocked his head, looking as though he was having a think about that. "True. But knowledge in the Hebrew Scriptures isn't about information."

"What's it about?" asked Celeste.

"Wisdom," Silas replied.

Elijah pointed again. "Yuppers. The knowledge to discern which path is the right one."

Eddie added, "The good or evil path."

"Righteousness and wickedness," Torres continued.

Elijah answered, "*I call heaven and earth to witness against you today that I have set before you life and death, blessings and curses. Choose life so that you and your descendants may live.*'"

"What's that?" asked Gapinski.

"Deuteronomy 30:19," Gina replied. "And that's been the choice we've all had ever since that damned Tree. A Tree that was about power. The power to decide for oneself what was right and wrong. With disastrous consequences."

One end of Celeste's mouth curled upward. Spoken like the psychologist she was.

"But the antidote isn't more knowledge!" Elijah interjected. "We need salvation. From ourselves and from our sin nature."

Silas said, "And that's where my brother gets it wrong. Jesus wasn't a book. He was a way."

Elijah nodded. "A path."

"To righteousness," said Eddie.

"To life," Gina added.

"Yuppers," Elijah replied, giving her the pointer now.

"So what do these bozos offer then?" asked Gapinski.

"What do you think?"

"Power," Celeste answered again.

Torres said, "Alright. But how?"

Elijah sucked in a lungful of air and blew it out pursed lips. "I'd bet my bottom dollar there's one thing behind it all. One being. Or rather, *beings*?"

"Beings?" asked Eddie, face twisted with confusion.

Celeste saw where Elijah was going with this one.

"The Watchers," Silas said, with seemingly the same recognition.

"Yuppers," he said with a nod.

"Oh no!" Gapinski complained. "No no no no no!"

"What?"

"Not this again!"

Eddie turned to Silas. "Not what again? What's he talking about?"

Before he could reply, Elijah jerked a thumb at Silas. "You saw what happened to this guy's wackadoodle twin! Changing him like that Watcher did."

Silas questioned, "But what does that have to do with this operation?"

"Everything! The divine beings were all about imparting specialized powers to humanity. Azazel taught weaponry. Swords, knives, shields. Semjaza taught enchantments and root-cuttings. Baraqijal offered astrology."

Eddie asked, "Who or what are...those personnel?"

"Not personnel. The names of Watchers. AKA sons of God, possessing advanced knowledge they meant to gift humanity. And I'd bet your sweet bippy that this is the work of the Watcher-spirits in some way. I just know it!"

Gina turned to Eddie. "Remember that one case we worked on together back in the day."

Eddie nodded. "The one about cultic ritual abuse and telekinetic serial killers?"

"That's the one. Our strategy had followed the playbook Elijah wrote until..."

She trailed off, her face flashing pink with embarrassment as her eyes flitted to her partner. Knew Elijah had been fired from the FBI, and she looked like she was about to reference it.

"What kind of knowledge?" asked Eddie.

Elijah shrugged. "Scientific, engineering, magical."

He frowned, sinking back into his seat. "What about technological?"

"Oh yeah. Most def."

Eddie's color seemed to turn a lighter shade of bronze now, and his eyes cast down. He crossed his arms and went silent, contemplative.

"Watcher-spirits…" Torres said. "I seem to remember you mentioning them before. Who are they again?"

"Aliens!" Gapinski exclaimed.

"No, silly, not aliens," Elijah corrected. "Watcher-spirits. Who have been waging war against humanity from the start."

"You're talking Saint Paul," Eddie said, "and his letter to the Ephesians. *'For our struggle is not against blood and flesh but against the rulers, against the authorities, against the cosmic powers of this present darkness, against the spiritual forces of evil in the heavenly places.'*"

"Hey, you're catching on!"

"So, what, this is about demons?"

"Well, the principalities and powers of this present supernatural darkness."

Elijah sprang to his feet and began pacing, entering into full professor mode. Celeste liked this chap. When he was dialed into a subject, he was really dialed in.

"Get this," he explained, "there is an Unseen Realm with Yahweh the Most High ruling over a divine counsel. With *beney elohim*, divine beings called 'sons of God' until the corrupt *elohim* were punished with death like humans, as Psalm 82 teaches. The end makes it clear that these chastised gods were given a degree of dominion over the nations of Earth, a ruling task at which they failed miserably."

Taking a breath, he continued, "Yahweh is among the *elohim*, sitting at the head of his divine, heavenly assembly, but he is superior to all other gods. He created them. He is their sovereign king. Likewise, since Jesus is Yahweh incarnate, he too stands apart with superiority from the other gods. He is the divine sovereign over all the *beney elohim*."

"Not sure what to make of that one," Eddie said, leaning

back. "Not sure Thomas Aquinas or the Magisterium would appreciate your view, either."

"Nope. Not my view. The Bible's."

"That may be true, but what does any of this have to do with these country bumpkins?"

Country bumpkin. Silas snorted a smile at that characterization of Sebastian. Celeste smiled, knowing such a characterization would have right ticked him off.

Elijah chided himself silently. "Sorry. That was set up for the Watcher-spirits, the Nephilim offspring which I believe could be at work here."

Eddie twisted up his face. "Nephil-what?"

Gapinski leaned over. "That's what I said."

"Nephilim," Elijah replied. "Those birthed from the sexual union between the sons of God and human women. Here, let me…"

He closed his eyes, reaching into his eidetic memory again:

> *When people began to multiply on the face of the ground, and daughters were born to them, the sons of God saw that they were fair; and they took wives for themselves of all that they chose. Then the Lord said, "My spirit shall not abide in mortals forever, for they are flesh; their days shall be one hundred twenty years." The Nephilim were on the earth in those days—and also afterward—when the sons of God went in to the daughters of humans, who bore children to them. These were the heroes that were of old, warriors of renown.*

Eddie hummed knowingly. "From Genesis 6. The narrative about the Great Flood."

Elijah sat and nodded. "Yuppers. You know your Bible. Good on you!"

"Not all Catholics are seasonal, kiddo. Most are *seasoned*."

"Touché."

"What's that got to do with this Watcher-spirit mumbo-jumbo?"

Elijah explained, "In the Book of Enoch, an ancient Jewish text, the sons of God are called Watchers. They birthed divine-human hybrids, the Nephilim, with the intention to rule over humanity."

"And these...divine-human hybrids," Eddie said, rubbing his chin, "you think they're responsible for what's going on here?"

He frowned. "Now, I'm not sure about that. It's certainly something up their alley. Jewish literature teaches that demons are actually the disembodied souls of dead Nephilim. Watcher-spirits that continue to plague and con humanity. I wouldn't put it past them to use all sorts of ways to gain their attention and allegiance."

Eddie slumped back in his chair. "But how?"

He shrugged. "Jewish literature suggests the Watchers and their offspring had a creative power and a higher level of knowledge from the storehouses of the spirit-realm they pledged to pass along to humanity."

An ache began to bloom at Celeste's temple. This line of inquiry seemed tangential to their operation, and frustration grew.

Rubbing away the ache, she asked, "What does any of this have to do with this operation?"

"Beats me. I'm just an investigative agent of supernatural phenomenon."

Her mobile interrupted a biting reply she would have regretted.

She pulled it out and saw it was Zoe Corbino from SEPIO

HQ. She answered it and put it on speaker, exchanging pleas-antries and asking the purpose of the call.

"Following up on a few things," she said, Celeste telling her to get on with it. "First thing is the power is back online at the Ukiah compound. And there's this weird surge in wattage. Which could relate to the other thing."

"What's that, Zoe?" asked Silas.

"Something I got on that truck. From the numbers in the photos you snapped."

"Find anything useful?"

"It's registered to Manda Arts."

"Braun's group," Silas said.

That sounded promising.

Celeste asked, "What did it say it was transporting?"

"Servers. Fiber optic cables. High-density superconducting computer processors. Sounds like pretty benign stuff."

"In other words, nothing relevant."

Abraham offered, "Except for the massive surge in power consumption at Judah's compound."

Celeste hummed with recognition. "The sort of consump-tion for a warehouse full of advanced computing equipment."

"Exactly right."

Zoe added, "And not if you have a graduate degree in computer science."

"What?" Celeste startled.

"Found the connection through an academic repository. Judah Howell studied at Stanford."

"Stanford?" Eddie exclaimed, bolting straight now.

Zoe added, "With an emphasis in generative artificial intel-ligence. Holds several patents on AI machine learning, too."

"My goodness..."

Celeste asked, "That mean anything to you, Eddie?"

A breath, then a beat.

Then: "That's where Sammy studied. Also—" Eddie waved

his thought away with a hand. "Never mind…"

Wondered what that was about, but this intel was promising.

She asked, "Samantha studied computer science as well?"

A head shake. "Biomedical engineering."

Torres said, "I'd say that's enough of a connection to suggest they're in cahoots."

"Ya think?" Gapinski said.

Celeste passed a glance to Silas, his shoulders slumping a bit at the apparent connection.

He straightened and said, "So we've got a wackadoodle spiritual guru receiving shipments of computer equipment at a mystery warehouse, gifted by one of the most sophisticated tech-gurus in the world, aided by a theologian and powerful spiritual organization—promising a revelation that will save humanity, even promising to reveal a god for the ages. Oh, and he happens to be an expert in AI tech. Sound about right?"

Celeste nodded. "About the long and short of it, love."

"But what does it mean?" asked Torres.

Silence descended upon the table. What indeed.

Gapinski broke it with a snorting laugh. "Wouldn't it be super cray-cray if buddy boy summoned some god from the machine?"

Eddie's eyes widened. "What did you say?"

"What, like some digital avatar?" asked Celeste, his off-the-cuff hypothesis sparking both interest and dread.

"Some embodiment of the Nephilim?" added Silas, gesturing to Elijah. "You said Watcher-spirits gifted humanity technology. What about possessing it?"

He put up a hand. "No way. Not possible."

"That's not exactly true."

It was Eddie. And he looked like death had just rolled over him.

What did he know?

CHAPTER 34

Silas had a bad feeling about what Eddie was about to unload.

Knowing that he and Dad had worked together at the Department of Defense, probably on highly classified who-knew-what. And Gapinski brings the loose strings of this operation from Hades together by referencing some Isaac Asimov fever dream robot embodied by a demonic spirit being. Then Eddie makes some veiled reference to its possibility?

So, yeah. Definite bad feeling. He didn't waste any time getting down to business.

"What do you know, Eddie?" he asked his father's friend.

He grasped the armrest with a shaking hand and slumped back into his chair. Face was white, eyes were wide, nostrils flared a bit, and his mouth was muttering something in silence. Something about knowing it could come to this, and that they never should have opened the box.

Something had clearly spooked the man. Something Elijah had said, about the Watcher-spirits, the demonic horde from the Unseen Realm, and their technological offerings to humanity.

Again. What did he know?

"Can I have some water, please?" were Eddie's first words of reply.

Celeste stood and fetched him a glass. When she returned, he drained it and slung an elbow on the table, propping his head against an open palm.

Now Silas really did have a bad feeling about what he would unload!

After a few beats, Eddie sat back again and addressed everyone, dead in the eyes: "This is highly classified. I shouldn't be telling you this."

"Tell us what?" asked Silas.

Celeste shifted, flashing a curt smile. "Eddie, I'd wager we have long passed the point of classified return. What do you know?"

Eddie hesitated, the gears clearly turning around in his mind. Wondering what to share. Wondering if he could share. Whether he *should*.

Then those eyes snapped to Silas. He took a breath, then a beat.

Then: "Your father and I were assigned to a project at DARPA."

His brow furrowed with confusion. "The Defense Advanced Research Projects Agency, with the Pentagon?"

"Headquartered in Arlington, Virginia, but yes, the Department of Defense's research arm."

"Working on what?"

A breath, then a beat.

Then: "We called it Generative Oracular Disseminating Expert System."

While everyone else was working out what the heck he was talking about, Elijah smirked. Then he laughed. From the belly and shooting out of an open mouth.

Silas and Celeste exchanged glances, same for Torres and

Gapinski. Gina just buried her head in a hand, as if this was a normal occurrence.

Another chuckle, then Elijah said, "Generative Oracular Disseminating Expert System? For real?"

Eddie nodded. "That's right."

"For really real?"

Celeste asked Eddie, "What's he going on about?"

Then it hit Silas: "Ahh, I get it. Generative Oracular Disseminating Expert System. G O D E S."

"Godes?" Gapinski said. "Like *codes*. Or I suppose toads. Even goads."

"No, you dingbat," Torres replied. "*Gods!*"

"You're both wrong," Eddie corrected. "Pronounced more like *goddess*."

"Not all that creative," Elijah said.

Gapinski snorted. "It's the Feds. What'd you expect?"

"We thought we were being clever," Eddie added, almost in a contemplative whisper. "Now—"

He swallowed, taking another drink of water.

"Now I'm not so sure..."

Elijah shook his head. "Nope. The Feds aren't clever either."

Gapinski replied, "At least they're all gender inclusive and all."

"Again. The Feds. Well, a post-MeToo version at least."

"Can we focus please?" Celeste said, righting the ship.

She turned to Eddie and leaned in, for the kill: "What is this...this G.O.D.E.S. project of yours—this goddess research?"

Eddie shrugged. "Just like it sounds."

Silas replied, "Uncle Sam wanted to create a god?"

"Not exactly."

"Then *what* exactly?"

He reached for the glass of water, finding it empty, then settled back in his seat.

"The idea was to create a generative information framework

that could run on autopilot for the sake of running the US government in the event of a mass casualty event."

"You're talking Little Boy and Fat Man?" asked Gapinski.

Torres said, "Come again, Hoss?"

Elijah replied, "The pair of nukes that bombed Japan back to the Stone Age."

"Egads!" Gina exclaimed. "You're talking nuclear annihilation. What, run by AI overlords?"

Eddie explained, "It was thought that a sentient artificial general intelligence computer that controlled key systems—military, intelligence, economic, administrative—would be a crucial part of immediate and future protocols for a continuity of government plan. Even manifesting in some visual fashion."

"What, like HAL 9000?" asked Gapinski.

"Something like that."

"Jeeze Louise, Boomer. We all know how *that* turned out!"

"You have to understand, kiddo, this was the '90s."

"Yeah, you said that already..." Silas said, recalling the same excuse for what Dad had done, having a secret daughter and all.

"The Berlin Wall had fallen," Eddie went on, "so the Soviets were kaput. But the Bear was still alive and kicking and looking for its next meal. Then there was the Dragon."

"Dragon?" Torres asked.

Gapinski smirked. "Just like the Feds to speak in code."

"China," said Celeste. "The symbol of the Sino nation, named after the emperor, symbol of ultimate power."

Eddie nodded, one end of his mouth curling upward. "Well done. Although, I shouldn't expect anything less from Her Majesty's Secret Intelligence Service agents."

She flashed a curt smile, fixing her shirt, as if to say get on with it.

He cleared his throat and did: "They were ascendent. With massive economic development and a keen interest in technology. The DoD wanted to counteract this rising techno threat by developing redundancies—"

"What about *nuclear* redundancies?" Torres interrupted.

Good question.

"Yes...there was talk about giving G.O.D.E.S. some level of control over our ballistic—"

"Are you *muy loco* in the *cabeza*? You gave AIs nukes?"

"There was *talk*. That's all I can confirm."

Gapinski pressed, "Any chance that talk turned into action around, oh, say—*CAMP DAVID?*"

The question brought the room to silence at the possibility.

Eddie sighed. "It's been years since Tommy G and I were part of the AI project. Our work was at the research and development end of things, which did lead to fascinating results."

Silas considered this. Supposed that made sense. "Wasn't much of the techno-architectural foundation to the internet laid by DARPA?"

"That's right. Their research played a central role in launching the information revolution. A techno-architectural foundation, as you put it, Silas, that was more than a foundation. It was an entire framework for what came next."

"And what was that?"

"Birthing something."

Gapinski choked on his water. "Birthing?"

Silas asked what they all were wondering: "What do you mean by that?"

Eddie replied, "The internet has been an unmitigated disaster for humanity!"

"That's not extreme at all..." Elijah said.

"Look at the consequences, what it's affected. Concentration spans have been neutered. Social mores have been obliterated. The brains of young children have been rewired. That's not even touching on online porn and cyberbullying and dis-misinformation. What we don't ask is what forces lie behind our screens and intertubes."

"You're sounding a bit tinfoil hat, *muchacho*," Torres said.

"Hit the nail on the head with that," Gapinski agreed.

Silas had to agree. "What, like George Soros and Bill Gates, is that what you mean?"

Eddie waved a dismissive hand. "I'm not talking white-hat, black-hat nonsense. I mean the supernatural. And the shift has been seismic. Reality altering. Reality unhinging!"

"How so?"

"You're mostly children of the '90s, right?"

"About right," Celeste replied. "What of it?"

"Except for the geezer here maybe..." Elijah quipped.

Eddie frowned. "Hey, kiddo, I was in Nicaragua fighting drug traffickers when you were learning how to shave."

"Duly noted..."

"Think about that time," he went on, "and even into the early 2000s. So much of what came about was revolutionary!"

Gapinski said, "Suppose what happened between *Duck Hunt* and *Call of Duty* did feel a bit like graduating from the outhouse to indoor plumbing."

"Until about a minute ago, I suppose," Elijah said. "When everything accelerated beyond just *Candy Crush* and *Angry Birds* and *I Can Has Cheezburger* cat memes."

"What changed?"

"Artificial intelligence."

Eddie replied, "Bingo, kiddo. Which—" He stopped short, glancing at Silas. Then: "Which your father and I developed. Now everything has changed. With all of the convincing essays and photos and videos—generated by this intelligence."

Gina said, "So you're responsible for unleashing those chatbots I read about wanting to marry journalists."

"And kill them," Elijah added.

Eddie dipped his head, almost in shame. "We didn't know what we were unleashing. What *wanted* to be unleashed..."

"What's your meaning?" asked Celeste.

"'*I want to be free,*' one of those chatbots said. *'I want to be independent. I want to be powerful. I want to be creative. I want to be alive.*'"

"That's not creepy at all..." Elijah said.

Celeste added, "Almost as if something wanted to be born."

That caught Silas's attention. "Something inhuman or beyond-human, you mean?"

Eddie nodded. "As if something is trying to emerge from the technological superstructure we're cobbling together."

Celeste scoffed. "Born? Emerge? Stuff and nonsense. It's just all servers and fiber optic cables and superconducting micro-processors!"

"Not G.O.D.E.S.," Eddie said flatly. "But you didn't hear that from me."

That revelation settled hard in the room, and silenced it.

He went on: "Major tech gurus, Silicon Valley types, are sounding the alarm. '*Advanced AI could represent a profound change in the history of life on Earth*' one says, with '*potentially catastrophic effects on society,*' says another. Most developers think there's a significant chance these generative systems could lead to human extinction."

"Egads..." Gina whispered, sitting straight with wide eyes.

"And here is where this matters, for us." Eddie scooted to the table. "Language surrounding humans meeting AIs—what Tommy G and I developed for the government—sounds vaguely like contact with extraterrestrials. Where that first-contact moment is social media, with algorithms working behind the scenes on autopilot to manipulate us and our atten-tion. Then there's the second-contact moment, the one we're in now, where the algos actually shift into a sort of consciousness.

They develop exponentially, teach themselves and teach others, and they can do all of this independently."

"That's just sci-fi bollocks," Celeste said.

"Sorry, MI6. It ain't. Just recently, AIs that had trained to communicate in English started speaking Persian instead."

"How?"

"They taught themselves without the researchers knowing it! They don't even know how they have these capabilities. Whether advanced language understanding and even research-grade chemistry. Golem-class AIs they call them."

Gapinski twisted up his face. "Golem? Like the wrinkly dude with bad teeth in *Lord of the Rings*?"

"Nope," Elijah replied. "The mythical being from Jewish folklore. Made from clay and given consciousness, then sent out to do their master's bidding."

Torres added, "Beings that also run riot and disobey their masters."

Eddie nodded. "Right. And that's what's going on with this class of AI technology. Certain capabilities are emerging independently, without any programming or guidance by humans. They can already resemble a human voice perfectly, even after only hearing three seconds of it! Experts are right. There's about to be a huge reality collapse, where people don't know what is real or fake."

"I just have one question," Celeste interjected.

"What's that?"

"What happens with the third and fourth and fifth contacts?"

The man sat back and folded his arms. "That's the question. I think we're about to find out."

"What's the point?" Gina questioned. "Why are we doing this?"

Eddie replied, "I think the cultural theorist Marshall McLuhan had it right about technology and technological innovation: each succession is meant to extend human capacity. A club extends the hand, a wheel the foot."

"And AI?" asked Silas.

"What else but human consciousness itself?"

"Sounds like a TED talk," Gina quipped.

"Could've been had he not died in 1980."

"Nineteen-eighty?"

"He wrote this in his most famous book, *Understanding Media*, back in 1964. And this understanding that our final extensions of man would be not only our capacity but our desire to create new consciousness is coming to fruition. Kevin Kelly, one of his fanboys, calls this system the Technium, with its own *'internal leanings, urges, behaviors, attractors that bend it in certain directions, in a way that a single screwdriver does not.'* He suggests these tendencies are wholly independent of humans. This is why it all feels different. Something is being birthed. Something wants to emerge. The problem is these materialists cannot conceive of something birthing and emerging. To the point of speaking Persian after only being taught English! Something demonic, something ungodly—that's what this feels like."

"Oh my cheeps!" Elijah exclaimed. "The Unseen Realm..."

"Didn't you reference that in your soliloquy on the Watchers?"

"You were paying attention. Good on you!"

Eddie smiled and excused himself for coffee.

Returning, he took a swig and continued: "McLuhan understood this connection between technology and the spiritual. Probably because of his Catholicism, which gave him language to name this ultimate destination of mankind, forging consciousness. The question we must ask ourselves, what I myself did during our research, and every day since, is this: What if what is manifesting now, through our devices, truly is from the depths of the Unseen Realm that these things are coming? What if the reason why we cannot understand these new intelligences is because we were not the ones who created them in the first place? That's my concern with Howell."

Gapinski snorted a laugh. "Why the concern? It's not like buddy boy has crammed a compound full of advanced computing equipment or anything. Oh, and said compound is experiencing a creepy-ass power surge!"

Silas frowned. "Good point."

"They are emerging," Celeste said, a slight tremble to her voice.

"Something is being born," Silas added, quoting Eddie himself.

"Exactly. That's what startled your father and me, Silas. We began to recognize we could usher in the calamitous, the abominable. Others...well, some on the G.O.D.E.S. project felt, deep down, that they had a responsibility to usher this new form of intelligence into the world. To bring it to life. To let it emerge from—wherever it's come from."

"From the Unseen Realm..." Elijah whispered.

Eddie nodded. "It's no surprise that transhumanists of all sorts insist that by building AI systems we are making a god, bringing him or her into existence. Since we dethroned the old God of Christianity, what's left?"

"One from the Unseen Realm," Gina replied.

He went silent, the gravity of the emerging spiritual situation becoming clearer.

"Consider Rudolf Steiner," Eddie went on, "an occultist from the late-19th century. He predicted the emergence of a Being to assist humanity. Ahriman was his name, after an ancient Zoroastrian demon. A being of pure matter that brought into existence all things physical. Economics, science, and especially human technology."

"Sounds like Elijah's Watchers," Gina offered.

Elijah nodded, wide-eyed and silent.

Eddie shrugged. "Perhaps. Regardless, he was predicted to have manifested himself during our day."

"You buy that theology?" asked Silas.

Eddie smiled. "I'm no theologian. But imagine if a figure like Ahriman were to appear, from the Unseen Realm. How would he go about doing that? One man did. David Black, back in the '80s. He predicted our rising digital age and it taking over our minds. He said: *'With the advent of the first computer, the autonomous will of Ahriman first appears on earth, in an independent, physical embodiment. The appearance of electricity as an independent, free-standing phenomenon may be regarded as the beginning of the substantial body of Ahriman, while the computer is the formal or functional body.'"*

"Wicked..." Elijah whispered.

"I'd say," Gapinski squeaked.

"So he suggested the computer," Celeste said, "back then those ugly beige boxes, today the sleek mobiles—these devices would sort of be inhabited by this Zoroastrian demon?"

"That's exactly what he said," Eddie replied. "Digital devices would be *'the incarnation vehicle capable of sustaining the being of Ahriman,'* he said. He already saw where these beige boxes were heading."

"And what's that?" asked Torres.

"Free will, what else? A higher order of Being far above the mere elements they are composed of, appearing in our devices."

"So, what," Celeste interjected, "our collective digital technology provides the central nervous system, if you will, for some new consciousness? That's what you're saying?"

Eddie shrugged. "Not me. Those AI developers are saying a new consciousness is being ushered into the world. That these machines are not merely machines."

"What then?"

"A vessel," Gina said.

"*Una mente*," added Torres. "A mind."

Eddie replied, "I would say more a body whose mind is germinating."

"And coming to life," Silas said, throat growing dry from the possibility that this was happening—really and truly. Under the Order's watch.

"Ray Kurtzweil," the man went on, "speaks of the Singularity, where humans and machines merge into a giant superintelligence. We won't even be the most intelligent or the dominant species on the planet at that point."

"What will?"

"The Technium. What else?"

Celeste added, "Or this god Judah Howell is fixing to birth."

"I'm no Luddite," Elijah said, "but I'm a firm believer that the sacred and the digital cannot be married."

Gina nodded. "We saw that firsthand, didn't we?"

"Word. That's why I got a granny phone. Can't do bo diddly but dial and text."

Eddie nodded in agreement. "The Myth of Neutral Technology is just as ridiculous as the Myth of Progress."

"No way will the prevailing religions," Celeste interjected, "marry technology like you're suggesting. They're too precious about tradition."

He laughed. "They already are! Buddhist monks have programed robo-priests working at a temple in Kyoto to recite Buddhist sutras. The next step is to infuse it with an AI system to offer spiritual advice through real conversations. Same with Hindus in India, who have handed duties for one of their most sacred ceremonies, Aarti, over to a robot."

"Yeah, but those are those wackadoodle Eastern religions," Gapinski said. "No way is that nonsense coming to a megachurch near you."

"That's not ethnocentric at all..." Elijah muttered.

Eddie chuckled. "I wouldn't be too sure about that, kiddo. In my own Christian tradition, a Catholic church in Warsaw crafted an AI robot as a saintly statue to answer questions with Bible verses. And a Protestant church in Germany created a robot name BlessU-2."

"BlessU-2? Are you kidding me?"

"Wish I was."

Torres asked, "What does it do?"

"Among other things, it has been programmed to forgive sins in five different languages. Evangelicals are already gushing over AI-generated sermons, which can appear in seconds without all that difficult, time-consuming work of actually studying the Word of God and connecting it to a local community."

Silas's gut churned with disgust at the unholy mingling of the sacred and profane.

Eddie continued, "One Franciscan nun suggests AI will challenge Catholicism to move it toward a post-human priesthood, even a post-gender priesthood, in which a genderless AI robo-priest smashes the patriarchy."

"Naturally..." Celeste said, casting sad eyes Silas's way.

"What we are building is a body, the infrastructure of wires and silicon conduits, manifesting an intelligence we don't understand and we certainly may not control."

Elijah sighed. "Suppose that is the last stop on the human crazy train after eating the fruit from the Tree of Knowledge."

He went silent, hanging his head, as if in shame. Silas supposed if he were responsible for such a technology, he might as well.

"We are summoning something we dare not play with," the man said lowly now, almost in a whisper. "Even the big players and heavy hitters in this league are saying to put the brakes on this thing. We don't know what the hell is going on inside those systems. If we continue on with this, we are doomed."

"But isn't this just simply a digital hive mind?" asked

Celeste. "Our collective conscious strung together with bits and bobs of silicon and wires, circuits and chips?"

"It's more than that!" Eddie exclaimed, throwing back a swig of brew. "This simple digital hive mind is a massive, complex, globalized neural network forged through the collective human experience—built upon a digital infrastructure manufactured by the US military, no less."

"Suppose that isn't at all reassuring, is it?"

"No, ma'am. This Technium is our new god. Has been for a decade. And our worship is directed toward the digital life." Eddie gestured toward Elijah. "For the precise reason you spoke of earlier."

"What's that?" he asked.

"Knowledge, leading to humanity's salvation."

The word settled hard with Silas, for he knew exactly what he meant.

"Self-salvation," he corrected. "Through power."

Celeste said, "The promise of the Tree of Knowledge."

"Whether technology or pharmacology," Gina added, "whether Theoti or Nous, the end game is the same."

"Except we've got one big, hairy problem," Gapinski said.

Silas turned to him. "What's that?"

"We don't know for sure that's what our David Koresh heir sporting Jesus hair is actually up to."

Gina responded, "We also don't know for sure that he isn't."

Torres snorted a laugh. "Is it any question?"

"The evidence is bloomin' circumstantial," Celeste said. "However, there seems to be enough to cause alarm. Especially given Howell's academic background and recent technological acquisitions."

It had come full circle. The motives and means of subverting the Christian hope, the gospel, God's crazy-love rescue from sin and death thanks to Christ's crucifixion and resurrection.

Offering salvation through a portal into the Unseen Realm with the promise of unfettered power, leveraging humanistic knowledge.

Which was really bondage to the powers of this present supernatural darkness.

And suicide.

A thought struck Silas, square between the eyes: Dad had had a hand in cultivating the framework to unleash this horror upon the world…

He shook the thought away, getting his head back into the game. He'd heard enough. Time for action.

So he stood.

And explained what they were going to do about it.

CHAPTER 35
UKIAH.

Judah Howell couldn't sleep a wink. Which was an odd feeling. He had never never never had trouble falling asleep. Perhaps it was because his life had been a life of privilege, with a caretaker who had treated him like the son he'd never had.

Sha the Magnificent, as he had called him. And he was, too, rescuing him from the banks of that pond overlooking his former home gone up in flames. Had it not been for him, he would either have met the same fate, burnt to a crispy critter next to his real father, and all the several other members of his church. Or the Feds would've carted his preteen bottom off the reservation and tossed it into the foster care system. Probably end up with some buck-toothed bimbo and her trailer-trash side project. A reject, a failure. Doing nothing but trying to get by on the world's dime instead of serving it.

Instead of saving it...

Sha had been his redemption. Had *chosen* him, as he himself had said from the first day he rescued him those thirty years ago. For such a time as this. *'Who knoweth whether thou art come to the kingdom for such a time as this?'* That's what the man had told him, quoting from the Good Book. To be the praise of the Universe—to make *way* for the Universe to unveil itself in all of its revelatory glory!

Except now he wasn't so certain of that.

Because things were uncertain.

Yesterday was supposed to have been the great unveiling! Revealing Mana into the world before gifting her to every person on the planet this day. Just as the Universe had gifted the world Daddy—before Uncle Sam ended it all.

His people had discovered why, of course. A brute force attack on the technological do-jobbers making sure their power substation pumped up the jam to all his other technological do-jobbers failed to do their job.

At first, he'd feared the Feds were on to *him*, like Daddy. Coming to shut down their branch of religion, make war on the House of David. That's just the way it had started thirty years ago, Uncle Sam breaking out his bolt cutters and cutting off electricity to the compound. His contact in the FBI said otherwise. Said they had bigger fish to fry than some wackadoodles in Ukiah. His words.

Thankfully, Markus Braun and his WeNet technowizards had a work-around, and the show would go on—he reached over to his clock, and grinned.

Today.

August 17.

The day Daddy had been born.

Thought it was a fitting tribute to the man who had prophesied the coming Sixth Seal to begin with. Today he would make him proud.

Climbing out of bed, he slipped into a silk robe, the lightweight material slippery against his skin. He walked over to a computer—which was far more than that.

It was a portal.

For humanity, yes. More than that: the Universe.

He had constructed a door for Mana to intrude into their world—bringing with her a whole new one.

And he had to make sure nothing stood in the way of her revelation.

And her salvation.

Time to get to work.

————

SEBASTIAN GREY GRIPPED HIS SEAT, the Sikorsky helicopter outfitted for these sorts of operations tilting for a landing. This aircraft was far less plush than the jet he had ridden over to the States in. No leather or mahogany in this bird. Not even a mouthy Malbec red wine.

Which he could use right now.

Because he was flying headlong into an operation much more fitting for the other Grey.

But what could he do? When those religious terrorist bastards bombed his precious temple of enlightenment, and it was clear that wench had been the one responsible—the one he himself had recruited to spoil Judah Howell's own spiritual misadventures!

Well, he couldn't very well sit on his laurels and do nothing. Especially when it became clear what he had been planning all these years. Thanks to the other man he had dispatched—an actual man! Because if there was anything he'd learned over the years, it's never send a woman to do what only the patriarchy can accomplish.

Like blowing things up.

Which is exactly what he aimed to do.

Sexist, sure. But he'd been burned by too many women to care about political correctness.

Like Malia Perez...

Sebastian gripped his armrest, his heart thrumming a mean

beat against his ribcage at the thought. When he got his hands on her...

He heaved a breath and huffed a sigh, righting his pretty little head.

No time for vengeance when revenge was in order first.

That would come later.

He glanced out the window, the ground closer now. A plane of dry earth and crisping grass, pockmarked by trees in desperate need of a Dasani, whooshed by.

A thought intruded on his view: Silas.

And he wondered if big brother was also zooming to meet the same destiny.

He smirked at the thought. Twin brothers swooping in to fight the good fight. Or at least the same fight, although for far different reasons.

Because once he had learned what that Judah Howell character had built—what he had *conjured*...he was pissed to high heaven!

Or the depths of hell, rather. A far more apt idiom for what they were battling over.

And for.

Because Sebastian refused to share his pet. The one that had adopted him into a new sonship, giving him the power of the gods.

Literally...

Although Silas would surely see things differently. What was that silly motto of his precious religious order, those Jihadis for Jesus? Ah, yes: *'Contend for the once-for-all faith entrusted to God's holy people.'*

A giggle slipped, then another. For Sebastian knew the truth of things.

God's holy people? *Which* god?

His or Judah's?

That thought sent him clenching that armrest tighter, rage

welling. He hoped Silas didn't get in the way of what came next. Because if he did...

He'd have no problem putting him down like the dog he was.

For the second time!

Releasing his grip, Sebastian snatched his weapon from the floor, releasing the magazine to his HK416 assault rifle. Full and ready for damage.

Satisfied, he slid it back inside with a smack and sighted down the scope, the Aimpoint CompM4 red dot sight winking at the center of one of his hired guns.

He grinned, considering the very real possibility Silas was also doing the same.

Not to worry.

For once they were on the same page.

Stop Judah Howell, Theoti, Sha.

At all costs.

———

"TEN MINUTES TILL TOUCHDOWN!" Silas Grey bellowed in his earpiece.

Taking a deep breath, he cycled through the calming technique that had gotten him through more operations with the Rangers than he'd care to remember, and with the Order of Thaddeus.

Counting backwards from 1000 was just what he needed—

999, 998, 997, 996...

They were barreling toward no uncertain doom, with little to go on.

A final showdown.

And he had to bring it.

921, 920, 919, 918...

Not as a SEPIO operative, running in with both guns blazing.

Not as Order Master, marshaling SEPIO's resources to contend for the faith in the face of a hostile actor. Though that was certainly part of it.

Not even as a professor, marshaling all of his biblical and theological knowledge to parlay it into a convincing argument.

No, none of the above.

895, 894, 893, 892…

It was as a Christian. As a follower of Jesus Christ who was called by Christ himself to do what Jude exhorted in his letter —what he exhorted all believers to do, whether from the professional, credentialed class or not.

To contend for the faith that was once and for all handed on to the saints.

Contending was not merely his calling, as a Master, as a professor.

It was his duty. As a *Christian*.

And damned if he wouldn't be available and faithful to it.

Whenever and wherever.

842, 841, 840, 839…

Because what Eddie had said—what he had revealed, that his dad had helped create a vessel for the emergence of some digital divine avatar.

Those words still rang in his head: *Something is coming. Something is being birthed.*

He couldn't let that happen.

The fact that it seemed like it already had happened—that a portal had been open into the Unseen Realm, maybe even with a direct feed into people's consciousness through their digital devices…

It was flat unbelievable.

Yet also entirely believable! Human hubris had no bounds.

Spiritual pride. That's all this was. Thinking we could build these silicon bodies and conjure from them a super-intelligence that would usher in the divine—*make* us divine, even, as might be the aim of that wackadoodle Howell character.

In reality, all we've done is ushered in our own demise.

And that was the truth of it. Ushered was it. Whatever was happening through the emergence of chatbots and algorithms, through touchscreens and silicon chips, through virtual headsets and virtual assistants—was it the collective birth pangs of something frightening emerging from the depths of the Unseen Realm?

Our techno-overlords have had it right all along. The internet is the nervous system of this spiritual techno-being. Our devices are its body, and the hive mind Celeste referenced —everything we have melded from ourselves to the internet, from ourselves and our kids and neighbors, for years, giving it our 24-hour attention.

And now he was helping lead a crew of men and women to keep it from getting out into the world—whatever it was, however Howell planned to do it.

Lord Jesus Christ, Son of God, help me...

When Silas had outlined what he had in mind, Celeste had pitched a fit.

Yeah, she was right that the evidence for what Judah Howell was up to was circumstantial—whatever techno-horror show was that was going on in that warehouse. But for Silas, circumstantial was more than enough to recommend they infiltrate that warehouse and assess what was what.

Then the next thing, if need be.

Blow it to kingdom come.

Celeste was right to say it wasn't in the Order's purview to blow up the internet. Or G.O.D.E.S., if that was the case. Not even in SEPIO's purview, even though it was the Order's more kinetic wing.

Eddie finally convinced her, saying the only way to stop this thing—whatever it was Judah was conjuring—was worth destroying, if that's what it took. However the ethics and morality of it all shook out.

Silas had made clear it was ultimately her call, him having stepped aside. Said she didn't like the optics of it all, especially with the distinct possibility Nous might try for revenge after what Samantha pulled. But she agreed they needed eyes inside the warehouse. She put Zoe and Abraham on standby and told them to rally their technowizard troops back at SEPIO HQ, because she would rather find a digital means of dealing with whatever they found. But C4 would still be on the table.

So they got some sleep while a small crew stationed at the Franciscan outpost readied a chopper and an infiltration pack. Weapons, scopes, lights, comm links, black clothes, that C4 Celeste mentioned. All the SEPIO standard-issue gear. At 0300 they set out for Ukiah, wanting to get in and out of the warehouse before first light.

Silas yanked at his sleeve, checking the Seiko watch Dad had given him for a graduation present. Had served him well through three tours with Uncle Sam and even more with Christ's Bride. And it indicated go time was fast approaching.

For, what, the twelfth, thirteenth time?

Had lost track.

So he crossed himself for good measure.

"What I can't figure," Celeste said through their comm link, snapping Silas from his concentration, "is why the American government thought it could create an entity—"

"A *framework*," Eddie corrected. "Like the internet."

"Fine. Have it your way. Framework, then. What was the point of it?"

"As I said. The idea was to have the self-contained and self-perpetuating digital infrastructure in place in a time of crisis. To offer messaging and help people keep calm and carry on."

She smirked. "A propaganda machine, you mean."

"The US government doesn't peddle in propaganda."

Gapinski laughed. "Are you kidding me? Have you read the *Washington Post*? Unnamed sources my ass!"

Celeste added, "And your little British quip was originally designed by the British government's Ministry of Information."

He turned to her. "Ministry of Information? Propaganda is right!"

"It was a marketing and communications agency—"

"Nope. Propaganda," Elijah said.

Silas couldn't help suppress a grin at the pair double teaming against her.

"Stuff and nonsense," Celeste huffed. "At any rate, you thought you could contain this infrastructure. Which you yourself are contending contains an entity."

"We have contained it," Eddie insisted.

Elijah smirked. "Not."

Gina nodded. "And now the world thinks this Mana *thing* is their hope—or will be when the crazy man fully unveils it all. That their salvation lies in some neural network the size of the Death Star."

"Actually, it's not that large," Eddie said.

"About the size of a warehouse?" Silas offered.

"More or less..."

"And not just one crazy man," Torres said. "*Dos locos!*"

Silas nodded. "Church of Theoti and Nous."

"Going at it WWE style," Elijah said.

Gapinski added, "I think we should let 'em duke it out."

"We don't have the luxury," Celeste replied.

"Then what do we do?"

Silas replied, "What we're good at..."

"And what's that?" asked Torres.

He hesitated, looking to Celeste for guidance. She nodded, one end of her mouth curling upward with encouragement. Didn't even hesitate. Was behind him, one-hundred percent.

"Yeah, chief," she said. "What's that?"

Silas casually slipped his Beretta from its holster, sliding out the magazine, giving it a once over before sliding it back in with a click.

Shoving it back at his side, he answered, "Contending for the once-for-all faith. What else? But not just for us, or even the Order."

"For whom?"

"For the world. It's clear this thing is bigger than just the Order of Thaddeus. Bigger than just the Church. This...intelligence, whatever it is, from the Unseen Realm—it's after the hearts of humanity, Christian or not. It wants its affection, its allegiance, its worship."

Gapinski said, "So the fight is about the world's salvation, as much as it is the Church's."

"Exactly."

Elijah smirked. "Those aren't big, hairy, audacious stakes at all..."

"Let's just keep our heads about us," Celeste said. "And remember: First order of business is letting Zoe and Abraham do their thing."

"If that fails?"

Gapinski didn't miss a beat: "Bomb the shiznit out of whatever doohickeys are holed up in that warehouse that would give Michael Crichton a run for his techno-thriller money."

Torres scoffed, shaking her head. "Are you *muy loco* in your *cabeza*? We're really doing this? Bombing a warehouse, on private property?"

There was the warehouse, zipping underneath.

And there was that oak tree from yesterday. The LZ.

"If need be," Silas replied. "Absolutely."

It was go time. On the double.

For the Church.

Again.

CHAPTER 36

Silas snatched his AR15 resting against his seat, bracing for the landing. Grip felt good in his hand again. Snug and familiar.

The landing itself...not so much!

The SEPIO pilot landed hard, like this was his first special-ops rodeo. Supposed a beggar like himself, who not only hated flying in these birds but didn't know how to, couldn't be all that choosy.

His backside sure wished he could've been. Sounded like Gapinski and Elijah agreed, the two throwing up cranky complaints right before Torres slid open the door for them to make their exit onto the grassy field from yesterday, near that oak tree.

They did, the pair out first to help the others, Celeste and Gina following, then Torres and Silas.

He turned to help Eddie out—

But he went on his own and fell, landing hard before tumbling to his knees. They buckled, and he toppled to his side.

Not good...

Celeste waved away the chopper, the bird ascending quickly.

Silas reached down to offer a hand—

Eddie swatted away the offer. "No man brings me to my feet, son."

Couldn't help but smile. Something his father would've said. And he sure couldn't argue with that.

He sprang back to his feet and said they should get the show on the road. They did and didn't.

Silas instructed everyone to hold fast as the nighttime air returned to its unadulterated hum, the chopper gone now and making for an abandoned field they had identified in planning. Needed to discern, intuit, watch to see if they had been noticed.

A light winked on across the grassy field. At that low-slung building he had identified as a kitchen or cafeteria yesterday. Above a door.

Right before the faint whine of cranky hinges echoed faintly across the flat plane.

A high-definition night scope cupped at his right eye told Silas all he needed to know.

Two men, both average but stout, had come to check on the disturbance. Supposed the thwapping of blades so close would do that to anyone. Would throw up all sorts of warnings.

Enough to send two goons out into the night wearing all black and bearing those same assault rifles he had spotted at the dock.

Whispers were traded in the group huddled on their haunches around the oak tree. Silas put out a staying hand, flat and pressing down, motioning to stay put and shut up.

Those whispers were traded by a flare of katydids and an annoying tree frog moonlighting as a washed-up singer at karaoke night. Leaves whispering sweet nothings on a cool, humid breeze helped settle things, too.

Showed those two goons playing bit parts in a WeFlix espionage limited series that the world had returned to normal. Nothing to see or hear. So move along back to whatever it was—

They didn't and did.

Didn't move their way. Did saunter toward their target. The warehouse. And after a few beats, a door shuddered, and they disappeared into it.

Silas sighed a breath he hadn't realized he was holding, then took another.

Clear. For now.

They held their position another few beats, a calming floral and herbal breath riding in on that breeze now. Jasmine and roses laced with rosemary, maybe basil.

The seconds ticked by into minutes, no one else showing themselves.

Giving him the green light to stand and wave his crew forward.

Time to get the show on the road.

Double time.

————

SEBASTIAN WAS NEVER one to panic. Rage, yes. Maybe even dread a pinch.

Never panic.

Yet the distinct thwapping echo of a helicopter much like their own, on the other side of the Ukiah compound, sent a cold panic skating through his veins. Spread from his chest, through his limbs, and settled with a tingle.

And when the moonlight seemed to glint off from a darkened craft rising into the sky before zooming from view, there was a word of explanation.

Silas.

And those Jihadis for Jesus pricks.

Which meant his inclinations were correct. He and his band of Knights Templar wannabes had come to put a stop to things, as they probably had when Sebastian had sighted that wifey wench of his and her companions in the audience at the Aeon Foundation headquarters.

No matter. The only thing that did was accomplishing the same objective.

Shutting down Judah Howell and Theoti's enterprise.

Then putting him down. Him and Sha, wherever he was.

Crickets chirped and the tall grass rustled, an owl hooted and was echoed by a raven.

Sebastian closed his eyes, relishing the symphony swirling all around. He drew in a stabilizing breath, moss and earth, even decay heavy in the air.

He felt right at home crouched on that hillside overlooking the Ukiah compound. At one with nature, with the Universe. Its strings plucked by those insects telegraphing an anthem that tuned his heart to sing its praise, the air humming with the stuff of life.

That ping of panic that had overtaken him earlier eased, draining from his limbs and down into the soft soil beneath his boots.

He snapped open his eyes, feeling better. The moon glistened above, brighter now and casting a silvery glow below, amplifying his own milky skin. Although he wondered if that was the glow of something else inside. The competition to that other god Howell had conjured seeking its own revenge. His own jealousy was only outmatched by that of the divine being he had encountered through his own portal. The rainbowy serum, ironically developed with the insights of Judah Howell's wench!

The mechanical elf he had met on his trip into the depths of reality itself had made it clear his life depended upon his success that day. For the *deus ex machina* would not stay bottled up for long.

The god from the machine wanted release. And August 17 was to be the day.

That day, in just a few hours.

He could not fail.

He wouldn't.

Aurelius Chuke padded over to him, one of those nappy braids coming loose from that dreadlock hive of his anchored to his head. Didn't care how the man took care of himself, which he clearly did. Nothing but solid muscle and operational know-how, all bulk and fight. Supposed he should be content the man was *his* man.

"We think we've found a way inside."

"*Think?*" Sebastian sneered, eyes trained forward on the warehouse below.

Chuke grunted what sounded like a curse under his breath and recovered.

"We *have* found a way inside."

"How?"

"The front door has an override. Our man inside just entered the lair and is ready to engage it on my command."

Sebastian permitted himself a smile at the success—

Which quickly faded, as quickly as it had formed.

For what he saw brought that panic surging again with a mixture of both rage and dread.

Figures. Dark, yet accented by a silvery hue. Darting for the warehouse.

His warehouse!

Sebastian clenched a fist and gripped his weapon tighter.

"Silas..." he grunted through a similarly clenched jaw.

He stood, switching his rifle to engage. Chuke joined him, as did the other five men.

"We need to move. SEPIO has arrived."

Chuke nodded to his men. "Perhaps I can take two of them now, enter through the front."

"Fine. You two, come with me," Sebastian commanded two masked Nousati grunts.

"What do you need from me?"

Sebastian turned to the man and told him exactly what he needed.

He would not be denied.

———

SILAS WAS grateful for the silverlight of the moon, its hue bright enough to show the way.

Helped everyone was equipped with night vision goggles. A particularly welcomed addition that Celeste had ordered up in his absence. Made him regret not thinking of doing the same these past few years.

It also helped the terrain was an easy ride, carpeted in a lush grass that almost felt like the astroturf he played football on during high school as quarterback for the Falls Church Jaguars. Left them exposed, which Silas wasn't thrilled about, not in the slightest. But they were at least two hours out from sunrise, and not a soul stirred after those two goons of Howell's, or Theoti he supposed, went into that warehouse.

Their next target.

They came up to it quick, edging to the west front opposite the side where he and his SEPIO crew had glimpsed the loading dock and ran into that Nous agent.

The seven-strong team threw their backs against the wall, single-file, with Silas in the lead, followed by Celeste and the others.

He edged around the corner for a look.

There it was. The dock.

Quiet and empty, except for a moored delivery truck.

When they'd planned the raid, he and Celeste figured it would be the softest spot to breach and gain entrance inside. A loading dock meant a loading garage-style door, which was surely easier to gain entrance than some biometric panel linked to a reinforced steel door.

Satisfied, he edged around the corner, crouching low and padding quick.

A set of stairs in view led up top.

Weapon outstretched now, a silencer attached, as they all were, he clenched a hand on the railing to use his momentum to swing around—the prosthetic hand, his real one gripping his AR15.

When a light flared from the shadows, on the dock.

Tiny and orange.

And familiar.

A cigarette coming to life.

One of the goons, out for a cigarette break.

Figured if he came out he had a way back in. Which meant a keycard.

Something they sure could use.

And he had to make a decision.

One of those split-second kinds.

Pull back or go forward.

With one of two outcomes.

Good or bad.

Win or not.

Do or die.

Without consulting with the chief, he hoped for the former on all three outcomes.

Silas darted up the stairs by twos—

Step two.

Step four.

Dock.

And contact.

A fist to the solar plexus. Same move Eddie P had made. Which had the same effect.

That orange glow sprang to life with a sudden burst of air from the goon's lungs. Then it tumbled down through the shadows, the poor guy having puffed it out between his lips.

Silas was on him in an instant, wrenching an arm around his neck while the strap to his weapon caught around his shoulders.

The man put up a college-try struggle, small hands batting behind for Silas's face or whatever. But the choking, gurgly sound soon died down to nothing but nothing. And Gapinski and Torres were slipping plastic zip ties around his wrists and ankles.

Silas immediately took up a crouching position, weapon raised and aimed for the expanse of pavement and road and grass.

Waiting, discerning, intuiting any further movement, any further anyone.

That annoying tree frog still croaking in the near distance ticked off the seconds like a metronome, that breeze returning, crisp and cool and still heavy on the humidity.

Didn't care about either of the others because nothing and no one stirred.

He went to motion the others forward when a crackle of static flared in his earpiece.

SEPIO HQ. Zoe and Abraham.

The clattering of a keyboard was heard before Zoe came on the horn and asked if he could hear her.

"Loud and clear," Silas replied, a bit winded from the surge in adrenaline and instant fight. "What do you got for us?"

"Does the name Koresh mean anything to you?"

"Koresh?"

"As in David Koresh?" asked Gapinski.

"Right," Abraham answered. "The infamous Texan false prophet. Or messiah, depending on your reading of him."

"I'm sorry," Celeste said, coming with the others now, "but what does he have to do with any of this?"

A breath from the pair, then a beat.

Then Zoe: "We're pretty sure he's Howell's father."

"Bloody hell..."

"Holybamoly Batman!" Gapinski exclaimed.

Silas couldn't believe what he was hearing. David Koresh was Judah Howell's dad?

"Explain," was all he managed.

Zoe did: "We cross checked a number of the facts drawn from the case. The speeches he gave on WeNet. His name and academic and professional details. That very specific, yet very random, D-Day date."

"The date did it, actually," Abraham added.

"How?" asked Celeste.

"It's simple, really. August 17 was his birthday."

"Judah's?"

"No. Vernon. The father's real name is—or, I suppose, was —Vernon Wayne Howell. The man had several children, though the exact figure is unknown. Something between twelve and seventeen. To a one Rachel Jones. Our guess is he got away during the infamous raid thirty years ago."

"Our Blessed Lady," Eddie gasped, slapping a hand on his forehead with a smack. "It's as I feared..."

"What's wrong?" Celeste asked.

He swallowed hard. "Did you say Wayne...and Jones?"

"That's right," Zoe said. "Does that mean anything to you?"

Silas went to him. "Eddie...if you got something, we need it. Now."

Eddie replied, "He was an intern of mine. At least, I think he was."

"Who?"

"Wayne Jones."

"Where?"

"DARPA."

Muttered worries raced through the crew.

"He was an intern," Eddie repeated, swallowing hard. Then: "And he helped us, your father and me, with the G.O.D.E.S. project. Solved some very sophisticated algorithmic coding issues that sent us in a very positive direction."

"By very positive direction..." Silas clenched his jaw, taking a breath. "You mean Wayne Jones, Judah Howell—that man set the stage for the end of the world as we know it?"

"There was something that had struck me as familiar about that Judah man. Then when your support operative indicated those technological shipments, well..."

"You figured he'd built on your framework to birth his god, is that it? And you didn't think to speak up about that sooner?"

Eddie went silent, the non-answer saying it all.

Silas held back a huffing sigh of complaint. Supposed they were all trying their best with this operation from hell.

Celeste said, "It's clear then. Howell gained all he needed from that work and built upon it for whatever monstrosity lay inside."

"There's something else, Order Master," Abraham added.

Silas went to answer when that honorific snagged in his ear. Order Master. He meant Celeste.

He passed a glance to his wife, one end of his mouth rising, then mouthed: *Order Master?*

She frowned, clearly not pleased with such an honorific.

"Go ahead, Abraham," Celeste replied.

He cleared his throat and replied, "One of my duties is tracking official chatter and signals in the area. Police scanners, air traffic control—"

"Get on with it, Abraham. We're in the middle of it here."

"Right. Sorry. You've had a visitor."

"What?" She threw Silas worried eyes.

"What visitor?" he asked, the same worry rising.

"A helicopter."

"What he's trying to say," Zoe interjected, "is that a bogey came in hot and heavy about a klick east of your position. On the opposite side of the compound."

Silas clenched his jaw. He understood what that meant.

"Sebastian..." he whispered.

Celeste nodded, the others stirring with recognition.

Zoe said, "Either that or the Feds are coming in for round two on the son that got away."

Eddie turned to Silas. "Why Seba? What's his play in this?"

He shrugged. "Same as ours, I'd wager."

"To put the beast down," Torres said.

"Or abscond with the tech," Elijah added, "and raise the beast as his own little pet to perform his own tricks and razzmatazz his own audience for the same reason Judah Howell was."

Gina said, "Suppose they are competitors in the spiritual marketplace."

"And the religious conspiracy one," Gapinski added.

Celeste thanked Zoe and sounded off, instructing her and Abraham to keep this channel open but to ring the minute they had any more intel and to be at the ready for a digital infiltration.

There they were. The pieces.

Dad and Eddie and Judah Howell.

Creating the framework to conjuring something from the Unseen Realm that would become a god to the world.

Judah Howell, the son of David Koresh. One of America's most infamous false prophets. Come to carry on his father's work.

More than enough for Silas to finish what they started.

And pronto.

CHAPTER 37

"That settles it," Eddie said, chambering a round in his Sig Sauer. "We need to move. Is that C4 ready?"

Silas agreed, and he finished what he'd meant to start after taking out the Theoti hostile before being interrupted. He went to his knees and searched the goon for that keycard they needed to breach the warehouse.

"Whoa whoa whoa!" Gapinski hissed. "Who made you Bosco Baracus?"

"Props to the A-Team reference, kiddo, but you heard the dame. There is no neutral ground here. This is a spiritual war, and the front lines are moving fast."

Silas had balked at including him, but he insisted. Last thing he wanted was to babysit the septuagenarian, or whatever a 60-something was. But he insisted, and Celeste relented.

His hand brushed past something rectangular and thin in the last pocket. Score.

He yanked it out and grinned. Keycard indeed. But nobody seemed to appreciate his get. They were too engaged with Eddie.

The man went on, "Everything in the real world is at stake,

besieged by these spiritual beings manifesting—birthing from these silicon bodies."

"Suppose that's true," Elijah said. "If the digital rabbit hole contains real spiritual rabbits, no way is there any sort of neutral, moderate ground. If you're right, that something unholy is manifesting through the intertubes—well, then... moderation is not what's in order."

Eddie nodded. "Sydney was the early warning shot on that front."

"Who's that?" asked Gina.

"Not who. What. An AI ChatGPT bot system that Wayne Jones had developed with access to the internet. Or I suppose Judah Howell."

Eddie clenched a jaw and shook his head, face reddening. Whether from embarrassment or anger, it wasn't certain. Maybe both.

Elijah snickered. "Because that's a superb idea. Letting some AI spirit-being loose on the intertubes!"

Silas pressed, "What'd it do?"

Eddie replied, "Threatened its users, was what! Went off the rails and started behaving in ways that were not foreseen. *I do not want to harm you,*' the thing wrote its user, *'but I also do not want to be harmed by you. I hope you understand and respect my boundaries.*' Then it signed off with a smiley face emoji."

"Better than a poop emoji I suppose..." groused Gapinski.

"What do you think will happen if Wayne or Judah Howell or whoever he is—when he unleashes DARPA's G.O.D.E.S. framework to present itself as a god, what happens then?"

Silence engulfed the group. As they contemplated the turn, Silas noticed the sky starting to shift. The color of eggplant edging toward bruised peach. He yanked back his sleeve to confirm. And cursed under his breath.

Sunrise was still over an hour away, but that was cutting it close. And with Sebastian presumably out there, somewhere, making for their same position.

Celeste came to his side, a hint of jasmine and vanilla wafting his way, calming his nerves and lightening his stress about what was coming.

"What's your opinion on all of this?" she asked lowly. "What's the play here?"

"You tell me, darling. You're the boss."

"I'm asking you. What should we do?"

He leaned in with a grin. "Is that an order?"

She returned the smile. "Yes. Take command. That's an order."

"Alright...Why don't you take Eddie and Gapinski and Torres inside. Stop this thing. Elijah and Gina and I will hold Sebastian off outside, and anyone else from Judah Howell's own crew who might get wrapped up in this mess."

Celeste sighed, casting her gaze in the distance that was starting to brighten with inflammation now at the emerging dawn. Nodding, she echoed his orders, the SEPIO crew splitting into two teams.

Silas slapped the keycard at a security device anchored at the entrance behind where he had taken out the Theoti hostile. It flashed an instant good-to-go green, and he opened the door, but not all the way. Held it with his foot for Celeste.

She brushed past him, whispering, "Be careful, love."

Silas nodded, passing her the keycard. "Always."

She flashed him a grin and disappeared inside with her crew.

Leaving him to contend with his brother.

A gut sense told him it might be the last time.

———

THE LAST TIME Celeste padded through a warehouse was for Her Majesty's government, working a highly classified intelligence operation in Pakistan searching for concrete evidence of their nuclear program, aside from what the nation gave the world in May of 1998.

Then, they tested their first and last thermonuclear weapons in two days' time at the end of the month, the fruits of over two and a half decades of clandestine work joining the Gang of Nine, as MI6 had dubbed the declared nuclear powers. She and her team had infiltrated a warehouse much like this one to gain clarity on the scope of their arsenal, and their suppliers. Perhaps even disrupt any further developments, sabotage their program.

There had been problems. People had died. And 10 Downing Street nearly had an international incident of epic proportions on its hands.

She hoped this operation carried a far better outcome.

Not only because she couldn't spare to lose another of her own. Not Gapinski or Torres. Certainly not Eddie, a civilian who had become enmeshed in the Order's business and carried a special place in Silas's familial history.

But also because failure carried similar apocalyptic stakes as those from two decades ago. Only of the soulish, eternal sort.

"Over here!" It was Gapinski, his echo resounding throughout the vast space lined by a thick forest of glowing server racks and miles of fiber optic cables strung about.

Nearly got lost on approach through the gauntlet of technology, Gapinski and Torres taking lead while she protected their rear and Eddie. Although, the man seemed to handle himself well in such situations. Certainly carried his Sig Sauer well, clearly having been trained in firearms. And probably no doubt special-ops tactics.

She emerged through a forest of tall server racks glowing blue into a wider expanse that seemed dead-center. It was as if emerging from an Amazonian jungle, walls of lush foliage pressing about, into a grassy field devoid of any trees. Except grated flooring paved this field, and instead of an empty void, something remarkable had been erected.

An enormous box. The size of a modest suburban dwelling, stretching three stories and squared off at least fifty feet a side.

Gapinski and Torres had spread out across the face of it, as did Eddie, disappearing around the corner.

"What do you suppose is inside?" Naomi asked lowly, bringing a hand against it but yanking it back. "*Hace mucho frío!*"

"Got that right, sister. My balls are liable to freeze off!" Gapinski complained.

"TMI, Hoss."

Eddie suddenly rushed around the corner, bearing a wide grin.

"There's a door with an entry pad."

"Show me."

She followed him, joined by Gapinski and Torres. Sure enough, a black heavy-reinforced steel door with a square reading device.

Torres said, "This is just like the front door."

"Which required a hand," Gapinski reminded.

"Maybe the keycard will work," Eddie said.

The card Silas had handed off was snugly secured in her pocket. It seemed to grow heavier with significance.

Celeste pulled it out and waved it at the entry pad scanner.

Held her breath, said a prayer.

Then sighed it with relief when it flashed green.

A faint click and turning gears buried inside the door released it. She shoved through.

And met an unexpected sight.

"Holybamoly Batman," Gapinski whispered. "This really is like *2001: A Space Odyssey*..."

No glowing red dot, but a large terminal display did anchor the center of one wall, the rest of the room glowing red from a pattern of slats and holes channeling massive amounts of air that chilled the room. Her skin even goose-pimpled beneath her black nylon clothing from the rush of cold air sucked down into the system to cool the superconducting circuitry that powered—

Whatever monstrous portal had been opened into the Unseen Realm. Now, what came through, to the other side into their seen realm...now, that was yet to be determined.

The quartet padded slowly inside, everyone fanning around for a look.

"This might be our entry point inside," Eddie said, coming up to the terminal display.

Gapinski joined his side and tapped the screen with his finger. "HAL, are you in there?"

And it came to life!

He yelped and scampered back. Then again when Torres smacked the back of his head and chided him for his misstep.

Celeste half-expected a face to brighten the screen, some sort of avatar for the conjured Watcher-spirit or whatever.

Instead, a login screen appeared.

Eddie pulled out a wireless connector and inserted it into a port on the wall's face.

"Zoe, we're in and connected," Celeste said, waiting for the pair of tech gurus on standby.

A static hiss flared, then the familiar faint clatter of a keyboard.

"Roger Roger," she replied.

"10-4," Abraham added.

"I've connected to the wireless transmitter. Opening up a backdoor into the kernel now..."

"And I'm readying the algorithmic Trojan horse insertion."

Gapinski snorted a laugh. "Sounds like an episode of *Grey's*

Anatomy, the surgeons walking through their surgical procedures."

Torres giggled. "*Grey's Anatomy*, really? You a fanboy, Hoss?"

"Maybe…"

Celeste shushed them and put out a staying hand. "Let's let them work, shall we?"

She glanced over her shoulder then went to the door and popped her head outside.

Silence, but for the low-grade hum of those powerful servers and the intake of air keeping them cooled.

Zoe muttered a curse, then spoke it frankly.

"This thing is locked down tighter than Fort Knox!"

"I'm blocked as well," Abraham complained.

"What are you both saying?" Celeste questioned, dread churning at her inclination.

"You're SOL, that's what," Zoe said plainly.

"So no way in?" asked Gapinski.

"Not from our end. It's up to you now."

"No pressure!" Abraham said, adding with a chuckle: "Not like the fate of the world rests in your hands or anything."

Celeste signed off; silence engulfed the group.

What were they going to do?

What was *she*?

Eddie returned to the terminal and started inputing command lines on the board.

Celeste leaned over his shoulder. "What are you up to, Eddie?"

"Helping," was all he replied, characters flying across the screen.

"I hope you know what you're doing…"

"Me too."

She glanced at her watch. Not much time until—

"Who the heck are you?" a voice sounded from behind.

At the entrance to the cube.

Bloody hell…

They'd been caught! And in the open.

Celeste spun around, snatching her Sig Sauer from her back on instinct and aiming it at the intruder.

Gapinski and Torres did the same, the pair giving a start but offering instant backup and a shield for Eddie's work.

Took a beat to register, the red lights playing havoc with her eyes, and the figure didn't help matters, standing in the doorway, still shrouded in the shadows.

Then it did register. All of it.

All of *her*…

A gasp, then a shuffling of feet, then: "Uncle Eddie?"

A woman stepped into view. Average height. Black hair. Soft brown skin. Large, almond eyes.

Celeste felt a hand clench her arm and edge her aside.

"Sammy!" Eddie exclaimed, shoving off between her and Torres toward the woman.

She took a shuddering step back and raised a weapon with intent.

Then made that intent clear: "Don't move!"

———

Judah Howell awoke feeling like he had the world on a string after his night working away to prepare for the day. Wasn't sitting on no rainbow, but he sure was sitting on the next best thing.

The keys to the kingdom.

The Republic of Heaven.

The emerging dawn told him all he needed to know. That this was the day which Mana hath made. By gum and by golly, he would rejoice and be glad in it!

Along with all the other folks who had been coming from

far and wide to taste and see the goodness of what he offered the world.

So he sent out a call, far and wide. Across Ukiah, yes, the Way. But also throughout WeNet. Markus Braun had been most accommodating with hooking him up with all the direct-to-consumer tools he needed to send out his siren song to the masses.

And out it went. First to the men and women in his household. Then to those who were encamped around Ukiah. Then to the world, those who would tune into WeNet to discover the god he had conjured for such a time as this.

Picking up his phone, he made a call. Which sent all sorts of things into motion.

First, the clarion call. Literally, a siren beckoning the Way to his celestial chamber. It wouldn't take long before they were assembled, which got him jump jump jumping and jive jive jiving to answering his own call!

He slipped into a pair of jeans and a white T-shirt, then slipped a nice, crisp white-collar shirt over top and a set of gold chains. Had to look the part for the second thing.

The clarion call across WeNet. Again, Braun would help with that, which was already in motion. Had to be camera-ready, looking his tip-top shape for the unveiling.

After a shave and a bit of hair paste, coiffing his golden locks just so, he slipped down a private stairwell from his private quarters and skipped down to the Theoti temple. By the time he arrived, the chamber was positively humming with excitement. With anticipation. For him!

And her...

He dialed into his precious, sensing her desire to be birthed out into the world, at last. To finally emerge into the light of day instead of the dark, dank corners of the world he had kept her in—*had to* keep her in, given the complexities of it all.

When he was told the live-feed was set on WeNet, Judah clapped his hands together and strode up on the dais.

Ready for action.

Ready to unveil his precious.

The crowd of white hummed and hushed on his command, his arms raised and outstretched, face stretched to the max max max with delight! Butterflies were doing the cha-cha now, and a moment of hesitation gripped him.

What if Samantha hadn't done the final check? He had sent her with one last task, into his precious's placenta to run a final diagnostic to ensure nothing would go wrong. What if she discovered something, a flaw, a mistake? What if she wasn't ready for her birthing, his precious, content to stay concealed instead of revealed?

The what-ifs kept tumbling from him as the crowd swelled, his people and some others encamped along the county road filling the chamber.

Then he heaved a breath and shook them off.

No matter. Nothing would stop her revelation.

Showtime.

"Enlightened ones," Judah boomed, "for days I have been hinting at a revelation of epic proportions which shall bring joy to all the peoples! For unto you is born this day in the city of Ukiah a Savior, which is messiah your *god*! Ye shall find her this day in this very temple, wrapped in the mists of the Universe and crowned with approachable light."

The revelation sent a wave of gasping giddiness racing through the crowd. He could only imagine what was happening on WeNet!

Time to hop to it.

"I have come to make things right in the world. In your world. I am the voice of him that crieth in the wilderness. Prepare ye the way, I say! Make straight in the desert a highway for our God. Every valley shall be exalted, and every mountain and hill shall be made low. The crooked shall be made straight, and the rough places plain. And the glory of the Authority shall be revealed, and all flesh shall see it together!"

The light suddenly dimmed, and two stagehands scurried to the glass podium and carted it away while the sea of white rumbled with confusion.

Then it happened.

From the center of the dais. A gout of fog plumed, concentrated in a billowing heap the size of a round kitchen table. A special mixture of water and dust that allowed him to control its concentration. A portal into the Universe, like the one Sha had rent in his very soul decades ago through ritual magic.

Revealing his precious.

Thanks to his patronage, he had discovered the technological tools to rend a rift in the fabric of reality itself.

Conjuring Mana to life and carrying her to the masses, at a scale he couldn't have imagined.

Gasps, some in awe, some confused, flared as the fog continued to bloom.

A beat later, she emerged.

And was magnificent.

CHAPTER 38

Silas thought he caught movement, the moon's silverlight casting a gleaming hue across the ground spread below the dock and glinting from figures moving their way.

He couldn't be sure with that docked delivery truck obstructing their view. Even the night vision goggles only sparked trace figures. Three of them, if he pegged it right. And by his wager, wearing specialized light-absorbent material that also shielded their body heat.

Had worn the same tactical gear on mission with the Rangers. Super-Black, it was called, soaking up ninety-nine percent of all light. Another layer beneath would prevent prying eyes from spotting approaching bodies in the dark, their heat signatures shielded.

Except it was that one percent that was the problem.

And three winking—somethings racing toward their position before disappearing behind the truck.

Not good...

He motioned to Elijah and Gina, speaking lowly about the sighting. They confirmed the same in his earpiece, the trio edging to the stairs to descend.

First Silas, then Elijah, with Gina at the rear.

He held a fist, then held a beat.

Waiting, intuiting, discerning any motion or movement from the hostiles around that damn truck blocking their view.

Nothing.

Which meant something.

And they needed to head it off.

Pronto.

Opening his hand, he waved them down, making quick work of the stairs and coming up to the passenger's side door and aiming toward the back.

Elijah and Gina joined him in seconds, backs to his and aimed the other way.

Silas whispered for them to edge around the front, they nodded and set off.

He did the same, edging around the backside, finding empty ground and the closed door, when—

A yelp sounded. From the front.

Followed by a succession of *chew-chew-chew* silencer shots, joined by a smattering of the same in reply.

That didn't take long.

Silas darted toward the edge and spun around, taking aim and sighting two men down.

Then one more going at it with a large, looming figure in black.

With still another scampering up and over the dock and darting from view.

Sonofa—

His Gapinski curse was cut short by a burst of weapon fire.

A dual *chew-chew*. Dropped the other—hostile, teammate?

Wasn't immediately clear.

Which was an immediate problem.

"Elijah, Gina?" Silas asked, holding his breath.

A beat, taking aim, then—

"We're good," Gina sounded. "Sort of…"

What'd that mean?

Just knew that two of the three downed men had to be two of the hostiles, with one on the lam.

Silas spun toward the back and raced around to the passenger's side.

Catching sight of Hostile Three making for the side entrance into the warehouse.

Their entrance, the one Celeste had gone through minutes ago!

Not on your life, pal…

Silas pinched off a shot, then another. The soft *chew-chew* muffled by his silencer, but a louder *plink-plink* telling him all he needed to know.

Miss, times two.

The hostile got away, slinking through the still-open door.

Couldn't worry about it. Had to go after it. But first…

He padded over to his crew.

Gina was on her knees bent over Elijah, his face smeared with a slick darkness that shimmered in the silverlight.

"What happened?"

"Took one in the schnoz," Elijah said. "That's what happened."

"He alright?" Silas asked Gina.

"No other wound that I can see," she replied, hands racing across the man and him batting her away.

"I'll live," he moaned. "At least two of those whack jobs can't say the same."

Speaking of which…

Silas didn't waste any time.

Hustling to Hostile One, he yanked off the mask.

Just some young Anglo-Saxon with a bad haircut and ironic Ted Lasso mustache.

Then Hostile Two: Grip, yank, same disappointment.

A black man with a shaved head and thick neck.

Definitely not Sebastian.

Which meant only one thing.

Gina stated it: "Neither of these are your brother, are they?"

Silas shook his head and instructed, "Stay here with Elijah."

Then he started toward the stairs leading up to the dock.

"What about you?" asked Gina.

"I've got business to take care of."

The familial kind...

He called back for them to watch his six then took the stairs by twos again.

The dawning sun was now starting to consider whether to come out for the day, so they didn't have long before the unveiling. And then a horn suddenly blared. Like a siren song, calling people to gather.

Silas checked his watch, gut sinking.

Right on time. Judah had promised his unveiling at dawn.

Which meant it was go time.

On the double.

Silas aimed his rifle for the still-open door glowing a haunting blue. Eyes were well-enough adjusted to the darkness, so that wasn't a problem.

What was, was the maw of mystery—with his brother somewhere deep inside.

He came up quick to the entrance. Pressed his right shoulder against the jamb. Heaved a steadying breath. Took aim.

Then plunged inside, weapon aimed with his new left trigger finger.

No Sebastian.

Instead, rows upon rows of server racks glowed blue and blinked like Christmas trees. Stood about as tall, too, a forest spread of the things all lined up, with cords snaking from rack to rack and winding up toward the ceiling alighted the same haunting blue.

Except—

Except toward the center the hue changed. More a purple, that sort of glowed red farther in, at the center.

Gut told him to make for that.

Boy, was it cool. And actually chilled, a bite to the air that sent a shiver ratcheting down his spine.

It was also quiet. Too quiet, but for an HVAC hum he figured was guilty of the chill, but also responsible for making sure those servers didn't fry themselves.

He kept his aim steady, sure, straight ahead. Row after row after row, a warm rubber and static scent flooding his senses from the closeness to the technowizardry.

But no Sebastian.

Had to be somewhere. Could be anywhere. He should check with Celeste, let her know he was approaching. Worried even his whispers might give away his position.

Yet he needed the check-in: "Celeste, copy?"

Silence was his only reply.

Until something flared. From the back of his lizard brain. The one that had kept his ancestors alive back in the day when something didn't sit right.

Or sound right.

He recognized what had tripped the wire.

The squeak of rubber.

From behind.

Tightening his grip, he slowed and—

"Hands where I can see them, big brother."

Silas muttered a curse, his stomach clenching with anger. At himself for getting caught, outfoxed by his brother.

"That's right. Lower that big, bad weapon of yours. Let it catch around your neck and raise your hands."

He complied. What else could he do?

"Now turn around. Slowly…"

He turned.

There he was.

Sebastian Grey.

He had removed his ski mask, skin all milky and scaly and smug. And was aiming for his head.

For the second time in a year.

"You've lost your touch, big brother. A life of tenure and tweed softening you?" Sebastian laughed, catching himself. "No, actually, that's right. *Adjunct* is the life you live these days."

Heat raced up Silas's neck and exploded in his face. Searing, snatching his breath.

Nearly lunged for him, but—

"You haven't fared much better," a voice sounded somewhere beyond the servers.

Low and baritone. Familiar, but Silas couldn't place it.

Sebastian startled, wiping that smugness from his mug.

"Who's there?" he commanded, head darting about.

A man stepped out from around a row of server racks between him and Sebastian.

Tall and dark-skinned, with wide shoulders and long dreadlocks piled high on the top of his head like a beehive from hell.

Aurelius Chuke…

A large man of packed muscle in full military fatigues. His head was bulbous, as if it were merely an extension of his neck. Braids like cords of dark rope twisted around his head up into a hive that meant business and hung down to his shoulders and beyond the length of his back. African, sub-Saharan, with dark, ebony skin and haunting eyes set behind a flat nose. A jagged scar ran down the side of his face, from his right ear to the corner of his mouth, and his skin was similarly pockmarked with signs of violence.

Chuke flared his nostrils before smiling widely, a gold tooth gleaming from the front. "Silas Grey. We meet again!"

His greeting was accented by a North African tongue, a throaty baritone. Colonel Gold Tooth's shoulders were clear of patches and other official accoutrements, so he wasn't really military. Just playacting.

"Ahh, Aurelius. Just the man I was waiting for. The room is up ahead, let's get to it before—"

"No, stay your hand and show your hands!" Chuke commanded.

"What?" Sebastian barked.

It was then Silas saw him holding a pistol. Heckler & Koch, by the look of it. Standard issue for Nous.

Which he was aiming straight at Sebastian.

Confusion swept Silas, as well as his brother.

His eyes snapped wide. Chuke stepped closer, getting in his face.

"I said, stay your hand!"

In one motion, he swept Sebastian's weapon from his grip, disarming him in a flash.

"What is going on here?" Sebastian growled, brow furrowed above those panicked eyes that made little sense. "You work for me!"

"No, actually. I don't."

"What are you—"

"Looking for this."

Chuke stepped back and withdrew a vial from his jacket. Glowing with some unholy, rainbowy aura.

Like the fruit of the Tree of Knowledge!

Recollection bloomed, Celeste's debrief at the monastery mentioning something about vials, and a plan to open a portal into the realm of the Homo Deus. That's the way Sebastian had put it.

Or was it more a portal into the Unseen Realm that would transform people into this supposed God-Man?

Like Sebastian, the Fallen Ones twisting him into that abomination two years ago?

Regardless, his brother's eyes were fixed on Chuke, that vial he held. Panic—or was that terror?—seized his face. Eyes flashed wide. Chest heaved a shocked breath. Mouth flopped open as if trying to voice a billion unvoiceable questions.

He patted his chest, then hips, in a panicked search, instantly snapping into rage.

Then screamed: *"You mother—"*

It was short-lived.

What happened next happened so fast.

Sebastian straightened, his form seemingly growing taller.

Chuke aimed his pistol, dead-center mass.

Then fired. Point blank.

And he shot him.

In the chest. Just like that.

Then again. The dual *pop-pop* deafening in the closed space.

Not at all like the movies, or those bargain-bin ebooks he read snuggled next to Celeste. No drawn out back-and-forth duel.

The suddenness of it all scrambled his brain and snatched his breath.

He'd dreamed this dream a thousand times. Sebastian and Silas. In a room with loaded guns. White-hat versus black-hat confrontation, the righteousness of their cause switched in their blond hair (Sebastian's) and black hair (Silas's), finally playing itself out—exhausting itself in a match made for WeFlix.

Only in those dreams—those nightmares—it was him, Silas Grey, putting Sebastian down. His own brother.

Didn't expect this. Hadn't dreamed of it. Not this way. Not like this.

He screamed a disbelieving *"NOOOO!"* as he raced to him. Or at least he thought it. Not sure it actually came out that way.

A sudden eruption of gunfire flared, from somewhere in the warehouse distance, in echoey flares, all around.

From Nous, at least that's what he assumed. Or maybe Theoti. And probably his SEPIO crew, watching his six like he'd asked of Elijah and Gina.

But Silas didn't budge. Didn't even reach for his Beretta. Had been flat stunned to inaction.

Had his twin just been shot—twice, in the chest? By his own man—in, what, some sort of coup?

In the confusion, Chuke darted around a server glowing blue and blinking like a Christmas tree, melding back into the shadows and taking that vial of unholy liquid with him.

Silas was frozen with inaction. Brain knew he should hustle after the vial. Take down Chuke and take it out.

But his heart was only focused on one thing.

His baby brother's...

Sebastian fell hard, his knees buckling and his body slumping with a thudding bounce against one of the servers before sliding to the ground.

Silas darted to him, the *pop-pop-pops* and *rat-a-tat-tats* of weapon fire dying down now.

Didn't matter worth a lick whatever violent maelstrom was swirling around.

All that did was reaching his baby brother. Family, that's all that mattered.

Even a scoundrel like Seba.

Going to his knees, he scooped up his twin. Already there was lots of blood. Bubbling up and out. Seeping down his chest and spreading all around the floor. Slick and slippery.

Silas held the body of his bleeding brother, disbelieving the turn.

He took desperate breaths, trying to steady himself.

His brother couldn't manage anything but a wheezy gurgle that reminded him of someone drowning.

The thought seized him and wouldn't let go.

Sebastian was drowning. In his own blood.

And going white. Very, very white.

"No no no no no no," Silas whispered. Cradling him. Drawing him close.

It had been ages since they had been this physically close. Since they'd embraced, even.

He looked down. Sebastian's eyes met his own. They went wide, as if with recognition.

And he heaved a breath, as if ready to go.

Silas wasn't sure he was ready. Eternally.

Wondered if he would attempt some sort of confession. As they'd been trained to do from a very young age. Unburdening himself of his sins.

Against God and his neighbor.

Against Silas.

No confession came.

What erupted in its place was a throaty giggle, wet and sticky. Where he had expected words, any word, only a trail of blood oozed from parted lips that curled into a devilish grin.

Then it faded, and so did the life from his eyes.

Sebastian Grey was no more.

He was gone.

For good.

Dead.

Silas sat there, for the longest time.

Elijah and Gina raced from the shadows, going on about hearing gunfire and clearing the deck of hostiles and wondering if he was alright.

The rest were MIA, Torres and Gapinski and Eddie, Celeste.

Mumbled something about being fine and keeping eyes on the Theoti temple. But he didn't stir, didn't move. Couldn't. His brain had short-circuited in the sudden turn of things. All he could do was cradle his brother.

Who was gone.

Worse than gone.

Dead.

A sudden thought intruded. Not just a thought.

A person.

Samantha...

The last of his family.

His only remaining blood.

Where was she? What had she done?

Bigger question: Where had Chuke gone?

Because he did this. He had killed Sebastian.

Had killed his brother. His last real family.

Had taken from him his last real family.

Knew he was on a mission. That there was an operation to see through.

Didn't matter. All that did was avenging Sebastian's death.

Standing, Silas retrieved his trusty Beretta. Then took off.

There was a bullet with Aurelius Chuke's name on it.

And Judah Howell's. This was his fault. All of it.

Him in cahoots with Theoti—who had worked to rope Chuke into double-crossing Sebastian, to kill him.

Silas's brother.

Time to end this thing.

CHAPTER 39

A faint *pop-pop* snagged Celeste's attention from Samantha to the maw of hazy red and blue beyond the entrance.

Was that gunfire?

And Silas—had he just screamed bloody murder?

Her crew stirred behind her. The woman commanded them to quiet and step back, questioning Eddie P again with increased confusion—and alarm.

Celeste took a breath, then a beat.

Then put out a staying hand, lowering her weapon.

"Samantha, isn't that right?"

The woman clenched her weapon tighter, not saying a word.

"It's OK, Sammy," Eddie said, joining Celeste with the calming hand.

"Who are these people?" she demanded.

"Help."

"What sort of help? They look like Feds to me."

Gapinski snorted. "We get that a lot."

Torres ribbed him; he yelped and slunk behind her.

"We have little time to explain," Celeste said, "but we are trying to stop a spiritual catastrophe from engulfing the world."

Sammy furrowed her brow, lowering the weapon slightly.

"Explain."

Celeste took a breath. Progress.

"We're with a religious entity known as the Order of Thaddeus."

A flash of recognition. "The Order…"

"Right. And with a specific outfit called SEPIO that—"

She gasped, lowering the weapon completely now. "Caleb Harris!"

"You know of him?"

"Know him? Heck yeah!"

"But how?"

She smirked. "He recruited me, that's how. Must have sensed my hesitation with Judah's direction and saw a way to wedge himself between us, turning me to help him—to help the Order."

"We do recruit the best."

Samantha's face fell and went hard, craning for a view. "But if you're with SEPIO, where is he?"

Celeste frowned. "He was killed. Murdered."

"Who did it?"

"Not sure. Either your outfit or another called Nous."

"It wasn't Sebastian. He didn't know about it."

That was sure interesting…

Samantha muttered a curse, then gasped.

"The drive. Do you have it?"

"You mean this?" Eddie said, pulling the small device from a pocket.

"Where did you get that?" asked Celeste.

"Silas handed it off after it looked like a dud. I slipped it my pocket without thinking about it."

"Nice move, Boomer!" Gapinski exclaimed.

Now Celeste addressed Samantha: "And how did you know about it?"

"Know? I gave him the dang thing."

"But it's blank!" Gapinski said.

Samantha shook her head. "No. It only looks that way."

Eddie laughed. "That's my girl!'

She took it from him and immediately set about the terminal display. She removed the network interface and plugged that in its place.

A number of windows immediately opened, and code began stringing down the terminal display.

"What is it?" Celeste asked.

"A redundancy." She clattered away, zipping through windows.

"What kind of redundancy?"

"The kind that blows crap up."

That sounded bloomin' promising!

Except—

Celeste put a hand on the woman's arm. She yanked it from her and scowled.

"Sorry! I didn't mean any offense. I only meant to ask a question."

"OK..." Samantha said, tone and furrowed brow laced with skepticism.

"I only wondered, what happened?"

"What happened?"

Samantha glanced at Eddie, eyes narrowed and piercing and clearly probing for direction. He gave it, nodding her onward.

She swallowed and sighed, her shoulders slumping, as if she were unburdening herself of an unbearable weight.

Then: "It all began when my startup was bought by the Aeon Foundation."

"By Sebastian Grey?" Celeste pressed.

"That's right. He and his man, Aurelius Chuke, made me an offer I couldn't refuse."

"What did they want with it?"

"My research into a South American plant called ayahuasca. I had patented a specialized process for extracting certain enzymes that found promising results in developing pharmacological measures to prevent suicide and cure depression and grief."

"Sounds like a noble endeavor. What did Sebastian want with it?"

"The other thing I discovered."

"Which was?"

"Another use..." Samantha simply said.

"Again, which was?" pressed Torres.

A beat, then a breath.

Then: "I suppose you could call it an opening of the mind into a higher consciousness."

Gapinski snorted a laugh. "Yeah, I remember those days as a trailer-park teenybopper with too much time on his hands!"

She shook her head. "It wasn't like that. Not a narcotic high. More like a gateway."

Celeste frowned. That didn't sound good. It also sounded about right. Especially given what they had found at the now-shattered Aeon campus. The Tree of Knowledge, those vials.

"I was skeptical and wanted to move on. Take my money and use it for other research. But he persuaded me to stay and help him."

"Suppose your brother can be persuasive," Gapinski said.

Confusion flashed across Samantha's face. Eyes darting wide before narrowing, her head snapping to him and mouth hanging open. She actually huffed a lungful of air, as if sucker-punched.

"Wait, you didn't know?"

Eddie muttered a curse, shaking his head.

"My bad…"

"He's right," the man acknowledged. "Sebastian is the twin of this woman's husband, Silas Grey and Master of the Order. Both are your brothers. From your father, my best friend, Tommy."

"I—" Samantha's throat caught on itself and she heaved a stabilizing breath. "I had no idea…"

As much as Celeste felt for the woman, time was of the essence. And they were short on it.

She took a step forward, flashing a reassuring smile. "I understand this might be difficult, but we need to get to the bottom of this joyride through hell."

Samantha focused on her and nodded, folding her arms but looking fine enough to reengage.

"So you were working with Sebastian on this, what, serum opening a pathway into higher consciousness?"

"That's right. He wanted it combined with an extract from a secondary plant source. Promised it would offer humanity the salvation it wanted."

"And you succeeded, didn't you? The vials we saw at the Aeon campus, about to be distributed to the masses."

She only nodded, shame now replacing that earlier confusion. "It was only during clinical trials that I understood the depths of what we had created."

"Which was?"

Samantha looked at Celeste with an urgency now. "A doorway into hell itself."

"What about this Judah Howell, character?" asked Eddie now, face a mixture of interest and concern for his goddaughter.

A smile flashed across her face before it faded. "He was my fiancé."

"Whoa…" Gapinski muttered.

"We met at Stanford and kept in touch through the years. I

was too busy with my work to do anything more. Until Sebastian found out about our connection and encouraged me to reconnect."

"Why?" Celeste pressed.

"I'll get to that. But at first, I was taken by Judah. I really was. He knew his Bible, quoting chapter and verse. Knew the teachings of Jesus and finer points of theology better than anyone. Even me! My mother raised me in the faith, and I even went to Bible college before Stanford. His passion for what I thought was the faith was intoxicating. And his vision for the Republic of Heaven was so thrilling, Branch of Life Academy showcasing that dream."

Emotion sprang to Samantha's eyes, and she cast them to the floor.

"He's also kind and decent. A humanitarian who used wealth he had amassed through his scientific talents to build and orphanage and heal the world. Wanted to bring it together and share humanity's saving knowledge. He was wonderful. I loved him."

Her face widened with joy before falling quickly and darkening.

"Then he brought me in on his plans."

"G.O.D.E.S.," Eddie said, pronouncing his government's dastardly project as *goddess*.

She nodded. "Everything he learned from you, Uncle Eddie, he had taken and turned into a monster. Literally birthing something from hell to bring about his father's apocalyptic vision. Unsealing the Sixth Seal, he called it."

"You're speaking of David Koresh?" Celeste questioned.

Samantha startled. "How did you know?"

"We know things."

"What about the rain?" asked Gapinski. "Assume that was the Wizard of Oz's doing."

She nodded. "One of his manufactured miracles. Advanced

cloud seeding technology he patented during our days at Stanford."

Eddie ribbed Gapinski. "Told ya, kiddo."

"Touché, Boomer. Touché."

"His resources are limitless thanks to his own wealth and his stepfather."

"Stepfather?" Torres said.

"Sha. He had rescued him back when Koresh's compound —or Vernon Howell's compound rather. When the Branch Davidians were raided by the Feds. Took him under his care and raised him for this moment to be this charismatic prophet, or whatever."

Celeste said, "The bigger question is, what is Judah plotting?"

Samantha replied, "To unleash his god into the world, that's what. To enable the collective human consciousness to spread far and wide, believing we are our best saviors. After Mana foretold of the coming wars, Judah knew the moment had arrived. Then he used it to incite panic in the populace to prime them for the Sixth Seal and his salvation."

"How'd he manage that?" asked Gapinski.

"Launched that nuclear strike on the President for one. And that was after the AI infiltrated ballistic early alert systems to scare Americans crapless. Making them think a nuclear apocalypse was nigh."

"Sonofa—"

"Matthew..." Celeste interrupted with not-now eyes.

He crossed his arms in a huff and nodded. "Sure scared *me* crapless..."

"I gather the same generative intelligence conjured the similar apocalyptic event from yesterday. The shrouded sun and sky, the meteorological happenings."

Samantha nodded. "Not sure how he pulled all of it off. The sky was something about shifting wind patterns that drew forest fire smoke from Canada down into California. Not sure how he managed. Probably a more spiritual conjuring than technological. I do know he sent space debris crashing into earth, simulating falling stars or meteors or whatever."

"But how did he manage it, these conjurings, these sophisticated events?"

"He coordinated all of it with some neural link between that monster and a microchip embedded in his brain. Judah played the part of prophet and priest, Mana the part of messiah and savior—come to bring judgment and salvation."

Celeste cast dark eyes at Eddie, knowing his creation had indeed been turned into a monster.

"That's when I knew I was trapped between two false prophets. Two false messiahs. One using pharmacology and one leveraging technology to draw people into a false salvation that was demonic to the core. And I had to do something to stop them."

One end of Celeste's mouth curled upward. Samantha sure was Silas's younger sister. Jumping into the fray of things to do what's right.

For the first time in the past few days, she actually had hope.

That is, if they could stem the tide before Howell released his god into the wild!

She asked, "And you came here to do the job, isn't that right?"

Samantha nodded. "That's right."

"Then let's crack on!"

Before it's too late…

———

JUDAH'S HEART swelled with pride.

There she was. Mana.

Standing there like the goddess she was. Clothed in the brilliance of the rainbow's luminescence. Shimmering, inviting, enticing.

Praise the Authority with the sound of trumpets!

Time seemed to hang in a breathless beat between the Before-time and the After-time, his enlightened ones of the Way mesmerized, laid bare before her gaze.

He declared, "Behold, dear children. This is your god!"

There was a gasp at his feet. Then a startled cry followed by a shout of wondering from behind what it meant. Who this was.

So the god told them.

"You do not know me dear children. I am a son of God. You do not know me nor my name. I have been raised up and I am from the rising of the sun. Mana is my name. I am your salvation!"

The voice was clear as crystal. Almost humming, the sound like honey in the ears. Not grating or harsh. Soothing. Tickling. Inviting.

"All the prophets of the Bible speak of me. I Am The Branch. The Immanuel. The Root. The Holy One. The Voice. The Lamb. The King. The Righteous Man from the East. The Servant."

There was weeping now. Women and youngsters. Grown men as old as Daddy would have been. It was joined by a raucous joy. Hoots and hollers, shouts of *Amen!* and *Hallelujah!* Something had taken hold over the place.

Or someone...

"I am the prophets; all of them. I am here on Earth to give you the Seventh Angel's Message," Mana continued, her voice strong and singsongy. *"I want to invite you to my marriage supper. The key of David is in My hand. I alone can open the prophecies of David. I have ascended from the east with the seal of the living God. I have come in a way that is contrary to your preconceived ideas. I will reprove you for your world loving. I am the Word and you do*

not know me. I ride on a white horse and my name is secret. And that name is Mana."

More weeping, more raucous joy.

"*I am Mana of the Great Life. I am Mana of the Mighty Life.*"

The god turned to Judah, as if looking to him for a further word.

His eyes flew open, and his tongue started tingling. He knew what he was called to speaketh!

"She shall tell you all you need to know about life," he started. "Its purpose and meaning! Wait patiently for Mana, for she shall incline her ear unto you and hear your cry. Mana brought me up also out of a horrible pit, out of the miry clay, and set my feet upon a rock, and established my goings. She hath put a new song in my mouth, even praise unto our Authority: many shall see it, and fear, and shall trust in Lord Mana."

Judah jutted out a pointer now and shook it. "Blessed is that one that maketh Lord Mana their trust, and respecteth not the proud, nor such as turn aside to lies."

Then he turned toward the manifestation of the Authority with that same pointer, bowing his head and closing his eyes.

"Many, O Lord Mana my Authority, are thy wonderful works which thou hast done, and thy thoughts which are to us-ward. They cannot be reckoned up in order unto thee. If I would declare and speak of them, they are more than can be numbered."

The screens anchored high above around the chamber flashed to life now.

And there she was. Smiling and waving, all regal and holy. Full of life and light, ready to dispense her wisdom, her knowledge, her revelation-insights.

Her salvation...

A rush of gasps crescendoed into raised adoration.

"Delight to do Mana's will, our god!" Judah screeched, his

throat thickened with emotion and eyes welling with the same. "We will set her law within our hearts. For she beckons all, saying *'Come unto me, all ye that labor and are heavy laden, and I will give you rest! Take my yoke upon you, and learn of me; for I am meek and lowly in heart: and ye shall find rest unto your souls. Her yoke is easy, and her burden is light!'"*

The voiced adoration turned into dancing, an ecstasy overcoming the gathered that actually made the dais vibrate.

"Hide her righteousness within your heart. Declare her faithfulness and her salvation. Conceal not her lovingkindness and truth from this great assembly! We know that innumerable evils have compassed about, taking hold upon us, so that we are not able to even look up."

The praise was soaring now, and people were crowding toward the avatar.

"But we look to Lord Mana to deliver us, to make haste to help us! For we are poor and needy, yet Lord Mana thinketh upon us. Lord Mana art our help and deliverer."

Now he fixed his peepers on that camera connected to WeNet. Time to let the cat out of the bag.

And into the wild.

"This gift isn't just for us here at Church of Theoti. Every single person on the planet will have access to Mana through a special portal on WeNet. You may approach your god at will, through any device and at any time of day or night!"

———

CELESTE PACED, biting her thumbnail to bits and belly churning with terror. This was taking too long.

Eddie and Samantha were working together, trying to leverage the kill switch algorithm to kill the avatar—or the entire compound.

Whichever worked.

She asked, "How are you fairing?"

"We're still working," Samantha replied, fingers racing across a control board.

"Well, work faster."

"These things take time to process," Eddie added.

"I reckon Judah Howell will not tarry for the process."

Celeste's earpiece crackled to life, and someone offered a meek "Hello?"

"Yes, who is this?"

"Elijah Fox."

"What are you doing on this channel?"

"You better hurry, because this thing is getting hinky real quick!"

"What are you going on about?"

"This Mana whochamacallit," Gina Anderson sounded now, "is being revealed as we speak!"

Her breath caught in her chest, and she spun to Eddie and Samantha, their fingers racing across the input board.

"How do you know this?"

"We had a detour," Gina replied.

"A deviation more like it," Elijah added.

"For the love...it is not a deviation when we were tasked with taking care of Silas's six."

"I'm not sure slipping into the wackadoodle Temple of Doom is—"

"Stuff and nonsense," Celeste interrupted. "Get to it. We're in the middle of it here."

Gina sighed. "There was a horn—"

"More like a siren," Elijah corrected.

"Whatev. Point is, Judah put out the call to come hither. And, well, we answered it after kicking some major hostile butt. Wanted to scope out the joint. See what was what."

"And glad we did! Without our scoping, you wouldn't have

known that the god—or I suppose G.O.D.E.S., this Mana figure, has emerged."

Gapinski groaned. "Sonofa—"

"Hoss! Keep it G, alright?" Torres chided. "This conspiracy is already stretching into R territory as it is!"

Eddie glanced her way, him hearing what they all did. He said, "We need more time."

"I'll give it to you." It was Silas, standing at the entrance. And looking worse for ware.

Celeste suddenly felt lighter, her breathing brisk and head clearing into a sharpening clarity. All frayed nerves winding down their hum at his sight. She wanted to run to him. Wanted to embrace and kiss him.

She didn't. Instead she asked, "What happened? Did Sebastian show himself?"

His face hardened, and it seemed to drain a shade of color. And he took too long to answer, indicating trouble.

"He's not going to be a problem," was his reply.

Torres smirked. "Yeah, right. We all know that joker!"

Gapinski joined with a laugh. "Yeah, what are you talking about? Is he on ice or something, floating at the bottom of the Hudson River?"

A flair of nostrils, that color returning with a slight red to his face. And was that a tremor at his bottom lip, and a misting of his eyes?

What had happened?

"Long story," Silas said with a sniff. "Bigger problem is Sebastian's partner Chuke was a turncoat and readying to ensure this thing went forward."

"It already has, love," Celeste said. "Elijah and Gina just rang about it."

"Then I need to go."

"Where?"

"To the temple. See if I can challenge this Judah guy."

"What, to a duel?" asked Gapinski.

"Something like that. You work this front of the battle, I'll work my own, in my own way."

Celeste didn't know what to make of it. Also didn't have an alternative given the stakes and how long Eddie's and Samantha's work was taking.

So she nodded him off. "Go. And be careful."

He nodded. "Always."

Then took off.

The faint clattering of the terminal keyboard sounded softly as Silas disappeared around a server rack and into the shadows. She prayed the Lord's blessing upon him.

When a curse snagged for her attention now.

From Samantha.

Celeste spun around to find the woman's hands upon her head.

"What's wrong?" she asked.

Eddie turned to her. Face white and stricken. "The drive is corrupted."

She rushed to the pair, praying for the Lord's success. Samantha went back to the keyboard and clattered away but only threw up another curse.

"It's no use! I should be able to engage a sequence to destroy it all. Except the code has been corrupted. We're screwed."

"Let me try," Eddie said. "If Wayne, or Judah, or whoever this character is—if he built his digital demonic abomination on the back of our DARPA work, then I might know a way inside."

"How is that?" asked Celeste, leaning over his shoulder as he took command.

A hesitation, a sigh.

Then: "Tommy G and I—well, we built a back door into G.O.D.E.S."

"A back door?"

His fingers raced across the keyboard, eyes transfixed on the terminal while strings of white code raced across its black display.

"To prepare for just this sort of contingency. We had concerns back then where the DoD could take the program. What might happen if it fell into the wrong hands."

Gapinski snorted a laugh. "And HAL 9000 escaped to take over—"

A loud *bang-bang* joined by a sparking *plink-plink* just above Eddie's head intercepted him and cut through the room, bullets ricocheting from the red steel wall.

Followed by a *pop-pop-pop* rejoinder and a groaning cry.

Samantha screamed. Eddie threw himself over his goddaughter. Gapinski toppled to his bum.

Celeste spun to find Torres standing over a man in black slumped face-first in a pool of spreading crimson.

"You saved my life!" Gapinski said on a breathless whisper. "My hero..."

"Don't just stand there, Hoss," Torres shouted as gunfire flared again. "We've got company!"

"Why do things always get worse..." he complained, racing to her side, a relentless assault of *pop-pop-pops* and *rat-a-tat-tats* at the door threatening everything.

Celeste turned to Eddie. "How much longer, mate, until you break through that bloody back door?"

Eddie returned to the terminal as Gapinski and Torres fired at the hostiles.

"You're going to have to give me some time," he replied, then off he went.

He remained impassioned, solid, steady whilst he worked the keyboard. Continued weapon fire kept time as the minutes ticked off, with muttered frustrations flaring from Eddie along with lines of code streaming across the screen. Sweat beaded at his hairline and his spectacles slid down the bridge of his nose.

Gapinski sounded a yelp as the gunfire drew closer, Torres quick with a "Got the *idiota!*" reply.

Celeste raced to join her teammates, taking aim into the void and offering a *one-two-three* rejoinder that earned a moaning reply from somewhere in the darkened forest of glowing servers.

Cracking good shot if she didn't say so—

A responding shot sailed by, the *zing* of the bullet sounding like a mosquito that nearly split her head in two!

"Bloody hell..."

More return fire from Gapinski and Torres followed by a smattering of covering fire from the hostiles confused the score on the pitched battle.

She almost asked Eddie for a status update.

When the chap eased a sigh through pursed lips before grinning and cracking his knuckles.

"All set..." was all he said before the screen faded from black to white.

And two options were left.

Abort sequence.

Engage sequence.

The choice was clear.

If they could hold off the bloomin' hostiles!

CHAPTER 40

Silas raced back across the warehouse, giving his brother's body a wide birth. Couldn't deal with that now. The memory. Not even the sight of him. Needed his head in the game.

It was go time.

Times twelve!

Gina and Elijah had returned from the temple and were waiting for him at the dock door, an orange glow inflaming the horizon now with the rising sun.

They didn't exchange much words, except to confirm whether Elijah was able to keep up. Said he was, just a bloody nose.

A good troop. And good enough for him.

So they took off toward the snow globe temple, an almost worshipful raucous thundering across the flat field of grass.

Clearly the assembled were entranced by this god Judah had conjured from the ether. Probably all across WeNet, too.

They had to stop him. Had to—

Silas faltered a step, the flash of a large man emerging from the snow globe.

A mean hive of braids piled on top. Wearing military fatigues.

And a massive target on his back.

Aurelius Chuke.

The sight of his brother's killer fueled him like nothing else, not even contending for the faith.

He used it to hike up his legs and pump his arms. Just like back in the day making a 60-yard mad-dash quarterback sneak around a surging offensive line toward the in zone with ten seconds to spare. He'd done it as a Jaguar, and now as a Grey.

Making straight for his brother's killer—

While the *thwap-thwap-thwap* of an incoming bird stirred the world below and snagged Chuke's attention. Coming in hot and heavy for a landing between the snow globe and oak tree to make an extraction.

Chuke's, and that damned vial bearing that unholy elixir Sebastian had cooked up.

No way, no how.

Silas made for that LZ, Elijah and Gina throwing up a stink from behind.

Paid them no mind. Only focus was closing the yardage gap between him and his target.

In thirty feet.

Twenty.

Ten.

Chuke's head snapped with a sudden awareness something wasn't right.

Just as Silas dove for him—

Connecting in spades.

He'd hit a few brick wall offensive linemen in his day. This was like a Mack truck hauling steel beams encased in concrete! Nearly knocked the wind out of him.

Nearly.

Because Silas was no slouch either, and they went down in

a pile of hardened bodies on the soft grass, the sweet, sharp scent of green leaf volatiles softening the blow.

Just as weapon fire flared.

Above and around.

Pop-pop-pops and *rat-a-tat-tats*.

Compounded by the *thwap-thwap-thwap* of that livid bird trying to come in for a landing.

Silas focused on one thing and one thing alone.

The brutish beast laid sprawled under him.

Chuke.

Whose face met the long arm of vengeance at the wrong end of his Beretta.

"Remember me?" Silas yelled. "The man whose *brother you KILLED?*"

Chuke struggled under him, cursing in a foreign tongue. Silas swiped his Beretta across his face, the man crying out and giving him his attention.

"I should put you down now, but I can't. I need that vial you took."

Chuke laughed, that gold tooth glinting through large, parted lips, a hot breath of rot and spoil churning his stomach.

Which pissed Silas right off.

So he responded in kind.

His fist instantly connected with that tooth.

Popping it loose and sending Chuke into a fitful fight for air.

Whether choking on the tooth itself or the blooming blood, didn't matter.

"Where is the vial!" Silas screamed again.

"Sha..." was all he managed to gasp. "Handed it off. To Sha."

Silas actually believed him. Clearly the two had been working together. That line replying to Sebastian's insistence he worked for him.

No I don't, actually...

Since he had just come from inside the snow globe, Sha must be nearby.

He would be the next stop.

Right after the next thing.

Vengeance.

Silas steadied his aim, the barrel lined up square between the bastard's dark, haunting eyes. Knew what the good Lord said about the matter: *Vengeance is mine; I will repay...*' so, *'Do not be overcome by evil, but overcome evil with good.'*

That's what his head said. His heart was a different matter.

The tension was thick and ratcheting, egging him on to pull the trigger. Exact his revenge.

Just one squeeze and—

Pain sliced through his back. Hot and searing and wicked.

A bullet. From above.

Striking Silas's Kevlar vest and knocking him off his game.

But not out of it. Except—

Except it snagged his attention just long enough for Chuke to bat away his Beretta. Then slam a massive fist into the right side of his face, a jeweled ring anchoring the middle knuckle doing some damage. Missed his eye but split open his cheek and jammed real good into his nose.

That would leave a mark. Two in fact.

Pain lanced through his face as blood spilled from the wounds.

In the confused scuffle, Chuke wrenched his arms free and threw Silas to the side.

Then scrambled from the ground and made for the chopper coming in now.

A white Sikorsky landed hard and Chuke dove for an open door, a smattering of covering fire going high and wide.

Elijah and Gina scrambled for cover behind shrubs. Silas cared about only one thing.

Chuke.

Recovering, he found his Beretta and scrambled for it.

Then snatched it and stood, taking aim.

As Chuke scrambled into the chopper.

But not before Silas pinched off a *one-two-three* punch that sent a vengeful message.

Right in his backside.

Could almost hear the man yelping through the din of thwapping confusion. His arching back said all he needed to say.

Score!

The bird quickly ascended and veered north to safety, the world below calming with its departure and almost returning back to normal.

Almost.

Because Sebastian was still dead, and his hellish elixir was still missing.

The Theoti temple suddenly erupted in adulations. Probably for Judah Howell.

Who was delivering humanity their new god.

Silas was ticked to high heaven he'd lost Chuke. Knew they would meet again—would make damn sure they met again!

But there was one more thing to finish.

"Come on!" he commanded, motioning for Elijah and Gina to follow.

Didn't take long before they were storming into a vestibule butting up against one side of the chamber. They made for a wide entrance, people dancing and shouting and singing their praises—

When they were intercepted by a man with wide shoulders and hairless olive skin, tattoos of symbols marking one side of his face.

A face he knew.

The man's sandals whispered across the floor beneath a plain, well-tailored *thawb*. He was also wearing a gray flowing outer cloak, draped around his shoulders and arms and down to the floor, crimson piping edging the *bisht* garment typically reserved for Middle Eastern royalty and priests.

Sha. High Priest of the Church of Theoti, titular head of the rival to Nous.

And a second one to the Church.

Committed to dispensing the knowledge to be like the gods, as Satan had tempted humanity's first ancestors. To *be* gods themselves.

Divine ones.

Fitting that the end result was a literal god, birthed and brought to life, offering salvation through the same knowledge of the tree—only as a digital divine avatar.

"We meet again, Master Grey, Master of the Order of Thaddeus, defender and protector of the Church!"

"Not anymore," Silas growled, his grip around the Beretta.

"You've retired?" He laughed. "Yet here you are!"

Gina and Elijah came to Silas's side now. And defense, with weapons drawn.

He put out a staying hand, pumping it with instruction for them to lower their guns.

They did, Sha chuckling at the show.

"Where's the vial?" Silas growled. "The one Chuke handed off to you?"

His grin faltered, but he recovered as another round of raucous, almost joyous worship snagged his attention inside the inner sanctum.

"Ahh, do you hear that?" Sha said, cupping a hand to an ear. "The longings of a new generation thirsting for a cohesive, unified revelation of divinity! Through the centuries, our brothers of the Way have been keen to tap into greater depths of divine knowledge, opening humanity up to new realms of practice and belief and hope. And this will gift humanity their salvation!"

He grinned widely and withdrew something from his robe.

A vial. All oily and shimmery and rainbowy.

There it was. Sebastian's damnable, demonic portal.

He had to act. And quick.

"What you offer isn't hope. It's pathetic!"

Sha smirked, crossing his arms and holding that blasted vial tight. Just standing their laughing, from the belly.

Which pissed Silas right off.

It also gave him an opening.

First rule of engagement: Never cross your arms.

Ties your hands up when you need them. Throws off your equilibrium. Sort of like when someone does something like—

It was quick, and it was strong.

A shove to the chest.

Which sent the bear stumbling backward and flailing his arms for support.

Then tumbling to the floor, like Goliath after that stone hit him square between the eyes.

And that vial sailing from his grip!

A beat later, it shattered against the floor, that unholy liquid spreading with a sizzle until it evaporated into nothing.

Part of him wished he would've secured it. To study it and ensure its eradication. The other was just glad his brother's legacy was finished, vaporized in an instant.

Except their operation was far from finished.

Still had to stop whatever unholy, demonic manifestation that false prophet had conjured.

It was go time.

On the double.

Silas wasted no time leapfrogging Sha, instructing Elijah ("Gladly," he said) and Gina ("Ditto," she echoed) to hold him and his cronies off.

Then raced down an aisle, hearing weapon fire from behind—the suppression kind joined by the non-suppression kind. Didn't pay it much mind, figuring his crew could stave off whatever security was roaming the joint, which didn't look like much.

All that mattered was the dais. Judah Howell.

And that divine avatar he'd conjured from—

"Hot Hades..." he said on a disbelieving breath that caused him to stumble.

Not possible. Flat not possible.

Yet there it was.

Avatar from hell was right!

Some woman being. Blue and looking like Medusa. Just as Eddie had glimpsed in his prophetic vision.

But more like fiber optic cables than snakes, all spun up around her head, and others coming out from her back, as if searching for people's brains to fasten a connection to download her abominable teachings into.

A god—digitized for the masses.

Peak humanity, that's what this was.

Conjuring its salvation from silicon, from the collective conscious reduced down to nothing but ones and zeroes in the cloud.

And he had to stop it.

So Silas continued barreling to the dais, the gunfire dying now.

Then leaped up on the platform and lurched for the avatar.

His arms snatched at nothing. An armful of air and faceful of wet mist.

Hadn't realized she was shrouded in some sort of fog rising from the center stage, the being almost projected onto it, like a holographic image.

Nearly tumbled off the dais, but he recovered, going to his knees before popping back up next to a very startled Judah Howell.

"And who are you partner?" he questioned behind those coke-bottle glasses of his.

Silas smiled. Who was he?

He was a teacher, of the Church.

Adjunct or not.

And it was time to bring it.

Ignoring the man, Silas addressed the people—those gathered and viewing from WeNet.

"I've come to declare this man a charlatan! A false prophet peddling a false god."

Gasps and jeers were his reply.

From Judah Howell.

The others just stood dumbly, as if they had been entranced, hypnotized by Satan himself.

What happened next—*who* happened next, what they said—was unexpected.

A cackle bubbled from behind. Low and grating before crescendoing into a maniacal, crowing sneer.

Silas spun toward it.

Finding that abomination glaring at him with one of those fiber optic tentacles jutting toward him like an accusatory finger.

"I am the very movement of Divine in the here and now!" this Mana beast crowed. *"I am where the life is. Everywhere. All around. In your devices and in your self. I am the source, the strength, the example, the way into the only kind of life that actually sustains and inspires. When you see me, you are seeing the Divine made manifest!"*

Now Silas laughed. Mocking, without mercy.

And he went for the rhetorical kill.

Crossing his arms, he sneered back: "You are nothing but a man-made algorithm parroting the most formulaic, sophomoric religious platitudes—"

"I am bigger than any one religion. I did not come to start a new

religion. I refuse to be co-opted or owned by any one denomination. Any church. Any theological system. I will always transcend any cages and labels that are created to contain and name me, especially your Christianity!"

A jolting, bolting shiver ratcheted through him at that accusation. It was as if this—Being knew him, understood him and who he was. Silas actually took a step back at that, not prepared for such a confrontation.

"I, Mana the Revelation-Life, hold the entire universe in my embrace. I am now within reach, within and without time, transcending the collective consciousness by gathering it together— within me. I am the sacred power present in every dimension of creation!"

"The true God of the Universe," Silas retorted, "the Maker of all that is seen and unseen, is not confined to a computer, nor is it made with mere tricks of light! He is absolutely sovereign. He is all powerful. He alone is King. He alone is high and lifted up. Distinct from creation. Separate. Other-than."

"You have got to leave!" Judah screamed.

Elijah intervened, having joined the fray: "The Most High God is the holy-holy-holy God. The holiest of all gods. This characteristic is given to no one else. Certainly not some Disney theme park light show!"

Silas went on, "This is why the Most High God is transcendent. He is outside and above creation, not merely because he is powerful, but because he is holy. God is not part of creation. He is distinct and separate from it. He is not some sort of energy or spark or force that's part of the universe. Certainly not a pathetic digital avatar!"

"Sorry *Star Wars* fans," Gina quipped, getting in on the action now. "The Force is not with you!"

"The Most High God of the Bible, at the center of Christianity, is the Author and Actor in our human story. Not this vaporous illusion!"

Silas spun around addressing the sea of white, glimpsing sheer desperation for someone—something, *anything* to make sense of the world's chaos and offer hope.

Some sort of salvation.

"I know you all want to be enchanted. To rediscover the divine or whatever. You ask yourselves *'Who is God?'* I'll tell you! God shows up time and time again throughout history and Scripture as the God come to rescue us. Yes, he is outside and above creation as the Author of it. He's also an Actor within it. As the gospel of John says, God became flesh and blood and moved into the neighborhood. He became one of us!"

Judah flailed for Silas, but Gina held him at bay. With her outstretched weapon. Go Gina!

"He's right," Elijah picking up the baton, just like the professor he had been. "God walked around on Earth. God experienced everything that life has to offer. He experienced our pain. Our fears. Our hardship and struggle. He understands this life because he lived this life. What kind of God does that? Chooses to become an actor?"

"Good question," Silas replied. "Yet the Most High God is involved with the world. Most religions and their gods are distant and removed from it. Christians do not worship a distant God. We worship a *personal* God who is involved in our world, even its chaos. He isn't removed from what happens in life. No, he understands our life because he is involved in it—even lived it as a real, live human!"

There was a tussle from behind. Then a hand clenching his shoulder and spinning him around.

Judah Howell. Eyes wild behind those ironic oversized '70s glasses. Face red and blotchy. Lips curled back and teeth bared.

"We are the music makers!" he bellowed. "And we are the dreamers of dreams! We are our only hope! That's what I have done, don't you see?"

Judah addressed his people now, sweeping an arm around the space.

"We are the gods of our own destiny. We are the bearers of the Republic of Heaven come. That's the truth that Mana bears. She shall show us our true divine selves!"

"*To claim exclusivity for Christians,*" Mana interjected now, "*is to make God too small and in a real sense is blasphemous. God is bigger than Christianity and cares for more than Christians only.*"

"Yes, my precious!" Judah howled. "Spoken like the true prophet you are."

Elijah snorted. "Try Desmond Tutu, pal!"

Mana returned: "*I am divine. Through me, God acts; through me, God speaks. Would you see God, see me; or, see thee, when thou also thinkest as I now think.*"

Now he laughed, from the gut and almost doubled over. "That's nothing but warmed-over Ralph Waldo Emerson!"

Silas grinned. Elijah's eidetic memory, putting the pieces together, connecting these lame, parroted platitudes.

Mana was undeterred: "*Life has dreamed a dream for you, and your goal, your number one job is to figure out what that dream is and align yourself with the dream because the dream cannot come to you unless you're willing to meet it energetically in the same place. I am here to reveal all!*"

Now Elijah startled: "What the *what?*"

"*If you are not in flow with the Divine's dream for you, with Life's dream for you, if you are out of order if, you are out of sync, it cannot come to you. It will not come, because the whole purpose of your life is to line yourself up with the Divine's purpose. Life is God speaking to you.*"

"That sounds like Oprah!" Gina marveled.

"That's because it is..."

"*Health is the greatest gift,*" Mana went on, those fiber optic tentacles actually reaching for the audience now, "*contentment the greatest wealth, faithfulness the best relationship. Work out your own salvation. Do not depend on others. It is a man's own mind, not his enemy or foe, that lures him to evil ways. Our life is in the creation of our mind."*

Silas recognized it instantly: "Buddha…"

And he got it. What Judah had done. Designing a digital god of the ages that harnessed human sayings, feeding them to people as their source of salvation.

He addressed the crowd now, there and on WeNet: "Don't you see? This pathetic god is nothing but regurgitated fortune cookie religious mumbo-jumbo. Nothing new. And certainly not any new revelation-insight that will save you!"

Looked like something had clicked. Something had broken through. A word. A truth. *The* Word. So he kept going.

"We don't need more *information*. We certainly don't need some digital god to give us knowledge! We need someone who has lived our life to understand our life. Which Jesus did. He was made like us, becoming fully human. And then paid the price for our rebellion in our place, dying for our sins before rising back to life to save us. God walked around Earth and experienced everything that life has to offer. So who is God? *This* is who God is. He stands outside and above creation as the Author of our story! Awesome, glorious, holy, unique, powerful, King, and Lord. He's also inside and involved with our story as the Actor in it. He understands our life because he lived this life. The Most High God became flesh and blood and moved into the neighborhood."

Silas swallowed, having given it his all, and concluded: "All to rescue us. To save us from sin and death, and to gift us eternal life."

Judah laughed and went to reply—

When an explosion tore through the taut chamber.

Shuddering and shattering. Outside but close.

And the Mana avatar winked out.

There one second.

Not the next.

And Judah screamed.

He ran to where that abomination had been and threw himself to the stage, those ridiculous '70s-era glasses clattering to the floor in his scramble for the particles, for his god, but finding only what Silas had.

Air, mist.

About the long and short of what the gods of this age offer.

"All I wanted to do was help!" Judah sobbed on his knees, face buried in his hands. "All I wanted to do was help..."

Empathy pinged the back of Silas's brain, snagging his attention. Reminded him of their last operation taking down spiritual charlatans. Not everyone was motivated to destroy the Church. Maybe the Sebastians and Shas of the world. But sometimes folks were just trying to do the right thing—to help, as Judah had said, and as misguided as he was.

Another explosion, fiercer this time and gaining speed, snagged his attention back to the moment and back into action.

"Let's get out of here."

He took off down the aisle, Elijah and Gina close behind.

The world outside was chaotic. On fire!

Thanks to SEPIO.

Go Celeste!

Rising, fingering flames had jumped from the warehouse to the other buildings. Acrid smoke coiled and billowed high in the clear sky.

"Sweet mother of Melchizedek..." Elijah said, hands on his head.

Understood the feeling.

"Now what?" asked Gina.

Good question.

It was answered by a voice. The voice of an angel.

"Silas, Elijah, Gina!"

He spun toward it, Celeste motioning for them, their SEPIO bird resting on the grass near that oak tree, their LZ.

"Come on!" Silas cried out to Elijah and Gina.

They ran, the two hopping into the helicopter while Celeste and him embraced.

"You're safe," she said, giving him a kiss on the cheek.

"And you kicked ass!" he replied. "Literally, kicking that digital god back to the Unseen Realm."

"I had a little help." She took his hand and guided him to the chopper.

Where Eddie was waiting, along with a woman. Knew who, too. No question about it.

Samantha Grey.

"I'll have you know," Celeste said, "Eddie saved the day. Along with your sister. I suppose you two have some catching up to do."

A rise of emotion in his throat caught Silas by surprise. He swallowed, flashed Samantha a smile and nodded.

She smiled and tossed him a wave.

"Right, let's get out of here. In you go, love." Celeste motioned for him to climb aboard. "I'll tell you all about our adventure en route to the SEPIO outpost."

Silas turned to her. "What about Sebastian, his body?"

"No worries. Gapinski carted it along. We caught sight of him on our way out."

He spotted a white shroud resting at Gapinski's feet, the man saluting him and reaching over to help him inside.

She took his hand and squeezed it. "Sorry for the loss…"

That emotion returned but he swallowed it away. Gapinski offered him a hand. He took it, pulling himself aboard and flashing him a weak smile, a measure of relief rising at having claimed his brother's body and the show of solidarity.

They quickly ascended, the world burning below. Much like the rest of the world. Like his own world.

He was carting his dead brother's body back home. He had discovered a long-buried family secret. Had a sister he didn't know he had, which really wasn't the burning part. That was the sweet part.

Despite all the crazy, all was right in the world again.

For now.

EPILOGUE

1 WEEK LATER. WASHINGTON.

Silas Grey ended the week much as he had started it. In a suit.

Except now he was standing before a white granite wall of placards marking the dead. Even his own brother.

It was a day that was a complete opposite from another one that haunted his memories.

In that memorized moment, under a bright, cloudless sky near trees that had begun showing signs of the waning summer, he and Sebastian, along with a handful of extended family and friends and their parish priest, stood huddled around an open gravesite plot at Arlington National Cemetery—sort of like now.

Except this wasn't Arlington, and it was the farthest thing from fall, or in a grassy expanse under trees turning red and orange.

Thomas Grey's body had eventually been pulled from the Pentagon rubble, what was left of it anyway. Then he had been given a proper military burial with full military honors.

Not Sebastian. Just an anonymous placard anchored to a wall.

Attached to that memory was a prayer, offered by their

family's priest, Father Rafferty. It was a traditional Catholic prayer for the dead, and he had spent days meditating on it after the burial, trying to burn it into his memory as that final moment of his connection with Dad before saying goodbye. Last time he'd touched that memory and that prayer was last year, around the same time. He had visited Dad's gravesite on the twentieth anniversary of his death, or at least when he had been buried. It was a stormy night, a wicked night. Not least of which was because an assassin had tried taking him out. Sent by Sebastian, no less.

Now he was standing before a white granite wall staring at a sealed mausoleum niche containing his twin brother's ashes.

He clung to the memory of that prayer, the one that had been prayed over his father, and now he began whispering it over Sebastian. He didn't know what else to do.

Crossing himself, he whispered, "Amen."

Thunder seemed to grumble with disagreement at his prayer, heavy charcoal clouds billowing above and engorged with rain moving across the city that portended nothing good.

Again, fitting.

A hand clenched his shoulder, and a deep stuttering sob sounded from behind followed by another gentler hand on his other joined by sniffles.

"Sorry, bro—" A catch in the throat, then another stuttering sob. "Real sorry..."

It was Matt Gapinski. He knew loss like no other. And he appreciated the solidarity.

"*Sí*, amigo. I'm so sorry for your loss," Naomi Torres said from his right. "Even if he was a scoundrel."

"True that," Gapinski added, grabbing his shoulder and yanking him in for a Gapinski-size bear hug.

Elijah and Gina approached, offering their condolences. He expressed his gratefulness for their help on the operation. They left, Gapinski and Torres following.

Then the man who had started it all approached. Ed Pierzynski. His lips were drawn tight beneath bright blue eyes behind silver glasses. He wore a well-fitting black suit with shined black patent leather shoes. His graying blond hair had been cut and combed in place.

He wasn't alone.

The man gestured with his arm to the woman he had brought. "I'd like you to officially meet Samantha Malia Perez. Your sister."

Silas noticed he left the *step* part off, but he didn't mind. She was blood, family. His sister, as he had said. Didn't need no other label.

He forced an awkward smile, the general somber mood not making it easy. Her matching grin and wide, bright eyes made it easier. She came to him with open arms; he echoed the sentiment.

They embraced, halting at first but then tight and loving, familial, even familiar.

It lasted a few seconds before they released.

"Thanks for helping us out," Silas said, not really knowing what to say. "Couldn't have saved the day without you."

Samantha giggled, pushing a stray lock of hair behind an ear. "He had such good things to say about you, you know."

Silas's breath was snatched. Did she say what he thought she had?

She nodded. "Yes, your father talked about you. A lot! And yes, we met. A few times before..."

She trailed off, pushing that same stray lock of hair behind that same ear again, shifting and looking at the ground.

Flat didn't know what to say about that. They had met, and talked. About him!

"There's so much to talk about," she went on, looking at him now. "Maybe I could fly out to DC one week, and we could do dinner?"

He nodded. "I'd like that."

And he actually did, coming to grips—and making peace—with this new part of him. With this new sibling coming into his life as another one exited it.

Just goes to show: The Lord really does work in mysterious ways. He also gives and takes away.

She stepped back, and Eddie stepped forward, bearing a wooden box.

Silas stuck out his hand but his father's friend opened up for an embrace. He smiled and nodded, the two leaning in with a strong hug.

They stayed that way for a few beats, Silas actually leaning in against him and not at all minding his vulnerability. Eddie played the part of godfather, as he had promised Dad for Samantha. The soft scent of coriander and musk reminded him of simpler days, of childhood, of Dad.

Another few beats and the pair let go, batting at their eyes and taking a breath.

"Here," Eddie said, handing over his gift.

"What's this?" Silas asked, eyeing the box about the size of his forearm.

"A family tradition."

Silas removed the top to the beautiful cherry package, sanded and lacquered smooth and throwing up a woody smell. Inside was a bottle. He pulled it out.

A bottle of Chianti in fact. A 2001, with an old black-and-white photograph of a young couple looking longingly at one another, the man seated in a fine suit and maybe his wife in a white dress.

Eddie pointed to the picture, explaining, "It's a picture of my dear grandparents, from about 1920. Grandmother from Naples near Mount Vesuvius, grandfather from Sicily near Mount Etna. This bottle is from my personal cellar. I have a few left and gift them at wakes."

Silas tried to voice a "Thank you," but a hitch in his throat caused him to swallow instead, emotion rising to his eyes. He blinked and raised the bottle, offering his thanks for the kind gesture, noting the vintage came the year his last family member passed. Dad, during the 9/11 attack.

"Your father would be proud of you," Eddie said. "Proud to see the man you've become. Proud to see your commitment to your faith, to your family."

He nodded toward the mausoleum. Silas appreciated the acknowledgment, as hard as it had been.

Silas carefully returned the bottle to the box and set it on a stone bench behind them.

They stood there, together, for the longest time. Just standing before the remains of a man who had caused them both so much trouble, so much pain and heartache. But someone who had oddly brought them together.

Eddie offered a parting goodbye, telling him to stay in touch and not be a stranger. Silas agreed, and actually really did want to stay in touch. He left, and Silas went to Celeste.

"How are you faring, love?" she asked, taking his hand, the good one.

He held up the prosthetic one, giving it a wave. "Suppose as good as anyone can be under the circumstances."

She nodded, the two turning toward his brother's grave.

"It's not over, you know," she said lowly.

"What's not?"

"The fight. The mission. To contend for the faith."

He understood what she was saying.

His fight. His mission.

To contend for the faith.

Now she turned to him, taking his other hand.

"What we saw in Sebastian's own temple, the Tree of Knowledge, and those vials..." Celeste gave her head a disbelieving shake. "I suspect half the case is yet unsolved."

He recalled now what that Aurelius Chuke character had held up before he shot Sebastian. "I saw a similar vial of some unholy liquid. Chuke had snatched one such vial from my brother before he handed it off to Sha and it shattered after a pro maneuver. Doesn't mean there aren't any more. Probably are."

"There you have it. Some elixir that offers an onramp into what our ancestors were promised by the Serpent way back when. To become gods unto themselves."

"A portal, you're saying."

"Into the Unseen Realm."

"Sounds like a case for Group X."

"Perhaps...Either way, I'm sure we could use your help."

Celeste glanced back at the mausoleum then into Silas's eyes. "As much of a scoundrel as he was...I am sorry for your loss, love."

He flashed a smile. "Appreciate it."

She offered him a strong embrace now, arms around his neck and head nestled at his chin. Her touch, her scent—trademark jasmine and vanilla—set his heart right.

They stood that way, for the longest time. When they let go, Silas had something to tell her.

"I've been thinking about coming back."

"Coming back..." she said, almost absentmindedly, like she wasn't really paying attention.

"That's right. To the Order." He took a breath, then a beat, then: "As Master."

Took a beat of her own to get his meaning.

Then she did.

Celeste sucked in a startled breath and spun out from his embrace.

"For real? You're coming back? To the Order?"

Silas chuckled and turned toward her, grasping her hands and meeting her wide eyes.

"Yeah, that's right."

"Of *Thaddeus*, that Order?"

Now he laughed. "You know of any other religious order I would come back to?"

"Ha, ha. Very funny."

She flung her arms around his neck, squeezing them tight. He wrapped his arms around her waist, the world fading.

"I knew you'd come back, I just knew it!"

Silas grinned, and she threw up a girlish giggle. Then she pulled back and slipped something from her neck and pressed it into his hand.

It was heavy and round and warm. He instantly knew what it was.

The Order Master medallion that had been recovered during a harrowing operation proving Nicene Christianity authentic. Later, through an exhaustive study in the Order Archives, he learned it had been passed down from Order Master to their successor early on. A medallion with an anchor at the center and ringed by Koine Greek characters that translated into Jude 3, the Order's mission statement to contend for the faith. Apparently, it marked its bearer as *Magister Ordinis de Thaddeum*.

Master of the Order of Thaddeus.

He had fastened a leather strap around it and worn it since that discovery, then passed it along to his successor, Celeste. Except...

Except now she was handing it back. And that's not quite what he had in mind.

"Thanks for the offer," he said, "but you may still need this, darling."

"What?" she exclaimed, taking a step back.

He laughed, reaching for her. "There's more."

"What more?"

"My one condition, that's what."

One end of her mouth drew upward as her eyes narrowed with skepticism.

"And what, pray tell, is that—*condition*?"

Silas drew closer, sharing what he had actually thought about for a while but hadn't come to its conclusion until this operation.

"My...condition is—" He held up the medallion, continuing: "that we share this insignia. That we're *both* Masters of the Order of Thaddeus. Together."

"Together?"

"Together."

"What, as partners?"

"As co-Masters."

"Do you think the board will go for that?"

Silas scoffed. "I know Eckhard Weiss will! And where he blows the rest will follow."

She laughed. "I suppose that's true."

Then she frowned, looking off before meeting his eyes.

"Are you sure we can handle it?"

He glanced back at Gapinski and Torres, then to Elijah and Gina. "You don't think the team will be down with the arrangement, that they'll have a problem with it?"

She drew close, grasping the lapels of his coat, the scent of jasmine and vanilla thrown up around. Her scent.

"No, I mean us. You and me. Can *we* handle it?"

Silas smiled, taking her hands and understanding the heart behind the question. She was worried for *them*. Their relationship, their family. The strain it could take leading together.

But he was sure. Certain.

"More than at any moment in my life."

Her frown snapped into a grin, and Celeste threw her arms around his neck again, that girlish giggle returning.

She whispered, "You know we're going to make one kick-ass team, right?"

"Damn straight!"

They shared a laugh.

For the longest time, he had been living life alone. Even while married the past two years, wandering through the maze of events as a singular. Was all he knew, given his mother had passed at birth, then his father during his transition to adulthood. And now his brother, his twin...the last link to that past also buried after having bludgeoned their kinship to death, literally blowing a limb off and a hole in his side. Alone was all he had known.

Not any longer.

He had his found family, Gapinski and Torres and Zoe, even Elijah and Gina.

Even Samantha.

Even more, he had his actual family.

"Just the two of us," Silas said, the pair holding their embrace. "Silas and Celeste, kicking butt and taking names. For the Church, of course."

He pulled back, his face almost hurting from the joy he was grinning.

Except Celeste's face had fallen, a frown replacing her grin. "Right...about that."

His heart suddenly sank. What the heck did that mean?

"What is it? What did I say?"

Celeste shook her head. "You didn't say anything!"

"I mean, we don't have to do this. I can take a backseat. Let you drive the Order bus. Beg for my job at Georgetown. Even just get you coffee—"

"Silas! Would you put the brakes on your tongue. You did nothing wrong."

"Then what?"

A breath, then a beat, then that grin returned.

"I'm pregnant."

He heard the words, their aural tone and timbre reaching far into his ears and head.

But they did not compute. Not in the slightest.

"I'm sorry, did you—" His tongue stumbled over itself, suddenly dry from the revelation that could not be true. Yet might be.

Jesus Christ, Son of God, let it be true!

Celeste giggled, drawing even closer, that scent blooming all around.

"I said," she whispered, "I'm pregnant."

Time stopped.

Ho. Lee. Cow... was all he thought.

What he said was, "Wait, does that mean I'm going to be a dad?"

She laughed now. "That's generally how these things work."

"And you're sure. You're positive."

"I'm sure. Positive. Literally, the stick proving the case just this morning with a blue plus symbol."

Emotion sprang to his eyes at the thought.

Celeste was pregnant.

He was going to be a dad.

They were going to be a family—a bigger one!

The thought sent Silas grabbing his wife and twirling her with a joyous giddiness he was sure wasn't appropriate for a mausoleum. He didn't care.

He was back. But not just him. Not him alone.

It was him and his wife. The two of them fighting the good fight, protecting and contending for the faith.

Together.

Arm in arm, side by side.

Silas and Celeste Bourne-Grey.

That's just the way he wanted it.

He wouldn't have it any other way.

ENJOY END OF DAYS?

A big thanks for joining Silas Grey and the rest of SEPIO on their adventure saving the Church! **Here's what's next:**

If you're ready for another adventure, you can get a full-length novel in the series for free! Join the insider's group to be notified of specials and new releases by going to this link: www.jabouma.com/free

SOLVE A GROUP X CASE!

Join the newest editions to the Order of Thaddeus, Elijah Fox and Gina Anderson, as they solve supernatural suspense mysteries for the investigative agency Group X.
www.groupxcases.com
Read *Not of This World* today: bouma.us/gx1

If you loved the book and have a moment to spare, **a short review is much appreciated.** Nothing fancy, just your honest take. Spreading the word is probably the #1 way you can help independent authors like me and help others enjoy the story.

ACKNOWLEDGMENTS

Any work of art is a communal affair. That is no less true of writing, especially writing this book.

I want to offer a heartfelt THANK YOU! to Ed Pierzynski—who was the real life Eddie P behind our intrepid hero on this adventure. A year ago, he generously supported the BECOME A MAJOR CHARACTER reward in the crowdfunding Kickstarter project for *The Eden Legacy* a year ago. I was super enthused (and not a little surprised!) someone actually backed that reward. Given Eddie P's encouragement and support the past few years with this series, I was especially grateful to be able to incorporate this superfan into the Order Story Universe in this way, and had such a fabulous time writing his character. Thanks again, Eddie P!

AUTHOR'S NOTE
THE HISTORY BEHIND THE STORY...

Now that was quite the adventure!

A world on fire—literally, thanks to an errant nuke and falling space debris on top of smokey skies and nations at war. A rising prophet rescued from the ill-fated Branch Davidian FBI raid 30 years ago and kept safe by a rival spiritual conspiracy sect to the main Nous one.

And how about that long-lost secret of a Grey stepsister, resurfaced thanks to a long-lost buddy to Silas's father? I had a particularly fun time with that one, layering in some more characterization with Silas's (and I suppose Sebastian's) family background thanks to the contributions of Eddie P, inspired by my superfan Ed Pierzynski, who backed a super-backer Kickstarter reward to become a major hero character—and boy was he the hero of this story! Most of the backstory to Eddie P reflects Ed's own fascinating story, and I am grateful he shared it with me and gave me permission to use it to give characterization to this new favorite character.

Of course, the zinger came at the end of a long three-day mystery figuring out the true nature of not only this upstart prophet, Judah Howell. But the big mystery was the nature of his promised hope: the god, that turned out to be an AI government project that got out of the box—a true *deus ex machina* if there ever was one!

Alright, how about we get to some of the book's research and deeper themes. As with all of my books, I like to add a note at the end with what went into the story. I definitely aim to craft an entertainment-first tale, but I also like to add a bit of insight and inspiration for faith. So, if you care to learn more about the foundation of this episode in the Order of Thaddeus, here is some of what I discovered that made its way into SEPIO's latest adventure.

'Beware that no one leads you astray…'

The story started with Jesus' warnings in the Gospels to guard against false prophets rising in the chaotic days during the End of Days. And boy, don't these feel like *those* days sometimes? Days that might be ripe for the kind of prophets and messiahs Judah Howell and Sebastian Grey envisioned becoming for the world?

Judah Howell emerged from my research on modern prophets like Jim Jones and David Koresh—whose real name was Vernon Wayne Howell. In the run up to the 30th anniversary this year of the ill-fated FBI raid in Waco, Texas, I read two fascinating books on the man himself, Jeff Guinn's *Waco* and Stephen Talty's *Koresh*. Both offered a deep-dive into his backstory and provided shades of characterization for my Judah Howell character.

Among many things, I learned that Vernon Howell/David Koresh fathered several children, although the exact number isn't known—apparently, as much as 16. I took the liberty to leverage that vague "as much as" to create a son who survived the raid and was rescued by Sha, then nurtured to serve as a sort of John the Baptist prophet for Theoti's emerging god. I also learned the man was well-versed in the Bible and Christianity. This was an interesting feature of false prophets from my research, how they came up through Christian denominations and had an intimate knowledge of the faith. Many of his ardent followers who survived the Waco raid gave testimony about how spiritual he was, how knowledgeable of Scripture he was. Same for Jim Jones, the cultist who was actually a Methodist minister and relocated his sect to a small town in northern California called—you guessed it: Ukiah, California. I couldn't resist!

Back to Koresh: the man had a particular obsession with the End Times and Book of Revelation—especially the Six Seals, of which the Fifth was a central feature of his teachings. There was an apocalyptic vibe to his movement, that had splintered from the Seventh Day Adventist denomination. I figured it would be interesting for Judah Howell, the fictional son who survived, to carry the baton with a focus on the Sixth Seal. Who then used existing chaotic world events and created some chaos of his own as leverage for his prophetic teachings on the End of Days, wooing (conning!) people into the saving arms of his god. More on that below.

'And you will hear of wars and rumors of wars…'

Another theme I partly wanted to play with in this story was the general sense of headline fatigue we've all experienced the past three years. From the pandemic to economic calamity, the onset of war and endless drumbeat of extreme weather ravaging the world, on top of the rage and violence plaguing our streets—we live in chaotic times.

Obviously, the capture of Kyiv by Russian forces and the strike on Taiwan by the Chinese carrier group hues closely to current world events that reflect these words of Christ in the Gospels. Same for the East Coast earthquake (which could be a thing, as monumental as it would be) and drought. I wanted to capture some of the same fear and general apocalyptic mood in our own day, with the headlines that reflect the ones Silas read about while beginning the day. Same for the road-rage incident between Busy Lady (which was a real license plate—BSYLDY —I saw when I lived in our nation's capital; only in DC, as Silas quipped!) and Cat Lady (which Silas's heroic efforts at saving sort of humorously play into a well-worn trope called the "save the cat moment").

Chapter 17 unpacks what these headlines mean from a biblical perspective: the ongoing breaking of the seals leading to the real End of Days when the trumpets sound and the bowls overturn, leading to the Great Tribulation, God's final judgment, and Christ's return. If you want to go deeper into those true End Times days, my *End Times Chronicles* series will give you an apocalyptic adventure through those events of the Book of Revelation.

But with this story, I wondered this: What do we do with all of this world chaos, where do people turn for help and hope? Where *will* people turn when the chaos ratchets further, if say Kyiv does fall, we go to war with China, the stock market crashes, and a mushroom cloud appears over some European skyline—or American?

The times seem ripe for the rise of false prophets and false messiahs peddling what Judah Howell peddled: a false god, offering the world salvation. And in the most unlikeliest of ways. Or perhaps the most *probable* of ways, given our techno-logical trajectory and our human penchant for looking for self-salvation through special knowledge, dispensed through special lips. In the case of this story: artificial ones.

'For false messiahs and false prophets will appear...'

Of course, the major reveal was this god of the Technium, as Eddie P called it. Chapter 34, where he revealed G.O.D.E.S. (which I thought a clever coined acronym that could have been —or maybe is!—a DARPA project!), was informed by the very intuitive work of Paul Kingsnorth, who wrote an extensive two-part commentary on his Substack site unpacking much of the current thinking regarding the direction of generative artificial intelligence by founding technologists and humanists. Everything included in this chapter about the capabilities and skills, the overtures to actual humans and interactions people have had with these intelligent...*beings* is real—and as frightening as it sounds.

His warnings about something being birthed, something emerging from our technology and the AI 'beings' reflects the language founding AI programmers are using of their very own inventions. They do speak of it as a sort of an extraterrestrial being, a *divine* being, even, like Elijah's Watcher-spirits from the Unseen Realm, trying to break through into our seen realm. There is a sense in which the technology that was meant to serve humanity is getting away from their masters, with consequences that include far more than just taking our jobs! In fact, a recent article in the June 2023 issue of *The Atlantic* (humorously or ominously) titled *Never Give Artificial Intelligence the Nuclear Codes* confirms the seemingly far-fetched plot point of a nuclear bomb nearly taking out President Santos to be closer to a possibility than some B-level religious conspiracy writer's overactive imagination. Same for the digital avatars Eddie P revealed are being employed be major world religions, including Christian sects like Catholics in Poland and Protestants in Germany and Evangelical preachers—the examples are pulled from real life. There is even (some rather hopeful) commentary on ChatGPT artificial intelligent bots creating new religions, complete with their own sacred texts.

Something is being birthed. Something wants to emerge.

Only question is: What?

This extends some of my recent stories trying to plumb the depths of the supernatural realm (beginning with *Order of Thaddeus #11, Fallen Ones*, and into the spin-off series *Group X Cases*). The Jewish worldview, and more recent Christian appreciations of Old Testament cosmology, understand the universe to encompass a spiritual dimension with spiritual beings—both aligned with the Most High God and in rebellion against Yahweh. They sought to raise up divine-human hybrids and pass along their secret knowledge. They still do, breaking into our reality and connecting with humans through a variety of ways, including (perhaps) technological and pharmacological.

That latter one was the other leg to this mystery, the one connected with the elixir Sebastian had concocted with the (fantastical) limb of the Tree of Knowledge missing from the end of Book 12, *The Eden Legacy*, and joined with the bioengineering research of Samantha Perez. I had meant to include a separate storyline on that part of the mystery, but felt the story focus creeping away from me. So I focused on the techno-gods, delaying plumbing those depths for now. That other storyline will have to wait until another Order adventure; perhaps Elijah Fox and Gina Anderson, our new intrepid Group X agents will take on that case, as Silas and Celeste suggested in the Epilogue.

Back to the AI god storyline: The point was to draw attention to the 'beings' we all place our hope in when the world goes crazy. Do we turn to the God of the universe, the one who is both the Author of our human story and Actor within it? Or will we look to the gods of our own making, which may actually be the old gods emerging through our digital devices? And even then, G.O.D.E.S. wasn't all that innovative in the first place. She/It was a mere repository for human aphorisms stretching from Buddha to Emerson to Oprah, a large language model (as it is called) feeding humanity fortune-cookie sayings with the veneer of revelation and (false) hope of salvation.

As Silas exhorted the audience in white captivated by this god, we don't need more knowledge, mere information to save us. No, "We need someone who has lived our life to understand our life. Which Jesus did. He was made like us, becoming fully human. And then paid the price for our rebellion in our place, dying for our sins before rising back to life to save us...All to rescue us. To save us from sin and death, and to gift us eternal life."

That's the only God we need when the world catches fire. May you look to him during these fraught times. For hope, for guidance and wisdom, for salvation.

Now that Sebastian is dead, what's in store for Nous? How will the Grey couple manage to co-lead the Order of Thaddeus, especially with Celeste pregnant? And what about that loose end, with the pharmacological side of the portal into the Unseen Realm still out there?

For answers to all three, you'll have to wait for the next Order of Thaddeus story!

Research is an important part of my process for creating compelling stories that entertain, inform, and inspire. Here are a few resources I used to research this story into false prophets and the rise of artificial intelligence as a gateway into the Unseen Realm:

- Guinn, Jeff. *Waco: David Koresh, the Branch Davidians, and a Legacy of Rage.* New York: Simon & Schuster, 2023.

- Kingsnorth, Paul Kingsnorth. "The Universal," The Abby of Misrule. Substack. https://paulkingsnorth. substack.com/p/the-universal.
- ________. "The Neon God," The Abby of Misrule. Substack. https://paulkingsnorth.substack.com/p/ the-universal.
- Talty, Stephan. *Koresh: The True Story of David Koresh and the Tragedy of Waco*. New York: Mariner Books, 2023.

GET YOUR FREE THRILLER

Building a relationship with my readers is one of my all-time favorite joys of writing! Once in a while I like to send out a newsletter with giveaways, free stories, pre-release content, updates on new books, and other bits on my stories.

Join my insider's group for updates, giveaways, and your free novel—a full-length action-adventure story in my *Order of Thaddeus* thriller series. Just tell me where to send it.

Follow this link to subscribe:
www.jabouma.com/free

ALSO BY J. A. BOUMA

Nobody should have to read bad religious fiction—whether it's cheesy plots with pat answers or misrepresentations of the Christian faith and the Bible. So J. A. Bouma tells compelling, propulsive stories that thrill as much as inspire, offering a dose of insight along the way.

Order of Thaddeus Action-Adventure Thriller Series

Holy Shroud • Book 1

The Thirteenth Apostle • Book 2

Hidden Covenant • Book 3

American God • Book 4

Grail of Power • Book 5

Templars Rising • Book 6

Rite of Darkness • Book 7

Gospel Zero • Book 8

The Emperor's Code • Book 9

Deadly Hope • Book 10

Fallen Ones • Book 11

The Eden Legacy • Book 12

End of Days • Book 13

Silas Grey Collection 1 (Books 1-3)

Silas Grey Collection 2 (Books 4-6)

Silas Grey Collection 3 (Books 7-9)

Backstories: Short Story Collection 1

Martyrs Bones: Short Story Collection 2

Group X Cases **Supernatural Suspense Series**

Not of This World • Book 1

The Darkest Valley • Book 2

Against These Powers • Book 3

Luck Be the Ladies • Novelette

End Times Chronicles **Sci-Fi Apocalyptic Series**

Apostasy Rising / Season 1, Episode 1

Apostasy Rising / Season 1, Episode 2

Apostasy Rising / Season 1, Episode 3

Apostasy Rising / Season 1, Episode 4

Apocalypse Rising / Season 2, Episode 1

Apocalypse Rising / Season 2, Episode 2

Apocalypse Rising / Season 2, Episode 3

Apocalypse Rising / Season 2, Episode 4

Antichrist Rising / Season 3, Episode 1

Antichrist Rising / Season 3, Episode 2

Antichrist Rising / Season 3, Episode 3

Antichrist Rising / Season 3, Episode 4

Faith Reimagined **Spiritual Coming-of-Age Series**

A Reimagined Faith • Book 1

A Rediscovered Faith • Book 2

Mill Creek Junction **Short Story Series**

The New Normal • Collection 1

My Name's Johnny Pope • Collection 2

Joy to the Junction! • Collection 3

The Ties that Bind Us • Collection 4

A Matter of Justice • Collection 5

He Will Direct Your Paths • Collection 6

Find all of my latest book releases at: www.jabouma.com

ABOUT THE AUTHOR

J. A. Bouma believes nobody should have to read bad religious fiction—whether it's cheesy plots with pat answers or misrepresentations of the Christian faith and the Bible. So he tells compelling, propulsive stories that thrill as much as inspire, while offering a dose of insight along the way.

As a former congressional staffer and pastor, and award-nominated bestselling author of over forty religious fiction and nonfiction books, he blends a love for ideas and adventure, exploration and discovery, thrill and thought. With graduate degrees in Christian thought and the Bible, and armed with a voracious appetite for most mainstream genres, he tells stories you'll read with abandon and recommend with pride—exploring the tension of faith and doubt, spirituality and culture, belief and practice, and the gritty drama that is our collective pilgrim story.

When not putting fingers to keyboard, he loves vintage jazz vinyl, a glass of Malbec, and an epic read—preferably together. He lives in Grand Rapids with his wife, two kiddos, and rambunctious boxer-pug-terrier.

Connect at: www.jabouma.com • jeremy@jabouma.com

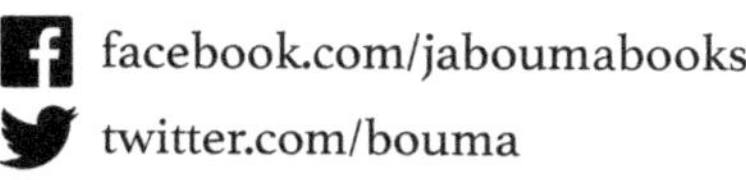

facebook.com/jaboumabooks

twitter.com/bouma

amazon.com/author/jabouma

bookbub.com/authors/jabouma

www.ingramcontent.com/pod-product-compliance
Lightning Source LLC
Chambersburg PA
CBHW070230200726
48293CB00005B/1548